FOUR OLD GEEZERS
AND A VALKYRIE

FOUR OLD GEEZERS AND A VALKYRIE

Gordon Lawrie

Comely Bank Publishing

First published 2012

This edition published by Comely Bank Publishing 2013

ISBN: 978-0-9573521-3-1

Copyright © 2012 Gordon Lawrie

The right of Gordon Lawrie to be identified as
author of this work has been identified by him in accordance
with the Copyright, Patents and Designs Act 1988.

All rights reserved. No part of this publication may be
reproduced, stored in or introduced into a retrieval system, or
transmitted, in any form, or by any means (electronic, mechanical,
photocopying, recording or otherwise) without the prior written
permission of the publisher. Any person who does any unauthorised
act in relation to this publication may be liable to criminal
prosecution and civil claims for damages.

Cover by Tayburn
Cover image by Vadym Drobot/Shutterstock
Text printed in Garamond by Printondemand (worldwide)

A CIP catalogue record for this book is available from
the British Library.

This book is sold subject to the condition that it shall not,
by way of trade or otherwise, be lent, re-sold, hired out,
or otherwise circulated without the publisher's prior consent
in any form or binding or cover other than that in which
it is published and without a similar condition including this
condition being imposed on the subsequent purchaser.

For Katherine

Gordon Lawrie spent thirty-six years teaching Modern Studies in the Edinburgh area, and has written on several educational topics including citizenship, the teaching of politics, and the relationship between education and society. In an earlier part of his life, he was briefly a mediocre pub-style folk singer, singing a mix of his own songs and covers of others.

Today he lives in Edinburgh city centre. The trams get in the way a bit.

All the songs mentioned in the story really exist. Some of Captain's completed ones can be found at the website www.flyingsaucers.eu.

CONTENTS

1	The Parabola of the Flying Saucer	9
2	The Nearly Man	13
3	Fleece	16
4	Mathers	24
5	Pentland Ale	28
6	The Letter	32
7	Getting in Shape for Sunday	37
8	Family Saturday	41
9	Waterstone's	47
10	Clark Kent	52
11	Supersomething Meets Gerry Rafferty	57
12	Paint Mixing at B&Q	64
13	Taking Stock with Harry	71
14	Bumping into Geoff	75
15	Another Encounter with the Siren	80
16	Na Na Na Na Nah Na	85
17	Lead Guitar	90
18	The Reminder	94
19	Geoff Meets the Band	100
20	Post Production	109
21	The Nerd	114
22	At Carmen's	118
23	What's in a Name?	123
24	Legal Aid	128
25	Dreaming of Christmas	134
26	The Ghost of Christmas Past	140
27	Ding-Dong Merrily	146
28	The Real Deal	152
29	The Real Costa Coffee	159
30	Fresh Start	167
31	An Attachment	173
32	New Material	179
33	Manager	186
34	The World's my Oyster	193

35	Citizens' Advice Bureau.................	199
36	The Labours of Geoff.....................	206
37	The Studio, Part One......................	212
38	The Studio, Part Two......................	220
39	Hard Negotiations........................	228
40	Harry Phones.............................	231
41	The Fruits of our Labour.................	236
42	Acting Out the Music.....................	241
43	Making Movies...........................	250
44	The Finishing Touch......................	254
45	Passing the Torch........................	261
46	The True Value of Fame.................	264
47	Courting Disaster........................	270
48	Thank God It's Thursday...............	273
49	Walnut Mobilised........................	277
50	A Grand Gathering at Bev's............	282
51	The Missing Link.........................	291
52	For Whom the Bell Tolls.................	300
53	The Prodigal Son.........................	303
54	At Cantina Mexicana.....................	313
55	Sacred Music..............................	318
56	Meet the Earl..............................	323
57	Desperate Measures.	331
58	Legal Correspondence....................	335
59	The Truth about Brian...................	338
60	Condemned Men Eat Cheese Scones......	343
61	Hidden Memories.........................	353
62	Curtains for Walnut......................	359
63	Doomsday.................................	363
64	Otis Farrell and The Upbeats............	369
65	Live from Peebles.........................	372
66	Encore.....................................	382
67	Travelodge.................................	384

1

The Parabola of the Flying Saucer

Ah, the saucers, the saucers.

Experience has taught me the properties of a range of Weapons of Domestic Violence. Light pans, for instance, make lots of noise but do little damage. Heavier ones such as frying pans and rolling pins enjoy an undeserved reputation but are likely to do lasting damage to the intended target. You might think that's a good thing, but it's essential that a thrower or a beater can retain the option to continue at will, as a key pleasure in doing anything enjoyable is to be able to do it again and again without feeling guilty. Le Creuset will probably be fatal, which defeats the object completely. Knives are also rather unsuited to being thrown. It's a matter of sheer chance whether the metal slices through dermis and epidermis to permanent and lasting effect, bounces off the target, or merely skims past and embeds itself in something else which the thrower actually quite values. Cutlery also has an unnerving habit of spinning vertically through the air.

Some people err on the safe side, making soft cushions, wet cloths, or perhaps oranges their weapons of choice. In my opinion, these people aren't really taking part in serious projectile-throwing at all, but instead are indulging in a perverse attempt to demonstrate affection. If the missile lands on target, it should cause pain, either physical or, better still, mental.

That's why fine crockery is made of porcelain and not plastic or enamelled metal. It's light enough to fit in the smallest of hands – even heavier teapots come with convenient handles – and fragile enough to shatter against any reasonably hard surface. If well-chosen, items can be of sentimental value to the target – like Great Aunt Ethel's Victorian hundred-piece tea-service – and can strike deep into the soul of the mark, perhaps also shattering on his or her skull. For this purpose it helps to select quality china; nothing from TK Maxx or Asda will do here.

But even within the range offered by a china tea-set, different pieces of china perform differently. Jugs and sugar bowls, both heavier objects, will travel through the air in a flat arc, barely deviating from their initial line of flight. A cup will be unbalanced in the air by its handle. Although its flight might straighten in much the same manner as a bullet fired from a rifle barrel, there remains a good chance that the thrower will catch a finger in the handle and make a complete mess of things. Plates – even side plates – can, like jugs, be a little heavy for effective use.

Which leaves the saucer. In fact, owners of tea-sets must wonder if there is any other purpose for saucers, especially in the modern era when tea- and coffee-drinkers are so wedded to mugs for everyday use. Let's face it – when did you last use a saucer when you didn't have guests in the house? These things sit in some difficult-to-reach corner of a cupboard or dresser. (Lower cupboards of dressers are really suited to nothing else, are they?) The chosen drinking vessels of the twenty-first century are the mug and the wine glass. Wine glasses throw well, too, by the way, and of course they shatter brilliantly, but nothing beats the saucer in the air. And who needs saucers? There are always more than you ever need, especially since cups and saucers seem to break in a ratio of three to one.

So there they sit, these saucers, ready for the next domestic dispute, ready to fulfill their true purpose, like butterflies whose finest hour is the instant before their death. Saucers are the Ferraris of the domestic projectile world, the go-to implements for all would-be pitchers. They can be hurled directly, just like teacups and jugs, but far more satisfyingly they can be slung backhanded. Instantly, they assume one of two extraordinary frisbee flight-paths. Right-way up, the right-handed thrower will see the saucer set off, bank slightly upwards to the left, then fall away to the floor and its certain destruction; upside-down, the saucer will bend left-to-right, then dip sharply downwards to the right and an even faster terminal impact. If you see a saucer flying upside-down towards you, it is fatal to duck – you'll duck *into* its flightpath like as not, increasing the impact speed. Instead, the correct technique is to sway smoothly backwards and forwards to allow it to pass harmlessly by. During the Falklands conflict, British naval helicopters used a similar technique to dodge Exocet missiles; in turn they probably picked up the trick from Spanish matadors.

By now you must be asking how I've become such an expert in the parabolas of flying crockery, and, yes, you'd be correct in guessing that I've been the target more than a few times myself. Picture the scene: Brunhilde, my wife of thirty-one years, has once again decided that I am a useless, no-good piece of manure fit only for the wheelie-bin. We're standing in the kitchen/dining-room of our rather nice house in Newington in the south side of Edinburgh, just off Minto Street to the left going down. She's thrown things before, but this time she's found the mother-lode, the aforementioned Aunt Ethel's tea-set. It had actually been worth quite a lot of money, at least while it was only in one hundred pieces. Brunhilde's not her real name, incidentally; her real name's Jane, but her valkyrie-like features make the nickname inevitable. Now she's gone, having swept out of the front door, leaving me behind to sweep up thousands of pieces of what was Aunt Ethel's pride and joy. Hopefully, there's no life after death and she can't be aware of its fate. Personally, I wasn't that bothered, thus displaying the very indifference that had driven Brunhilde mad in the first place. Indifference about my job, life, Brunhilde, the universe, whatever. Almost everything, but not quite everything.

She didn't leave for good. Later that evening she returned and demanded that I did instead, her reasoning being that the children needed her to be in the family home.

I could have debated this, especially since one of our children, Becky, was twenty-two at the time and coming to the end of a degree in French and Linguistic Studies at St. Andrews, while the older one, Harry, was well and truly off the payroll – with both a law and an accountancy degree – and safely settled in his own Bruntsfield flat with his long-term partner Danni. I certainly wasn't indifferent to them, but they weren't coming home in a hurry. And contesting the occupation of a home with so much grief attached was another thing I was indifferent to, so out I went, to find myself to rent a small basement flat in the West End. There, my life became quieter, safer, and – frankly – more boring.

For a while, at any rate.

2

The Nearly Man

There is no glory whatsoever in being the Depute Head of a secondary school. (The word is pronounced 'deh-pyoot' incidentally, as opposed to the word 'deputy', as in 'Deputy Dawg'.) In essence, Depute Heads are failures, all of them, poor sad cases who aspired to the stardom of a headship of their own, but fell short of the mark. Don't believe any of them who try to tell you they are 'happy where they are, thank you'; they'd all jump at the chance to give the orders themselves rather than be the dogsbodies beneath them. In Scotland, you can go on a course to become a headteacher, no matter how little talent you might have, wasting large amounts of local authority money that would be better spent on teaching five-year-olds how to tie their shoelaces or whatever. Local authorities decide who should go on the course, which in reality means your school's head; if your face fits, you're on. My face didn't fit, and perhaps I was lucky, not because I would have made a good head – I wouldn't have, by the way – but rather because I've seen what happens to the people who do get chosen: Stepford Wives, the lot of them, even the men. Perhaps especially the men. The women turn into Stepford Husbands who have created male robots to fulfill their needs, so the Ira Levin novel operates in reverse.

It's not even as if the money's that good. Don't get me wrong – teachers generally are not on the breadline, although that's often because there are two of them in the one household, and the hourly wage-rate isn't so attractive once you take the real length of the working week into account. No, the point I'm making is that Depute Heads aren't paid that much more than heads of department in a secondary school, and they get to do something I haven't done for years: teach the interesting classes. They get the fun classes, the 'sexy' classes if you like, the ones with the fancy certificates. Depute Heads get the leftovers, the second year classes full of malcontents, the bottom sets and the troublemakers. Depute Heads are treated like dogsbodies when it comes to teaching, too – do you detect a pattern here? Actually, department heads might well work longer hours, but they're doing stuff they want to do. Depute Heads have to do what they're told, by irate headteachers, by irate parents, by irate social workers, by irate community police – even by irate visiting speakers sometimes.

Sooner or later, most Depute Heads waken up to the fact that life has passed them by. No-one pays the slightest attention to them, and turning up to work has become a purgatory to be endured until the merciful release of retirement comes. Unless…

Unless you get really lucky. Once in a generation, some fool in an office somewhere decides that the solution to all of life's ills is to flush out all the dead wood – they mean people like me – and replace us with something younger, more dynamic, and – above all – cheaper. They think they can do without you, so they offer you a package to leave, which is sometimes attractive enough (very rarely these days, actually) to make it just about possible to up sticks and do something else. When I was fifty-six, a number of Depute Heads of my age were made an offer to leave. I couldn't get out quick enough. I'd been in the job too long and I knew it.

The difficulty was that what I received from my former employers was never going to be quite enough to keep me in the manner to which I'd become accustomed and with which I wanted to remain on speaking terms. I needed something to top up a smallish pension, and something to keep me occupied and out of mischief, away from bookshops and music stores. I tried sending articles to magazines and newspapers. The first paid very little and the second paid nothing at all, simply ignoring everything I fired at them. If the truth be told, I wasn't any better at writing than I was at teaching.

Then I did land a small job to keep me going. My local Costa coffee shop was looking for a part-time barista, and so on Tuesdays and Thursdays – they had students working at the weekend – I now find myself standing with a black apron trying to construct the best espressos and lattes the cut-price coffee would produce. I'm not too bad at making coffee, I reckon. I like talking to customers, passing the time of day, discussing the weather, some item of news, or even a football match, and they like talking to me. I've even served my own daughter Becky once, when she came in to see how I was getting on and give me moral support. I gave her a latte with vanilla syrup on the house in return. Jane has never come in, though, even although she knows I work there, which is maybe just as well; the cups would hurt too much if they hit me. Funny thing, though: I called her Brunhilde, sometimes even to her face, when we were married, but now she's gone, she's 'Jane'.

Late one November Thursday afternoon, I'm clearing up some tables and getting ready to load up another dishwasher when a voice from the past whispers in my ear.

"Aye, aye, Captain, fancy finding you in here of all places!" Did I say the voice whispers? It's a cross between heavy breathing and a bellow. A moment or so ago I was all alone.

Even before I look round I know who it is.

3

Fleece

In fact it's as well that I recognise Fleece's voice before I see him. He's utterly different from the figure who was my best man when I married Jane. He's put on a ton of weight, grown a beard of sorts, and his once-blond hair has turned a pinkish shade of grey. Frankly, the man's a mess, and his clothing – never the tidiest at the best of times – would allow him to pass as a street beggar. He doesn't look fat as such, he's just bulked out, and it's difficult to say if he's developed a beer belly because he's so large in directions otherwise. He looks like a cross between Gérard Depardieu and Brian Blessed, and like the latter he roars with laughter, a characteristic which caused his friends embarrassment in many a pub and restaurant in younger days. But now that I study him again, he remains in the same broad proportions as when we first met at university. Back then he was on the first of four university courses (I did say four, yes) that he'd try out for size. Fleece had money, or at least his parents did, so he was able to chop and change like Goldilocks and the three degrees. He did eventually finish the last one, something in business management, I heard. Not that it mattered. His dad owned a collection of snooker and pool rooms in Glasgow which he knew would keep him more than provided for.

The first degree attempt was in French and Law, for goodness' sake. Can you imagine Fleece – whose real name is Big Josh Mackay, by the way, although his parents called him Joshua and omitted the 'Big' – with his beer-stained jumpers, entertaining clients in a Queen Street law office? There was never any danger that he'd be allowed out in the open where he could possibly ruin a corporate image. But there he was, mid-1970s, supposedly studying law and even a little French until the time came when he had to sit some exams at the end of the first year. And that was that.

He's talking to me, but I'm not listening properly, I'm just adjusting to the deafening presence of this gorilla in the West End Costa. He's in my domain, he's invaded my space, and he knows it, just as he knows I'm not happy.

"Look Captain, I know you're not listening, you don't need to answer," he says, punching me in the shoulder. "I'll just turn round and leave the same way as I came in. I know when I'm not wanted."

I've missed something, but I've no idea what. "No, no, please – stay. How are you, Fleece?" Why do people say things they don't mean just so as not to appear rude? Of course it would be nice if he turned around and left. But instead I say, "Haven't seen you for years – it must be…?"

"That's just what I was saying, you daft twit. Don't you ever listen? Are you going deaf in your old age as well as putting on weight?" He delivers an almighty backhanded wallop to my stomach. "I saw you at Walnut's fiftieth, remember?"

Yes, I do remember. Walnut's real name is Duncan, and Fleece had christened him Walnut 'in loving memory' of the Walnut Whips that were once made in the Duncan's chocolate factory in Canonmills, just down the road from where we stand as he reminds me. Nowadays, they're made somewhere in darkest Yorkshire, I believe. Duncan hated being called 'Walnut', in fact, and he was acutely embarrassed when a number of his old university chums turned up at his function in the Roxburghe Hotel at the end of George Street. Duncan, you see, had started the same law course as Fleece, but he'd actually gone on to be a successful part of the Edinburgh legal establishment. For a while I'd got to know Duncan quite well after Fleece had dropped out for the first time. Duncan and I were rugby fans, the only ones in our little group, and we ended up going to internationals together. Even a couple of away games – Twickenham and Paris.

That was in the days when you had to stand on giant terracings. Duncan was good at picking up girls from nowhere, so we always had a good time. A very good time.

But our worlds drifted far apart until I bumped into him at Murrayfield one February Saturday, dressed in a Barbour jacket and now bald apart from a neat fringe around his ears. He'd greeted me like a long-lost friend, called me 'Brian', my real name, and asked after Brunhilde. He invited us to his fiftieth, which by chance was to be the following Friday night. Jane and I were still together then, so we both turned up, and sure enough Duncan had invited a number of his old university friends; there, in all his glory, was Fleece. That night, Fleece had his second wife Hannah on his arm. His first wife was Carla (the main result of his second attempt to gain a degree, Italian Studies), and they had had two daughters, but then Carla had thrown Fleece out in much the same way that Brunhilde would later eject me.

Fleece only wears Barbour jackets when he feels he should look smart. Most of the time, he wears... a fleece. Surprisingly for a closet Hibs fan, he used to wear maroon ones quite a bit, although one of his daughters once gave him a nice green Hibs fleece for a birthday and for a while he felt obliged to wear it. "I look a prat in this, don't I, Captain? I look a prat." Fleece has a habit of repeating himself, although he insists that was my habit, and in particular he claims I have a habit of agreeing in a 'knowledgeable' way, nodding my head sagely and simply saying "Aye", often several times, usually because I could never get a word in while he was talking. Get the nickname now? Then Fleece repeats it over and over again until it sticks. I suppose he thought it was funny. Fleece thinks most of what he says is funny, and no-one's got the heart to tell him otherwise.

"Heard you and Brunhilde split, old boy," he yells, just about loud enough for the other barista, who's busy washing up in the kitchen, almost to hear. "Sorry to hear about that.

She was a bit wild, wasn't she? I often wondered what you saw in each other to be honest, you had so little in common."

"Did we?"

"You can always tell how well couples will get on by how well their tastes in music match up. Take me and Carla. I like cowboy music and southern rock" – Fleece loved everything by The Band – "and she liked pop music. Marriage made in heaven."

I wait for him to square this logic with the fact that his first marriage to Carla disappeared in flames even quicker than mine years ago. I am not to be disappointed.

"Well it should have been," he explains, "until pop music went over to that New Romantic stuff. Beat's in a different place. It needs to be da-da-*dah*. Da-da-*dah*." He emphasises the last 'dah' each time. "Think of Neil Young in *Southern Man*. So that was that for Carla and me. Led astray by Spandau Ballet and so on." He pauses, then throws his head back and roars with laughter again. Meanwhile I am reminded that Fleece was a recreational drummer in a past life, conjuring up an image of the hairy drummer beast from *The Muppet Show*. For some reason I ask him if he's still beating the skins.

"Hell, yeah!" he exclaims, mimicking some wild west cowboy who almost certainly never existed by slapping his thigh. On second thoughts, maybe Doris Day in *Calamity Jane*. "How's a man supposed to give vent to his frustrations if he doesn't smash a drum-kit regularly? Helped me get through Carla all those years ago, in fact. Me and Little Joe still jam regularly, would you believe?"

"Really?" I feign interest.

'Little Joe' is in fact Joe Mackay, Fleece's younger brother, whom I do see from time to time. He and I happen to belong the same squash club, although he's at least ten leagues higher than me (most of my opponents are beginners or over seventy, in fact) and in squash terms he treats me like something he's just scraped off the sole of his shoe. Joe is

'Little' in the sense that he is six years younger, and a whole heap thinner, although as it happens he is also three inches taller at six feet three. He confuses everyone by being bald, too – not as bald as Walnut, certainly, but with a massively receding hairline. He's attempted to deal with this by cropping what he has left really closely, so that with a vest on he probably takes after Bruce Willis; it just about works, I think. Joe could be any age, and when he's not smiling he can look evil. Joe may not be little but then again Fleece is a *Bonanza* fan, especially since he's found repeats of his favourite childhood western series on ITV 6 or some other obscure satellite channel.

The very mention of Joe sets Fleece off.

"Da, duddle ah, duddle ah, duddle ah, duddle ah-dah –
Da, duddle ah, da, duddle ah, da duddle ah dah dah."

he sings, belting out the *Bonanza* theme tune. As he does so, I'm reminded that Fleece's drumming skills require him to hold a rhythm better than a tune. I humour him by smiling politely.

"Little Joe was the youngest of the four Cartwrights in *Bonanza*," I remind him. "There were only two of you, although you'd make a good Hoss Cartwright given a decent ten-gallon hat."

"I believe you're making reference to my increased stature, Captain. I can't tell a lie, I've put the beef on a bit. But there's life in me yet, I'll have you know. I turned out for Old Wanderers two weeks ago." Fleece used to be a very good rugby second-row forward, but this still amazes me. He amplifies. "I lasted all of thirty-five minutes."

"Really?" I'm amazed.

"Yes. Although in two instalments. The first one lasted three minutes then I had to sit down to get my breath back. A wee while later I came back on and ran around for a while at a more sensible speed."

"So what are you up to these days?" I ask. "Last I heard you were refusing benefits to lots of needy people in the Department of Social Security."

"Still am, I'm afraid. Not like you, you lucky bugger, getting paid to get out. The government intends to make me complete all my sentence. Nelson Mandela only got twenty-seven years and they treated him like a hero!"

"So you've around three years to go?"

"Two years, seven months and seventeen days." He looks at his watch. "Less the eighteen minutes it took me to walk here from Market Street." He roars again. I notice a customer has appeared, a mother and child, bringing some welcome relief from this continuing assault on my eardrums. She orders a latte with an extra shot – a good choice, the coffee's like dishwasher today – and an organic orange juice for her son. They share a packet of assorted mini-muffins, before the child, who's probably aged around three, sets off to play with the toys that I've both cleaned and tidied up for the day. Or so I'd thought.

Meanwhile Fleece is standing around like a spare part and, finally taking the hint, puts his hand in his pocket to buy a ristretto, which is not only the smallest but also the cheapest thing I sell. He wants a glass of water to go with it, which is not surprising since the effort of laughing has forced him into a sweat, while his always-red face now looks a deep crimson.

"How's Hannah?" I ask. Hannah and he met and married in a whirlwind romance after the demise of Carla, and she and Brunhilde always got on well.

He shifts his weight uneasily from one foot to the other and then back again. For a moment I wish I hadn't asked. "Well that's the thing, Captain, that's the thing. You see, Captain…" – dropping his voice for the first time, he fumbles for the right words and looks away from me – "she's only gone and left me, hasn't she. So there we are, the pair of us."

"Jane didn't leave me," I correct him. "She threw me out. Where are you staying?"

"Ah well, Hannah and I had already downsized after the kids left, and we moved into a modern small flat off the Canongate three years ago. Very nice. A wee garden, even. Unfortunately it left Hannah with loads of money to lavish on a toy-boy. Fucked off with him in June. Probably literally."

"A toy-boy? Hannah?"

"Well, she's about six months older than him."

I try to make a comparison between Hannah and Fleece's sister-in-law. "Joe's two years younger than Bev. Is Joe a toy-boy?"

Fleece considers the question carefully. "Possibly. But it doesn't matter because Bev is drop-dead gorgeous and Joe actually looks about five years older than her." Actually, this is cruel, but spot-on.

"I'm shocked, Fleece," I say. "I'm sorry to hear that, my friend. That's the two of us in much the same situation, I suppose."

"Indeed it is, Captain, indeed it is," Fleece intones. He pauses, shuffles around. He's got something on his mind. Then he asks, "What time do you clock off tonight, Captain?"

I'm not sure I've heard this right and decide to play safe. "I'm not sure what you're asking, Fleece, and I know you're probably desperate, but I should make it clear that I'm not. At least not that desperate."

Fleece looks at me blankly, then roars with laughter. "Nice one, Captain, nice one. No, all I was suggesting was a quiet drink. How about Mathers just up the road? Seven-fifteen?" Mathers is a classic old working men's pub of the type where any self-respecting woman can now swan in and order a large glass of chilled sauvignon blanc. To go with olives and a scotch pie. It's perfect.

"OK, I'm doing nothing tonight," I say. In fact I'm doing nothing tomorrow night, the night after, or the night after that...

4

Mathers

I'm sitting alone in Mathers in a dark corner. I made a point of turning up fifteen minutes late because Fleece is absolutely always late by a quarter of an hour at least, but it's past a quarter to eight when he appears.

"Hope I haven't kept you waiting, Captain," he greets me. "I didn't rush because I knew you'd be late. What's the recommendation?" Considerate of you, Fleece, I think. You're one pint behind already.

"Stewart's Pentland Ale seems to be a guest beer," I suggest. "Good. Like treacle, bitter." I omit the fact that it's got a low alcohol-by-volume of under four per cent as well, a major plus point in any strategic entanglement with Fleece in a public house.

He returns with a pint of something entirely different, of course.

"You didn't tell me they had Old Speckled Hen."

"By the way, Fleece, they have Old Speckled Hen," I inform him.

He plants his ample rear on a slightly unconvincing chair across from me. "So, then, Captain, what's the news? Kids well?"

I'm surprised he's remembered to ask about anything outside his immediate orbit. I give him a very brief summary before he loses interest.

"Harry and Danni still live in Bruntsfield, making shed-loads of money now. Becky's got a man, too – Tommy – and they live in Bathgate. She's working in what she calls 'public affairs', but I call her a lobbyist for an obscure charity."

"What's the obscure charity?"

"Oxfam."

"Right." It's a test to see if he's still listening. Turns out he is, just; he smiles after a brief delay. "But she's not earning shed-loads?"

"Nobody in that sort of job earns shed-loads unless they're with a very, very special firm, Fleece. That's why they live out in the sticks. Can't afford Edinburgh prices."

He's paying attention again. "And I suppose the Bank of Mum and Dad is experiencing a bit of a credit crisis at the moment?"

"Like all the other major high street banks. Being separated is a financial disaster, I've discovered."

"Tell me about it," he agrees. "Remind me what Danni does?"

"You probably wouldn't ever have known, actually. She's a stockbroker and financial adviser, although she works in a law firm, in fact. Little old ladies looking for advice from their family solicitor on what to do with their savings get sent to her."

"Where they get ripped off?" he asks, a cynical smile spreading across his face.

"Of course," I reassure him. "And she takes her commission for ripping them off and hands it over to the firm. She's a valued employee."

"I bet she does a roaring trade in divorces as well," he laughs.

"Naturally. Think of all those nest-eggs that have to be turned into hard cash so that the proceeds can be divided up properly."

"Do you like her?"

"Of course." And I do, actually, and not only because she makes my son extremely happy. "I like Tommy, too. He's a cabinet-maker. An up-market joiner if you prefer. Works for a wee firm out in West Lothian making and selling nice pine furniture."

"A horny-handed son of the soil, then?"

"Not a bit of it. He was in Becky's year at university."

"Did he drop out?"

"No, no, he finished his course all right. Did fine, actually – got the bog-standard two-one that everyone seems to get nowadays. Then he discovered that in the present economic climate, there's not much demand for Metaphysics graduates, honours or otherwise."

"Metaphysics! Christ, I didn't know anyone still did that."

"No-one with any sense does." Then I reconsider. "Actually, perhaps courses like Moral Phil and Metaphysics are the only courses worth doing at university these days. At least when you leave you already know how useless you are in the world."

"Perhaps, so, Captain, perhaps so. So how did he end up as a joiner?"

"He got a good grade in Standard Grade woodwork, it seems."

Fleece smiles, then slightly shifts the angle of the conversation. "How did they take it when you and Brunhilde? You know…"

"On the surface they were OK about it. But I could tell they were upset, even although they knew Jane and I were fighting non-stop."

"Fighting non-stop? I think that's putting it mildly, Captain. Listen, though, I notice you call her 'Jane' these days. When did that start? Feeling wistful, all of a sudden?"

I look into my Pentland Ale. "Perhaps."

He knocks the table abruptly with the knuckles of his right hand. He ticks me off. "Cut it out, my boy. Absence may make the heart grow fonder, but you began from a low starting point. It wasn't safe in the Reid household."

"It certainly wasn't. But there are things about her I miss."

"Like her contribution to the family finances, perhaps."

I smile ruefully. "Indeed. But I miss having someone to talk to at times. And I miss the company. You know."

He knows, but he won't let me feel sorry for myself. "Well," he says, "I don't think she misses you. She missed you plenty when she was throwing the cups," he says, roaring with laughter. "And in the meantime you've just found me to talk to."

"That's nice," I reply, although 'nice' is actually not a word I'd use in relation to Fleece at all. Curiously, though, it's turning out to be nice to have run into him. There's a brief pause in the conversation, and I know that now's the time to ask.

"Tell me about Hannah, Fleece. It's why you wanted a drink, isn't it? You wanted to talk about Hannah."

5

Pentland Ale

Fleece has returned from the bar with a second pint, and for once I agree to have a second as well, although my first isn't actually finished. Fleece can lap me comfortably every fourth pint, actually; it's why he's the size he is. This time he's followed my lead and bought the Stewart's Pentland.

"Damn good this, Captain, damned good this," he says, gulping back a huge mouthful of the dark nectar.

I decide to keep pressing, quietly. "You were about to tell me about Hannah, Fleece."

"Yes I was, wasn't I? I don't know what to tell you, Captain. Some of it's sort of... personal, you know."

"Spare me the sordid details if you want."

It's Fleece's turn to look down at the floor. "To cut a long story short, I've been a bit careless, Captain. I didn't pay her enough attention. I drank with the lads when I should have spent time in with her and a bottle of wine. I played drums with Little Joe when I should have taken her to the theatre or the cinema. I drank pies and pints in pubs when I should have eaten oysters and champagne. So some other guy got in there and did it all for Hannah instead."

"Very eloquent," I say to him, "and utter bullshit. True, you've let yourself go to seed a bit" – I glance at his midriff and stained jumper – "but that stuff comes after, not before, a marriage grows cold. There's no point in getting married if you can't tell your partner what you really think of them."

"You're saying she might have been looking for an excuse?"

"Well, I can't say that for sure – "

"I even went to see a doctor, although not till after she'd gone." He hesitates. "You know, about..."

"Are we talking about erectile dysfunction here, Fleece?"

He looks around, ssh-ing me. This is a new experience for me; normally I'm the one who's mortified at the thought that my conversations with Fleece might be overheard. "They call it 'ED' now, Captain."

"VD?" I ask, mischievously. I've heard him all right.

"You heard me, you bugger, and keep your voice down," he says. "Anyway, I went to the GP. Trust my luck to get a woman, but actually she was very nice."

"Very nice?"

"I should have said 'very good', you dirty so-and-so. Said I should lose weight and do some exercise."

"Hence the rugby?"

"Hence the rugby. And I go hillwalking. And I've started playing golf again. Fancy a game sometime?"

Actually, Fleece's golf used to be both entertaining and awful. That might work if we can find somewhere that will have us. I promise to consider it.

"So Hannah found someone else?"

"Would you believe, she went off with an airline pilot?"

I can't help but make the joke. "Up, up and away with him?"

Fleece ignores me. "I've met him, Captain. I met him at a party once. Hannah was actually shagging him at the time and I didn't know it. He was the most boring man you'll ever meet. Spent the whole time telling me how difficult it was to land a plane in Gibraltar."

"Is it difficult to land a plane in Gibraltar?" I ask.

"Apparently."

"Then that's Gibraltar crossed off my holiday list."

"Anyway, I found out too late that she was two-timing me. She was off with him."

"To Gibraltar and other places."

"Well, they get free travel. How's a civil servant supposed to match that?"

"Do you miss her?" I ask. The conversation has gone full circle. "Feeling wistful?"

He looks at me intently for a moment. Surely he's not about to shed a tear? Then suddenly he throws his head back and – laughing – roars, "Hell yeah," slapping his thigh. "Gawd-dammit, she done make a mean apple-pie!"

"Can't you be serious for just a minute?"

"I miss Hannah, Captain."

"Does she still sing with The Blonde Bombshelles?" Hannah was the singer in a band, a proper one, which played lucrative gigs like weddings. All the band members were female – that was its special feature – and Jane/Brunhilde sang screeching valkyrie-like backing vocals while playing guitar and bass. Brunhilde was heavily influenced by Joan Jett. Her playing was unsubtle, it was fair to say.

"That's been put on the back burner for the moment, I gather. Hannah never seems to know whether she's going to be in Tranent or Tokyo."

"And all for free. What about you? Have you been beating the drums again?"

"Quite a bit. You should get into it yourself. Come to think of it, you used to play guitar yourself. Remember?"

"I remember." How could I forget? Every Tuesday night in the Southsider Bar in Newington. Got paid a fiver a night, which seemed a lot when I was a student. Just me and an acoustic guitar with an impossibly high action and which was almost impossible to tune. That must have been almost forty years ago, I think.

He can read my mind. "The beer was shite then, too," he says. It's the word 'too' that's the problem in that sentence. "Listen," he says, "me and Little Joe are having our weekly jam on Sunday. Fancy joining us? Just for old time's sake?" He punches me in shoulder, to emphasise the invitation I suppose. I can think of no other reason.

God knows what 'old time's sake' Fleece is referring to. We have never played musical instruments together, ever, in our entire lives. He is a passable drummer who sweats a lot.

He has always treated my three-chord guitar playing and folk-singing with utter contempt.

With devastating logic, I agree. Then I get cold feet and want to lessen the torture. "But I'm busy earlier in the afternoon. Can I come later?"

"Jesus, you come when you fancy, Captain, you come when you fancy. Your turn for another Pentland, please. And a packet of cheese and onion crisps if they've got any."

6

The Letter

Of course Fleece leads me astray, as I knew he would. Thankfully neither of us need drive home and in fact all I have to do is stagger across the Dean Bridge – I always look over the parapet at the hundred-foot drop for some reason, which is stupid when you're the worse for wear – to my Eton Terrace flat. Doesn't Eton Terrace sound a grand address? It *is* a grand address, in fact, but my particular flat's a small basement thing with a tiny paved patio at the back and an even tinier paved area at the front. It suits me, and I suppose it's home. In any case, it's all I can afford.

Anyway, I've been out all day and it's after half past eleven when I unlock my front door, which has had three separate locks ever since I was broken into in the first week there. I haven't been home all day, so I have to climb over the usual pile of junk mail and the local free newspaper, the *Herald and Post*. That and the equally cost-free the *Metro* form my newspaper reading, supplemented for quality by internet versions of the newspapers I wish I could afford. There's a couple of proper letters addressed to me, but I've decided I like junk mail as well; it makes me feel more valued. I even like the leaflets. This time there's a couple for takeaways, the Sun Palace Chinese, and Shazia's 'genuine Bangladeshi', which I notice has all the same 'genuine' dishes as every other bog-standard Indian restaurant. I'll maybe give the Chinese a shot sometime, but I make my own curries, and with a lot less oil. Both do free deliveries without a minimum order, though, which is a plus point and probably speaks volumes about their need to compete in the current recession.

One of the proper letters is handwritten, and I open it first. It's from a nephew and his wife, thanking me for a present I sent to their newborn daughter, and for the twenty-pound note I sent them, too. Young couples need a treat in that situation, I remember. One of those takeaways would do the trick perfectly. I put it on the mantelpiece as I put the lights and living room gas fire on.

The other letter comes in a heavyweight envelope, and I assume it must contain several sheets of paper but when I open it, it turns out there's only one. I look at it but I take a minute or two to absorb it. It's from a firm of solicitors that I know only too well, the magnificently named Robb Merriman. They're Brunhilde's solicitors, and how appropriate that their very name implies that they act like a reverse-gear version of Robin Hood: they take from poor people like me and give to rich people like Brunhilde. My heart always sinks when I see their letterhead at the top of the page, and this is no exception.

ROBB MERRIMAN, W.S.
18, Rutland Square
Edinburgh, EH1 2BB
11th November 2011

Brian Reid,
19A, Eton Terrace,
Edinburgh, EH4 1QD
Dear Mr Reid,

I write regarding our client Mrs Jane Reid (née Forrest), your former wife.

It has come to our attention that you recently retired from your employment as a teacher with the City of Edinburgh Council, and are now in receipt of a pension as a result. You will be aware that under the terms of your separation from Mrs Reid, she is entitled to a share of this pension, in accordance with the number of years you contributing while you were married.

Our client has informed us that she is not receiving any share of your pension, although she ought to be, and has asked us to write to you to clarify and rectify this situation.

I look forward to hearing your reply by return. Should you have any concerns regarding this matter, please do not hesitate to contact me.

Yours sincerely,

Susan Gunn
(Partner, Robb Merriman)

I re-read the letter three times. Is this the effect of drink? If so, I'll sign up for Alcoholics Anonymous first thing Monday. But it's not the booze. Brunhilde wants half my pension, I think. She's got plenty herself, but she wants half of what I've got as well. This is why we fell out.

Why did I agree to this? Who knows, but I must have, just to get rid of the cow. Bitch cow bitch cow bitch cow. May she rot in hell. It occurs to me that I could always go back and take the hundred-foot jump off the Dean Bridge and then she'd get half of nothing, but then it also occurs to me that I probably wouldn't get anything either. Although knowing my luck and general incompetence, I'd survive anyway. That's what Brunhilde would say, now that I think about it.

I scrunch the letter up into a ball and throw into the corner. It belongs with the fluff I've never got round to hoovering up, and I've got more important things to do, like make myself some toast, the ultimate comfort food. Four nice slices of Kingsmill brown bread, with loads of butter and a big hunk of cheddar will help me forget Brunhilde, Robb and his Merrimen. Five minutes later, I'm feeling better, and – perhaps fuelled by some Pentland Ale – at the top of my voice I start singing the only suitable song I know, *The Letter*, as in The Box Tops' hit from 1967. It's one of my earliest memories, and because it's one of my earliest memories, I've completely forgotten all the words. Who cares? No-one can hear me.

Da-da-da-de-da-de-da-de-da-de-da,
Da-de-da-de-da-de-da-de-da-de-da,
Da-de-da-de-da, Da-de-da-de-da -

Actually, it's all wrong, I think, and I stop singing almost at exactly the same time as the old boy upstairs bangs on my ceiling to tell me to shut up at this late hour of night. It seems someone can hear me after all. Shut up yourself, I think, you haven't just opened a letter from your ex-wife. Actually that's a bit harsh too given that his wife died eight years ago; he'd probably either love to get a letter or die on the spot of a heart attack. Anyway, one way or another, I'm being asked for money that I've no hope of providing, and that's only the beginning of my problems.

More pressing still is, how am I going to get out of this jam session with Fleece and Little Joe? In all of our chat, I forgot to mention that I haven't actually played the guitar for over thirty years, although I still have the thing I used to use in its original case, presumably with thirty-year-old strings. I've not been idle in the interim: I tried to learn to play the piano, but Brunhilde will testify that as piano player I was a good guitarist, and as a guitarist I was a good piano player. There's a lot of stuff you can try to play on the piano, though, and I have any amount of sheet music that I can't play piled up around my pride and joy, a Technics SX PC-26 that I've had for years. By the way, the music I play on the piano is classical stuff, or something that Messrs Chopin, Bach, Ravel, Handel and co. might vaguely recognise as their own given enough clues. I can't play modern stuff – rock, R&B, jazz, that sort of thing. I'm really not very good, but I work on the principle that, since no-one will ever hear me, no harm can be done. You can turn the volume right down on a Technics SX PC-26, or better still plug in some headphones.

The guitar is an 'Angelica', an entry-level thing with a rounded neck produced by Boosey and Hawkes in the early

1970s, and I discover it in a cupboard under some welly boots, my toolkit, and – for some reason – a bag of potting compost. (Inside the actual half-filled bag of compost there's a mouse-trap. I've no idea how that could have found its way in there. The guitar is probably more of a hazard to mice.) The case is caked in dust, but inside the guitar itself is just as I last saw it in the 1980s, and to my amazement, five out of the six strings are on the guitar, with only the top one missing. That's not a bad start, and there are spares in a little compartment in the middle of the case; the bad news is that three of the strings are actually at the same pitch, and as I start to tighten the strings a little, two more snap. That's all right – there's a music shop in Queensferry Street which I can visit tomorrow, and in the meantime I might be able to do something with what I have in the case if I can just prevent the little twiddly things at the end that you use to tune the strings stop slipping. Remember all of this is happening when it's almost midnight.

I manage to get the guitar vaguely in tune with the help of a few reminders from the internet and my Technics SX PC-26. I strum it with my right hand, then I place the fingers of my left hand one by one in the appropriate positions for the chord of C. This needs assistance from my right hand for the fourth finger to help it get to the third fret on the A string, and then I'm ready. The tips of my fingers are in agony as the metal carves through them like cheese-wire, but I know I must suffer for my art. Hopefully, I play the chord with my right hand, and it sounds like someone's put a wet sock over all the strings.

I decide it's bedtime, and I don't want the old boy above me complaining again, but I realise there is work to do tomorrow. And Saturday. And Sunday morning, too. What have I agreed to?

Meanwhile, Brunhilde's lawyer can wait.

7

Getting in Shape for Sunday

By the next morning – Friday – I have become utterly obsessed with trying to avoid making a fool of myself in the coming Sunday session. I rise early and, quickly downing a coffee and what remains of the loaf, toasted, I dive up the road to the music shop where I buy two sets of brand-new strings for my beloved Angelica. Actually, I already know how awful a guitar it is. The strings sit miles away from the fretboard, and there is an ominous bulge behind the bridge, which suggests that it might one day part company with the rest of the guitar. I suspect that the two problems might be connected.

In the meantime I get back to the flat and tune up. I have decided on a plan: I'll stick to a very small number of chords, major and minor, and use a capo to do everything else such as changing key. I'm not going to try to be smart here, as Little Joe and Fleece will have had thirty years' more practice than me. I discover that, surprisingly, I can just about remember the important ones: C, F, G, D, and I can still do A minor, D minor and E minor, too. As a bonus, the seventh chords C7, G7 and D7 come back to me, too, although I can remember nothing of the mysterious F7. Later, I can remember E and A major, as well. They're not so hard, either. I will do nothing at all except strum with right hand, either using what nails I have left or perhaps a plectrum (is that called a 'pick'?). The whole of the period leading up to lunchtime is chords, chords, more chords, changing chords, with my fingertips in agony, but the fact that I can remember more of this than I expected is a major compensation. Adrenalin carries me through the afternoon – I'm almost excited, and I've still got two days to go – and I very nearly forget that I've got nothing for tonight's evening meal.

My inspiration with the guitar carries over into my cuisine, and I decide to make myself a fish curry, something I haven't done for, well, years. I nip across the Dean Bridge again to collect some fish from the fishmonger, and using a small tin of potatoes, some coconut milk, leaf coriander and spices such as turmeric and chilli I contrive to create something I could even have served to a guest. It's a pity I don't have a guest to show off to, but my feeling of loneliness is compensated for by the fact that there's more for me to tuck into. But I decide to drink no alcohol, although I'm not going out, because I want to be at my best for my practising.

Then it's back to the guitar for the evening. My fingers don't seem quite so sore tonight, which could be down to better technique, or it could simply be that calluses are already forming on the tips of my precious digits. That's good, but now the new problem is occasional cramp in my left hand. I remember that used to happen in the old days, too, when I was trying too hard. The secret is to relax, but it's easier said than done.

By around eight or so I feel confident that I've got the main chords pretty well in shape, and I'm ready to try out a few songs. For some reason, *The Letter* is still in my mind, although I can't for the life of me remember why. Off I go, starting it in E minor...

Dum-de-dum-de-dum (change to C) *dum*
(change to D) *Dum-de-dum* (change to A) *Dum*
(back to E minor) *Dum-de-dum-de-dum* (now C) *Dum-de-dum* -

What the fuck chord is that? A chord from the planet Mars? I go up and down the fretboard, desperately trying to construct something from nothing, but playing from ear I get nowhere. I can't play anything on the guitar that remotely sounds right.

Defeated, I can think of nothing better than to look up the idiot's friend, the internet. Surely there must be somewhere that tells you what chord comes after what in *The Letter*. "There ain't no point in the internet," I sing to myself as I Google, only to come up with the immediately miraculous site chordsforeverything.com site, which turns out to be a companion site to lyricsforeverything.com. Where have these been hiding? I needed to look up the lyrics anyway.

But 'Chords For Everything' tells me that the chord I'm looking for – in the 'Easiplay Version', by the way, how insulting – is the remote B7, a chord that I'm sure I never once played in my entire career as a pub-singer. It even gives me no fewer than eleven, yes eleven, different ways of playing the precious B7, so I spend half an hour trying to find a version that I can both play and at the same time sounds right. But I'm right up for *The Letter* now, and I shall never surrender. I went for a few piano lessons when I started playing my Technics SX PC-26, but when my teacher described my playing as 'dogged' one time, I knew it was time to give up any hopes of being good. The strength of my musicality is that, like Sylvester Stallone in Rocky, I bravely keep coming back for more punishment when the instrument has given me a severe beating. Besides, I've made the effort to print out the words from 'Lyrics For Everything', and I'm not going to waste a good sheet of printed A4.

By the third attempt, I've just about got the hang of it, so I decide to stand up and do a dress rehearsal. I successfully lay waste to all three verses and chorus, and even manage to come up with great series of chord changes to finish with, which I celebrate with a Pete Townshend windmill flourish. To my horror, this performance is greeted with rapturous applause from a drunk in the street – it is Friday night, you will recall – who I discover has been standing on the pavement gazing down into my basement living room at my moronic display. Jesus, he must have been able to hear me, too.

"Bravo," he slurs. "Bravo!"

I'm mortified, but all I can do is to wave back in thanks.

Next morning, I wake up to discover that in fact he was urinating into my basement area.

8

Family Saturday

Once I've hosed down the basement on the Saturday morning – it's the seventh time this year I've had to do it – I feel less inclined to practise my guitar skills. I have a leisurely breakfast. Actually, all my breakfasts are leisurely these days, but this time I nip up to the newsagent to pick up a couple of rolls to supplement my Oat Krunchies and grapefruit juice, so that breakfast is a long enough experience to make it worth scanning the internet versions of the morning papers. I always start with the BBC itself, studying the main news, then the sports headlines, and finally anything to do with Hibs. Hibs are playing at home today, but I'll be avoiding Easter Road Stadium since they haven't won there for almost a year. That's another one to follow on the internet.

Then I move on to the *Guardian*'s website, where I follow the same routine, except that they won't have anything on Hibs, of course, being a parochial English newspaper. (To those who suggest that it is I who am being parochial, I present to you a list of football teams – Barcelona, Real Madrid, Inter Milan, Ajax Amsterdam, Bayern Munich and Shamrock Rovers – which don't make it into today's *Guardian* either.) This absence of true sporting football news gives me an excuse to visit the *Scotsman* and *Edinburgh Evening News* site to catch up on the latest local gossip, and also to see if anyone I know locally has died. Fortunately, I haven't discovered my own name there yet.

I use the search engine in the newspaper to see if anyone called 'Reid' has been given a mention this week – it's a secret vice of mine that I hope I'll eventually attain my fifteen minutes of Andy Warhol fame – and to my amazement Brunhilde's name comes up. (She's not under 'Brunhilde', of course, but 'Jane Reid'.) Jane is the head of the City Library services, a juicily-paid job I might add, and she makes it into Tuesday's edition of the *Evening News* with a statement about the closure of a public library in Craigentinny. She gets two mentions, in fact, because the newspaper editorial has a go at the city council for its short-sighted ending of a valuable free service at a time when reading is declining, blah, blah, blah, and as Brunhilde is in the firing line she catches it as the bureaucrat in charge of such stupidity. Good, I think, she deserves it.

Today will be in fact be dominated by a plan to meet Harry and Becky, together with the respective partners, for lunch. I may be the poorest of the five of us, but that doesn't mean I won't be paying. Harry says that he's trying to help me avoid paying inheritance tax, and he may have a point, but I don't plan to die just yet and in the meantime it would be nice if one of them took me out now and again. Anyway, we're due to meet at Café Andaluz in George Street, which we can all get to without too much effort by public transport because it's nice and central, which will allow us to have something to drink. I know that Becky's boyfriend Tommy will down tools in a hurry for Spanish beer, which is fun to watch, and there's a collective spirit about sharing tapas which is usually good at breaking the ice for any group. It'll be good to go out as five. (Yes, I know, it would have been better if there had been six, but Brunhilde wouldn't make for a happy sixth.)

We're due to meet at one, and, just as Fleece is always late, there's a little palaver that accompanies any meeting of my two children. Becky is always early, at least fifteen minutes, sometimes more, while Harry is always five minutes late. Each in turn demands that their respective partner toes the party line, which means that I already know that Becky and Tommy will have arrived at twelve forty-five, and you could set your watch for Harry and Danni to walk in at five past one on the dot. He does this purely to wind her up. I was late myself one time for of these little dances, and I caught sight of Harry standing round the corner, clearly insisting to Danni that they mustn't arrive on time. What happens when they arrive is that Becky berates him for being late – not five minutes late, though, but twenty minutes, quite illogically factoring in the fifteen minutes that Becky has chosen to arrive early.

Today I make a point of turning up at exactly one o'clock, timing my arrival exactly to coincide with the castle gun's daily blast. It's a good dramatic entrance, I feel, and into the bargain steers a nice neutral path between the about-to-be-warring siblings. Becky and I hug and kiss each other on the cheek, and Tommy shakes my hand politely. As we sit, I study her, my daughter. Today she's wearing tight-fitting jeans and a bright red jumper, showing off a figure that she works on extensively in the gym and by pounding miles of Bathgate streets whenever she can. She's a daughter to be proud of, and I am. Tommy depends on his work to keep him fit; he has plenty of furniture to shift. He's wearing what he always wears whether he's working or not, a fawn crew-neck sweater, and his 'best' blue jeans, and both of them appear to have quite smart coats draped over the back of the chairs they occupy. He's not really shorter than Becky – he's all of five foot ten, actually – but her preference for high heels allows her to peer over his head when they stand together in the street.

True to form, Harry and Danni keep us waiting in Café Andaluz, and Becky greets them both with a kiss then says, "Good of you to join us for dessert, Harry." But she smiles as she says it, which I think might be a promising sign, although in the past Harry has talked of his sister's 'assassin smile'. I suspect all brothers say things like that about their sisters, just as sisters complain about their brothers' smelly socks.

Danni has dressed for the occasion, slipping her coat off to reveal a smart green knee-length dress under which she's wearing a black top with long sleeves to keep the November cold out. It gives her a slight sixties look, I feel, but I don't dare say so. The golden rule for fathers with their children is 'speak only when you have to'; fathers would make great secret agents. Like Becky, Danni gives me a chaste kiss on the cheek. Meanwhile Harry can read my mind and knows that some sort of thought has flitted across my brain, probably about Danni.

"Out with it then, old boy, what are you thinking?" he asks. Harry's first move in any conversation with me is to metaphorically pin me to the floor.

Of course I plead innocence. "Eh?" is usually effective in these situations, followed by, if I'm sharp enough, a response such as "I'm just thinking what sort of idiot would ask a question like that." But I'm never sharp enough, and perhaps it's just as well, as I'd no doubt regret it within fifteen seconds. Harry, meantime, has chosen to wear a jacket and an open-necked shirt, so he must be perishing in today's freezing cold, but of course Harry always dresses as though he lives in the tropics.

His conversation returns to semi-normal as he and Danni sit down. As expected, I'm at one end of the table, while he and Danni sit facing Becky and Tommy. This simple strategy has already ensured one thing: I've been manoeuvred into the seat that asks for the waiter, orders the wine, asks for the bill, and, most importantly, has to pay it. These people are in the wrong job, they have the tactical acumen of military generals.

"So how are you, old boy? You and Mum still behaving like total fuckwits?" Another of Harry's special talents is that he cuts brilliantly to the chase.

That would usually stump me, but for once I have an answer. "Why not ask your mum?"

"So the answer's 'yes', then," he counters.

"Leave him alone, you big bully," Danni says. "How would you like it if somebody was giving you a hard time like that?" Thank you, Danni, I appreciate your calling an ambulance for me.

But they do ask how things are, and they sound genuinely interested, so I tell them about Brunhilde's lawyer's letter, which threatens to leave me selling copies of the *Big Issue* before long. Again, I get little sympathy from Harry or even Danni, who seem to feel I should have known what was what before I signed the bits of paper. I point out that Brunhilde – I don't describe her as 'Brunhilde' to them, you understand – now has a pretty good job, and it seems unfair. Becky, who generally takes my side, agrees, whereas Harry says that, well life is unfair, isn't it? But I suspect that deep down they're all a little concerned for me, which I don't want. I don't want them to worry about me. I just need a little understanding in a difficult situation.

We order lunch. Chorizo and white beans, black pudding, prawns in garlic, several salads, sea bass, some pork cheeks, lamb chops, patatas bravas, white anchovies, tortilla and a paella, the last of which will come at the end because it takes longer. Even Tommy joins us in drinking the house red, which in the circumstances has to be a tempranillo, although from a more obscure area. It's another of my 'restaurant rules' – always choose the house wine unless you have a really good reason not to. The restaurant will almost certainly know its own house wines best, and be negotiating the best bulk order discounts on them as they buy them wholesale. And sure enough, this is a good choice, at least for lunchtime quaffing. It's great that everyone has come by public transport today, and in no time our worries are washed away in a sea of strong flavours. By the time the paella arrives we already need more wine to wash it down. This is the life.

Becky and Harry demand dessert, and – offered the chance – Tommy decides to join them, but Danni pleads that she's watching her figure. I plead that I just don't fancy dessert. Two ice creams and a crème brulée follow, followed shortly by a medley of teas and coffees. Tommy, who has taken to the wine big-style, orders another glass of red. I breathe in and ask for the bill.

When it comes, it's suitably large, but then that's what a credit card's for isn't it, to get you out of embarrassing situations you shouldn't have got yourself into in the first place? Harry offers a contribution towards the tip, so I make the suggestion that they each contribute a tenner. Harry reckons that must amount to a generous tip but it was a great meal, but I don't enlighten them that tapas and wine for five, even at lunchtime, can come to quite a large amount if everyone eats like horses. But I have to agree I had a good time. I can work how to pay for the good time later.

9

Waterstone's

After lunch, we get up and wander towards another of our collective happy places, Waterstone's bookstore in George Street. All five of us like books, and for some reason the George Street Waterstone's seems the best of the bunch. I like its open, airy layout: although it's a modern shop, it still has an old-fashioned bookshop feel.

We're standing looking at the crime section, Harry and I, when he casually asks if I have any plans for the weekend. I tell him that I've met Fleece and that I'm going to jam with him and Little Joe the next day. He's genuinely astonished.

"I didn't know you still saw either of them," he says. "And the guitar, too – do you still play that? I thought that was just an urban legend."

I've never been quite sure what an 'urban legend' is, but in case it's not complimentary, I ignore it. I come straight to the point – it's a family trait, I've discovered.

"I don't," I explain.

"Which?"

"Neither. I don't see them, and I don't play the guitar. Not any more, anyway."

"This is going to be an interesting jam session, then," he observes. "The invisible meets the inaudible." Harry's cynical brand of humour is lacerating at times.

"Have you read the latest Michael Connolly?" I ask him, trying to divert him away from the uncomfortable reality that I've got myself into a bit of a jam. Literally, of course. "There's a new Harry Bosch."

"I've taken to reading John Connolly recently. Better, I think. Stop changing the subject."

"Too brutal for me. I'm not changing the subject," I lie. "I don't know what I've let myself in for, to be honest, but

I've nothing to lose. Read any of those Italian authors I mentioned last time?"

"A couple. Thanks, by the way, for giving me those two Montalbano books completely in the wrong order. I think you're supposed to read each one in turn."

"Did I get it wrong? Sorry." I am sorry, actually, they're good books and I want Harry to enjoy them. "It's a while since I read them."

"Obviously. So are you looking forward to tomorrow?"

"Not sure. A bit nervous. I've been practising my three chords furiously."

Harry smiles; he knows I'm better than that, marginally.

"Do they know you play the piano these days?" he asks.

"Do I?" I wonder. "That's a question I ask myself every day, you know."

"I think most people would have you down as a piano player," he says, kindly. "You're not as bad as you like to make out. You even passed an exam."

"I don't think Grade 3 piano counts. It's only one level higher than 'Twinkle, twinkle little star'. And to answer your question, no, they don't know. Thankfully."

"Do you still practise?"

"Piano? Yes, believe it or not, every day."

"But no more lessons since your teacher called you 'dogged'," Harry chuckles. He knows the story.

"No. I've gone into retreat as a piano player."

"Well I hope you have a nice time tomorrow. Give Josh my regards." Harry says, using Fleece's real name. I almost don't know who he's referring to.

"Thanks. I will."

"What are you going to do about Mum?" he asks.

"No idea, Harry. I don't have the sort of cash she's looking for, to be honest. I feel she's trying to bleed me dry."

He studies a Harlan Coben novel. *Long Lost.* "Not sure I've read this," he says. "I wish you and Mum could behave like grown-ups."

"I thought Harlan Coben died of a drugs overdose long ago. Nirvana?" It's a useless, forced joke, the sort I know fathers tell to annoy their children, and I regret it immediately. Harry just ignores me with a contemptuous shake of the head.

"I'm not sure whether to offer you the benefit of my expertise or not. At one level I feel I should be helping my dad cope with a crisis in his life, especially if it's in my financial field. At another level, I want to keep out of the war zone that you and Mum have become."

"Became," I correct him. "Long ago. And before you say it, at least as much my fault as hers, I know."

"Becky and I feel like UN emissaries here," he goes on. "We daren't get too close to either of you for fear that you'll think we're taking sides."

"Don't you?"

"No. Don't insult me. Or Becky, for that matter. See what I mean? Behaving like a fuckwit."

The anger in his voice upsets me and I look away in case he sees.

But he's seen me all right. "Don't give me the 'upset' routine. You and Mum both deserve to be upset the way you're both behaving. There are too many innocent civilian casualties as you and Mum lob grenades at each other."

"By 'innocent civilian casualties' I presume you mean you and Becky?"

"And Danni and Tommy," he says. "Tommy doesn't dare say a word these days in case it's out of place."

Danni appears; she knows Harry only too well and she's come to rescue me. She lays a quiet hand on my arm, a feminine touch that is all the more powerful for its gentleness.

"Leave him alone, Harry," she chides him. "We've had a lovely lunch and don't spoil it now. Your dad is a generous man and I for one love him dearly." She almost breathes the last few words in my ear to comfort me. Don't let go of this gem, Harry, I think. You don't know how lucky you are.

Becky and Tommy appear. Becky realises she's been missing something, and she's probably glad of it, but she asks anyway.

"Everything OK?"

"Fine," I lie. "Your brother has just been berating me for my behaviour towards your mum. Nothing new."

Harry bridles. "Come on, Dad, I merely said the fact that you and Mum didn't speak made it difficult for the rest of us."

"Well, I've had a lovely time, Dad," Becky says, "and thanks for a lovely lunch." She kisses me on the cheek.

Danni continues to try to be upbeat. "Well, Brian, I have no problems with either you or Jane." She turns to Tommy. "Do you have a problem, Tommy?"

Tommy is horrified to be put on the spot. He shrugs his shoulders and says, "The way I see it, Brian, if I can't see Jane, she's not around, and so she's not a problem. She hasn't been a problem for me today at all. When we visit Jane, you're not around so it's not a problem either." Four years of metaphysics have boiled down to this. I'm not sure how to take it, actually; it appears I come and go only in figments of Tommy's imagination.

Danni now knows why she shouldn't have involved Tommy, and being an intelligent young woman, will note that for the future.

"But thanks for the lovely lunch, by the way," Tommy adds as an afterthought.

"Look, it's been lovely to be with all of you," I say, genuinely. This has been the highlight of my week, at least until now.

Harry tries to ease his tone a little. "Look Dad, why not scan the relevant documents and fire them over to me in an email? At least I can tell you if Mum's lawyer's trying it on. But don't let on to Mum. We need to be – "

"Yes, I know. You need to be peace envoys. I understand."

10

Clark Kent

I rise on the Sunday morning with equal measures of excitement and trepidation. I need to rattle through my chord practice, so off I go to get the papers, some rolls and a packet of smoked bacon from the local Sainsburys Lite or whatever it calls itself. It never actually seems to have any of the things I want, so I end up with having to buy smoked back bacon when I think unsmoked works better for bacon rolls. I still manage to wolf down three of them; the condemned man eats a hearty breakfast.

I study the newspapers – on Sundays I treat myself to an *Observer* and to a *Scotland on Sunday* because they give me lots more reading material for the rest of the week, and, if I'm honest, because of all the sports news at weekends. The Hibs result was the usual. Leading 1-0 at home to St. Mirren three minutes from the end, they contrived to lose two late goals and already by mid-November we're in our usual relegation dogfight. The government swings wildly between smug incompetence and devious corruption. There's a music section in the *Observer* this week, and I pay a little more attention to it as I daydream that, at the ripe age of fifty-eight, I'm going to suddenly develop a career worthy of note with my three-chord guitar playing. There's a review of a concert by Tom Paxton, who must now well into his seventies, so there's time yet. Then again he didn't fritter away the first thirty-five years of his musical career in teaching.

I fetch my guitar and play a couple of tunes, singing along and playing the chords as best I can. Playing helps me keep the tune much better, although discovering a few scraps of paper at the foot of the guitar case reveals an interesting fact: my voice has dropped a couple of semitones. That turns out to be quite convenient, because now I can play songs without a capo when previously I needed one, which looks a lot better to those who aren't in the know. I've heard singers' voices often drop as they get older, and the great operatic tenor Placido Domingo has started taking on baritone roles in his dotage. I play a few of my 'golden oldies' from my pub-singing days: Ralph McTell, Dylan, and of course the greatest songwriter ever to emerge from Scotland, Gerry Rafferty. I had fun then, I remember. Maybe this will be, too. Living dangerously, I even try something much more recent, a little Snow Patrol, *Run*, a cover version in which I fill in all the words I don't know with "la-la-lahs". Then I realise I haven't a clue what any of the words are at all, although I like the song a lot and I have all of Snow Patrol's albums – it's all "la-la-lahs" and it grinds to a halt before I'm forced to pay a further visit to lyricsforeverything.com.

It'll be interesting to see what Fleece and Little Joe are like these days. By three o'clock, I decide it's time to stop pussyfooting around any longer and go. The journey takes less than twenty minutes on a Sunday afternoon when everyone with any sense is watching Manchester United play Liverpool on Sky Sports 2, so that the traffic is non-existent. I even have a moment to nip down to the brand new farmers' market that's opened by the bridge in Stockbridge, where I buy some unpasteurised Tomme de Savoie cheese from a French stallholder operating out of a white van. That can be my treat for later, washed down with a glug or two of red wine if it goes well. The whole bottle if I disgrace myself. Eventually, I find myself outside Little Joe's house.

I need to explain a couple of things about Little Joe – in fact there's a whole lot I need to explain about Little Joe. First of all, he lives in a very nice detached house in Merchiston – Merchiston Place, in fact, with his drop-dead-gorgeous wife of twenty years, Bev. They don't have any children – I've no idea why, it's none of my business – but it's a shame, because they'd make lovely parents. Bev really is a lovely looking brunette in her early fifties but she could pass for at least ten years younger, and she uses her soft middle-class Glaswegian lilt to devastating effect on anything male, me included. Secondly, Bev is also astonishingly well-off, having set up her own recruitment business – you'll have heard of Beverley Rome Employment – in her early twenties and built it up to such a level that five years ago she was made an offer of millions, lots of them, to sell and she just couldn't refuse. That came at a good time, in part because the recruitment business then went into a decline (Bev lost a little money, too, but nothing very serious) but it meant she could devote all of her time to loving Joe at a time when he needed all the love and affection she could offer.

Thirdly, Little Joe used to be a policeman, a job he loved doing, but eight years ago he arrested a young man one Friday night but was then himself accused of sexually assaulting the young man. The accusation was eventually dismissed, but not before Joe had been suspended for eight months, had a nervous breakdown, and eventually had to leave the job he adored on a medical discharge. He received compensation from Lothian and Borders Police – lots of it – but he's not really been the same since. The good thing is that, together with Bev's vast wealth, he really need never work again.

However, Bev was also smart enough to realise that Joe's self-esteem had been totally undermined by the entire police episode, and that he needed something to keep him occupied and, just as importantly, out of Bev's hair during the day. Joe had always been interested in all things household, tools, kitchenware and so on, and so when a few months later the chance came up to buy a retiring ironmonger's business near the foot of Morningside Road, Bev and Joe couldn't get in there fast enough. The old boy selling was delighted that the business was going to continue, and he even gave them all of his old stock for nothing. Three months later, with a complete refit inside and out, a brand-new 'MACKAY

IRONMONGERY' opened, Joe and Bev giving away helium-filled balloons to passing children all that Saturday. Joe was as happy as could be, and now spends every day except Sunday proudly walking down from Merchiston Place each morning to open his shop at nine, and proudly walking home again each night after closing up at five-thirty. In between times he sells precious little, but for Bev that isn't the point. Incidentally, it's the fact that they live in Merchiston that has led me to bump into Joe, because they actually live only four hundred yards or so from Harry and Danni's Bruntsfield flat.

So that's where we are with Joe now. To an outsider he looks a sad case, carrying a sad case (he carries his packed lunch and coffee flask in a briefcase to work each day), but Bev is proud of him, and she makes him feel good when he gets home at night, too. She's a saint, in truth, and the only thing she appears to get out of it is the sure and certain knowledge that she's making the man she loves utterly happy. But there might be more to it than that.

Joe's day off is therefore a Sunday, but it's not a day of leisure for him. If he behaves like Clark Kent the other six days a week — though let's be clear about this, Joe doesn't look like Clark Kent — Sunday is the day he becomes, well, Supersomething, although I've never seen him wearing a bright blue wetsuit or a red cape. So picture me: guitar case in hand, standing nervously outside his house while torrential rain combined with a cold, buffeting, easterly November wind trying to drop the hint that I might be about to do something stupid. I ring the doorbell, and after I hear the softest of footsteps in the stairs leading to their flat, I'm greeted by Bev, who certainly does bear a passing resemblance to Lois Lane.

"Hi, Brian," she breathes in my ear, giving me a lingering kiss on the lips, and at the same time softly draws her hand down my arm. "Lovely to see you. You look well," she lies. Bev's life is all about making men feel good, I think. I'm not kidding myself into thinking I'm being given any sort of special treatment here; she reserves that entirely for her husband.

It takes me a moment to come to my senses and say "Thanks, Bev – lovely to see you, too." I go on to comment that she seems to look even younger than when I last saw her, which might actually be true.

She shrugs off the compliment with yet another lovely smile and leads me by the hand along a passageway through to the back of the house towards the back door. I've not actually been in their house before and I've no idea what awaits me.

"I'm sorry you'll have to brave the elements from here to the outhouse. Watch your feet on the path, it's wet and slippy," she says, nodding her head in the direction of a brick building around the size of a small garage but with no garage doors. We enter instead by a conventional door from the back garden where I am greeted by

11

Supersomething Meets Gerry Rafferty

the most awful cacophonous racket the world has ever witnessed.

Bear in mind that there are only two people present, Fleece and Little Joe. Joe is playing something I've never heard before, at least I don't think I've ever heard it before, although it might on reflection be a distant cousin of Jimi Hendrix's *Hey Joe*. Remarkably, he might be singing it, too, although the jury's out on that: it could be that other Hendrix smash hit, *Mary Had A Little Lamb*. It has taken me less than eight seconds to calculate that singing is not Little Joe's strong point.

Fleece is, as expected, 'giein' it laldy' on the drums, that fine Scots term for thrashing the things so violently that he manages to shut out Joe's guitar playing and, best of all, Joe's singing. The difficulty this presents is that, because he's unable to hear what he's drumming to, Fleece merely adds to the battering my ears are receiving. To complete the picture, both brothers are lost in their muse, eyes closed in concentration. Bev and I simply have to wait politely until they make such a mess of things that they eventually have to stop. Amazingly, she continues to smile benignly while this happens, and I have enough time to recall that Rose West probably lured many young people to their deaths with just such a welcoming smile.

"Look who's here, you two! Please make yourself at home, Brian." Yes, Rose might well have said that. I am consequently much more suspicious than politeness requires when Bev says she's off to make some scones, and then leaves, giving me one of those fingery waves that women give sometimes.

"Captain, you made it at last! We thought you'd taken cold feet," Fleece roars.

I manage to avoid conceding how close Fleece is to the truth as Joe steps forward to shake my hand.

"Great to see you, Captain, and glad you could make it. How are you?"

"Bearing up. How's the ironmongery business?"

"Not bad at the moment, actually. I'm selling lots of mousetraps at the moment to the residents of Falcon Avenue, which seems overrun by the things. And there's an outbreak of clothes moth in the whole of south Morningside. I've had to buy in more stock of moth killer."

Affecting interest, I ask, "Does it make any difference?"

"The mousetraps are a waste of time. You need the professionals in for that. Or cats. Moths can be dealt with using moth killer, so long as the spray contains a decent percentage of Cypermethrin. If you use one of the others you kill the moths but not the larvae."

In speaking, Little Joe has gone back into Clark Kent mode. Amazing that moth killer can so diminish a man.

Little Joe waves his hand to show me the room we stand in. "So? Tell me then, what do you think?"

Actually, I think the room I'm looking at is astonishing, now that I've had a chance to take it all in. It has soundproof cladding all round the walls, except for a window to a next-door room in which there is clearly a giant recording console. The lighting looks good, and the studio – for that's what it is – has a number of microphones that look to be just a little expensive. Nothing in the room looks less than top-drawer in quality except for the following: Little Joe's playing and singing, Fleece's drumming, and my Angelica round-neck entry-level guitar, and they haven't seen that yet.

"We had it custom-built, Bev and me," Little Joe explains redundantly.

"It's great, Captain," Fleece adds, "when you're outside you can't possibly hear how bad we are."

"Speak for yourself," Little Joe says, a little hurt.

"OK, no-one outside could possibly hear how bad *you* are."

"Piss off, Josh," Little Joe says. He's the only person in the whole world who calls Fleece by his real name.

Turning to me, he says, "Great, Captain, you've brought your guitar! What sort of stuff do you play?"

I'd like to be able to answer that question myself but Fleece beats me to it.

"Captain's a folk singer, Little Joe, he used to sing in a pub years ago. Play *The Wild Rover* for us, will you, Captain?"

I still haven't had a chance to reply but suddenly I'm being ordered to get my guitar out and check it's in tune. Even before I manage that Little Joe and Fleece have launched into a vicious rendition and I'm expected to join in. Each time we sing – sort of – "No, nay, never," in the chorus, Fleece produces a ridiculous drum-roll. I manage to bring the wild horses under control just before the start of the third verse.

"No. I don't play *The Wild Rover*, and I never did," I say firmly.

"No?" Fleece looks amazed. "What, then?"

I know I need to get this in quickly before he loses interest. "Dylan Ralph McTell Gerry Rafferty The Band – "

"The Band!" he replies. Of course, Fleece fancies himself as Levon Helm, their wonderful drummer, and what's more, Levon could sing. Perhaps Fleece can, too. Anything's got to be better than Little Joe.

We discuss some possibilities and decide to have a bash at *The Night They Drove Ol' Dixie Down*, giving Fleece a chance to sing. He tests out his voice and then off we go, but we then run into another problem, which is that Fleece can't multi-task. He can sing or he can drum, but he can't do both. So I'm given the responsibility, so long as the others join in the chorus. Then I point out the problem with my guitar, which no-one can hear, not even me, which might be a good thing but I should really make the effort. Little Joe conjures up an electric pick-up for my Angelica from somewhere, and after playing the chords through we try it out. In the event no-one can hear anything of what anyone else is playing, it's just all too loud. I make it through *The Night They Drove Ol' Dixie Down* by a combination of mime and lip-reading.

"That was good," Little Joe says, and he might be right, because I couldn't hear him.

Out of politeness I ask Little Joe what sort of stuff he likes playing. Fleece shakes his head and closes his eyes; it transpires I have opened Pandora's Box.

"Funny you should ask that," Little Joe replies, thoughtfully. "I've been experimenting lately with a fusion of Scottish independent music and reggae. Imagine a cross between The Proclaimers and Bob Marley."

I spend some time trying to imagine a cross between The Proclaimers and Bob Marley and am no nearer a picture when I realise Little Joe's going on.

"You've got to get the beat first. It goes chung-cha-ka-chung-chung, chung-cha-ka-chung-chung then you lay that rhythm onto whatever Scottish tune you fancy. Try it with *Lock The Door Lariston*," he says, and off he goes, desperately trying to fit the words of an old Corries' folk song – one the Corries themselves had already messed with – into a reggae beat. It's possible that this could drive me mad even quicker than the 'wall of sound' that greeted me when I arrived.

But I have to give him credit for one thing: he has utterly mastered the moves to go with this performance. This Scots-reggae 'number' is played out to a convincing combination of deep knee-bends and guitar movements. Particularly impressive is the point in the bar where he pulls the neck of the guitar up and backwards in perfect time. I decide to encourage him by telling him that as music, it makes great theatre.

"Do you think so, Captain? Thanks. Actually, I thought it would look great if we all wore kilts, too. We could flip the sporrans and the front of the kilts up on the back beat."

"Yes," I say, thoughtfully. It's a thought, certainly.

"And it works in reverse, too," and he goes on to prove the point by playing The Wailers' *We're Jammin'* with a broad Proclaimers Craig/Charlie Reid accent. By now I've understood that Fleece's presence here is simply to support his little brother in his hour of need. He's doing a social service, a bit like visiting an old lady in a nursing home.

I listen politely, and eventually Joe's fusion experiment runs out of steam. Then Fleece lobs a grenade into the conversation.

"Sing something for us, Captain. Anything."

I've been dreading this moment, but it's what I've prepared for so extensively in the last forty-eight hours.

"I used to sing a Gerry Rafferty song. *I Can't Stop Now*. Join in if you want. Join in if you can. I need all the support I can get." I don't give them a chance to argue.

I Can't Stop Now, an old Humblebums number from around 1970, is a fairly quiet acoustic song which simply demands that no-one gets carried away with the volume, and to be fair, Little Joe manages to stick to strumming along with the volume right down on his amplifier, while Fleece brushes the cymbal. It's not right, but it could be worse, and if I'm being honest, I could be worse, too.

But the surprise I get is in the reaction from the others as I finish.

"You can still sing, Captain," Fleece says. "Your voice is still OK."

"I think that might be a compliment," I reply.

"You used to have a good voice forty years ago, but I'm surprised it's still there." I realise Fleece is being serious, and

I'm quite touched. Not for long. He adds, "The trouble was that you sang such crap."

"Gerry Rafferty is God," I insist.

"Nothing wrong with Gerry Rafferty. You sang some Dylan as well. And you played a couple of Ralph McTell numbers that I liked in those days."

"*Zimmerman Blues* and *This Time of Night*. I played a harmonica as well, to cover up how bad the guitar-playing was," I remind him. "Actually, I played all sorts of stuff, but people kept asking me to play *Flower of Scotland* and so on. I preferred to leave that sort of stuff to the professionals."

"You've remembered the words of these all this time?" Little Joe asks me.

"No," I confess. "I found all sorts of scraps of paper with the lyrics in the guitar case under the guitar. In those days you had to play the vinyl over and over again to pick up the words. 'LyrsRus' didn't exist back then."

"You could tell a real musician's record collection by the amount of scratched vinyl it had," Fleece agrees. "There was often no alternative to wrecking the record." Fleece is on his feet, walking towards my guitar case as he's talking, and, too late, I realise what he's after. He's down on knees scrabbling about in the inside of my cheap cardboard case and he emerges with a couple of four-decade-old pieces of paper which were never intended to be shared with the world.

"What have we here, I wonder?" Fleece announces, with a wild, excited look in his eyes. "Here we are – the words and chords to the aforementioned *Zimmerman Blues*. And what's this underneath? The title of this thing is *The Saturday Blues*. This is all coming back to me, Captain. You used to write songs yourself, didn't you? Lots of self-indulgent dross, probably."

"Probably," I say defensively. "Everyone was writing self-indulgent dross in those days. I was just in fashion."

"If you'd been any good you'd still be doing it," Fleece points out. "Take Leonard Cohen. You would think that everyone who's ever liked his stuff must have already committed suicide by now, but still they keep coming, and he's in his seventies." I laugh, but although he's correct about Leonard Cohen, he's wrong about something else.

12

Paint Mixing at B&Q

"Play this thing *The Saturday Blues* for us," Little Joe asks nicely. "Ignore my older brother. He's just jealous of your ability to sing."

Fleece doesn't argue. "Play it, Captain. For old time's sake." Fleece also thinks *Casablanca* is the greatest movie ever shot; I've seen him cry more than once while watching it.

"Of all the gin joints, in all the towns, in all the world, I happen to walk into this one," I reply. I snatch the piece of paper and run through the chords with Little Joe. Then I take my courage in my hands and set off on *The Saturday Blues*, being given its first airing since my early twenties. I know it's not great, and its main plus on this particular occasion is that it has enough of a rock beat to allow Fleece and Little Joe to play along. They're even kind enough to join in singing the last chorus. But when it grinds to a halt, nobody seems keen to try it again, and when all's said and done it's sat in my guitar case for forty years and no-one's missed it.

So I suggest *The Letter* which refuses to leave my head for some reason I can't work out. Little Joe's delighted, and immediately starts to play it reggae-style. It sounds execrable, but now it's my turn to sound politely enthusiastic, and try to play along, although each time I catch Fleece's eye I'm aware that he's shaking his head not only in time with the beat but also in laughter at the pair of us: Little Joe for his performance, me for encouraging him, however inadvertently. Joe compounds the felony by singing in his Proclaimers accent.

When it finishes, Fleece's only comment is, "Different."

I ask Little Joe where he got this idea of Scots-Reggae.

"It's obvious, Captain, don't you see?" he replies. I don't, but that's fine because there's no escaping him explaining it anyway. "It all goes back to the slave-trade era. You're aware Scots were big in the slave trade." I am indeed very aware that we in Scotland have an excellent record in screwing up the rest of the world, and slavery was a fine example. On he goes. "You see, everyone goes on about how migrants influence music. You know, the Cajuns were French from Canada, and jazz was black African music, as was the whole of rock and roll. But what were they influencing? What was the canvas they painted on?"

He has my rapt attention.

"Think of music like one of those paint-mixing machines in B&Q." He repeats, "Yes, B&Q."

I wonder what he's going to come up with here. Little Joe explains. "Well, you need to think of Jamaican reggae, hip-hop, Blues and so on as the pigments. But what do you add the pigments to? Tell me that – what do you add the pigments to?"

I can't begin to guess. It's hard to believe that this lunatic is the same sedate Morningside ironmonger who carries his lunch and coffee flask in a briefcase every day.

"The base, Captain, the base! And what is the base of all American music? It's the music you don't hear, it's Scottish music."

To say I'm struggling with this is an understatement. "You're saying you know it's there because you can't hear it? Is that what you're telling me?"

"Yes, Captain, exactly! I knew you'd understand! That's why I want to explore the true roots of American music through Scottish music."

"The Proclaimers?" I blink.

"Gerry Rafferty, too, if you like. Donovan. Wet Wet Wet. The Corries. The whole jing-bang."

Thankfully, I'm saved from further comment by the merciful arrival of the wonderful Bev, who to add to her lustre is carrying a tray of mugs of coffee together with cheese scones, already buttered. There must be at least twenty-four, and even now I can tell that every one will be eaten.

"Thank you," I say to her, meaning for everything. "Looks wonderful." I could also be talking about the scones.

"Going well?" she asks me.

"It's proving to be an education," I tell her.

"Brian was telling us that he used to write his own songs," Joe says.

Fleece intervenes. "That was a long time ago, thank God. There's no need to rake over old coals," he says, roaring with laughter.

"That's not very kind," Bev says, encouragingly. "I'm sure they were very good."

"They weren't very good, I'm afraid. You've just been fortunate enough to miss me playing one," I tell her. I'm actually slightly irritated by Fleece, though. It's all right for me to take the piss out of my own songs, but not him, no matter how bad they are.

"I'm actually very sorry to have missed it, Brian," Bev says quietly, looking at me and pointedly ignoring Fleece. "I'd like to have made my own mind up. Can I hear something else?" Meanwhile, Joe is quietly starting to play a reggae version of *Annie Laurie* in one corner of the room.

"For Christ's sake, Bev, don't give Captain a chance," Fleece says. "It's bad enough with Desperate Dan Marley there. No wonder they were called The Wailers."

"*Maxwel – ton Braes – are bon-nie, Where ear-ly – fa's – the dew – It was there – that Ann – ie – Laurie -*"

Fleece's eyes are rolling. This is beyond the call of duty.

"Please play something for me, Brian, please," Bev says in an even more sexy voice. She seems to mean it, too, even if we all know she's just being nice. As she is to everyone.

"*– gave me – her pro – mise true – Gave me – her pro – mise true -*" squeals Little Joe in the corner.

"For fuck's sake, Little Joe," an exasperated Fleece yells, "that verse ends with you promising to lay me doon and die! Is that the plan? It sounds like it, the way you're singing. I might do the deed myself if you don't shut up."

Little Joe looks only a little disappointed. "Perhaps *Annie Laurie* is too pure to be influenced by the powerful flavours of the Caribbean," he suggests. "I wonder if you can play Desmond Decker stuff on the bagpipes…"

Bev is still breathing at me. "Go on, Brian." I love the way that she's calling me 'Brian'. "Let me hear something before I leave."

"Go on, Fleece. You might as well. It's either that or the Jock jerk across there."

"Fleece says your song was forty years old," Bev persists. "Why did you stop? I'm sure they weren't that bad."

Fleece is about to make yet another rude remark when I suddenly blurt out, "Actually, I suppose I didn't."

Bev smiles with big wide, surprised eyes. "Really? Are you still writing then? What sort of stuff do you write these days?"

I'm stuck on this question; I've never known how to describe my songs. I'm a bit embarrassed, and say, "I don't know…"

"Well, now we have to hear something, Brian. Please. Please don't let me down now." This is emotional blackmail, and I'm not very good at resisting any sort of pressure anyway. She's so close to me now that she can almost whisper in my ear, and she has her hand on my arm to boot.

"Play it, Brian. Play it for me." That's it. She's pressed the magic button. I give in.

"OK, if I must. You can tell me it's crap if you like, but remember you asked for it."

Fleece agrees. "Got to be better than Little Joe's last performance there." Little Joe's eyebrows rise a little.

"That's the second time today someone has used 'Play it' to get me to play something. Fleece tried it earlier," I point out.

Little Joe points out that Bev looks more like Ingrid Bergman than Fleece does.

"Get on with it then, Captain. Don't hang about – there's all these cheese scones to eat," Fleece yells.

I pick up my Angelica round-neck guitar – sticking the old cloth strap over my head to get it out of the way – and start to strum a few chords in C. I stop briefly to explain that the song is called 'Bird', just 'Bird', and then I start again with the intro, then into the quiet first verse…

Please understand I wouldn't hurt you
Please understand I mean no ill
Please try to listen when I tell you
The love in my heart remains there still

That line is then repeated as a sort of link –

The love in my heart remains there still -

rising in pitch towards the chorus -

Set me free,
Set me free,
Let me spread my wings,
And fly like a bird,
And soar beyond the sea,
A world is calling,
A world is calling,
A world is calling, calling to me.

Then it goes into a second quiet verse -

Nobody came to try and tempt me

Nobody tried to turn my head,
You're not to blame that this has happened
Leave me to take the fall instead,
Leave me to take the fall instead.

The chorus is repeated, then it goes quickly into a middle section, louder and higher -

No matter how near, no matter how far
It doesn't matter, you know I won't care,
I'll still be with you wherever you are,
There, I'll still be with you there,
I'll still be with you there.

Then there's the final verse -

All that I want is space to wander,
All that I need is room to roam,
Give me a chance and if you'll have me,
It won't be long before I'm home.
It won't be long before I'm home.

The last line of the final chorus rises a little to a top C, which I just about manage to hold so long as I'm strumming the guitar at the same time. It's a slow tune, so it lasts a little while – maybe six minutes. I haven't noticed that they've all listened in silence, but when it comes to an end, there's a continuing silence that I'm not ready for and which I find a little unsettling.

Eventually, I say, "What did I do? Kill somebody?"

"It's beautiful," Bev says, looking into my eyes and softly touching my sleeve yet again. "It's really beautiful, Brian. Thank you for playing it for me." I notice how she uses the 'me' in that sentence. I want to say a number of things in response to her but none of them are appropriate. The woman's commitment to her husband, and her utter unavailability to others, is part of her allure.

"You left a bit of yourself in that one, Captain, didn't you?" Fleece comments. He doesn't repeat himself, which means he's not trying to be funny.

"Thank you," I say to them both, and I mean it; I'm genuinely touched. "I'm sure you're just being very kind, but I'd prefer to take it as a compliment, however undeserved."

"I said it's beautiful, Brian," Bev says, surprisingly firmly. "Please don't think I was just being polite. I could listen to that again, and what's more I could listen to you singing it. You *do* have a lovely voice. Don't be self-deprecating." Bev's eyes look as big as ever, and her hand is on my sleeve again, but now there's a firmer pressure on my arm. I sense she wants something, in a really nice way, and she'll make it happen. I'm experiencing why Bev was so successful as a businesswoman – she got people to do things because they experienced the joy of pleasing her. There is an electrifying magnetism about her that drives all those who come near her, and that power is on full throttle at the moment.

Little Joe has been silent so far, and I suspect he may not be quite as enthusiastic as the others.

"Hey there, Little Joe, you're real quiet. What d'ya make of that?" Fleece asks him in a Bonanza accent.

"Oh, it was good, it was good, Captain. I liked it. Well done."

"But?" I ask him.

"Well," he replies, "I was just turning over in my mind whether a different rhythm would work better." He starts playing some chords on his guitar. "How about combining it with a little reggae? -"

"Joe – " his wife immediately tries to say.

"Em – " I try to butt in.

"FUCK OFF, JOE, YOU STUPID CRETIN!!" Fleece roars at the top of his voice, and I have to say that for once I approve completely.

13

Taking Stock with Harry

"You asked me to look at your stuff regarding Mum."

Harry has shocked me by appearing in my West End Costa on the Tuesday following the jam session with Fleece and Little Joe. He's never come in before, but now he's come in and has scrounged a flat white out of me.

"I knew I could find you here. It saved me the bother of phoning you to make an appointment," he explains. Dear me. We have to make appointments to meet? I suppose his iPhone demands it.

"I'm supposed to be working. And all the customers will be able to hear."

"For another five minutes, I understand. Then your shift ends and you can do whatever you want. By the way, in the meantime there's no-one here." He looks around very slowly indeed to make the point, with a smug smile on his face.

"Seven o'clock or not, I still have to tidy up for a bit, but I suppose it's OK. Did you make any progress?"

"Sort of. I spoke to a pal in the office and asked him to look at it, too, and of course asked Danni for a second opinion." He stops to consider. "Third, really, when you think about it... but everyone just calls it a 'second' opinion, don't they?" Harry has this habit of philosophising on his own speech, which can be irritating when you want him to supply you with the simplest of detail.

"Sure," I say. "No problem. I'm thinking of publishing the whole lot on the web for free download."

Harry looks at me and smiles. "Do you want the benefit of our collective advice or don't you, you stupid old fart?"

Once again I feel myself reeling from another mental blow to my solar plexus.

"Of course. Thank you. I'm grateful for your help."

"Well... well... the way I see it, we see it, is that you're utterly fucked."

"Really?"

"What the fuck did you agree to this for, Dad? You've signed your life away here," he says, waving his hand at the file lying before us on the little round Costa coffee table at which we're seated.

"The lawyer advised me that was for the best."

"Whose lawyer? Mum's or yours?"

"Well... at the time we only had the one. Look, I just wanted the whole sordid business to be done and dusted as quickly as possible. I did eventually get my own solicitor, and now that I remember that he tried to get me to cancel the agreement on the grounds that I'd signed under duress, but I said it was OK."

"You should have listened to him."

"Is there anything that can be done?"

"Yes, I can think of one thing. Two actually, but I'd rather you didn't do the second."

"What are your recommendations?"

"Win the National Lottery. That would be good."

"Given that I don't do the National Lottery, that may present problems. What's the other suggestion?"

"Shoot Mum. I'm sure there's a section for 'Contract Killers' in the Yellow Pages."

"I can understand why you might prefer I didn't do that."

"Quite. Although at the moment I'm feeling just a little bit sorry for you, old boy. I wouldn't wish this on my worst enemy, if I'm honest."

"Is it that bad?"

"Deep shit. Nice coffee, by the way. Good hit."

"There are three shots in it. You wanted double coffee, remember? That would have been six hits."

"That would have had even me buzzing, I think. What will you do now?"

"I think I asked you myself that very question a moment ago, remember? No idea. No idea at all. Look for some ways of earning money, I suppose. But that'll be tough in the recession. Who's going to want to train a fifty-seven-year-old new worker?"

"I thought you were fifty-eight."

"I can always lie about my age."

He smiles. "Really, Dad, I'm sorry to be the bearer of such bad tidings. Do you want me to see if I get some sort of proper professional advice for you?"

"No, it's all right, thanks. They'd charge a fee just to tell me something I already know now, and money to burn is just what I don't have at present."

"OK, fair enough. But the offer stands." He changes the subject to something lighter. "How did Sunday go, by the way?"

"Fine. Actually, I really enjoyed it."

"How was Fleece?"

"Unchanged."

"Give him my regards if you see him again. Will you see him again?"

"Next Sunday, believe it or not. Same time, same place."

"Really? What's his brother like?"

"Bonkers. Runs an ironmongers' shop in Morningside Road."

"The one near the foot on the right? I've been in there. That guy plays the guitar? And he's Fleece's brother? This is too much – you're having me on." Harry is genuinely interested. "What on earth is going on here?"

I give him a very brief potted history of the Mackay family.

"So let me get this straight – last Sunday, you, Fleece, and the Morningside ironmonger were to be found in the ironmonger's personal studio in Merchiston, playing your hearts out to old seventies numbers?"

"Ancient and modern. Some old, some new."

"What new stuff? This gets more and more intriguing."

I tell him about Little Joe's flirtation with rasta-jock.

"I can see that," Harry says. "I can picture a Jamaican Rastafarian spaced out on the ganja lying back in the long grass and saying, 'Hoots Mon'."

"I'll refrain from telling him that if you don't mind. I don't want to encourage him."

"Better not. Did you play one of your old numbers, by any chance?" Harry gives a little smile. It's a running joke between us, perhaps even deep down a running sore, that I've told him I used to write my own songs in the seventies but he's never heard any of them. He's always tried to suggest that they don't exist, presumably to wind me up into playing one, which he can then laugh at.

"Yes, we did. One of the old ones from away back. A newer one, too."

"A newer one? Are you still at it? Oh wait a minute – this'll be on the piano, won't it. Chopin? Mozart? Elton John?"

"Nope," I say. "Guitar. The new one went down better than I'd expected."

"Can I hear it?"

"No."

"Nothing changes then," he says, sitting back in his seat.

14

Bumping into Geoff

The following Thursday's a bit chaotic at the café, but actually I don't mind that at the moment. The Costa days at least provide some shape to my week, helping me tell what day of the week it is without having to look at my watch and then consult a calendar. Without a structure to my life, I would tend to get up and do whatever suits me – read books, go for a walk, go to the cinema perhaps. If the mood doesn't suit, I'll often do nothing, although I have improved my skills on my Technics SX PC-26 by making a point of playing it every day: scales in the morning, tunes in the afternoon. Sometimes I take my car – which by the way is a silver five-year-old Honda Jazz, nothing very interesting there – into the countryside and go for a long walk, places like the Fife Coastal Path or the John Muir Way. However, walking for the sake of it, even climbing mountains, has always seemed a little bit mindless to me. I prefer setting off in search of something, looking for some sort of wildlife, perhaps. I've even been known to get some pleasure out of a round of golf, but that palls after a bit, too. I could probably get into fishing.

But the real problem is that I crave company, and the Costa days, however frenetic, provide human interaction, something I've missed badly since Brunhilde and I split up and then I gave up teaching. In the café, at least, there's a constant stream of chatter with my fellow baristas, who on my days on duty are invariably either students earning an extra crust to help eke out their loans, or recent graduates trying to pay the loans back.

Then of course there are always the customers. They want lattes, skinny lattes, espressos, double espressos, cappuccinos, macchiatos, mocha lattes, vanilla lattes; teas –

herbal and conventional; hot chocolate, with or without marshmallow; fruit juices; then there are all the ice-cold drinks, which personally I find putrescent but I serve with the same bright smile as all the rest. You'd be surprised that I rarely get asked for the same order twice in the space of twenty minutes – lattes are the most popular, though – and in addition there's always the possibility of tempting the customer with a cake on the side. I recommend the biscotti, personally, to be dunked in a simple espresso shot. There's nothing to beat a classic.

And my week might have taken for the better with the prospect of regular Sundays at Bev and Little Joe's house. I can't deny that I surprised myself by how *Bird* sounded on its first outing. I'm not one of those who often sings at the top of his voice in my basement flat, partly because the old boy above bangs his walking stick to complain, but more, if I'm honest, because I'm just a little shy. Even on my own, I know, it's completely ridiculous.

The most immediate effect of the praise received for *Bird* – warranted or not – is that a fair part of my free time this week is taken up with reacquainting myself with a whole range of guitar chords. I practise changing them quickly and efficiently in all sorts of combinations, sometimes random, sometimes in chord progressions which are likely to appear in a number of songs. In the meantime, I've also experimented with strumming, with a plectrum and without, and I'm trying out some finger-picking again, although that's pretty useless in an electric or rock situation.

But a new feature of my Costa day is that I make up little tunes – fragments, more like it – which might have the promise to develop into future numbers for the 'band'. I've got miles ahead of myself here of course, I know, but that's just the way it is – don't destroy my dream in its infancy, please. Whenever I come up with something, I take the first moment when there's no customer waiting to dive off into the kitchen or the staff toilet to sing some little ditty into my iPhone as a 'voice memo', and by the Thursday after the jam session I already have eleven different ideas. (Later, I discover that three of these are almost exactly the same, and that four more are actually near-copies of things I've heard elsewhere.) But it means that I sound really happy to all my customers.

Towards the end of my shift, I'm emerging from the kitchen singing a potential chorus which has one-and-a-half lines and no more, when a voice I should recognise asks for a latte to go and a toasted cheese and ham panini.

"Geoff!"

"Brian!" Geoff replies. "Goodness me! Are you working here? I'd absolutely no idea."

Geoff is an old pal of mine, a few years older, from my old school, where he was the head of the art department. He's English, from Lincolnshire or somewhere down there, and although he's lived up here with his Scottish wife Sheila since he was twenty-two, his accent has picked up nothing of his adopted country at all. I always got on well with Geoff, and he and I would sit in each other's offices and chew the fat several times a week. When he retired, I missed his company, actually, and life as a depute head became that much more difficult when I lost a fellow traveller with whom I could share my troubles.

Geoff hasn't changed much. He's still thin and wiry, about my height, has most of his hair left, and he has a habit of smiling and frowning alternately, which these days shows up a few more wrinkles. He looks a great advert for retirement if I can only sort my life out the way he has.

"Goodness me," Geoff says again. "Goodness me" is something Geoff says rather a lot. "So how long have you been working here, then?"

I explain that I've been there for some months trying to boost my pension and stop getting bored.

"Good for you, Brian, good for you." He steps back. "Goodness me," he says, almost inevitably.

Then I commit the cardinal sin when speaking to Geoff: I ask him how he is. When you ask someone "How are you?" in English, the only answer you expect to receive is "Fine." In truth, you don't really care how the other person 'is', it's just a way of starting the conversational ball rolling, the pawn to king four of the chat world. The trouble with Geoff is that when you ask him how he is, he actually tells you, giving every sordid detail, and since Geoff is a Michelin-starred hypochondriac, that's going to include a few pieces of information you'd rather not hear. I just pray that he hasn't been having trouble with his bowels again. Not in Costa, please. But it could be worse.

"Could be worse, Brian, yes, goodness me, could be a lot worse. Trouble with my left knee all last week, woke with a crick in my neck twice at the weekend, strange kind of mark on my shin where I bumped myself on Monday, and of course the old trouble with the water works."

Geoff always has trouble with his water works. Goodness me, yes.

While I'm putting his latte together and toasting his panini, I manage to ask Geoff what he's doing with his own spare time, and I'm surprised to hear that he, too, has the guitar bug in his system. He tells me he's always had an unusual ambition; he wants to make a CD, and to design his own CD cover for it, although in fact that's not so odd when you remember he was an art teacher.

"Would you believe it, Brian, I'm still getting lessons every week? Goodness me, that must have been ten years I've been going now. Same teacher. Goodness me, though, he's a hard task-master. Scales and arpeggios, scales and arpeggios, that's what I have to practise all the time. Goodness me, yes." He frown-smiles, and makes an upwardy point with his index finger. "Doesn't mean I'm getting any better, though."

I suggest that it's a little unlikely that he hasn't improved over the last few years.

"Perhaps a little, Brian, perhaps a little. What about you? Still playing the piano?"

I admit that I still am, badly and without lessons, but I keep very quiet about my latest foray with my round-necked Angelica guitar. I don't want Geoff getting any bright ideas.

"Listen, Brian," he says, "let's keep in touch. You've got my number, haven't you?"

I assure him I have, but his latte to go is now ready and I place a lid on the cardboard container.

He picks it up and gives another cheery frown-smile. "Well, I'll be off then. Goodness me, wait till I tell Sheila where I bumped into you. Hope to see you soon, Brian!"

I wish him well and turn to serve the next customer. Then I realise that Geoff has left his panini on the counter, so I'm forced to dash out into the street to call him back. He returns looking a little flustered and embarrassed, full of frown-smiles and apologies to everyone in the queue.

"Goodness me!" he says, shaking his head in disbelief. "Goodness me!"

15

Another Encounter with the Siren

Why do the days pass so slowly sometimes? I can't wait for the next Sunday afternoon musical encounter, and this time there will be no 'waiting till later' – I'll be there from the start this time. I'm really hoping that *Bird* – do you notice how it's already acquired italics, by the way? – will get another airing, and I've got other things up my sleeve as well. I'm going to take them by storm.

The silver Honda Jazz arrives at the front door of the Merchiston house, and Bev once again greets me with one of her drop-dead-gorgeous smiles. Today I just about manage to notice that everything she's wearing fits her perfectly, and she's made up perfectly as well, subtly, discreetly, sexily. I'm aware she's wearing a perfume, but only just, as she kisses me on both cheeks, lingering a little as she does so.

"How good of you to come again, Brian. Joe and Josh are already there in the studio. They're so looking forward to seeing you," she breathes, huskily. This just isn't fair, I think, as once again she leads me by the hand – there's that touch again – through the house to the back garden, and then to the studio. Thankfully, it's a better day than the last time, so nobody's getting either wet or blown away, although Bev seems not to be affected by the weather anyway. She makes her excuses after a quick word with Joe, which I think is about the timing of the cheese scones, leaving the three of us to set things up. Not that there's even that much of that to be done – I hadn't realised that Fleece just left his drum-kit permanently ready to go in Little Joe's studio.

"So, Captain," Fleece says at a level that could be heard twenty metres away, although I'm actually right next to him, "what surprises have you got for us this week? What surprises have you got for us this week?"

"What do you want?" I reply, trying to sound intriguing.

"Are you trying to sound intriguing?" Fleece replies, "Because if you are, you're being a pain in the arse. I don't like intriguing people very much."

I ask him which side of the bed he got out of this morning.

"The point is, Captain, I had a choice which side of the bed I got out of. I mean with my masculine… attributes and demands, I shouldn't have such a choice." He switches into *Bonanza* mode. "A man's gotta do what a man's gotta do."

Ignoring the fact that the hairy monster before me might have only a niche appeal to the opposite gender, I try to point out that that there are a number of bodily functions that 'a man's gotta do' and that I don't need to hear about his success rate in any of them. Briefly, for some reason, that seems to quieten him, but I try to distract him by appealing to his sense of music.

"Come on," I say, "let's try something. Warm up with *Take It Easy*?" Eagle's numbers offer several attractions, including the fact that the bass isn't too obvious and we don't actually have one at all. For a first number, it also gets us all singing, although Fleece – who really is in a grumpy mood today – complains that *Take It Easy* comes from the wrong part of the States for his taste. Equally grumpily, I remind him that a Canadian, Neil Young, wrote his beloved *Southern Man*.

Little Joe, meantime, is irrepressible. He's really excited because he feels he's making progress with his exploration of 'rasta-jock' as he's now termed his fusion of Scottish folk music and reggae.

"Listen to this, Captain," he says. "There I was, listening to an old LP of the McCalmans singing *Willie's Gone Tae Melville Castle* and it suddenly all fell into place." He picks up his guitar – he's already on his feet – and starts playing a chung – chanka – chan – ka West Indian rhythm, then launches into the first couple of lines -

Wullie's gone tae Melville Castle
Boots an' spurs an' a'
Tae bid the ladies a' fareweel,
Afore he gaes awa'

I concentrate on the guitar-pulls and the deep knee bends in an attempt to take my mind off the pain, and indeed the 'mind over matter' policy might be working. I spot Fleece's tactic, which appears to be to dig his fingernails deep into his upper thighs, although to his credit he's managing to smile benignly at the same time

Wullie's young and blythe and bonnie
Loved by ane and a'
O what will all the lassies dae
When Wullie gaes awa'

This must come to an end, soon, I pray, but no, Little Joe actually tries to launch into a second verse -

The first he met was Lady Kate,
She led him through the ha',
And wi' a sad and sorry heart
She let the teardrops fa' -

By now, however, Fleece has thought of a different approach: to join in. Using a variety of simple drums, especially the hi-hat and a couple of other strange things he's had tucked away, he manages to drag Little Joe's performance through to an end. As it happens, I know the words of *Willie's Gone Tae Melville Castle*, too, so we can all sing along right to the point where the McCalmans would do three-part harmonies, still retaining the reggae beat. Incidentally, I've discovered that it is utterly impossible to sing reggae without moving to the beat at the same time. We're all going in different directions, sure, but we're all moving.

In the meantime, the music is just atrocious, and Little Joe has a lot of work to do yet. Thank goodness the studio is soundproof. If we ever make a recording, it'll have to be secretly stored at the Ministry of Defence establishment at Porton Down where they keep dangerous chemical weapons.

After this Fleece deserves a treat, something that involves straightforward rock drumming. Amazingly, it turns out after some discussion that we all know the words of the Free classic *All Right Now*, although in fact it doesn't really matter that only I really know all the verses, because it's the chorus where everyone joins in. We make it through, but the absence of a bass in rock numbers is posing a problem, and other things either turn out to be unsuitable for Fleece's drum-kit or my Angelica guitar apart from – frighteningly – Little Joe's rasta-jock.

Eventually, not a moment too soon, the gorgeous Bev appears with mugs of coffee and cheese scones which she seems to have anointed with her personal magnetism. As I consume them, the irreverent idea flits into my mind that they might represent 'the body of Bev' and 'the blood of Bev', but thankfully the thought flits out again quickly before I've eaten too many scones.

As during the previous week, she sits down to join us for a moment to grace us with her presence, politely asking Fleece how the Civil Service is, and me about Costa. We exchange the usual small talk – I have to confess I'm enjoying the café, still, and then she suddenly changes the subject – and her voice with it.

"Tell me, Brian," she husks at me, "are you going to play that song of yours again?"

I smile. "It's not a rock band number really, Bev. I'm sure you'd rather hear something all of us were playing." Actually, she probably has heard stuff all of us were playing and is getting desperate.

"I'd like to hear something of yours, though, Brian. Please play something of yours for me," she adds. There's that Ingrid Bergman voice again. If this woman were a rocky outcrop in the middle of the sea, ships would run aground every day.

Fatally, I hesitate.

"Please, Brian, play something of you for me," she repeats. Something in that last sentence has changed, I'm sure, but I can't work out what, because I'm so confused.

Little Joe chips in. "Bev means it," he says quietly. "Why not play your song? Fleece? Agree?"

"Go, Captain, go!" yells Fleece, and roars with laughter, releasing the tension at the same time. Actually, I've noticed he doesn't laugh so much when he's jamming – drumming is quite a serious business for him.

Bev touches my sleeve again, softly, but she's won already.

"Look," I say, "what if we sing something else that I wrote recently?"

"Another one!" cries Fleece, "My God, is there no end to this man's talents?"

"I'd simply love to hear another of your songs, Brian," Bev sighs. "If it's half as good as your last one, it'll be wonderful." I just don't know how to handle praise like this from her. I'm putty, I'm in a trance.

16

Na Na Na Na Nah Na

"Well," I say, "I do have another song, much more upbeat this time, called 'Right Here Lovin' Me'. Shall I play it? It's got a chorus that goes like this" – and I start to play it. It has a straight rock-pop beat.

And if the night is cold, if the night is dark,
There's only one place you should be
So from now until dawn I'll be hanging on,
I want you right here lovin' me.

"I like the sound of this already," Bev says, sounding surprisingly animated. For a moment the siren voice has gone and she sounds human.

"Good one, Captain," which is high praise from Little Joe, although I can already see his mind turning over. He continues, "How about – "

"How about if you play the whole fucking thing, Captain, your way, and not with some Jamaican beat?" Fleece jumps in quickly to save the world. "We could join in with this, couldn't we? You're right about that."

I play the chorus again and they get the hang of the words. Bev actually writes them down and goes over to stand beside Little Joe to hold them up so that he can see them – he needs a pair of reading glasses, so there's a brief delay as he returns to Clark Kent ironmonger mode again. But we play it through, everyone seems to enjoy singing it, and Bev gives us a one-woman round of applause. Fleece makes the interesting observation that it's likely that no-one has ever applauded our music before, so Bev claps again and demands an encore.

"You've not heard the whole song yet, Bev. It's got three verses, each with a chorus, which is repeated the last time, although I haven't got a proper introduction for it. I'd like a sort of quick 'na-na-na-na-nah-na', followed by a real heavy series of chord changes. That would be fun, but I can't play it. Can you do it Joe?"

Little Joe tries, several times, and is still trying when Fleece interrupts to say he'd quite like to hear the song some time before Christmas.

Bev comes up with a suggestion. "Why don't you just sing 'na-na-na-na-nah-na' just now, and you can work on that bit later?"

"I suppose so, Bev," I say. "It's a small point really."

I start to play the introductory chords of the song of *Right Here Lovin' Me*, feeling a complete twit singing "na-na-na-na-nah-na" at the same time, but I can't help but smile at the stupidity of it and I'm helped a lot as Fleece, Little Joe, and even Bev help by singing "na-na-na-na-nah-na" to keep me company. I launch into the first verse –

I've got you thinking, I've got you wondering what's inside my mind
We're just beginning, we're only starting, we can do as we feel inclined
You'll have to take me just as you see me to see what lies behind
So try me baby, dance with me baby, you never know what you'll find

Then the chorus

And if the night is cold, if the night is dark,
There's only one place you should be,
So from now until dawn, I'll still be hanging on,
I want you right here lovin' me.

Then verse two -

Slow down, what's the hurry? There's a long, long way to go
Just take it easy, take it as you feel it, just let the music flow
We're going nowhere, this is where it happens, this is the only show
Just enjoy it, you and me together,
Where we're heading I don't know

Then the chorus again, then the third verse -

It's getting later, it's getting darker, it's time now to beware
The band is playing to a different rhythm, something else is there
Can you sense it, sense a little danger? There's danger in the air -
So come on closer, just a little closer, closer still if you dare

Then the chorus is sung twice, and there's a few 'right here lovin' me' lines sung, as well as 'na-na-na-na-nah-nas'. The song does have a certain 'join-in' quality, but the other three make the most of it as well. Bev and Fleece both finish laughing uproariously, and in Bev's case this again cracks her image a little. She manages to seem less sexy when she's laughing, but nicer at the same time.

"It's definitely a cracker, Captain, definitely a cracker," Fleece says. "It's a pity we don't play anywhere or it would be a winner for weddings."

Little Joe can see the pound signs in that statement.

"We could start a band," he says.

Fleece, ever the practical, begs to differ. "Don't be so fucking stupid, Little Joe. This is a band with a drummer, a rhythm guitar who can't play any lead, a singer who needs to play acoustic guitar to sing in tune, and no bass."

"Succinctly put, Fleece," I agree. "Having no bass is a bit of a problem, I think." Fleece appears to believe that as a drummer he has no limitations, by the way, and to be fair he's probably the least bad amongst us.

"What we need is Suzi Quattro," he says. "That would solve all our problems. All mine, at least, if she was willing."

"I rather doubt Suzi can make it this afternoon, Fleece," I suggest. "Can you play the bass, Bev?"

She laughs, but she's already returned to husky mode. "I stick to cheese scones," she says. I bet she does.

Little Joe hasn't given up. "We could record it anyway," he says, hopefully. "It would be good to hear what it sounds like. You could record the other one, too – what's it called?"

"*Bird.*"

"OK, *Bird* and, this one as well. And while we're at it, we could try out some rasta-jock."

Now it's all clear, and Fleece and I groan, and although I manage to do it inwardly, both Little Joe and Bev can see it in my eyes – I'm too transparent. Fleece is about to go on a rant when Bev surprisingly intervenes.

"Why not, boys? What have you got to lose? It's only for your own ears anyway."

"My ears have been seared by 'rasta-jock', Bev." Fleece spits the term out. "I think it's a sort of cultural meltdown."

But Bev knows who the weak link is and it's me she's eyeing.

"What do you think, Brian?"

What I think at the moment is whatever Bev wants me to think, and therefore I think it's a great idea to record a bit of rasta-jock.

"I think it's a great idea to record a bit of rasta-jock," I say, as if the words have been spoken by an alien who has invaded my whole being. Bev, meantime, gives me the faintest of nods; I have done well, it says.

"Oh fuck," Fleece says, studying me. Then he suddenly throws his head back and roars with laughter, repeating "Oh, fuck." Strange how two such similar sentences can sound so utterly different, especially when he contrives to laugh so much that he falls backwards off his stool at the very thought. Fleece does nothing quietly.

"Great!" says Little Joe, ecstatic at the thought that his brainchild is to be laid down for posterity. "When can we start, Captain? Now?"

"I think a little practice might be a good idea. Next week, perhaps. Anyway, Joe, which of your many numbers would you want to record?"

"Now that you mention it, I don't know. Give me a week to think about it."

"Then we'll need to practise whatever you choose. Heaven knows what I can do on an acoustic guitar. Maybe nothing. By the way, I meant to say – that other song, *Bird*, I really imagined as an electric number."

"Really?" Joe sounds surprised. "We could all join in?"

"That would be the idea. There's a small problem, though."

"Let me guess," Fleece says, "it needs a bass, and we need someone to play lead guitar."

"Right on both counts," I confirm.

"I go for Quattro on the bass," he says, helpfully. "Anyone know someone who can play lead guitar?"

As it happens, I do.

17

Lead Guitar

"Goodness me, Brian! Fancy hearing from you again. Fancy that – goodness me, yes. How are you? Nice of you to phone me."

"Not too bad, Geoff," I reply. "You?" I've taken the precaution of finding a comfortable chair to sit on, and I've made myself a cup of coffee to boot – Nescafé Instant Espresso, one-and-a-half spoonfuls with a little milk. I can do some deep breathing exercises while he replies to this one as well.

"Well, Brian, funny you should mention that. Goodness me, yes, what a coincidence! In fact I've been struggling with a strange tingle in my left toe – the one between the little one and the middle one – which has kept me awake a couple of nights this last week. Doesn't sound much but goodness me wasn't it a pest? And I've still not managed to completely deal with that cricked neck I told you about in the café – I did tell you about my cricked neck didn't I? – goodness me yes of course I did – but the strange mark on my shin seems to have been a bruise and it's fading so that's one thing less. Now in the last few days I've been having a few toilet problems too – you know what I mean, I think – which might be related to a plate of curried lamb Sheila made last Friday. Sheila makes a lovely plate of curried lamb but at my age I'm not sure it's really such a good idea to be eating such exotic food. At least that's what I keep telling her, and goodness me has it played havoc when I've been going – you know. You never know what's going to happen next. And of course I've still got the usual problems with the water works! Did I mention the water works?"

I think there's a pause at the other end of the line, although I'm not certain because I've been drifting in and out of consciousness. Geoff should have been a hypnotist: "Now just relax while I tell you about my bowels…" But on balance I think that's a pause, so now I've got to say something, which in turn means I've got to guess the right answer.

"Yes, Geoff."

"Oh, I suppose I will have. Goodness me, I suppose so. But you didn't call to enquire after my state of health, Brian, goodness me, no."

Was it that obvious? "No, Geoff. Actually, I'm looking for a favour, but you might like to help anyway."

"I'm intrigued, Brian. I'm intrigued."

I explain about the little jam sessions Fleece, Little Joe and I have had these last couple of weeks, and that we need a bit of lead guitar if we're going to record my songs.

"So you've been writing little ditties, Brian? Goodness me, there's a thing now. You really do have me interested. When did you say?"

"Sunday afternoon coming."

"Let me speak to Sheila for a minute and I'll see if we're doing anything." A minute later he returns to the phone. "Looks like I can make it, Brian! Goodness me, what an adventure! I hope you don't expect me to be any good."

"However good or bad you are, Geoff, you'll be the best musician there. Rest easy."

We chat for a few more minutes and I give him Little Joe's address before we ring off, agreeing to see each other at two o'clock.

I return to my guitar and run through the two songs I've played with the band, although others are swirling around in my head as well. I'm looking forward to hearing what they sound like, but a little part of me also wants to hear what I sound like personally, because I don't want to embarrass myself in front of the others, especially as we're now up to four.

Over in the corner of my living room is yet another of my boy's toys, my state-of-the-art laptop, an Apple Macbook Pro with bucketloads of memory and enough processing power to take me to the moon. I bought it when I left teaching, but so far I've done little more with it than surf the internet, look at television programmes I've missed, write letters and check my emails. I don't even have any photographs to process. I'm hardly making the most of it, although it looks beautiful on the coffee table beside a table lamp which Brunhilde thought was ugly but I thought was extremely stylish. Anyway, I suddenly remember that there are two computer applications on it which might be of use – something called *Sibelius*, and another called Garageband. The first one – which is used to write sheet music – I paid quite a bit of money for, then hardly used at all; astonishingly, the second is free and I've never used it even once.

These things come with tutorials, and sure enough it quickly emerges that with a little effort – not all that much, actually – it's possible to create backing tracks to support virtually anything I want. I even find how to record myself on the laptop, and it's not bad, although I discover that I don't know the words of my own songs as well as I should, and it takes several efforts to get the balance right between guitar and voice. (The microphone needs to be higher up, which means the laptop needs to be on a shelf somewhere. It also seems to work best doing the recording in my bedroom, which has less disturbance from passing cars and urinating onlookers as well.)

Once I get myself onto the laptop – I record both *Bird* and *Right Here Lovin' Me* – I then try adding some effects. The most pressing is the bass, but this proves to be easy because I have no imagination with the bass, and I can get the notes I want by attaching the laptop to my Technics SX PC-26 and creating a series of 'loops' – little sections of music that I can join together to accompany my singing and acoustic guitar. I do some similar things with the lead guitar, and although it's not quite as easy as the manual claims it should be, I eventually manage to make it sound not too bad, especially with the addition of a little percussion.

Feeling rather pleased with myself, I turn the whole thing into a file that I can load up onto my iPod. It could be useful on Sunday.

18

The Reminder

When I come back from my Costa duty on the following Tuesday evening, there's the usual junk mail behind the front door waiting for me – I love junk mail, it makes me feel wanted – a letter from the doctor telling me it's time I had my blood-pressure checked, and a heavyweight piece of stationery that immediately sends it soaring.

> ROBB MERRIMAN, W.S.
> 18, Rutland Square
> Edinburgh, EH1 2BB
> 25th November, 2011

Brian Reid,
19A, Eton Terrace,
Edinburgh, EH4 1QD

Dear Mr Reid,

I write further regarding our client Mrs Jane Reid (née Forrest), your former wife.

You will recall that we wrote to you on the eleventh of this month concerning your recent retirement as a teacher, and that you are now in receipt of a pension, a share of which Mrs Reid is entitled in accordance with the your divorce settlement. We understand from our client that she is still not receiving this share of your pension.

We are concerned not to have made progress on this issue, nor even, as we understand, even to have received an acknowledgement. It is of course possible that the contact details we have for you are now out of date, and therefore it is of the utmost importance that you make contact with me at the earliest opportunity. Time is of the essence in this matter.

I look forward to hearing your reply by return. Should you have any concerns regarding this matter, please do not hesitate to contact me.

Yours sincerely,
Susan Gunn
(Partner, Robb Merriman)

Perhaps 'time is of the essence in this matter', but I've managed to put it to the back of my mind, even if not out of it altogether where it belongs. All the same, I remember to file the letter with the other one, in the corner behind the sofa with the other one and the balls of fluff. Brunhilde can whistle for my hard-earned pension, and what's more her solicitor has just presented me with a great idea – I can pretend I don't live here any more. That'll buy a little time. In the meantime, the only sign that 'time is of the essence' is that this letter has a first-class stamp on it whereas the previous one had a second. In keeping with the traditions of Royal Mail, it took just as long to reach me as the first one did.

My life has gained a meaning beyond flat whites and skinny lattes, although it's not that I dislike my work in Costa at all, and indeed the café offers even greater joy now that it's not the only thing I have to look forward to each week. Above all, it beats teaching for a lark.

I've texted the others to say Geoff has agreed to come on Sunday and had positive, if a little muted, responses. They've never met him and I can understand they're a little concerned that they might be losing control of things; I would be in their shoes. In the meantime there's nothing for it but to practise, find more material to play, and to play around with Garageband.

Wednesday brings a phone call from Becky, who wants to meet me after work. Her office is in the Grassmarket, and each night she walks down Morrison Street to Haymarket station, so I suggest we meet in Ryrie's, right at the station itself, so she doesn't have to worry about time. I know that way I'll also be seeing her down onto the platform and onto the train itself, which gives me the maximum time possible with her. It goes without saying that I miss her, although of course she effectively left the nest years ago when she went off to St. Andrews; now, the brutal truth is that she has to share her 'family time' between her mother and me. These are the times when I kick myself for the way I let my marriage go, but then a letter arrives through my door like the one today from Robb Merriman which reminds me that there was no alternative.

I'm glad Becky is my only daughter, because she would be bound to be my favourite anyway. She's touchy-feely towards me, knowing that she'll be probably be the only person in the world who really can be, and sure enough, when she walks in through the doors of Ryrie's bar at around five forty-five and spots me, the first thing she does is to give me a great big hug and a kiss. The idea flits through my head that not so long ago a woman wouldn't be seen dead inside a pub like Ryrie's, far less engage in any sort of intimacy, family or not. How times have changed for the better: women in pubs, no smoking, wine, soft drinks, or coffee if you want without so much as an eyelid batted behind the bar. Then I look outside over Becky's shoulder and smile at the roadworks for the trams project, known locally by all as 'the Fucking Trams'. Not everything is better.

Becky is dressed for work this time, and as she removes her coat and scarf and hangs it over the back of the seat I've kept for her, I see she's wearing a skirt and jumper underneath together with long boots to keep the November cold out.

"Been waiting long?"

"No," I lie, "I've just got here." Of course I got here ages ago. I didn't want to miss out on precious time with my daughter. "What can I get you?"

"I shouldn't," she says – she always she says she shouldn't but she always does, I've noticed – "but I think on a cold night like this I'd like something to warm me up. Could I have a whisky mac?"

"Goodness!" I say, realising immediately that I sound like Geoff, "of course you can."

I return a few minutes later with the whisky/Crabbies Green Ginger combination. I'm delighted that the barmaid, an Australian by the sound of things, knows her job well enough that she doesn't need to ask me what a 'whisky mac' is.

"Tell me, Becky," I wonder as I set the glass down on the table before her, "why do we call male bar staff 'barmen' but females are 'barmaids'? How about that for discrimination? Yet nobody says a word against it."

"Thanks for the drink, Dad. Haven't a clue – you're right, I've never given it a moment's thought." She's smiling, laughing at me. "Anyway, these ones should be baristas, because they all serve fancy coffee, too. How are things, then?"

"As you see me, my love. I think your mum is about to rack up the pressure on me. To me she seems vindictive, but I don't want you to get involved."

"I'd rather not get too involved, either. She still seems very angry with you."

"I've noticed."

Becky wants to say something, but she's holding herself back, I can see.

"Out with it, Becky. What's eating you? I know you too well."

She smiles, but there's sadness in her eyes and she looks down quickly. That look devastates me every time I see it. "You know what it is, Dad. I just want you and Mum to…"

"We'll never get back together, you know."

"To get on, then. For us. For me and for Harry. For Tommy and Danni, for that matter, too. To make matters worse, neither Harry or me ever worked out why you fought."

"She threw crockery at me, Becky."

"Yes, but we don't know why she threw crockery at you. OK, Mum has a temper sometimes, but she's also got a really upbeat sense of humour, and usually she's full of life."

Yes, I remember she was once like that with me, too. A long time ago. "Harry called your mum and me a 'war zone' the other Saturday."

"He's got a point. In which case the four of us are the 'collateral damage'."

"I was paying for your lunch at the time and he still said it."

Becky takes it as the joke I mean it to be and decides to move on to a happier theme. "How's the rock star, then? When are you going to release your first album?" One joke deserves another.

"I think we're just a little bit late for that. Besides which, we have two further problems. First we have no bass player; second we have no talent."

Becky, who happens to be drinking at the time, thinks this is pricelessly funny and ends up in a coughing fit.

"You can't be that bad."

"I'd advise you not to try and find out." I suddenly remember that Becky and Tommy are both fans of Monty Python. "Have you ever seen that sketch 'The Joke That Killed'?"

This sets her off again, but when she manages to calm down she says, "I'd be willing to take a chance. Not many people get to hear their fathers play in a band. If you ever make a recording…"

"I'll let you know if we ever make it on to *Top Of The Pops*."

"Now you are too late for that. That ended years ago."

"Really? And *The Old Grey Whistle Test*?"

"And *Laurel and Hardy*. And *Bilko*. And Buddy Holly's dead, by the way, too, if you'd missed it."

"Is Don McLean gone, too? You know, *American Pie*?"

"Still going, I think. He was on telly just the other week. He's nearly seventy."

"Sweet Jesus," I say, shocked. "I'd better move fast then with the rest of my life."

Becky laughs at me again. "I'll tell you what you should do. Make a YouTube clip of your music. You might end up like that American band that had all the success when their guitar got broken by an airline."

"Sons of Maxwell."

"Sorry?"

"That was the band's name – Sons of Maxwell. And they were Canadian. But they were different from us in one huge respect."

"Go on."

"Talent."

She laughs.

Meanwhile I'm thinking YouTube.

19

Geoff Meets the Band

The following Sunday, Geoff and I agree to meet for a couple of hours or so before we both go up to Little Joe's house in Merchiston. Around midday, Geoff arrives in a newish car, a convertible of some sort totally unsuited to Scotland in early December, and makes his way down the steps to my flat. As well as his guitar, he's also carrying something I'm not ready for – a music stand.

"Hi, Geoff, good of you to come round early like this."

"Hi, Brian. Goodness me, but it's no trouble at all. This seems a good idea, if you ask me. You said there were one or two numbers I wouldn't have heard before, and it makes sense to run through them at least."

I show him into the living room. I've already tried to warn the old boy in the flat above me that it might be a bit noisy for a short while but he doesn't seem to be answering the door. His problem – I did my best. Geoff gets his guitar case out.

"You look all very organised, Geoff," I say. "A music stand as well. That's for your... music, I suppose?"

Other people would take the mickey out of me for that question but taking the mickey is not part of Geoff's armoury.

"Yes. I need my music."

"I was just planning on running through a couple of songs and I was hoping you could pick it up as you go along."

"The problem with that, Brian, is that I don't play by ear."

"Sorry?"

"I really can't – sorry. I've been taught all the time to sight-read. My teacher is a real stickler, actually," he frown-smiles.

"You mean I'll need to write out the music for you?" Please answer 'no' to that question, Geoff.

"Yes, I'm afraid so. Goodness me, yes, I definitely need the music."

"So if you ever did a live gig, you'd need a music stand beside you?" I say, incredulously.

"Goodness me, of course. Is that a problem?"

I'm trying to imagine Jimmy Page, live at Wembley, with a music stand in front before him.

"Can you memorise music you've learned?" I ask in desperation.

"Eventually."

"So if you had to, you could shut your eyes and read the music in your mind's eye?"

"I suppose so. I've done it before, and I suppose I could still do it if I had to."

"In that case I might ask you to shut your eyes eventually and do just that." I might be able to sell Geoff to the others as 'lost in the music'. In the meantime this is a major pain in the backside, because now things are going to have to be written out for Geoff's benefit, and there's only one person who can do that; I'm the only one of the 'Merchiston three' who reads music, courtesy of Grade 3 piano exams.

I play Geoff my two songs and he's suitably polite about them ("Goodness me, I didn't know you had the talent, Brian"). I've had some ideas for little bits of lead guitar, and I write them down on scraps of paper on makeshift staves, and when he plays them over the recorded versions with the bass, sure enough they do make a difference. This might be going somewhere, but it's a big 'might'.

Eventually, it's time to face the music at Little Joe's house. Geoff has come from his home in Cramond in the north-west corner of Edinburgh and he insists that it makes sense that he gives me a lift there and back, especially since I can give him directions as we go. I've decided that I'll take my laptop as well as my guitar, and I've also loaded up an ancient briefcase with some cables and one or two nifty little converters which might prove useful later. There's plenty of room in the boot of Geoff's car for all the kit – he's already been told he won't need any amplifiers of his own, he can use Little Joe's – but the real problem lies in getting me into the front passenger seat. It takes fully five minutes to shoe-horn me in, and he has to fold back the soft-top roof of his Nissan Micra Sport especially to let it happen.

We arrive at Little Joe and Bev's at two as promised. Once again, it's Bev who answers the door, and Geoff is completely bowled over by her; he says "Goodness me" six times in his first seven sentences of their introductions, and, unsurprisingly, can't take his eyes off her. She leads us through to the back of the house – it's Geoff who gets the 'hand' treatment this time and I'm about to be jealous when Bev leaves him briefly and gasping a "Lovely to see you, Brian," in my ear, reaches up to kiss me on the lips. As a result I fail to notice that the back garden path is an icy death trap and nearly go my length as we make our way to the studio.

"Are you all right, Brian?" Bev pants at me desperately. "I thought I'd lost you there."

If I had indeed died and gone to heaven, heaven would be full of Bevs, but I reassure her I'm still in the land of the living. She exhales that she'd better sprinkle some salt on the path before she brings the cheese scones.

We eventually teeter into the studio, where Fleece and Little Joe are in full flow. I forget that I've already grown accustomed to this intergalactic blast, but Geoff is struggling to cope with what his ears are letting in. Suddenly, Fleece stops in mid-batter, and Little Joe grinds to a merciful end soon after.

"Captain!!" Fleece roars. "How great to see you. Thought you'd never get here!"

Only for a second do I mistake this for a genuine urge to see me personally – a nod of his head towards Little Joe is enough to tell me that rasta-jock has been particularly trying so far and my arrival brings relief.

I introduce Geoff to his two new 'jammin' cousins', and they engage in a little small talk about how they each know me, which parts of the city they live in, and the Fucking Trams. The last is always a wonderful twenty-first century ice-breaker, I find. Borrowing a phrase I've heard before – I can't quite remember where – I suggest that 'time is of the essence', and that we ought to get down do to the music. In the case of rasta-jock, a very long way down. I have warned Geoff about rasta-jock, by the way, and he has brought an interesting ear-plugs in the form of his iPod headphones, which look quite professional the way he wears them.

I'm already beginning to be the one who keeps things moving in this ensemble, and I'm the one who seems to be making the suggestions as to what we play, but I'm aware of my responsibilities to keep everyone interested, especially Little Joe, whose ego remains the most fragile. As a result we start as ever with a couple of rocky numbers for Fleece, then Little Joe gets to try out his latest rasta-jock offering, and then I invite Geoff to play something for us. It turns out he has a small arsenal of crackerjack instrumentals, including Carlos Santana's *Samba Pa Te* and Focus's *Hocus Pocus*, all played from sheet music propped up on his music stand. Those of us with suitable electric instruments can join in, so I'm left out.

"Ok, it's your turn now, Brian – or do I call you Captain here? Yes, goodness me, do I call you Captain?"

"I answer to both," I reply, then go on to explain to everyone that Geoff and I ran through these earlier.

We're going to try *Right Here Lovin' Me* first, partly because it's got a simpler structure, and as I open up the laptop and plug one of many cables into one of Little Joe's many amplifiers, Fleece peers over his cymbals and looks down.

"What's this, Captain? What's this?"

"It's our bass player."

"I thought you were going to try to get Suzi Quattro."

"I tried to get her but she had something on this afternoon," I reply, not paying much attention.

"Pity," Fleece burbles on, "I like Suzi better when she's got nothing on." I suppose that was predictable.

"Think of Suzi down here, any way you like. Close your eyes and she's right there in front of you," I suggest, pointing to the laptop.

He closes his eyes. "Now I can't see her," he complains, and opens his eyes.

"She's hiding behind your drums down here, but she'll only be here if you don't look." I wonder what Tommy the carpenter-metaphysician would make of this conversation.

"Surreal," Fleece says. Actually, that's what Tommy would say, too.

"Tell you what," I suggest, "let's call the laptop Suzi when she's playing the bass. They're a bit alike, actually, small, nice to look at, and in a shiny case."

Fleece roars with laughter. "You're calling a dumb machine 'she' already'! You've made my day, Captain, you've made my day. Fancy having Suzi Quattro as our bass player. How's a man supposed to concentrate on his drumming?"

"By keeping your eyes closed."

"Which is where we came in."

I tell them the plan, which is to set Suzi off on the floor, playing her bass through the amp between Fleece and Little Joe, and then I join in, then each of them in turn playing the basic beat. Then I'm to launch into the first verse. In the end, it takes two false starts before we get it right, but we do eventually manage to plough our way to the end, including the repeat of the chorus and a few extra bits. As always happens when something sounds good, there's a generally warm self-congratulatory smugness all round, which means nothing. Suzi, sitting on the floor, is none too impressed on the other hand: her screen has gone to sleep. Meanwhile, there's been a knock on the outside door, and Bev pops her head round.

"I've been listening outside – I didn't want to disturb you." She emerges with... cheese scones and mugs of coffee, and there are extra of course because we have Geoff with us.

"Goodness me, Brian," he exclaims, "you didn't tell me about the cheese scones."

There's a lot I didn't tell you about Bev, Geoff, for your own safety, I think, but I let Bev reply for herself.

"I do hope you like cheese scones, Geoff. It's so nice of you to come," she says softly.

Geoff doesn't know what has hit him, but manfully he turns his frown-smile gauge to maximum and says, "The pleasure's mine, Bev, goodness me it's all mine. And I don't know a man on this earth who wouldn't die for a cheese scone like this."

"If you decide to die, Geoff, do it soon will you so that I can eat your share," yells Fleece.

Geoff finds this funny, and gets up to show a polite interest in Fleece's drum-kit. He's been well brought up in the art of socialisation and small talk, and I know I can rely on him to make a lot of effort with these two half-wits I've introduced him to. Meanwhile, Little Joe comes across towards me, and therefore also Bev who has pulled a stool up close to me, tantalisingly just on the edge of my personal space.

"Captain, I've been meaning to have a word," he begins. "Just you and me," then, looking at Bev, "and Bev, of course."

This bodes ill. "Which word would you like to have, Joe? I can offer you words like 'yes' or 'no', or longer ones such as 'perhaps'."

Bev, in a rare show of violence, gives my thigh a playful slap. Gorgeous. Sensibly, Joe ignores everything and carries on to elaborate. "It's about my rasta-jock project."

I'd feared it might be, but let's be optimistic, he might be about to say he's abandoned it. "Tell me."

"I think I've found the missing link."

"Sorry?"

"The missing link. The song that proves my theory about black West-Indian music and its impact on Scottish folk music."

"Really?" I look at Bev, who's clearly heard this gibberish already and yet still looks as excited as her husband.

"I told you I'd find it, and I knew you had the most faith in me. Didn't I say that, Bev? Didn't I tell you that Captain was on my side?"

"You did, my love. Many times," Bev agrees, nodding her head as she gazes at me.

"So what's the song?" This I must hear. Actually, on second thoughts this I mustn't hear if I can help it.

"That's just the trouble," Little Joe says, his voice down a bit. "I don't know about it."

"Just tell me, Joe! I'm listening."

"It's *Ho-ro, My Nut Brown Maiden...*," he says. "But..., but... is it racist?" He's genuinely worried.

I manage to keep a straight face about Joe's 'discovery'. My guess is that the 'nut-brown' maiden has 'nut-brown hair', but I don't want to disappoint him. "It may be an early example of Scottish multiculturalism, perhaps, extolling the virtues of a mixed marriage. Have you done any research on the song?"

"It seems to be a Gaelic song, and the one we know from the Corries is just a translation."

"Probably a waulking song," I suggest. It's got the right rhythm.

"Do you mean a sort of march?" he asks.

"I don't mean that kind of 'walking'," and I go on to explain how the women of the Western Isles used to stretch and beat the living daylights and natural oils out of the wool they had turned into tweed, and that they kept in time with each other by singing songs. "They say that the women used a solution of their own urine to work the cloth. These days it's the songs themselves that are pish." I apologise to Bev for my language, but she brushes a hand across my knee and reassures me that she's not offended at all.

"What about it, Captain?" Little Joe pleads. He's imploring me to sound enthusiastic, and the magnetic field to my left is urging me to be supportive, too.

"Okay," I reply, "We'll try it later, perhaps?"

"Great, Captain, great!" He's so excited, and Bev again gives me a discreet nod to say "well done", followed by a longer, more lingering brush of the knee.

Bev wants to hear the original material, bless her, and she even wants to hear Little Joe's latest rasta-jock. "Play it again, Brian, play it." There she goes again, pressing the magic buttons.

This time we attempt to record something as we play *Right Here Lovin' Me*, which takes two further attempts but we get there in the end. Flushed with success, we then turn to *Bird*, which demands a little more practice. Again, the lead guitar is no problem – Geoff is turning out to be good, if a little pedestrian, he has to have instructions for everything – but the vocals are a big issue this time. It sounds better if we sing the last chorus twice, with everyone contributing the very last time – even Bev joins in. But there's a middle eight that just isn't right at all. The whole process is taking ages.

"Listen, Brian," Geoff says, "I don't mean to be rude but I said to Sheila that I'd be home by six-thirty for my dinner. Goodness me – but she'll be getting worried. Can we just try something just now and see how it goes? Anything?"

He's desperate, and so is the music, to be honest. We might as well, I suggest, and see what it sounds like when we play it back, but I'm not hopeful – Little Joe is no natural harmoniser, although I can hardly say that. We set off, with me strumming the guitar in a simple intro again, while all the rest join in as Suzi keeps the beat on the bass. She at least doesn't cause any bother. If only the others were laptops as well, I think, but laptops still don't sing very well.

Little Joe joins in the middle eight, totally out of tune but we've agreed to keep going no matter what so that Geoff can get home. Of course he's giving me a lift home, too, and I still have to work out how to squeeze back into that tent-on-wheels of his, but at least it's now dark rather than broad daylight, so my embarrassment will not be seen unless I'm unlucky.

Little Joe looks crestfallen. "You promised," he says. Bev looks at me, crushed. You promised, she's thinking.

"Can we quickly record Little Joe's *Nut Brown Maiden*, Geoff?" I turn to Joe. "Will it take long?" I ask hopefully. Bev seems to have forgiven me.

Mercifully, it really doesn't take long to get something down, partly because so few people can add anything to it – just the drums, and a couple of rhythm guitar sounds from Joe and me. I promise to listen to it at home and perhaps add a bass. But Geoff's tugging at my arm.

"Come on, Brian, we've got to go. Goodness me, yes please. Let's go," and he's already on his way out with Bev leading, giving a cheery see-you-next-week wave as he goes.

20

Post Production

My job as Depyoot Head at my school landed me with responsibility for 'IT' – information technology in all its forms, shapes and sizes. This didn't mean I was ever particularly adept at IT, but it did mean that I got to know all the people in my school who were. It also meant I could bring gadgetry home – especially the latest gadgetry – to become 'familiar' with it, so for around twenty years I've become a computer nerd. But the problem with information technology is that most people only bother to learn how to use it when they can see a point – in other words, they discover they want to do something, and then want to learn the computer skills to help them achieve it. I've discovered that I'm no different from anyone else, in fact, and that my knowledge of the music program *Garageband* is proving quite inadequate for my needs. I'm struggling with the process of mixing the real recording with the synthetic bass I need to add to make it

Of course I do know someone who can help me, someone at my old school, and unsurprisingly it's not the head of computer studies, it's the head of music, Lex Maddison. Rid your head now of any preconceptions of 'computer whizz-kids'; Lex is an attractive woman in her early- to mid-thirties with shortish dark hair and an incredibly sunny disposition, as well as two children of her own under five. Lex is a brilliant violinist – although the school would hardly know because her work compels her to play endless piano and keyboard accompaniments for her pupils – but her other passion is music production using *Garageband*, and a couple of other programs, including *Sibelius*.

Lex has agreed to help me with some technical problems regarding different types of music – especially combining what we sing and play with Sue Zee, as the 'laptop' bass player has now become known. She wants me to come into the music department one lunchtime, and I reluctantly agree. I have no wish to revisit the old school, to be honest, and I particularly wish to avoid my old headteacher Dr Genevieve Forbes-Marr, she and I not having parted on the best of terms. On the surface, Dr Genevieve ("call me Jenny") Forbes-Marr is a blonde, personable, five-foot-three's worth of excellent company, but underneath she's a cold, stupid, talentless bitch. She is, in fact, loathed by ninety percent of the staff, mostly openly; the remaining ten per cent want the promotion she can give them. She particularly dislikes me, because it was I who discovered – courtesy of a random visit to the online Scottish birth certificate service – that she was actually christened 'Jennifer', and that the 'Forbes-Marr' bit is also simply a combination of her middle name and that of her ex-husband. Flushed with that success, I blundered on to find that her PhD was actually attained from a correspondence course with Lewisberg University in Tennessee, at a grand total cost of eight hundred and fifty-nine dollars, including postage and packing.

Fortunately, Lex's music department lies in a little wing of its own, so it gives me the chance to slip in a back door unnoticed. It takes her five minutes to demonstrate what I need to know, and another thirty before I can do it myself.

"Let's listen to the music, Brian," she says.

"It's awful, believe me."

"Then at least I'll get a good laugh. Consider it as payment for the lesson you've just had."

There's no answer to that, so I start to let her hear the three items we have. She gives *Right Here Lovin' Me* a "not bad, not bad at all" – high praise in Scotland – then we listen to *Bird*. I warn her that that Little Joe's backing vocals will fall short of her own high standards. Just a little. But she surprises me.

"I'm not sure I agree with you about the backing vocals, Brian," she says. "They're different, sure, but I think they really work. There's an urgency about them that's missing in most of these sorts of things."

"Call it desperation, Lex. He's desperately trying to sing the right notes."

"Whatever. Personally, I think it's genius."

Genius? I ask if I can feel her forehead to check if she's running a temperature.

"No," she says, "I'd leave that as it is. It's got something."

"I'm not sure Joe can sing the same something twice on purpose."

"That's a problem, I'll give you."

"Thanks anyway. Do you want a laugh? Shall I play the rasta-jock?"

"What???"

Sure enough, *Ho-ro, My Nut Brown Maiden* has her in hysterics in no time. "It would make a great karaoke competition, though."

"Eh? Karaoke?"

"It's a good test to see if anyone can sing along with it," she explains. "The ultimate challenge, the Everest of karaoke."

"It would be an interesting selling point."

"Meantime," Lex goes on, "have you thought how you're going to publish this stuff?"

"By which you mean...?"

"Let the world hear it?"

"I'd thought about YouTube, but thinking about it is as far as I'd got. I haven't a clue how, though."

"YouTube's one idea, certainly. A website would be a good idea as well, so that anyone who hears one of your tracks can go and listen to others if they want."

"But our stuff is crap, Lex. I'm not sure we shouldn't be hiding it rather than publicising it."

"You know it's not that bad, Brian. Otherwise you wouldn't be here, would you?"

"No. I suppose I wouldn't," I admit, a bit sheepishly.

"In any case, whether it's any good or not is for the listener to decide, not you," she says, quietly.

"Does that even apply to rasta-jock?"

"Don't be silly, Brian. There's a limit. Being serious for a moment, what you need is video."

"Why?" I'm thinking: Why? What is there to video?

Lex explains. "It doesn't have to be a video of you or the band."

I'm confused, and tell her so.

"It doesn't really matter what it's a video of, actually, as long as the listener can look at something while they listen. That *Bird* song, for instance, could have film of a soaring bird. An eagle, perhaps, even just a buzzard."

"Are they different?" I ask.

"Yes," she says, "one's an eagle and the other's a buzzard."

"Thanks. That explains everything."

"As I say, though, nobody really pays much attention to the film, but if it's there people think it's a more professional recording."

"Seriously?"

"Definitely. Heaven knows how you're going to find something to go with rasta-jock. What about a film of the band itself?"

"Hardly. A bunch of geriatrics playing in a converted garage? A laptop instead of a bass player? How do we brush that away?"

Lex ponders for a moment. "The Traveling Wilburys had a rocking chair where Roy Orbison should have been."

"That was Roy Orbison. He was a legend, a bit like Buddy Holly and John Lennon. Shut your eyes and you can still see him. People will shut their eyes in case they see us."

"You'll come up with something. Animation? If you're desperate, try one of these things that generates colourful pattern to match your music. Anything's better then nothing."

Eventually, Lex hints that it's time I left, pointing out she has a class after lunch but insisting she'd be "delighted to help any time". As I gather up my equipment, she says insistently, "Don't forget the website, Brian. Create a website. It's not that expensive, really. What's your band called?"

It occurs to me we haven't got a name. "Do we need one?"

"I rather think so. Nobody wants to hear 'anonymous' playing. Sometimes just calling the band the first thing that comes into your head gets the best results."

The thought makes me smile. "My ex-wife would have said you'd have to wait a long time for anything to come into my head."

"That's not very nice of her," Lex says, concerned. "Prove her wrong right now. What are you thinking of right at the moment?"

Right at the moment, the very mention of the wild Brunhilde and her sarky remarks conjures up an intriguing picture. But Lex wants the first thing that comes into my head, so that means...

21

The Nerd

A new problem has developed in the last few days. Three scrunched-letters from Robb Merriman now lie with the fluff behind the living-room sofa, but I suspect the postie – a very cheery woman in her thirties who, remarkably, wears shorts all the year round – wants to deliver a fourth, because she's been ringing my doorbell these last three days, and by creeping up in my stocking soles and peering through the peephole I can see she has a recorded delivery letter in her hand. As a matter of policy I try never to accept recorded delivery letters unless I'm due for a new credit card; they always bring bad news, a bit like receiving a telegram during the war. My fears are confirmed by Thursday when I see her casually in the street on another round.

"I've been looking for you this week," she says, breezily. It's December, freezing, and she's still in shorts. I'm cold just looking at her.

"Oh, I've been out a lot lately," I tell her, which is actually even less true than usual.

"Funny, I could have sworn I saw a light go on in your front room this morning."

"No, not me." So she knows. "I've got one of these timers that switches lights on and off to fool the burglars."

"Good idea," she smiles. She knows I'm lying and I was there all the time. "You can't be too careful. Maybe I'll catch you tomorrow then?"

"Maybe. Hope so." Another lie to end the conversation. I need to get a grip of my life, I tell myself as I wave her a friendly 'cheerio'.

Meanwhile, Lex has filled me with all sorts of ideas, most of which prove far harder to make happen than they really should, but in the week leading up to the next session I have become that completely anti-social being, the computer bore. The only saving grace is that I have no-one to bore, and only once do I have to take Lex up on her kind offer to phone her in the evening for help. (Lex's husband, by the way, is very understanding, as it turns out he too makes an exceptional living out of being a computer geek, testing games before they're released on the market. Lex tells me he's been responsible for the hugely successful *Death Crash Racing Track Star 1* and *Death Crash Racing Track Star 2*, and something else which I don't quite catch.) This computer stuff is certainly engrossing, and by Friday I've not only managed to make *Bird* sound better than it deserves – complete with 'Sue Zee the bass' – I've found enough free video footage of soaring birds to go with it. I'm quite pleased with the result, in fact, although all the footage is plastered either with 'Freefootage.com' or the equally inventive 'Footageforfree.com'. On the other hand, although *Right Here Lovin' Me* sounds all right – thanks again, Suzi, for the bass – I'm no further forward with the video footage. Film of the band is out, though, partly because we haven't got a decent camera and partly because we're all old and ugly.

It can be compulsive pastime, and it's as well that I have my Costa days to bring me to my senses, and on Friday night – Friday night can be a lonely night for divorced guys in their late fifties, by the way – the phone goes and it's Becky again. I say Becky again not because she's phoned every day or anything – I've not seen her since the Ryrie's meeting over a week ago – but simply because I haven't spoken to Harry for even longer. But I'm about to get a nice surprise.

"Hi, Dad," she says, "How are things?"

"Hi, Becky, nice to hear from you. I'm fine. You well?"

"Yes, yes," she said. "Tommy and I were wondering if you fancied meeting for lunch tomorrow."

My weekend has just got a little more expensive.

"I was going to suggest Harry and Danni come too." A lot more expensive. "It was great the last time at Café Andaluz," she continues.

"Sounds lovely," I reply, and it does, but I know who's paying already. "Did you have somewhere in mind?" Actually, I know Becky will have somewhere in mind or she wouldn't have phoned me. Becky plans.

"I thought we could try that new place in Commercial Street, Carmen's," she suggests.

"The one that's just got a Michelin star?" Jesus wept. Has she no shame?

"Yes," she says brightly, "but they do a great lunch deal for thirty pounds a head on Saturdays."

"*How much?*"

"It's supposed to be very good, Dad."

"I can make a whole month's lunchtime tuna mayonnaise sandwiches for thirty quid, Becky."

"OK, sorry" she says, disappointed.

Thirty seconds later, my guilt-ometer has reached such a level that I'm the one positively pleading with her to take me up on the offer to go to this dirt-cheap new Michelin-starred cafe in Leith I've just heard about and am dying to try. Why am I so weak? Is it a male thing? Probably.

In fairness it must be good – it's not that easy for Becky and Tommy to get to from Bathgate, although even that theory gets blown out of the water when Becky announces that Tommy's bringing his van. But at least that means we'll save on some wine or beer.

Our conversation ends after five minutes or so – I tell her to save her news for Carmen's, and also, I say, to save her phone bill, although both of us know she's on her mobile and has one of those contracts where you can call all day and all night and it costs just the same – a fortune. I wonder if I can really justify my own mobile. I suspect it suits us both – she and Tommy are off to see what the bright lights of Bathgate have to offer, and I'm quite hooked on this computer lark.

By nine-thirty, I realise the video of *Bird* is as good as it will ever be, and *Right Here Lovin' Me* will not be anything other than sound-only any time soon. Lex has already signed me up for YouTube – amazingly easy – and in no time I've uploaded both the songs to my new account. People can listen, now – anyone at all, which is a bit scary. I console myself that no-one will ever find us.

All that remains is the band's website, which is something I can manage myself. It's basic, and is based on a template I found on my own laptop as part of a program which does everything for you, but it'll do. In a final moment of whimsy, I create a separate page for Little Joe's *Ho-Ro, My Nut-Brown Maiden* and his rasta-jock. If you're unlucky enough to trip over the wrong page, you might actually hear him.

Heaven help you. You have been warned. Even the name I've given to his band says he's on another planet.

22

At Carmen's

Three of us are sitting in Carmen's, a discreetly furnished restaurant in the fashionable Dock area of Leith. Becky is getting agitated and has been looking relentlessly at her watch ever since we all arrived together at 12.45. There's no sign of Harry and Danni, although they're actually the only ones who have been told lunch was at a quarter to one. The table is actually booked for one o'clock, but Becky's hoping to trick Harry into turning up on time for once.

Until now the waiters have been almost invisible, a sign of class in a restaurant in my experience, but now one – he's wearing a rather expensive-looking suit so he might even be the head waiter – is approaching.

"Mr Reid? I have a message for you from your son. He's saying he'll be a few minutes late."

Becky is furious. "He's already twelve minutes late according to the time we gave him. Did he define 'a few minutes'?" I know this is going to end in tears.

"Ah, Mr Reid junior called earlier to check the time of the booking. I'm sorry, sir, we simply told him it was booked for one." The waiter can already tell he's been dragged into something, and is both looking and sounding uncomfortable.

"No, no," I reassure him, "you did the right thing."

As the waiter drifts away, all I can hear Becky say is "Bugger Harry, why does he have to do this?" This is an unusually violent response by her standards, although I understand her frustrations, and she's still not cooled down when Harry and Danni swan in at exactly four minutes past one.

"Nice to see you, Harry. At last," Becky hisses at him.

Harry looks at his watch. "I know," he says, with a smug smile, "We're a fashionable four minutes late." Nobody can miss the reference to the fact that he knows when the table was really booked for. Danni, to her credit, is looking away, embarrassed. Tommy just doesn't care, and has buried his head in the menu. For an expensive menu, it's surprisingly spartan – merely a handwritten menu which has been reproduced twenty times or so on an inkjet printer. I'm reminded that not being ostentatious is itself a sign of class.

While we're choosing, Harry announces that since I was rather 'bounced' into hosting this meal, he would pay for any drink involved, and, intriguingly, Tommy emerges from behind the menu to announce that they'd pay any tip. I go through the motions of refusing, then I realise that they've all been discussing this beforehand – probably in textspeak – and it's all arranged, so why should I worry? All I have to think about now is five times thirty.

The menu offers four options for each of the first two courses, and I've chosen oysters, followed by hare, one of my winter favourites. Only three of us are drinking, it turns out, since Danni is driving too, and I suggest the house red wine, partly to save Harry money and partly because I frankly don't recognise any of the wines on the list. Harry of course is delighted that we're being so frugal with his money, but he is careful not to say so. No sooner have we ordered than another waiter appears with the mandatory 'amuse-bouche', on this occasion some concoction involving a giant peeled prawn wrapped in black pudding. There's a chilli in there somewhere, too.

We exchange the usual small talk for a while, then Danni turns to me.

"So, Brian," she says, "how's the band going. Are you still playing?"

"Yup," I reply.

Harry looks up, interested. "So are you booked for Glastonbury yet?"

"Not yet. The world has yet to waken up to our massed talents."

"When are we going to hear you? Is there any chance that'll happen?" It's because he sounds genuinely interested that I let it slip.

"I've taken up a suggestion of your sister's."

Becky looks as amazed as Harry. "What did I suggest, for goodness' sake?"

"YouTube. You suggested we post something on YouTube. So I did."

"Away!" Harry says. They're all interested now, even Tommy.

"You can listen to it whenever you like. There's the beginning of a website, too."

"Really? Really?" Harry doesn't know whether he should laugh out loud or hide under the table in shame that he's my son. "This I must check out." He gets his iPhone out.

"I think that's probably frowned on in a place like this," I suggest.

"Do you mind if I go outside and have a look?"

I shrug my shoulders.

Now they all want to know. "What's the name of the band? What's the website called?" so I tell them.

"What???"

"It was the first name that came into my head." They all know why, and there's a further disbelieving laugh. "The rest of the band don't know yet, so it's very much a prototype. All the names might change later."

Seconds later I find myself alone in the restaurant while they all dive outside to hear the songs on YouTube. I'm feeling a little stunned.

"Would you like to try the wine, sir?" says a voice behind me.

"Looks like I'm the only one left." I explain that they've all gone out to look at their phones.

"That sums up the younger generation," the waiter muses. "They value their smartphones more than wonderful food and wine with a few friends."

"Don't worry," I reassure him, "they'll be back. I'm paying."

He laughs, pours me a glass from different bottle of red, and says quietly, "On the house, sir. This is another house wine we're thinking about introducing. I'd value your opinion. And I think you deserve the treat."

I thank him, already reminded that a top-class restaurant must do more than provide great food and wine; it must be a great experience as well. I could return here, assuming I can afford it, which in turn depends on whether Brunhilde manages to get her claws into my pension or not.

Then suddenly they're back. And they're excited.

"That's amazing, Dad," Becky says. "Well done. Did I really suggest YouTube?"

"In Ryrie's. Remember?"

"I do, but never in a million years did I think you'd do it."

"A man of many surprises," Harry says.

"OK?" I ask him, tentatively.

"Oh, you get all sorts of shite on YouTube these days. Singing dogs, fireworks going wrong, little kids getting run over – "

"Harry!" Danni and Becky say together.

"Sorry. Although remember that little girl who was run over in China? You can watch her – "

"Enough, Harry," says Danni. She's good for him, she's what he needs.

"Seriously, Dad, I've heard a lot worse. Tinie Tempah for a start."

"Is that praise? I can't tell," I confess.

"That's praise, Dad. Not bad. You might make the big-time. Who knows?"

"I might need to. Your mum wants to take me for all I'm worth."

"Half of what you're worth, to be precise," Harry corrects me.

"That won't leave very much. I could do with a new source of income."

Harry stops. "Dad, can we offer you some advice?" Harry asks, quietly.

Am I ready for this? "Go on. Remember I'm paying for the meal."

"You need a lawyer. Urgently. Please – and if you can't afford it, I'll pay for it."

Harry is trying to shame me into action. I don't like it, but he's right.

"OK, I'll go and see a solicitor," I say.

"Promise?"

I pause. "I promise." There's a tense silence.

"Well, I really liked the music," Tommy chirps up, suddenly sensing the need to lighten the mood. "I'm going to FB all my friends about it."

I'm thrown. "'FB'? Sorry?"

"Facebook. All my Facebook friends," he explains. "I'll put the word about."

"We can all do that. The website, too," Becky adds. "Is there a counter for hits?"

"There is, actually," Harry says. "I noticed you had one on the front page, Dad. I'm impressed."

"Seriously?"

"Seriously."

Later, choosing to walk home after a lovely lunch with my children – they all four feel like my children – I have to time think, I did something to make them proud of me. It's been a long time since I've made them proud of me, I guess, and it's a nice feeling. It's almost been worth one hundred and fifty pounds.

23

What's in a Name?

"*What* name did you give us?" It's Fleece who expresses the first official view on my suggestion for the band's name.

The others haven't quite taken it in. It's Sunday afternoon, and we're getting set up in Little Joe's studio, Bev having floated away.

"My colleague told me to think of the first thing that came into my head," I try to explain.

"In which case, why didn't you call the band 'I'm A Complete Fucking Moron' then? Or is that too many words for your tiny head?"

"I was thinking about Brunhilde at the time. Sorry. I thought you wouldn't mind."

Little Joe is slowly working out what I'm telling them; I can see the wheels turning behind his eyes. Geoff, however, feels the need to ask for clarification.

"I need to get this right, Brian," he says, frown-smiling, although on closer inspection it's more of a frown-frown-frown-smile this time. "Yes, goodness me, do I need to get this right. You're telling me that for the last few days, if someone knew where to look, they could go onto the internet and listen to that recording we made last week?"

"That utter shite we recorded last week," Fleece tries to make it clear for him. "And he's given us a name, just out of nowhere."

"The Flying Saucers seemed as good a name as any," I say, meekly. I appear to have misjudged the importance of the band's name. "Listen," I say quickly, "we can change it."

"In the meantime," Fleece says, "if any of my friends has heard that... that..." – he's so angry he can't speak – "that tripe, you'll be hearing from my solicitor. Which is Walnut, by the way."

That reminds me. "By the way, I need a solicitor, too," I say.

"You will, right enough," yells Fleece. "But you can't have Walnut. He can't represent both of us when I sue you."

Fleece marches over and stands right in front of me. There's a tense silence. Then suddenly, he roars with laughter and delivers a massive blow to my overblown stomach which doubles me up, winded, while Fleece simply shouts at the top of his voice, "FUCK!" He drags me upright.

"Are you all right, Captain? Speak to me, are you all right?" He sounds concerned.

"I... I think so," I gasp.

This time he wallops me on the shoulder, sending me sideways. "Well, you don't deserve to be!" he says, roaring with laughter.

Geoff is a little embarrassed by this show of violence from our drummer, and looks away. Little Joe has still said nothing, until now, but still looks as bewildered as ever.

There's a knock on the door. Miraculously, Saint Bev has returned to save us all.

"I'm so sorry, boys, I forgot to ask you – will you be wanting your cheese scones at the usual time?"

The ever-polite Geoff, of course, frown-smiles immediately, saying "Goodness me, Bev, the cheese scones of course! Goodness me! Whenever it suits you, of course." But he's the only one with manners.

"Is something wrong?" Bev asks, slightly worried.

"My dear sister-in-law Beverley," says Fleece at top volume, "our lead singer here, Captain no less, has christened our motley crew with the daftest name you'll ever hear. And to cap it, he's made a YouTube recording, and launched a website using the said daft name."

"That's good, surely?"

"The Flying Saucers?"

Even Bev has to stifle a laugh, but when she sees she's hurt me, she comes over and caresses my shoulder.

"I'm sorry, Brian," she whispers. "Actually, it's not such a bad name when you think about it?"

She's lying, but her lies are good too.

"Do we have to think about it at all?" Fleece wants to know.

Bev has noticed that Little Joe has still said nothing, and she makes her way towards him.

"How about you, darling, how do you feel about all of this?"

"I don't know," Little Joe says at last. He looks a little down. "What do your two songs sound like on YouTube?"

It's Bev who has the idea. "We've got Brian's laptop – can we hear them now, Brian?"

"I suppose so," I say.

I fire up the internet and go to YouTube, and using the search engine provided locate *Bird*. Bev notices that quite a few people appear to have watched it already.

"That'll be Harry and Becky and their pals," I explain. "And I think each time we watch it counts separately, too."

"It's a video…" Geoff says with surprise.

Four minutes later, Fleece has a surprise for me.

"OK, Captain, I take it back. You've managed to make a plastic purse out of a sow's ear."

"But not silk," I smile back at him.

"I don't ask for the impossible. But you've cleaned up the sound and added a few bits and pieces, covering up some of the worst bits. It's not as bad as I'd feared. Amazing, considering we don't have a bass player. Let's hear the other one." This is the highest praise from our bearded drummer.

It's just an audio upload, but I've attached a picture of a band to go with it; not us, I might add, just a cartoon I picked up free from the web. That goes down well, too.

"This is wonderful, Brian," Bev says softly. "And you say there's a website, too?"

"www.flyingsaucers.eu," I reply.

"Dot what?" Fleece asks.

"Dot e-u. As in European Union. All the proper ones had been claimed by the bampots that claim to see UFOs."

"As opposed to the bampots that play rubbish and then put it on the internet?"

"And it was only ninety-nine pence to register the domain name."

"That's a good reason. That's all we're worth."

"Let's see the website, too," Bev breathes at me. She's still concerned about Joe, though, I can tell.

I fire that up, too, and navigate around it, with its page about the band – no-one is now questioning that we are a band – the music to listen to, and a contact page.

"Looks great," says Little Joe.

I know he feels he's losing control of his dream, but I haven't forgotten him. "Here's something for you, Little Joe."

There's a page within the site for 'Little Joe and the Martians', in which I've given him a little write-up about rasta-jock, and the download of *Ho-Ro, My Nut Brown Maiden*. Joe's reaction is electric.

"It's great, Captain, it's great. Thanks a lot! That's just great." He is just so happy.

Fleece rolls his eyes. Bev squeezes my arm with her hand. If it's possible for a hand and an arm to have sex together, it's just happened.

"I'm sorry about the name, Joe," I tell him, "I couldn't think of anything else at the time. We'll change it."

"No," he says, "I like it. I like it, really." He's like a little boy who's found the sweetie jar.

"And I'm warming to the name, 'The Flying Saucers'," Bev says. She's not the only one getting a little warm. "You might end up being known just as 'The Saucers' by your adoring fans."

"I think you might be our only 'adoring fan'," I point out. "And you're biased, Bev."

"Better than none at all," she whispers softly in my ear. She's still right beside me and it's almost unbearable.

Suddenly, she stands up. "OK, back to business. Cheese scones in an hour sound good?"

Fleece – who remains dazed by *Ho-Ro, My Nut-Brown Maiden* – Little Joe, and I are, for different reasons, unable to speak, but Geoff manages to answer on our behalf.

"Goodness me, thanks, Bev, yes, cheese scones in an hour. Goodness me, that would be very good."

24

Legal Aid

My week is beginning to settle into a rhythm, forming itself around my work in Costa, and the visits to Little Joe's studio on Sundays, interspersed with contact with my children, either in person or through the ether (the ether's cheaper). What's more I'm enjoying it. About the only fly in the ointment is my ongoing struggle to avoid the postie: stuck in the shower, pretending to be asleep, and hiding behind the living-room sofa have all been used as reasons to refuse to answer the door when I've seen her beshorted legs start to descend the steps to my basement flat.

One December day, around three in the afternoon, a very large van draws up outside the gate, and a delivery man gets out. A minute or so later, he emerges from the rear of the van carrying a large box, and starts – with some difficulty – to descend my stairway. The box is emblazoned with the words 'A GIFT FROM MARTINS'. Understandably, I'm intrigued. Even before he's halfway down, I'm opening my door to help him.

"Thanks, pal," he says, although of course I'm not his pal. "I need you to sign for this." He produces one of those handheld computer things with a stylus, indicating that I should sign my grey name in the grey box. I'm reminded of those tablets I used to be given as a wee boy in my Christmas stocking, where you drew something on a grey plastic slate, then you pulled the slide out to make it all disappear to clear it and start again. I never got the point of those either.

I manhandle the box, bulky but surprisingly light, into my living-room, and on opening it I find it is filled with sheets of expanded plastic bubble-wrap which I love stamping on to explode. At first I think that's all that's in it, but when I get to the foot of the box, there's a letter and a leaflet. My heart sinks as I recognise the letter instantly, but my eye is caught first by the leaflet.

MARTIN'S DELIVERY SERVICE
THANK YOU FOR BEING OUR LATEST
SUCCESSFUL MARTIN'S RECIPIENT
WE DELIVER ANYTHING TO ANYONE
WE NEVER FAIL
THERE IS NO DEPTH TO WHICH WE WILL
NOT STOOP

Sure enough, the letter is from Robb Merriman, W.S.

> ROBB MERRIMAN, W.S.
> 18, Rutland Square
> Edinburgh, EH1 2BB
> 8th December, 2011

Brian Reid,
19A, Eton Terrace,
Edinburgh, EH4 1QD

Dear Mr Reid,

I write further regarding our client Mrs Jane Reid (née Forrest), your former wife. I have been trying to contact you now for some time but have received no reply.

You will recall that we wrote to you on the 11th November 2011 concerning your recent retirement as a teacher, and that you are now in receipt of a pension, a share of which Mrs Reid is entitled to in accordance with the your divorce settlement. We understand that to date she is still not receiving this share of your pension.

We are concerned not to have made progress on this issue. Time is of the essence in this matter, and it is my duty to inform you that our client intends to have recourse to court action to recover what is due to her, action which we have advised her is likely to be successful. We already intend to press for costs, which will considerably add to the expenses of the losing party.

I assume that you will have received this letter, and I look forward to hearing your reply by return. Should you have any concerns regarding this matter, please do not hesitate to contact me.

Yours sincerely,

Susan Gunn
(Partner, Robb Merriman)

OK, Harry, you're right. I need a lawyer. I only know one lawyer, Walnut, aka Duncan McIntyre, and the very first thing I do in my panic is to phone his office. He's a lawyer and it's after four – I pray he hasn't gone home.

"Marsden McKinlay McIntyre Bell," a voice on the other end of the phone answers me.

I'm reminded immediately that Walnut is not the 'McIntyre' of Marsden McKinlay McIntyre Bell – they all died long ago – but it's why he chose that practice to buy into. All his clients think he's one of the originals, and Walnut chooses not to inform them otherwise.

"Can I speak to Wal – I mean, can I speak to Mr McIntyre, please?"

"I'll see if he's still in the office," she says – told you. "Can I ask who's calling, please?"

"Tell him it's Brian Reid."

There's quite a delay. Vivaldi's *Four Seasons* plays five times over.

"Mr Reid? How can I help you?"

Good start, Walnut. "Duncan," I say, "it's me, Brian Reid."

"Captain!" he says. "My dear boy, I'm so sorry." I want to call him Walnut now but I'm sure it'll put his fee up.

"To what do I owe the pleasure?" he says, trying to sound about eight socio-economic classes higher than me.

"I think I might need your professional advice, Duncan."

There's a heavily pregnant pause, after which Walnut says, "You make it sound serious." I appreciate that this is a clever opening gambit designed to find out exactly how serious it is.

"I have a problem with Jane," I explain.

"As I recall, you've had a lot of problems with your ex-wife."

"Indeed. But to cut to the chase, having grabbed most of what I had already, now she's trying to take the rest."

"Really? That doesn't sound right."

"That's why I need your advice. Can I come and see you?"

"Of course, old boy, and my first consultation is on the house, by the way. Between old friends."

In fact, this unctuous offer somehow makes feel extremely queasy. There has to be a catch.

"You'll appreciate that I'll need to charge for subsequent consultations, and for any work undertaken. Will that be OK, Brian?" Walnut continues.

As I was saying, there has to be a catch.

"I wouldn't have it any other way. I need advice, Duncan. Quickly, if possible."

"I see," he said, slowly. Over the phone I can hear his brain cells rubbing thoughts together. "I could fit you in first thing Friday morning. Could you manage eight thirty?"

"Of course."

"Look forward to seeing you then."

Which is the reason I now find myself sitting in Walnut's office in a modern office block in Multrees Walk, a newish – and very upmarket – shopping area in Edinburgh's previously less fashionable East End. Sure enough, it's only eight-thirty, but I'm here on time, which is more than can be said for my new legal adviser, who only bothers to make it around a quarter to nine. There's barely an apology.

"Sorry, old boy, delay trying to find a parking space this morning," which I know is a lie because the receptionist has already let slip that only the partners – therefore including Walnut – have reserved parking spaces in the car park. "Did you bring all the documentation?" he breezily enquires.

"I think so," not that there's very much, but I hand over what there is to him.

Walnut browses over it for a while, allowing the low December sun to stream through his office and light up his shiny bald pate. "Hmm," he says. "Hmmm," he says. Then, after a long pause, he comes to a clear conclusion.

"Hmmmm."

"Can you translate 'hmm' for me, please?"

"Your son – Harry, is that right? – looked at this already. Yes?"

"Yes."

"His opinion was?"

"I'm 'utterly fucked' was his exact opinion."

Walnut studies the papers again. "Well I think... I think... he's right. You're utterly fucked. His understanding of the law here seems quite good."

"He does have a law degree."

"What's that got to do with anything?" Walnut looks genuinely mystified. He carries on, "I think she's got you, old boy. A practising solicitor wouldn't use a term like 'utterly fucked' of course. We'd use the correct legal term in Scots law. You know, a bit of Latin like in loco parentis or interim interdict."

"And the correct legal term in this case would be?"

"Perfututum maximum." My knowledge of Latin is good enough to know he's simply come up with a direct translation. Walnut thinks it's faintly amusing to have a laugh at a client's expense, I realise.

"Is there nothing you can do to help me?"

"Did you have a gun pointed at your head?"

"Why? Most of time I felt like I wanted to shoot myself, right enough."

"We could try to say you signed the agreement under duress."

"Under duress? Of course I was under duress," I reply. "Who wouldn't be under duress trying to negotiate a divorce from a mad valkyrie who throws saucers at you for fun?"

"It would be a long shot," Walnut says. "A very long shot. A very, very long shot indeed."

"I get the picture. But do I have anything to lose?"

"Only my fee," Walnut replies quietly. "At seventy pounds per hour."

"How much?"

Walnut shrugs his shoulders apologetically. "We all have to make a living somehow, Brian. How else could we afford to have an office in Multrees Walk?"

I give the matter some thought, but something in me makes me think Walnut is up for a bit of fun.

"On the other hand," he says, "it could be entertaining." He reads my mind almost as well as Bev.

"I'm not sure entertainment is what I'm really looking for, Duncan."

"But I might be," he says. "Which means I might do it on a no-win-no-fee basis as a favour for an old pal. And I genuinely feel sorry for you. Would you like me to reply to Jane's solicitor on your behalf?"

Look out, Brunhilde, the fightback starts here.

25

Dreaming of Christmas

"Will I see you at Christmas?"

As soon as I ask the question, I know how sad it sounds, but there's no way round it. If I ask it, I sound a sad bastard, if I don't, I sound an uncaring bastard. And in any case I'd like to see my children at Christmas.

"You know we don't want to take sides between you and Mum, Dad," Harry replies at the other end of the phone.

"Will you spend Christmas with her? I quite understand." I quite understand, but I'll be very hurt.

"Why can't you two stop behaving like – "

"Total fuckwits, I know. And I know there's only a little over a week till Christmas, but I've been putting off asking you. I presume your mum's got in first."

"She hasn't actually – she's not been in touch with me, at any rate. Becky, perhaps, I couldn't say. Mum seems every bit as much an idiot as you." Harry is not known for mincing his words. "Listen," he says in a more conciliatory tone, Danni and I will try to come round for a bit to see you on the day itself. I'm not sure when, exactly."

"Thanks. I'd like that."

Harry moves the conversation on. "How did the meeting with your lawyer friend go?"

"Should I tell you? Won't you just blab to Mum?"

Harry gets slightly cross in reply. "Look, Dad, when are you going get it into that pea-sized brain of yours that I really don't want to take sides between the pair of you. The last thing I'd do is run off to tell her what you're planning."

I pause to think for a minute weighing up the pros and cons. In the end, I decide it's more important that Harry feels I've trusted him.

"Duncan thinks I can challenge the agreement," I tell him.

"Really?"

"I can say I signed under duress."

"Actually, I think you'd have to have had a gun at your head to agree to what you gave away, Dad."

"Funnily enough, that's what Duncan said."

We talk for a bit about the meeting. He's interested in Walnut, the sort of person he is, and why he's acquired the nickname. Then he turns the conversation away again to another topic.

"How's the band?" I notice – with some satisfaction – that there's no irony this time in his voice as he uses the term 'band'.

"Fine. We're taking a break till after Christmas, and we'll meet while everyone's off between Christmas and New Year."

"I told my FBs about you all."

"Your FBs – ?" until I remember his 'Facebook Friends'.

"Yeah," he says, "they think it's really safe that my dad has a band on YouTube."

"'Safe'?"

"It's the new 'cool'."

"What was wrong with the old 'cool'? Has it warmed up?"

"Like an inferno. You'll have to learn to keep up, old-timer." I can hear him quietly laughing at me at the other end of the phone. "Seriously, have you checked the site lately?"

"Which site? The YouTube clip or the website?"

"Both. They go to one then the other."

"Who do?"

"All the people who want to hear you play, twit."

"Do people want to hear us play?"

"Seems like it. Lots of them, too. If you check the counters, you'll see they often want to listen to the second tune once they've heard the first, whichever way round it is."

"And these are all your friends?"

"No, don't be daft. I don't have seven thousand friends, not even Facebook Friends."

"Seven thousand?"

"I'm telling you, people are listening. 'If you build it, they will come.'"

I'm not quite sure what to make of all of this. Keeping Harry on the end of the phone – what did we do before cordless handsets? – I go the internet on my computer and look up our YouTube songs and our website. The boy's right enough, except that now the visitors have topped eight thousand.

"OK," I say to him. "What now?"

"Good question," he says. "Why did you do it in the first place?"

"Haven't a clue. Because I could perhaps, like climbing Mount Everest?"

"I think climbing Mount Everest was more of an achievement, Dad."

"I'm not sure what took more nerve."

"Perhaps. And there's that awful rasta-jock stuff. Where did you get that idea from?" he asks.

"I'm completely innocent there. Fleece's brother cooked that one up."

"This is 'ironmonger Little Joe' who's actually taller than Fleece, right?" Harry's struggling with the concept of the ironmonger-by-day-rock-star-by-night.

"In the Edinburgh tradition with Deacon Brodie and Stevenson's *Jekyll and Hyde*."

"*Jekyll and Hyde* was set in London, Dad."

"You know what I mean. Stevenson was from Edinburgh, too."

"OK, let's not split hairs. In the meantime, it's always possible that what's really got everyone interested is Joe's excruciating drivel."

There's a brief silence. "So when will I know about Christmas?" I ask him quietly.

There's another brief silence. "Christmas Eve, if you're lucky?" He can be really irritating; but then he lets me off the hook. "Look, Becky and I will put our heads together and arrange something. Would you prefer if we all came together and then left you to go to Mum's, or do you want one of us to go to Mum's while the other's with you, and then swap? Does that make sense?"

"It makes sense, and I really don't mind either way. I suppose if I can't be with you all day, the next best thing is to know that the four of you are together," I say, although actually I'm aware that this will condemn me to a considerable period of Christmas Day alone. Perhaps I'll invite the cantankerous old boy upstairs down for a glass of whisky or something in a neighbourly gesture.

We talk for a while about his work, which at least seems to be going well, and then about Danni, whose work just seems to involve making ever more money for her firm.

"OK, Dad," Harry replies, "I'd better go now. I'll see what I can do about Christmas. This is all because you and Mum – "

"Because we insist on behaving like complete fuckwits, I know."

Harry sighs. "Listen, I'll speak to Becky and she'll get back to you later. Will that be OK?"

I say it's fine, and we say our goodbyes.

I don't have to wait long, less than half an hour in fact, before the phone rang again, this time Becky.

"Hi, Dad. How are you?"

"Hi, Becky. Nice to hear from you. I'm fine – you?" Of course, the answer to such a question has to be 'fine'.

"I'm fine, thanks." Originality is of little value in this situation. In any case I've managed to become quite anxious about whether I'll see my children at Christmas; indeed I've been able to think of little else since my conversation with Harry ended. "So," I say, "have you and Harry been talking?"

"We've just spoken for the second time. He said you would rather we all came together, so we gave Mum the choice of whether we'd go to her first or second. She said she'd like to see us in the evening out of preference."

So would I, Jane, I think, but it's not my call.

Becky is not insensitive to my disappointment, betrayed in a slight hesitation. I'm disappointed, but at the same time relieved to be seeing them at all; it's a confusingly powerful mix of emotions.

"Dad," she says. "Will that be all right?"

"Of course, that's wonderful. I'll be so pleased to see you. Will you eat with me?"

Again, Becky pauses. "How about some champagne and some nice nibbles, Dad? We can't do what we did last year again, eating Christmas lunch with you, followed by Christmas dinner with Mum. The four of us just about died that day."

I laugh at the memory, and she's right: this is our selfish decision to divorce, Brunhilde and me, and we must live with the consequences. I suspect every parted couple who has children must live with them.

"No, I suppose not. That was all a bit silly, wasn't it?"

"So that's it settled then?" Becky says, rather hopefully.

"That's it settled, Becky, and thanks for being so understanding."

"I think you're being the understanding one." She's right, I understand only too well.

There's a pause in the conversation, just as there was in the one with Harry earlier.

"Harry told me about your visit to your lawyer," Becky says.

"Good." I can't think of anything else to add.

"How's your band going?" Becky asks.

I repeat what I said to her brother, that we're on hold just now, but as I say it, I'm very aware that where my children and their loved ones spend Christmas is a million times more important than YouTube, The Flying Saucers or rasta-jock will ever be.

"OK, Dad." It's almost as though Becky's run out of things to say to her own father, and I can hardly blame her. "I'd better be going," she says.

"OK, Becky. Thanks for phoning, it was nice to hear from you."

The conversation ends, leaving me alone with my emptiness.

26

The Ghost of Christmas Past

Despite everything, in the three years Brunhilde and I have been apart, I've tried to maintain some sort of civilised point of contact with her. I always remember her birthday, and buy her a Christmas present, although buying presents for your ex-wife can be tricky. Flowers look like an attempt to woo her back, whereas gloves or a scarf might be fine from one of the children or a favourite aunt, but a loved one – even a an ex-loved one – should offer something a little 'closer'. In the end, I've ended up sending her a book, a DVD, or both. Brunhilde gave me nothing for a year, then she started giving me gloves and scarves, which curiously I now wear throughout the winter. I'm not sure what to make of my behaviour there.

This year, then, promises to bring all the usual difficulties for Christmas presents. I think long and hard, visit several shops in town, and then settle on the following: Tommy and Becky will each receive a book and a DVD, while Danni and Harry will each get a DVD and a book. That'll keep everyone happy. Tommy is actually very appreciative of any old movies I give him – Bogart, Hitchcock, Orson Welles – and I can buy Danni virtually anything from the current Booker shortlist. Becky and Harry often get a little something else thrown in over and above – a nice little cheque each to spend with their partners however they please. It barely matters what I send Brunhilde, and I get quite upset that I don't know if she appreciates getting anything or not, another agonising feature of being an ex-husband. Even Christmas cards take some choosing, and I try to spend some money on cards which are both tasteful and have a charity element. It seems such a futile pastime, sometimes, sending cards to people one barely ever sees from year to year, only for these cards to end up on mantelpieces, bookshelves, or hanging from strings on a living-room wall. Then again, Christmas cards act as annual 'I am not dead yet' notices, so perhaps I should simply take out a small ad in all the main newspapers, "This Christmas, I, Brian Reid, am pleased to announce that I have not snuffed it," and leave it at that.

So by early in the week before Christmas, my presents are wrapped, all my cards are long gone, and I'm 'ready for Christmas'. Isn't that exciting? Truth be told, Christmas preparation are easy because there's so little scope for variation that I can do virtually everything in the space of a couple of hours, or, at most, spread over two days. It's just a pity about Christmas Day itself.

On the other hand, lots of people want to tell me that they're still alive, or to 'remember' me with little gifts. Fleece and I have exchanged perfectly-wrapped bottle-of-whisky shaped gifts with great amusement. Little Joe and Bev have given me something which Bev says I've to keep cool, easier said than done when she herself is ratcheting the room temperature up by several degrees with her very presence. And as she handed it over, she gave me a kiss on the lips that was just a little more lingering than average, presumably as an hors d'oeuvre for the present itself. I'd like to suggest that she goes into business selling bottles of Essence de Bev – she and Little Joe would make a fortune – but the right moment hasn't yet come.

And of course there are the cards. There are the robins, the Santas, the holly, the reindeer, the snow, the snowmen, the penguins, the polar bears, the Victorian scenes, the wise men, the shepherds, the bright stars, the nativities, the winter scenes, the summer scenes (from Australia, that one), the glitter, and cards supporting every good cause imaginable. In addition, I've been sent, courtesy of Oxfam, Save the Children, Christian Aid and Barnardos, a grand total of five goats, two fresh water wells and three school desks (original for an ex-teacher). Then there's the circular letters, usually from some mystery member of the family who doesn't exist – "John has been doing this while Jill has been doing that" – or even cringe-worthier, written by the pet dog or cat. Only at Christmas does email spam turn into hard-copy tripe.

On the other hand, the plethora of Christmas junk-mail allows people like me to ignore things I don't want to know about, such as bills, letters from Brunhilde, or letters from Brunhilde's lawyer, although Jane's card made it through the maze and onto a remote part of my bookcase. My concession to the spirit of Christmas is not to start a fire with her card.

It so happens that Christmas Day will be a Sunday this year, so that the day will be even more depressing than it might otherwise have been. I've bought my *Radio Times* – the Christmas edition seems to come out in November these days and I nearly missed it – and a brief look at the Christmas night viewing schedules reveals that I'll need something to watch that night. Of course I might be given a DVD as a present, but I can't count on it. Choosing what to watch is tricky in my present frame of mind, though. Romantic comedies naturally make me feel maudlin, all the more so on Christmas Day; likewise sad movies. Last year I tried a foreign-language movie, *The Diving-Bell and the Butterfly* about a stroke victim with 'locked-in syndrome', on the basis that watching someone in a worse state than me might make me grateful for what I have, but in the end I switched it off and still haven't finished it. All-action might work, though, and because I've enjoyed Daniel Craig as James Bond, I decide to take myself into town on the Friday before Christmas to pick up a boxed set of the three 'Jason Bourne' films, none of which I've seen. To get myself into the mood, I decide to watch the first of the three, *The Bourne Identity*, that very same night. Not bad, and two more to come.

The next morning then, Saturday, brings Christmas Eve. I need something to eat each night, of course, and I decide on treats all the way through to Tuesday – four nights altogether – to be bought for in the morning. A good part of the day, then, will spent shopping in supermarkets seeming along with half the entire planet standing in checkout queues ahead of me; shellfish and pasta for tonight, and for Christmas Day some smoked salmon, to be followed by Marks and Spencer turkey breast and all the trimmings. I can never be bothered with puddings normally, so I choose a piece of Stilton to enjoy with a little tawny port, and at least if I've got no-one to answer to, I can get rat-arsed on Christmas Day. I've got steak and a steak pie lined up for Boxing Day and the Tuesday after, although Tuesday is set for another band practice. When I get home, I feel relieved to be back in my own flat again as I kick off my shoes and flop into a chair to read some newspapers, which are particularly good value at this time of year.

Eventually, I decide to make myself a cup of coffee and a whim takes me to the computer to check the website and YouTube to see if people have lost interest in our songs yet. I've heard that most of the 'hits' happen in the first week, and I expect the novelty – the amusement of Becky's and Harry's friends, in other words – to have worn off, but when I check out the figures I find I'm rubbing my eyes in disbelief: well over twenty thousand people have clocked on to the Flying Saucers songs. Twenty thousand! I refresh the page and the figure has increased by six, so that even as I've been looking at my own website, others have been checking us out, too. That's one really unexpected Christmas present I've had this year.

I long for a call, but the phone is silent, and as the day wears on I feel increasingly depressed that I've actually spoken to no-one, and in a moment of quite out-of-character kindheartedness – I'm really not this sort of person, honestly – I decide that perhaps the cantankerous old boy up the stairs might like to be invited to see Christmas in with me at midnight. Around eight, I make my way up my steps towards his flat, and after noting that the rooms are in darkness and that the curtains remain open, I ring his bell. He doesn't look in, and after a couple of further feeble attempts I decide he isn't. He's probably been invited to stay with one of his children for Christmas, I think. Lucky him.

As I make my way down the steps to my basement flat again, I can hear the phone ringing. One of my children is at last calling me. I fumble a way back into my house – why does it always take longer to get the key into a lock when your phone is ringing? – and grab the phone.

"Hello?" I gasp.

"You useless, duplicitous, miserable skunk-like piece of shit!" a voice yells at me.

"Sorry?"

"I said that of the lowest of the low, you really are the pits, you miserable little scumbag," the voice explains, a little more rationally.

Of course I've identified the voice now.

"Compliments of the season to you, too, Jane. How nice to hear your sweet voice."

"'Signed under duress?'"

"Ah. I'm acting on my solicitor's advice, there, Jane."

"You acted on your solicitor's advice when you signed the agreement before."

"That was your solicitor, Jane."

"Yours, too. And remember, we both said you should get your own lawyer, but no, not you, you insisted that mine would do for both of us. You said it would save money, as I recall."

"I'm sure it did, too."

"But you can't go back on the agreement!"

"I think that's the idea, Jane. You are ripping me off when all's said and done."

"Ripping you off, you lard-head?" Jane has not called me a 'lard-head' before; this is new. "You deserve everything you get, which is nothing."

"Jane – "

"And as for this... this... under duress. I'll give you 'under duress', yes, just you wait, I'll give you 'under duress'."

"Jane, can't we talk about this? Please?" There's no reply. "Jane, are you there? Can we talk for a moment? Jane?"

I think she might have put the phone down for a moment, although I'm not sure why.

"Jane? Jane? Happy Christmas, Jane?"

Suddenly, there's a loud crashing noise from the other end of the phone, then another, then another in quick succession.

"Jane? JANE, ARE YOU ALL RIGHT?" I yell, but the response is four more ear-splitting crashes at the other end of the phone.

Then I make the connection. At the other end of the line, Jane Brunhilde Reid, my ex-wife, is actually throwing crockery directly at the phone, which is being used as a substitute for yours truly. My guess is that most of the missiles are saucers.

27

Ding-Dong Merrily

If you've no special reason to rise early then don't is my motto, and on Christmas Day I decide to stay in bed till past ten o'clock. Opening my present to myself – I've wrapped it, how sad is that? – it occurs to me that there might be a market for a firm like Amazon or John Lewis to offer a 'Sad And Lonely Person's Surprise Gift Service'. As it is, I'm overwhelmed with surprise at how generous I was to myself only last Thursday when I picked up a Robert Goddard thriller and Michael Connolly's latest Harry Bosch story, and I've also promised to treat myself to some iTunes music during the morning, because at least that will be some sort of Christmas Day surprise. I almost forget my new coat, which has been sitting in the spare room for four weeks and I can now wear at last. Needless to say, that wasn't wrapped.

I keep the real surprise presents for the end. Bev and Little Joe's 'keep cool in the fridge' gift turns out to be a nice cheese selection and a little jar of pickle, while Fleece and I have at least exchanged different bottles of whisky, about as different as possible, in fact: he's given me Glenkinchie, while I gave him an Islay.

Television is great company for the lonely in the first part of Christmas Day, and with a huge seam of old favourites to mine I choose Spencer Tracy in *Inherit The Wind* and *Guys and Dolls*, the latter a fabulous musical too often forgotten these days, in my opinion. Watching *Guys and Dolls* is a little bizarre, actually, because I have it in my collection in the cupboard but somehow there's nothing quite like watching a movie when someone else puts it on for you. I sit eating my breakfast – also a Christmas Day treat of croissants and proper coffee – as I watch Spencer Tracy take on Frederic March in the 'Monkey Trial' movie, a film which

I read somewhere actually began life in the 1950s as a play against MacCarthyism. That was in the days when the bad guys ruled but the good guys eventually won. Now, it seems the bad guys rule, only to be beaten by even worse guys.

Guys and Dolls is still going when I spot Tommy and Becky coming down the steps to my flat, but there's a delay before they make it to the foot and I realise that Danni and Harry have by chance arrived at the same time. I've already opened the door as they descend the last few steps and come into my house, all Happy-Christmas-kisses-and-smiles, and laden with presents for me, they slide past me at the front door and into my living room. As I go to put the telly off, it's Harry who says it; nothing gets past him, it seems.

"Em, isn't that *Guys and Dolls*, Dad?"

"Yes," I say sheepishly.

"But you've got that DVD already. You could watch it any time."

"Yes, but it was on…"

Thankfully Danni comes to my rescue. "Leave him alone, Harry. He can watch whatever he wants in his own house. And it's Christmas Day."

"What's that got to do with things?" he asks, mischievously.

"Even the British and the Germans managed to stop fighting for a bit on Christmas Day in the First World War, Harry." It's Tommy who says this, to Becky's obvious surprise and pride.

"Then they went back to war. The England versus Germany game kept going to replays till the World Cup final in 1966. Which England won with Russian help, just like World War Two, as I understand. You're the only one here old enough to remember, Dad – is that right? You can probably remember them all."

"Harry, leave him alone." Becky this time.

As they all sit down, Harry spreads his arms, smiles even more broadly, and looks at me in appeal. "They're all ganging up on me, Dad. Help me."

"Let me get this straight, son," I say to him, scratching my head. "You want to bully me and you want me to prevent the others from stopping you. Is that it?" Actually, I enjoy this mental sparring that goes on more than the others realise. Most of the time.

He laughs. "That's about it. How are you, by the way?"

"As you see me."

Harry looks closely and says nothing. He sees a great deal, more than I'd like to reveal. Offering them drinks, there's a lack of interest in alcohol, but I've planned for drivers by concocting a non-alcoholic Buck's Fizz made with orange juice, elderflower cordial and chilled sparkling water. We've all settled to drink this when Becky leans forward in her chair.

"We've brought you some presents." They certainly have, two big bags. Handing over my carefully-wrapped DVD/book parcels, I feel quite miserly, although my ultra-thin cheques for each of them will help a little there.

"Let me guess, Dad," Harry says, waving his parcel. "Could it be a DVD, or could it be a book, I wonder? Aha, a combination of both!" Then he relents and says thanks very much, seriously, as do all the others. I apologise for being predictable, and that sometimes it's quite hard to select presents for them when I'm not sure what their tastes are, but that's actually code for 'the problem is that with no-one to discuss what to buy you, my confidence is shot'. I can tell that they know that, too.

Meanwhile, their presents to me include a towel dressing gown (from Becky and Tommy) and, intriguingly, a bread-making machine from Harry and Danni, as well as, from all four, a Blu-Ray player. To go with the Blu-Ray player, each has bought me a boxed set of Blu-Ray discs: Harry and Danni have bought me the original Star Wars movies, and Becky and Tommy have bought me… the boxed set of the Bourne films. I'm delighted, of course, leading to more thanks and kisses as appropriate, but with a deft flick of my left heel I kick my Bourne DVD boxed set under my own chair and fully out of sight, hoping that neither Becky nor Tommy have noticed it. In the meantime, the four of them have finally spotted the cheques that I've written for them. At the last moment I decided to double the amounts I was giving each of the couples, cupboard love I suppose, but why not?

"That's very generous, Dad," Harry says, and he means it. "You shouldn't have." He probably means that as well, since he's fully aware of my impoverished circumstances, made the more so by the impending doom of Brunhilde's pursuit of half of my meagre pension. I give them my standard reply, that they should look on it as a way of avoiding inheritance tax when I die.

The four of us talk small talk for a while. It's amazing how little people have to say at Christmas once they've exchanged information on presents received, and what their plans are for the rest of the day, plans I don't really want to know much about anyway. After visiting Brunhilde and eating with her, Becky and Tommy will spend the evening at Tommy's parents' house in Grangemouth, but Harry and Danni have opted to spend the whole of the rest of the day with Jane. Good, I say, not meaning good at all.

"Any plans for your band over the holidays, Brian?" Tommy asks to change the subject.

"Got a practice on Tuesday. Although what we're 'practising' for, God only knows."

"I haven't checked your hits on YouTube lately. Are people still interested?"

"It seems so. I actually got an email from someone yesterday who wanted to have a chat about the band over the phone I think there were more than twenty thousand hits yesterday when I looked. I don't know how that rates."

There's a four-way chorus. "Twenty thousand!"

"It's a lot, then, I take it."

"Fuck me, Dad," says Harry. "Let's see!" He grabs my laptop from the coffee table and opens up YouTube. This is my laptop, mind you, and without so much as a by-your-leave he's onto it. "Fuck me! It's up to twenty-three thousand now! What's going on here, Dad? Are you sitting up all night pressing the 'refresh' button?"

"Would that have had the same effect?"

"Yes, if you were pathetic enough."

"Well it wasn't me, although I suppose it could have been someone else," I point out. "I don't think so, though."

"Harry's only joking, Dad," Becky says. "Something's happening here, for sure. How exciting!" She seems really pleased for me, indeed they all do, even Harry, who quietly whispers in my ear, "I'm impressed, Dad, I'm really impressed." In fact, I've noticed that whenever he calls me 'Dad' rather than 'old boy', 'turnip-head' or 'pea-brain', he's usually trying to be nice to me. And he's called me 'Dad' twice in the last minute.

"Wait till Mum hears about this," Becky says. For some reason, I hesitate.

"I'm not sure I wouldn't rather you kept quiet for the moment," I say quietly.

"Why?"

"I don't know, Becky. It's just a gut feeling. Maybe soon, but not just yet. Please."

Becky pauses to look at the others, then says, "OK, Dad, if that's what you'd prefer."

"I think so. Thank you."

Their departure leaves an even larger void in my flat than usual, and with a significant amount of alcohol still completely un-drunk in the kitchen, I decide that the time might again be appropriate to try to invite my cantankerous upstairs neighbour down for a Christmas libation. I make my way upstairs and ring his bell, although again I see no lights on inside, I keep trying.

I'm still there when another neighbour, Maggie from the flat directly across the landing from the old boy, opens her front door and pops her head out.

"Hello, Brian, and Happy Christmas!"

"Yes, Happy Christmas, Maggie. You're well?"

"Yes, thanks. You're not looking for the Major, are you?"

"The Major?"

"Old Bob Russell. He was a major in the Malayan War. Didn't you know?"

"No. I was just calling to invite him down for a drink."

"Brave of you," Maggie smiles, implying a similar experience of the man's temper. "But a bit late, Brian, I'm afraid."

"Late?"

"You obviously don't know. Bob died a couple of weeks ago."

"Ah." I'm thinking, I'm not the only late one, but fortunately I manage to bite back an inappropriate joke.

Maggie sighs. "Such a shame. But on the other hand he would have been alone at Christmas, so he was spared that, at least."

"Yes, I suppose he was, I suppose he was."

28

The Real Deal

It's the Wednesday after Christmas.

The Tuesday jam session went well, and justified my day off Costa, which wasn't all that hard to arrange because a couple of the students were just desperate for extra cash having been deprived of work on Christmas Day and therefore keen to take my shift. The Christmas holiday crowd is a bit different anyway, with most of the customers proving to be refugees from the sales or from 'Edinburgh's Christmas', a tacky addition to the calendar including an open-air ice rink and a big wheel. It makes a lot of money but as Fleece likes to say, "no-one ever went broke underestimating the intelligence of the public", a quote he routinely attributes to Phineas Barnum, Sam Goldwyn, and Louis Mayer in strict rotation, wrongly in each case.

Speaking of Fleece, he was in fine form after he discovered that our recordings were attracting so much attention, while Geoff frown-smiled far less and frown-smile-smiled much more, even managing a couple of real smile-smile moments despite the trouble he claimed to be 'having with the water works'. Little Joe took more convincing. He felt a little worried that there might be less interest in rasta-jock, although he seemed much better when I gently suggested that the numbers visiting the website indicated otherwise, with one of the largest numbers of hits being on the 'Little Joe and the Martians' page (a complete lie, by the way, but rewarded by yet another of Bev's tingling touches on my lower arm). He is continuing to seek further evidence of links between Scotland and the West Indies, and with the latest railway siding being the poems of Robert Burns, he's latched onto *Will Ye Go Tae The Indies, My Mary* as a likely candidate. Why me, Oh Lord? He's become a Burns bore in the process.

As for me, while I'm still working on a couple of improvements to the songs already written, I'm working on some new ideas. The tunes are easy, and my iPhone is full of little 'Voice Memos' where I've switched it on and la-di-lahhed little melodies into the speaker. But finding lyrics – or even subjects that I want to write about – is tough. I'm not sure I'm a poet at heart, although in truth I set my standards high, and one problem for songwriters is that they have to be write decent lyrics prolifically, whereas a great poet – not a tune in sight – can be remembered for single sonnet, or even less. Consider the poet E. E. Cummings' (or is that e. e. cummings?) masterpiece "Parsley, Is gharstly." The songwriter is forever chained to four-line verses, perhaps interspersed with the odd chorus, and the odd middle eight to break things up. Little wonder then, at my admiration for arguably the greatest poetic achievement of the twentieth century, Paul Simon's *America*.

But technology at least is on my side, not least of which is a more-than-useful little 'app' on my iPhone called RhymeFree, without which it would never have occurred to me that 'tune' happens to rhyme with 'prune', 'raccoon', 'pantaloon' or 'contrabassoon', and now the only problem left to me is how to combine these four words into a meaningful verse. Perhaps a song about an American woodwind player quietly having breakfast when he spots a visiting garden animal making off with his trousers while they're hanging out to dry. No? See what I mean, it's harder than it looks.

I'm about to sit down to watch the *Six O'Clock News* when the telephone goes. I don't recognise the number on the display, but who does now in these days of mobile numbers. I don't think it's Brunhilde but I'm braced for the possibility that it might be.

"Hello?" I say, tentatively, and ready to duck.

"Can I speak to the Captain, please?" Some sort of broadish Scottish accent from further west.

"Sorry?"

"Do I have the wrong number? I emailed you just before Christmas and you gave me your phone number in reply. Is it inconvenient just now?"

Of course it's inconvenient, I'm just sitting down with a bottle of Peroni – a large one, it's Christmas after all – to watch the news. "No it's not inconvenient at all," I say. "What was your name again?"

"Tam Cantlay. Tam Cantlay, from Falkirk Wheel Music?"

"Sorry?"

"Falkirk Wheel Music. I emailed you before Christmas and you were kind enough to send me your phone number?"

Why on earth did I do that? I'll regret that mistake, I know it already. "I did? Anyway, Mr Cantlay, how can I help you."

"Call me Tam, Captain. It's about your YouTube clip and your website, which we find very interesting."

I'm still suspicious. "Thank you… Tam."

"You might have heard of me. I used to be a singer myself – Long Tom Cantlay.."

"So you're tall, I presume."

"Five feet two. Some sort of marketing joke at my expense, and it worked, I suppose. I had a minor hit with *Any Way You Want Me I'm Ready*. I'm sure you'll remember it. It was also used as the music for a tea advert."

"Tea?" Nope, I do not remember it, or this bampot either. "Perhaps I was out of the country at the time."

"Ah, well. I'll maybe let you have a loan of a disc to let you hear it. I've got plenty left." I bet you have, I think. "These days, though, I devote my time to 'The Real Deal at Falkirk Wheel.'"

"Sorry?" I'm completely confused. Meanwhile, the News is on silent, George Alagiah is reading the news and I can't hear him at all. A bomb has gone off somewhere, there are pictures of money and banks with meaningless numbers beside them, and Wayne Rooney looks like he's been sent off in a football match.

"...thought you might be interested." I realise that the voice at the end of the line has been blabbering away and I've been paying no attention.

"I'm so sorry," I say, "I've got a cordless phone here and the reception is breaking up. Excuse me, can I try to move to another room?"

I try to stretch the phone cable into the kitchen, and 'Tam' can hear my struggles. "I'll see if I can make it stretch –"

"I thought it was a cordless phone."

"It is, but the aerial needs to stretch," I explain, compounding one lie with another. "Anyway, I'm all right now, I can hear you I think."

"Well as I was saying, I'm calling about your band's music. My company is Falkirk Wheel Music and we're the real deal."

"Yes, I remember that 'real deal' bit."

"It's our company slogan, 'We're Falkirk Wheel and we're the real deal'."

Right, I think, and you clearly have RhymeFree on your mobile as well. "Keep saying that and you might end up believing it," I say to him.

"I do believe it already. We're the real deal."

I decide politeness might complete this conversation more quickly. "I'll take your word for it. I'm sorry I don't know who you are, Tam, but please carry on. What can I do for you?"

"There's a lot of music out there, Captain, but the real money is in finding new bands, developing them and selling them on to other producers and agents. The big boys. We can't compete with them, but we can pass good acts on to them. For a fee, of course."

"Of course." He seems content to call me 'Captain' and I feel content to let him, for some reason. This guy called me cold, and I don't intend to let on any more about me than I have to. He might be about to steal my identity and sell it on to a gangster or an international terrorist, so we'll make that process a little more difficult by not letting him have my name.

"My firm trawls the social media, Facebook, Twitter and so on, for the new bands that are being talked about, and we try to help them along a bit."

"I see. New young talent." As I explained, I'm not giving away any more to this potential identity-stealer. Interesting that he can't guess my age from my voice.

"Exactly. And that's why I'm on the phone tonight. You've come to our notice."

"Really?"

"You're not bad for a five-piece band. A couple of nice songs, an interesting mix of guitars, the vocals are good, and the rhythm is very tight, especially the bass."

He likes the bass? The MacBook Pro laptop *Garageband* series of loops? "Sue Zee?" I'm about to tell him the truth, then I remember – this man may be about to swap my identity with that of an arms smuggler, and I hold my tongue.

"Suzi? Suzi? She's great, yes, she's a star turn, really."

"She's very reliable."

"Good. Great. Actually you sound really great. But we think you could be a lot better."

Here it comes. "How?"

"In the first instance, a more professional video, and one for each of the songs, too. That's what made *United Breaks Guitars*. You know, the guy that had his guitar broken – "

"Dave Carroll."

"Sorry?"

"The name of the band was Sons of Maxwell and it was their singer Dave Carroll who had his Taylor guitar broken."

"Right... right. Anyway, if we added really good video footage to your recordings, we could see what happened after that."

"What would we have to do?"

"For the moment, nothing."

"Really? What's in it for you, then?"

"As I said, we get the chance to be your manager if it's a success. There's no cost to you at all otherwise."

Am I hearing this right? Some guy who's never heard us wants to be our manager?

"Should we not be discussing this with a lawyer or something?" I ask him.

"No need just now. It's a trust thing, and it's up to us to do something to establish your trust in us. After all, I called you cold – I could be trying to steal your identity."

"The thought never occurred to me."

"You can't be too careful. I'd recommend you never give away more than you have to in this business."

"Thanks for the advice."

"So anyway, what the plan would be is that we'll make couple of small videos to fit on with your songs, and then you can upload them yourself. If they turn out to be successful, we'll maybe make some more. Perhaps bring the band in for a performance."

"Really? Somehow, I suspect it'll not come to that."

"I should warn you, the chances are nothing will come of it, Captain. Don't get your hopes up. But as my old Uncle Charlie used to say, if you don't speculate, you can't accumulate."

"What was your old Uncle Charlie? A high financier?"

"You could say that. He was a bank employee who threw himself off a high-rise block in Govan."

"I see." I could warm to this Tam from The Real Deal at Falkirk Wheel.

We talk about a few details, and then he says, "I don't know much about your band, but I'm interested in the bass player, Suzi." He pronounces it as in 'Suzi' or "Susie", not two separate words as in 'Soo Zee'. "She's very good. Where did you find her?"

I think for a moment. "She's a band secret. I promised."

"Really? Is Suzi the same Suzi as I think she might be? There aren't too many Suzis around playing bass."

"That depends on who you think Sue Zee is. And I'm not at liberty to say," I say mysteriously.

"I get your meaning, Captain, I get your meaning. And your secret's safe with me."

29

The Real Costa Coffee

The next day I really do have to work at Costa. I don't mind, actually, as it's almost therapeutic to be allowed to make lattes and espressos in between wiping down tables and sweeping floors, and it allows me sociable conversation without having to think (a) where the band is going (b) how to keep my children happy and (c) how to keep Brunhilde's hands off my minute pension. Perhaps I should be paying Costa?

But there are quiet periods, and it's almost as though Fleece has been lying waiting for one of these lulls when I'm suddenly aware of his fiery dragon breath on the back of my collar.

"Caught you there, Captain," he says triumphantly.

"What are you doing here, Fleece?" I don't mean to sound as if he's unwelcome – he's not really, I'm glad to see him – but I can never get anything done while his huge fleece-encased carcass is occupying more of the café than it should. And he has this irritating habit of rumbling around after me while I'm trying to get on with my work.

"I can tell I'm annoying you," he says.

"No, no, it's OK."

"Ah well, that's all right then," he says, head back roaring with laughter.

"No, I mean it. I'm glad I saw you. There's been an interesting development." I didn't mean to let this slip but I'm so weak, sometimes.

"An interesting development?" he says, deliberately taking the mickey out of me with wild staring eyes. "Tell me about your interesting development while you make me a free cappuccino on the house."

In between the fizzes of the espresso machine, I fill Fleece in on the previous night's call from Falkirk Wheel Music. Fleece, who has now spread his rear over two adjacent chairs, looks both doubtful and amused at the same time.

"Are you sure he wasn't just a bampot, Captain?"

"I'm sure he *was* a bampot, Fleece, but we've nothing to lose if he turns out to be. He said he would do the video clip for nothing as a goodwill gesture to show he was the real deal."

"The real deal at Falkirk Wheel."

"Exactly."

"Well, it's better than endless hassle at Edinburgh Castle."

"True."

"Or smelly feet on Arthur's Seat." Sometimes Fleece can be really tiresome.

"I think you've made your point, Fleece," I tell him, firmly.

"Suit yourself. When do you think you'll hear from this bampot?"

"He said it wouldn't take long to do, actually, certainly no more than a day. It's just a question of getting round to doing it."

"That's honest, anyway. The coffee's a bit weak today, by the way. Losing your touch?"

"It's free, you ungrateful bugger," I tell him.

"That's what Hannah used to say to me," he says, wryly. "You know, when…"

"Oh, I see." I think I do, anyway. "All set for Sunday?"

"Christ, Captain, I suppose so. Although Little Joe's driving me mad with this tripe of his."

"Rasta-jock."

"I can think of some better names for it. One of them rhymes with 'rasta-jock'," he says. "I have to put up with more of it than you do."

"He ain't heavy, he's your brother."

"That was a crap song, too. Nothing to drum to."

"Pity poor Bev, then."

"No, Bev's all right. He does all this out in his 'studio' as he likes to call it. Bev's entirely soundproofed so long as she stays put in the kitchen. What does your pal Geoff make of it?"

"Geoff's too polite to say anything much, Fleece. I think he's a bit bemused by it all."

"Barely surprising in the circumstances. Sundays in Little Joe's place is a complete madhouse. You've been a surprise package with your wee songs, though."

I'm assuming that this is praise from Fleece. "I'm working on some others."

"Really? Don't get carried away, now," and he roars with laughter yet again., terrifying a little boy who's arrived in a buggy pushed by his mother, the pair of them waiting to be served. It takes me a minute or two to serve them orange juice and a flat white; it's the mother who wants the coffee, thankfully.

The mother-and-son combination has taken cover in one corner of the café; Fleece is still occupying most of what remains. Costa is otherwise empty, and I feel obliged to give him a little more attention.

"Listen, Captain," he stage-whispers to me, "have you spoken to a lawyer about Brunhilde yet?"

"Please, Fleece," I answer. "Turn the volume down a bit. That woman over there might think I'm some sort of criminal."

"She might be able to offer you some free advice. You never know, she might even be a lawyer herself."

"I seem to be getting plenty of free advice as it is."

"Sorry," he replies, trying to sound hurt.

"I actually spoke to Duncan McIntyre just before Christmas."

"Walnut!" he roars. "Just the man! How is he?"

"Just as you last saw him."

Fleece goes into contemplation mode, stroking his scruffy beard. "Ah, yes, Walnut. A skilled solicitor from the Edinburgh establishment. Did you sew all your pockets up before you entered his office, Captain?"

"He was fine. He seems to be making plenty of money, right enough, although he hasn't actually charged me for that consultation. 'For an old friend' were his words, I think."

"Beware the Greeks and the gifts they bring, Captain. Beware the Greeks, I say!" Fleece is indeed saying it. "Tae sup wi' the devil ye need a lang spoon!"

"Any other well-known sayings you want to have taken into consideration?"

Fleece paused for thought. "How about Hibs nil, the other lot one?"

Even I have to laugh at that one; there have been nine full moons since the last home win at Easter Road.

"So what did Walnut have to suggest, Captain? Was he any use?"

"Not really. He agrees with Harry that things look bad. He's suggesting that I try to claim that the agreement with Brunhilde was signed 'under duress'. I might be able to get it annulled. It's rather a long shot."

"And knowing Walnut, he'll make it an expensive long shot, too," Fleece added.

"That's a very nice office he has in Multrees Walk," I point out. "Somebody has to pay for it."

"What are you going to do, Captain?"

"More hours in Costa?" I suggest, hopefully.

But I'm about to be distracted still further, because Harry has just popped his head round the front door of the café. I wave him in.

"I was just passing on a little office errand. I thought you said you'd be back on duty today and thought I'd look in." Then catching sight of Fleece, Harry greets him like a long-lost friend.

"Hi, Fleece, haven't seen you for ages! How are things?"

"Nice to see you too, Harry," Fleece replies.

These two separate compartments of my life then politely exchange small talk before Fleece blurts out, "Your ears must be burning. We were just talking about you earlier."

"Oh yes?" Harry looks at me, suspicious.

"Nothing sinister. Just that you and the legal establishment seem to agree that your old man here is well and truly screwed as far as your mum is concerned," Fleece says.

Harry gives me an angry glance, while I think my, what a big mouth you've got, Grandma Fleece.

"Come on Fleece, Harry's trying to keep out of this," I tell him. "It's not fair either on him or on Becky."

"Oops, excuse me. Big foot in it again," he says, laughing, and I can see this time it's quite ostentatiously to cover up his own embarrassment.

"Yes, big foot in it again, Fleece." He can think again if he thinks I'm going to make it easier for him.

There's an awkward silence. It would be really good if Fleece were to stand up and say he needed to go, and leave Harry and me to ourselves.

"I've got a great idea," he says, "How about if you went off and made each of us one of those fancy-dan flat whites, Captain, and your son will sit down with me at this table?"

It's certainly not what I wanted, but there's little more I can do than shrug my shoulders. While they sit and talk about goodness knows what, I'm left making them both coffees which eventually I take across.

"That'll be nine pounds ninety, please, Fleece. Four ninety-five each. Do you have a Costa loyalty card?"

Fleece looks at me, smiling in disbelief, but says nothing and merely rummages around in his pockets for change. He comes up seventy pence short, and looks at me pleadingly. Unfortunately for him, I've lost patience, I'm fed up being taken for granted, and – essentially – I stare him out.

Of course Harry's embarrassed, and he offers to pay.

"No, Harry, Mr Mackay ordered the coffee, Mr Mackay should be paying for it."

"Dad – " Now Harry's really embarrassed.

Fleece starts to mumble an apology. "Look, Captain, I'm sorry..." but I don't let him finish.

"It's all right this time, sir. But next time please don't place an order before checking that you have the means to pay," and I sweep up all the money lying on the table and put it in the till.

Fleece slugs back the coffee, silent but chastened – which was the idea of course – and utterly deflated. But a minute or so later, he comes up to me at the till and it emerges that there is a new problem.

"I should be getting along now, I think," he says, quietly by Fleece's standards. "I'm sorry about that business, Captain. I'm sorry about that. I just thought..."

"The matter's closed, Fleece. Let's say no more."

"It's just that... it's just that... can you lend me one pound thirty for the bus fare home? I'll pay you back on Monday." Because Sunday is New Year's Day, the next practice is scheduled for a day later.

I study him for a moment, taking the untidy mess that stands before me. No wonder Hannah gave up on him and left for another. But Fleece is a chicken-and-egg of a poor soul in many ways; no woman would have the shambles that Fleece has become, but equally without one, he's got no incentive to anything about it.

I open the till. "Here's your bus fare. See you Monday, Fleece."

He trudges slowly out of the front door back into the December cold, leaving me to feel a mixture of anger, power and guilt. Meanwhile, Harry is still sitting at the table, and as there is no queue, I sit down with him on one of Fleece's two chairs: the one which had been supporting his left buttock, I suggest.

"You were a bit harsh there, Dad."

I explain that Fleece has been taking advantage for a while and it was time it came to an end, while I in turn apologise that a friend of mine tried to involve him, Harry, in a dispute between his parents.

"He didn't mean any harm, Dad. He was just being clumsy old Fleece."

"I know, Harry. Deep down I really know that. Don't make me feel any more guilty than I do already. But your mum and me – well, it's a raw nerve still. And I don't want to lose my children as well as my wife. Maybe I'm losing my best friends, too."

Then Harry does something most un-Harry-like; he reaches across the table and pats my arm. He really isn't a touchy-feely person at all, and in its own way his touch is every bit as powerful as Bev's, and far more precious.

"Becky and I are a bit harder to get rid of than you think, Dad, don't worry."

I can say nothing, and I'm putting a lot of effort into not crying, but I succeed. Just.

We're still sitting there when the woman with the child in buggy whom I'd served earlier slides past me on her way out, and looking at me approvingly, touches my sleeve. That's another one – two in one minute, for goodness' sake. She has a first-class honours Stockbridge accent.

"Thanks for the coffee. It was lovely, by the way. But I wanted to congratulate you for the way you handled that beggar who wandered in from the street demanding coffee.

Perhaps he's been selling the *Big Issue* all day long, I don't know. You were really kind to him. Kind but firm, I heard some of your conversation. But you gave him a cheap cup of coffee anyway. It's the real spirit of Christmas, you know. Well done – I'll be writing to Costa head office to sing your praises."

"I don't think…"

"No, no, I insist. Thanks again, and see you soon."

Harry leaps up to help her as she struggles to manoeuvre her way out of the door with the buggy. As soon as she's gone, he lets the door close behind her; the two of us are all alone and we can't prevent ourselves from laughing hysterically, although the tears running down my cheeks are in fact a more complex mix of emotions.

30

Fresh Start

As I've got older, I've become less excited by New Year and more enthusiastic about Christmas. The trouble with being older at Hogmanay is that it's too easy to look back on the year past as another year wasted, on the missed opportunities, on the regrets rather than the achievements. That's a feeling multiplied many times if your marriage has split up and you're spending time your time alone when everyone else has company.

My New Year was brought in with a glass of cask-strength Caol Ila – only eight years old, but Caol Ila is one of the most reliable of all Islays, I think, and I particularly like the younger ones that the Malt Whisky Society sells, and they're cheaper, too. Contact with the outside world amounted to BBC Scotland with Phil Cunningham and Jackie Bird, and texts from Becky and from Harry wishing me all the best for the following year. Becky and Tommy stayed in Edinburgh with friends for the night, having parked Tommy's van somewhere near me, I believe, and they dropped in around lunchtime to say hello after they'd collected it again. Later in the afternoon Harry and Danni appeared, Harry looking rather the worse for wear, and in the course of the conversation Harry revealed that the pair of them had actually passed my house just after two in the morning, but saw no lights on and they didn't want to waken me. I'm not sure if that was true or not, but I said that they would have been most welcome anyway. I'm not sure that was true either.

So my New Year really begins today, Monday, after all the painful nonsense has passed over, and with the latest visit to Little Joe and Bev's house. Once again, Geoff picks me up at the flat to save petrol. But it's still New-Year-speak season .

"Happy New Year, Brian," he greets me as I get into his car, which still has its soft top fitted despite the freezing cold weather. Still, at least I can descend vertically into it if Geoff slips the top back a bit. "How are you?" he asks.

"Fine thanks, Geoff," I reply breezily and shaking his hand, "and a Happy New Year to you, too. You're well I hope?" It's a catastrophic blunder, of course, and proof that the new year has left me no wiser than the previous one.

"Thanks, and I suppose so, but you know I've had an awful lot of bother with the water works. Goodness me, yes, such a lot of bother. I wonder if it's all the booze over the holiday period, but you know you have to let your hair down a bit, don't you." He frown-smiles as he tells me this universal truth. "Might need to take a sample to the doc, perhaps. A bit of trouble with the bowels, too, to be honest, Brian, but goodness me that's only to be expected with all this rich food and these irregular hours at this time of year, isn't it?

"And then I'm still having trouble with my left knee and my right ankle, but I suppose that's to be expected at my age, isn't it?" The frown-smile is accompanied by a laugh this time; we're already at the West End and I haven't so much as had to nod yet. Seven detailed symptoms later, we're turning into Merchiston Place, and I'm exhausted already. And I'm more than a little anxious about how Fleece will greet me after the Costa encounter. Geoff helps me escape from his Nissan Micra Rabbit-Hutch Sport, and we stumble our way up the icy path to ring the doorbell. Bev answers as ever. I see the low winter setting sun from the window at the far end of the hallway catching her hair like a halo until I realise it's actually pitch dark.

"Happy New Year, boys, and come in. You're actually our first foot, would you believe?" As she says it, I notice that Little Joe is behind her ready to greet us with genuine handshakes. Bev kisses Geoff, but I've had the nous to remember something for their New Year – a bottle of Ardbeg for Little Joe, and a pretty extravagant bunch of flowers for Bev. I'm immediately repaid by Bev – on behalf of them both with something which is only vaguely related to a second Bev kiss, which involves contact only between lips but this time somehow seems to impact on every nerve-end in my body.

"You're so kind, Brian," she whispers in my ear, while the hand guiding me through the house to the living room is a little lower down my back than I ever previously recall. Could that really be referred to as my 'back' at all, I wonder?

Little Joe insists that we sit down and join Bev and himself in "one for the New Year", something I foresaw when I brought the Ardbeg on Hogmanay. Even Geoff agrees to have "a thimbleful, no more, goodness me". Incidentally I notice that neither Bev nor Little Joe has committed my error of asking how he is yet. Perhaps they've made a New Year resolution not to: now there's an idea.

"Fleece not here yet?" I ask as I sip the amber nectar, although it's actually the sherried version which is a near-maroon colour.

"No," Joe answers, although it's Bev who completes the sentence, "and he's usually first here, too."

We talk small talk, everyone carefully avoiding the dreaded "how are you" question in case Geoff answers, much to my relief. I may have been imagining this, but I'm sure one of the seven supplementary symptoms he mentioned on our journey involved something to do with stool samples. It's all a bit like the radio quiz game *Just A Minute*, where contestants have to talk for sixty seconds without mentioning urine, arthritis, or incipient bunions.

Then the bell rings, and everyone jumps up, although of course only Bev and Joe will be going to the door. There's a roar from the front door, and of course it's Fleece, and when in due course he's shown through to the living-room, he's looking perhaps slightly better than when I last saw him. He shakes hands warmly with Geoff to wish him all the best for the new year, then turns to me.

"Happy New Year, Captain," he says, although some of the warmth has gone. "And I've got something for you," he adds, firmly placing exactly one pound thirty pence in my right hand. "There, we're even, now. They say it's bad luck to carry a debt over from one year to the next. Well, I'll just have to live with the bad luck, won't I?"

I don't know what to say, so I say nothing; I've decided I'm going to have to ride out this little huffy spell from Fleece. Fleece joins us, planting himself on the sofa with more of the Ardbeg.

Little Joe is oblivious to the tension, Bev gives me a concerned look. She knows her brother-in-law.

"Something we should know about?" she asks.

"No, nothing at all," Fleece says. "I took advantage of a friend, it seems."

I still don't know what to say. I don't think he wants me to say "Yes", though.

"Well, the least I expected there was for you to say I was wrong, Captain!" I shrug my shoulders, so Fleece continues. "For those of you who are wondering, Captain here had got into the habit of giving me a cup of coffee on the house, and then last Thursday he suddenly asked for payment on the very day I didn't have enough to pay for it."

"Fleece – " Little Joe tries to interrupt.

"I had to beg for money for the bus home. Would you believe I had to beg for money!"

"Can I say something here?" I ask. I'm getting fed up with this, so I put my side of the story, pointing out the salient facts that he'd demanded a second and third cup on the house, and that it was I who had provided the bus fare home.

Joe laughs. "Sounds reasonable enough to me, Josh. You can't expect Captain here to keep making you coffee whenever you fancy."

"So that's all friendship's worth, is it? Not even the price of a coffee?"

I don't know what to say, and nor does anyone else, so there's another embarrassed silence. Bev is almost reduced to asking Geoff how he is, when suddenly Fleece roars with laughter and says,

"Fuck!! Who cares?" In the blink of an eye, his mood has turned, and he turns to me and says, "Have you told them yet, Captain?"

"Told us what, Captain?" Joe enquires.

I was going to leave it till later, but now I tell them about Long Tom Cantlay and his offer to tag a couple of better videos to The Flying Saucers' tunes.

"And you say he's doing this for free?" Geoff asks, frown-smiling, and scratching his head for good measure. "Goodness me, it seems too good to be true."

"It certainly does, Captain," adds Little Joe. "Is there any danger that we'll have to give him something in return?"

"It looks like he's just trying to gain our trust, Joe. I suppose if we were ever to make it big, he'd hope to manage us for a bit. And then sell us on to one of the big boys, he says."

"The big boys!" roars Fleece. "Big boys for big boys, eh Bev?"

Bev's reply is a playful purr.

"Equally, of course," I point out, "it may all be an elaborate wind-up. Perhaps we should believe it when we see it."

Little Joe has been looking at me and by now I know what's coming.

"Did he mention anything about *Ho-Ro, My Nut-Brown Maiden*?"

"No, Joe, he didn't," I reply honestly. Then I add, dishonestly, "I'm sure he'll do something at some point. Remember he's doing this for nothing so I don't want to put him off."

"Put him off?" Little Joe says sharply. I daren't look at Bev, but I can feel her knife-like stare sliding into my gut.

"No, I didn't mean he'd be put off, Joe," I lie again, inwardly cursing my careless choice of words, "I'm simply trying to say that, at the moment, whatever he offers to do is what we accept. Tam simply made no comment about your song at all." Little Joe seems partly satisfied with this answer, and I think I can feel Bev's blade removing itself again.

"I'm sure you'll look after everyone," Bev breathes, and I breathe an inward matching sigh of relief myself. The crisis has passed.

This prompts Little Joe to jump up enthusiastically. "Come on then," he says, "time for work. It sounds like somebody out there's listening, so let's not let them down."

"Cheese scones at four, everyone?" Bev asks.

"Goodness me, yes. Goodness me, that sounds great, thanks," says an English accent.

31

An Attachment

On Wednesday morning there are two attention-grabbing emails in my inbox. Because it's the more recent, the first one I open is from Walnut.

In it he explains that he's set out a line of defence to protect my pension from Brunhilde, firstly pleading that it was signed under duress, and secondly that it was incorrect that we should both have the same solicitor. Yes, I signed to say that I clearly understood what I was doing by allowing our family solicitor to draw the agreement up, and, yes, it was made clear to me that I was waiving my rights in this matter, but Walnut is going to suggest that this acquiescence was all down to the duress I was experiencing. Our solicitor should have insisted that I spend vastly more money and taken on my own agent. In essence, Walnut has portrayed me as too weak and stupid for my own good, a view which Brunhilde would no doubt share. It still seems a pitifully weak case to me, though.

He then goes on to say that he sent this to Brunhilde's solicitor, Susan Gunn of Robb Merriman, and although 'Sue' – a worrying chumminess there – has acknowledged his letter, she awaits instruction from Jane, my ex-wife. He warns me to try to avoid contact with Jane during this period as it will compromise any negotiations the two solicitors might have. I've tried, of course, but I immediately reply to tell him about Brunhilde's screaming Christmas Eve phone call, and he must be sitting beside his computer because within a couple of minutes he's got back to say that it's not a problem. On the contrary, he's logged the call, and it might even enhance our case for emotional distress, especially if she was throwing saucers at the phone. He signs off by repeating: do not call her. As if I would.

The second interesting email is from Falkirk Wheel Music. I almost don't notice it because ever since Tam has added my email address to the Falkirk Wheel mailing list, I've been inundated with 'latest news on the hot central Scotland scene' featuring names like The Pogo-Sticks, Diamond and the Walruses, Cinnamon, The Straw Cats, Mark Droid, and The Chocolate Fireguards, all of which seem to be fourth-rate bands Tam's company is paid to suck the life out of. But there is one which is simply entitled FAO Captain, and at the use of my band name it suddenly dawns on me that this is Saucers-related. It's from Tam, and it's very short, explaining that the video clips he's made up are too large to send by email, but that I can download them by visiting an online webspace site where he's placed them.

There's an underlined, blue-coloured link in his email and, clicking as instructed, a QuickTime movie clip appears on my desktop; in fact there are two links, and there are two clips to download. Clicking on the first reveals a movie with my song *Bird* as the soundtrack, which consists of some quite high-quality footage of first an eagle taking off from a clifftop, then an albatross soaring over the oceans, interspersed with some footage of the Earth taken from space. In concept it's not so very different from what I'd done myself, but it's done to so much a higher standard that it transforms the whole experience. But it's the second movie clip which brings the real surprise. The video Tam's company has produced to go with *Right Here Lovin' Me* is a cartoon, and the 'band's' singing and playing is surprisingly well synchronised with the music. There's been a great deal of work put into this, or at least a great deal of expertise. One small issue is that the band members mostly look about twenty. Another is that there are five members, in other words there's a real bass player rather than an Apple laptop, and the bass player in question has been allowed to look a little older because she looks a little like… Suzi Quattro, dressed in black leather, while a feature of the video clip is that the male cartoon members of the band appear to have the hots for the bass player. A brief flash of concern crosses my mind at this point: have I misled Tam?

However, Tam's message exhorts me not to waste time, and that if I approve of the video clips I should waste no time in uploading to them YouTube and to my website. I'm so excited – and let's be honest here, flattered – that I do so straight away, then immediately afterwards text the others to tell them about it. I only expect a reply from Fleece, though, and that's assuming he's not in a meeting, because I suspect Little Joe will be disappointed that there's no rasta-jock movie, and Geoff still hasn't got to grips with the concept of mobile phones yet and switches it off altogether when he's not using it himself ("goodness me, Brian, would you believe there were fourteen text messages on my phone when I switched it on yesterday afternoon?"). Fleece is not in a meeting, however, and I do get a reply within ten minutes, which, predictably, is "Fckme fancy bird in cartoon myself". Then again, I suppose he could be at a very boring meeting indeed.

Based on this one-out-of-one sample, I decide to phone Falkirk Wheel Music directly in the hope of getting Tam. I'm greeted with one of those irritating messages which welcomes the caller and invites him or her to press buttons one to five, or to hold to speak to an operative, which I choose to do, only to be subjected to fully thirty seconds of Long Tom Cantlay belting out *Any Way You Want Me I'm Ready*, just long enough to realise how curiously inappropriate title it is to have to endure while waiting in a queue. But the pain ends eventually.

"Hello," a completely fake telephone voice announces. "Thomas Cantlay speaking. How can I help you?"

"Tam, Tam?" I ask, quite confused.

The voice clears it's throat. "Em, here. With whom am I speaking?" Still the same voice.

"I'm trying to speak to Tam Cantlay, please. It's Brian Reid speaking."

"Who?"

"Captain from The Flying Saucers."

"Captain!" The voice immediately becomes a central Scotland accent that I recognise. "Why didn't you say?"

"Sorry, I was just a little confused. With the big staff there, keeping track of everything must be difficult."

"What do you mean?" Tam asks. He sounds as confused as I am now.

"How many staff are there at Falkirk Wheel Music?"

"Em, well there's just me in the office today."

"Really? How many would there be normally?"

"Well if you must know, just me."

"So tell me, Tam, what's with the five options when someone like me calls?"

"In this business, Captain, appearances are everything."

"So all the calls come through to you, no matter what button I press?"

"Unless you choose option one about opening hours, yes. You see, Captain, it's all about managing the delicate balance between reassuring the client that we're a reputable organisation while at the same time maintaining the personal link with the top man."

"You seem to come down pretty heavily on the latter side, Tam."

"Yes. Don't you agree that's more important?" Tam seems not to have noticed that he's just confessed to me that he might be a little disreputable. I choose not to answer.

Tam clearly is uncomfortable with the silence. "Did you get my email, then?" he asks a little apprehensively.

"Yes. The movie clips are great, both of them, and I've uploaded them already. I liked them both, but I was really taken with the cartoon. That was a bit of a surprise."

"Thanks," Tam says, sounding relieved to be on a different subject, I suppose. "I'm quite pleased with the cartoon myself."

"Did you do it all yourself? Must have taken ages."

"No, no," he says. "I out-source most of my graphic design work." I suppose he has to out-source almost everything, when you think about it.

"So who did the cartoon?"

"Ah. My son, Sam. He's a bit of a computer geek and just loves putting that sort of thing together. He uses some software that he's pirated from somewhere. It should cost a fortune, he says, but he's got hold of a Chinese version."

"He does it in Chinese? How old is he, this guy?"

"Fifteen. These young lads are brilliant. He doesn't understand a word of Chinese though, don't get me wrong, he just picks up how to do it by intuition."

"Like The Pinball Wizard?"

"Indeed. Although I don't think he uses his sense of smell, because if he did, the first thing he'd smell would be a bedroom-full of socks." Tam laughs as he says it, knowing we're back on good terms again.

"So what happens now?" I ask him.

"We wait and see, Captain, we wait and see. I noticed the number of hits on your first clip had stalled a bit on YouTube this week. Let's see if they take off again."

"Great," I reply. Then I take a deep breath. "Listen, Tam, I've got another request. Did you find the other page on the website? The one about the fusion music?"

"That shite? Little Joe Marley and the whatsits?"

"It's a fusion of Scottish folk and reggae. He's convinced there's some connection."

"Sam described it as the worst sound he'd ever heard in his life. I think his description was 'good music to torture to'."

"Sam sounds like he has a better sense of hearing than of smell. Listen, the thing is... could Sam create some sort of video to go with Joe's music?"

"You're taking the piss."

"I'm not, actually. It would mean a lot to Joe."

Tam is silent at the other end. "Maybe. I'd have to charge you, because Sam would have to listen to the music. Danger money."

"Maybe Joe will come up with something better to match a video to. I'm just trying to be nice to him. Joe's a nice guy, really."

"Let me think about it, Captain. Maybe we can bring him to do a video in the studio here."

"Thanks, Tam. I'm very grateful."

"No promises, mind you. I'm a responsible parent, and that music isn't very responsible. Don't say anything to your friend."

"I won't, I promise. It can be your surprise. And in the meantime, Tam, we still owe you nothing?"

"Not yet. If you take me on, of course, I'll want a cut of whatever you make."

"Seems fair, but I'm not the only one to be considered here, I'm sure you'll understand."

"Of course, there's four more of you."

It's only after we've rung off that I remember that there are only three others to consider.

32

New Material

By Sunday, everyone knows that we have professionally produced video YouTube clips for our music – even Geoff, whom I finally phoned on Friday to tell him to switch his mobile on again. By the time he picks me up on Sunday in his Nissan Matchbox Sport, it seems he's already seen it eight times.

"Goodness me, yes, Brian. It's really good, isn't it?"

We're on our way to Merchiston, and it's really icy. The main roads have been gritted and are fine, but any side streets are rutted and really difficult. Fortunately, Bev and Joe live on the level, and although I'm terrified of falling, I think I'll just about manage the pathway, and there's a good chance that Little Joe will have salted everything anyway. He knows my fear. But Geoff is being bothered by the cold in a different way.

"It's the cold, Brian, goodness me it's been cold. Plays havoc with the water works, you know, goodness me, yes." I'm trapped in the passenger seat, and I can do nothing to avoid this. "I've been in a bit of pain, too. I went to the doc on Friday, in fact, and she felt up... up there, you know?"

"Ah," I say.

"Well, I said 'ah' as well, now that you mention it, Captain." He frown-smiles at the joke, but I've noticed that generally he's been doing a lot more frowning than smiling while he's been driving me today. "It was a woman GP, too, which was a bit different."

"Is it?"

"Actually, it's not, now that you mention it." Geoff has gone several sentences without saying 'goodness me', a sure sign that he's not himself.

"You worried about this, Geoff?"

"The doc's sending me off for tests to the Royal Infirmary, you know. But they'll take ages, she says. Huge waiting list, she says."

I look at him. "Goodness me," I say, which must sound like I'm taking the mickey, although I'm not. I like Geoff, and I'm worried for him. He drives along without saying anything for a bit, and in fact we're actually at Merchiston Place walking up the path to the front door when he finally remembers the videos.

"Oh, by the way, well done about the video clips on YouTube. Sheila showed me how to watch them – they're very good. Goodness me, yes." He frown-smiles as he says it, but I can tell he's in discomfort. The door opens and it's Bev who greets us, but Geoff does little more than say 'hello' and then ask if he can use the toilet, which he occupies for some minutes. The upside of this is that I'm left alone with Bev.

"How lovely to see you, Brian," she purrs, giving me perhaps a slightly more lingering kiss on the lips than I might have received otherwise. "Is Geoff OK?"

"I think so. Man-problems, I think."

"Poor soul. Geoff's such a nice man, Brian. Have you been friends long?"

"We were soul-mates at school for many, many years, despite the slight difference in our ages. And when our new head came, he shared my view of her."

"I know you didn't like her."

"Dr Genevieve Forbes-Marr? No, a cold, stupid, talentless bitch."

Bev's quite taken aback, and I apologise immediately. "Sorry if my language shocked you, Bev. I didn't like her, but you don't deserve hearing me be so explicit."

Bev smiles, and treats me to another kiss on the cheek and a faint brush on my left hip with her right hand. "Yes, I'm shocked, Brian, but not by your language. I have Josh as a brother-in-law so I'm quite immune to bad language. No, what surprised me was the hatred in your voice. I've never heard you speak so savagely. You're usually so laid back."

Perhaps it's the tingling sensation that still reverberates through my pelvic area from that brush of the hand, or perhaps I'm just thrown by waiting for Geoff, but I want to tell her more.

"Bev, according to Jane, I was *too* laid-back. She used to say all I ever got worked up about were the bad things in life."

"Really?" Bev sounds surprised. "I don't see you as being negative."

"Perhaps school, or at least that job, wasn't the best place for me to be positive."

The toilet flushes, and in a moment or so Geoff emerges, although he looks no better than he went in. But Geoff being Geoff, he's frown-smiling furiously as he opens the door.

"Sorry about that, you two. Didn't mean to keep you both waiting, goodness me, no."

Bev leads us through to the back door, and then down the garden path to Joe's studio. Little Joe and Fleece are both there, both playing, but only questionably are they playing the same tune, and Fleece takes our arrival as a cue to stop immediately leaving Little Joe to grind to a halt ten seconds later when he finally realises he's on his own.

"Geoff! Captain! Thank Christ you're here!" Fleece yells. "We were just running through Little Joe's latest offering."

Geoff frown-smiles, but he simply nods. I can tell his mind is on other matters. "Go on, tell me all about it," I say, and I fear the worst. Little Joe's excitement is almost tangible.

"I've discovered a new song, Captain – it's perfect. It's *The Jute Mill Song* – you know the one about fairly making ye work for yer ten an' nine," and with that he sets off to play the rhythm guitar part to go with it. It nearly works, but nearly is a very big word sometimes.

"Not bad, Joe," I say, encouragingly. "Possibly the best yet." This doesn't actually mean much but I know it's what Little Joe, and by extension Bev, want to hear. I'm looking in the other direction but I receive a telepathic message from Bev: thank you, Brian. It occurs to me, however, that if I can read her thoughts, she can also read mine, which means she knows I actually think it's rubbish.

"Do you think so?" Joe says brightly.

Fleece answers for me. "Of course, you daft twit. It's the least bad thing you've come up with so far."

Little Joe is beside himself. "Least bad so far, Fleece? *Least bad so far?* Do you really mean that?"

Fleece is rocking with laughter. "Yes, I suppose it is."

Remarkably, Geoff tries to put a gloss of sanity on Little Joe's entire project. "I think I can see what Joe's trying to achieve here," he says. "Rock music, jazz, blues and so on – they all have the drums playing on the back beat, beats two and four in the bar, but reggae's like classical music, and therefore folk, and plays it on beats one and three."

"Does it?" I ask. "Grade Three piano didn't take me that far."

Little Joe looks bemused by what Geoff has just said. "Could you repeat that a bit more slowly please, Geoff?"

Fleece butts in very quickly. "If you repeat any of that last sentence, Geoff, I swear I'll kill you before you finish it. Do not encourage him."

Little Joe looks hurt. "You're my brother. You're supposed to be helping me, Fleece." Bev is angry with Fleece, but he's completely immune – he's family. He can say what the rest of us are too polite to say.

"I am helping you, Little Joe. I'm trying to save you from yourself. Look, even Captain there is coming up with better material than you, and his is bad enough."

"Thanks," I acknowledge, although I know he doesn't mean it. Fleece belongs to that proud Scottish tradition where the highest praise is 'no' bad'.

"Actually, your stuff is no' bad, Captain," Fleece clarifies. "Anything else in the pipeline?"

"Is that a request?"

"Well, have you written anything else?" he asks me.

"Well, there's a song called *Get A Grip Of My Life*, which is supposed to be faintly amusing. It's vaguely in the style of Rab Noakes." I play a verse and chorus, strumming the guitar with a plectrum in a rhythm which Rab uses quite a lot; in fact I must remember to write to the great man and check he hasn't written it already and I've just conjured it out of my memory of a past album. The words aren't quite complete yet, but there's enough of the song that we can play it, get the chords and so on. Once again Bev, who seems to like staying for the first airing of new things, breathes her approval afterwards, and to be honest, with a backing it really doesn't sound bad either.

It's Bev who brings us back to Tam Cantlay.

"Will you make that into a video, too, Brian?"

I'm a bit embarrassed by the video clips at the moment. "Who knows, Bev? They're just songs, maybe not that good, really, that other people are playing with."

"Stop running yourself down, Brian," she says to me sharply. "You've no right to hide your talents from others. When you're blessed with the ability to do something, you have a responsibility to do it and to do it as well as you can for the common good."

I'm taken aback by this – for Bev – tirade. Immediately she softens again and says, "Oh, I'm sorry. I overstepped the mark there."

"No, no," I say, "maybe it's just the boot up the backside I need. If you all think so."

Geoff usually keeps out of these exchanges of fire, but now he speaks up. "Personally, Brian, I think the new clips, with decent film and even with your rough recordings, are really good. I enjoyed watching them."

"They are, Captain," Little Joe acknowledges as well.

"To be honest, Captain, your stuff might be crap, but it's our crap, and it's the best crap we've got at the moment," Fleece roars, laughing again and shaking his head. "At least it's a change from the rock standards we were playing before." Once again I notice that Little Joe looks down; he desperately wants approval for his project.

"And perhaps Little Joe will hit the mother lode soon," I suggest, to lift his spirits a little.

With this, Bev gets up, and announces she will return with cheese scones in an hour.

"Listen, Bev," Fleece says, "out of interest, could you do us a favour? Go and look up YouTube and see how many hits our new clips have."

Bev readily agrees, saying she'll return in a minute or two. She goes to leave, choosing to pass very close by me, and as she does so, she whispers in my ear.

"I'm so sorry if I upset you, Brian, I didn't mean to. And thank you so much for supporting Joe." Did I say Bev had whispered in my ear? She almost licked it; if I could have untied my own tongue I might have said that her apology made it worth my while being offended, but she's gone before I can speak at all.

A couple of minutes later she returns.

"Those new clips – they have nineteen thousand hits each. I don't know how many of them are since you last looked, though, Brian."

I'm astonished. "Nineteen thousand? Each? They're new clips, Bev, they're all new since I last looked. I haven't checked since I loaded them up on Wednesday. I thought it would take a while to pick up."

There's a silence in the room as what Bev is telling us slowly sinks in. As ever, Fleece is the one breaks it in his own succinct manner.

"What the fuck is happening here?"

33

Manager

Tam's excited enough. When I get home after our Sunday session, there's a message on my answerphone asking me to phone him back, no matter how late, but the raised pitch of his voice gives away the likely subject. It's around eight when I get back to him.

"Hello, Captain!" he greets me. "How are you? Great news, yes?"

"You're referring to the new clips?" I guess.

"Dead right, Captain, dead right. Isn't it great?"

"Nineteen thousand hits is a lot, I suppose."

"Over twenty, Captain. Over twenty."

The numbers have obviously risen even since Bev checked YouTube earlier, and Tam and I spend a few minutes discuss their significance.

"We mustn't lose momentum here, Captain," Tam says. "People are interested in what you have to offer, and we need to keep them interested."

"How do we do that?" I ask.

There's a moment's silence from Tam, then he replies, "That's where I come in, Captain."

"I think you're trying to tell me something here, Tam," I suggest, and when I hear nothing in reply, "Like this is the moment when it starts to cost money."

That does produce a reply. "Falkirk Wheel Music isn't a charity, Captain," Tam says; I'm interested that he never calls me by my real name, by the way. "I – I mean 'we' – need to make a living somehow."

"I understand that. How much?"

"Twenty per cent."

"That's quite a large percentage," I suggest. Actually, I've no idea if it's a large percentage or not.

"It is," he says, "but remember that I take much of the risk with groups that are starting up. Eventually, I'll pass you on to a bigger management group, something like IMG, who might charge a lot less. At that point I lose you."

"Although you get a fee for selling us to them?"

"Yes, but that's between me and them. As long as you're happy, that's all that matters."

"Does this involve a proper contract? Written and so on?"

"Yes, although tonight I can accept your word as a gentleman."

"Er, Tam, do you realise we've never actually met? Never clapped eyes on each other?"

"I'm all right with that at the moment. We'll meet soon enough."

"When, exactly?"

"Are you taking me on?"

"I suppose so. I've no idea what I'm letting myself in for, far less the others."

"It'll be fine, Captain. I'll tell you what I think you should do. I think we should make a video of the band, and at the same time we can sign a contract."

"Shouldn't our lawyer see it first?"

"It's just a standard thing. I'll send something to you and you can study it at your leisure. By all means show it to a lawyer. You can sign on behalf of the band if you want." I'm not actually sure I do want to, in fact. Tam continues, "And in any case, the songs are yours, so they're yours to sell."

"I suppose so."

"In the meantime, I'll take your word as your bond. If you break it, I'll send some heavies round," he says, laughing. I don't like the sound of a man I've never met sending heavies round.

"I hope that's a joke," I say. "So, once again, what happens next?"

"I think we should make a proper video of your band. Something which shows you playing."

"Us playing?" I'm not sure about this, it's been good to hide behind anonymity so far. I've also spotted that he hasn't confirmed that the heavies are a joke.

"Of course. Time to put you all out there for real. And a proper studio recording."

"Right... and who pays for this?"

"Ah well, that's at the band's expense," Tam says. "I put up the first thing. Now it's your turn."

"I'm not sure I can spend the rest of the band's money for them just like this, Tam. How much are we talking about here?"

"Well I can get you a deal there, as it happens," Tam says. "A friend of mine has a recording studio in Leith and he gives me discounted rates."

"Which are? Cut to the chase, Tam." I'm getting impatient here.

"Three hundred for a day in the studio. Another fifty for the video while you're playing it. Sam should be paid to edit it."

I take a deep breath. I suppose it could be worse and if the recording's any good, it's a once-in-lifetime experience. I can just about manage on my own if I have to keep Tam's heavies at bay.

"OK. I'm in."

"See? That was easy. The studio guy's got contacts, too. He acts as a scout for recording companies, people putting on gigs and so on. There are always people looking out for new talent."

"Fine, fine," I say. I'm sure I've just thrown several hundred pounds away on a vanity kick. "When will this happen?"

"Sooner the better. Like I said, we need to keep the momentum going. Take those two songs – could you record them straight away?"

"Just about, I think. A couple of finishing touches, maybe, that's all."

We discuss dates, and agree that if his mate in Leith can do it, we could provisionally record something in a fortnight. We're about to ring off when Tam suddenly has a final thought.

"Captain, we'll be in the studio for the whole day. If it goes well, we might record the two songs fairly quickly and have quite a bit of time left over. Do you have anything else we might record?"

"There are one or two other things in the pipeline, actually, although they're at the early stage." In a couple of cases, so early a stage that they're still in my head, but I'm not letting on yet." Tam's delighted. "And of course there's also Little Joe's stuff. Little Joe Mackay and the Martians," I add.

"I'm not that desperate, Captain. It is, though." I have to laugh at that one. "Let's see how it goes with your stuff, shall we? By the way," he adds, "in case I forget, can you remember something? Please try not to laugh at the sound engineer's name – he's quite sensitive about it."

"Well you'll have to tell me what it is now," I point out.

"His name is Coates. Duffy Coates."

"Duffy Coates," I repeat back at him. "So everyone calls him – "

" – You got it, 'Duffle'. He hates it, but we all do it. Duffy is actually his middle name, but it's better than his first name," which he then reveals. "Jesus – it's a common name in Gibraltar, apparently," Tam adds.

"Jesus? Poor guy. I won't say anything. As for 'Duffle', I'll try my best. Can't promise that the others will manage, though."

"Do your best. He's a nice guy and a good mate. Tell you what, I'll text Duffy now and see if he can do a fortnight today, and then I'll email you confirmation and that contract I was talking about."

He rings off. Less than five minutes later, my email inbox has a new message:

Hi Captain,
All go for studio recording a fortnight today. Contract attached, to be signed on day by all. Look forward to meeting the five of you at last.
Kind regards
Tam

Immediately, I forward Tam's email to everyone else, as well as texting them to bring them up to date, and both Little Joe and Fleece get back to me this time. Little Joe texts to say "snds grt in dry ctch ltr" which I assume means "That sounds great, Brian, I've put it in my diary. I'll catch up with you later." Like so many people, Little Joe has predictive text on his phone, so he's actually had to train it to talk this gobbledegook. Fleece, on the other hand, treats me to his mellifluous tones only a moment or two later.

"Holy Mary Mother of Hell!" are his very first words to me. Fleece has a penchant for mixed-metaphor swearing.

"Evening, Fleece, how are you?"

"What in the name of God have you signed us up for?"

"I thought we should take the plunge. Why not?"

"Because it'll cost us money, that's why not. Are you offering to pay?"

"Only if I have to," I reply. "I'm rather hoping we can all pitch up towards it, and after all, if anyone should be short of money, it should be me – I'm the poor pensioner, after all, whose ex-wife is trying to make him even poorer. But I'll pay your share if you want."

Fleece grunts at the other end of the phone. "Well, we'll see. Let me think about it." Actually, I know Fleece pretty well, and for him it's worth coughing up seventy or eighty pounds to be able to moan and give me a hard time.

"Nine hours is a long time," I point out. "Tam said we might be able to record some other stuff. I've got a couple of other songs if there's time, but we'd need to practise them."

"We can manage that on Sunday, Captain. And we could maybe fit in an emergency extra session if we think we need it, I suppose. Let's see how we feel on Sunday. But there's one thing in the email that bothers me."

"Yes?"

"This guy Tam – he seems to be expecting five of us in a fortnight."

I take a deep breath. "Yes, I think he might be. I haven't told him about Sue Zee."

"He thinks 'Sue Zee' is for real?"

"I'm afraid he might."

Fleece bursts out laughing. "He's going to get a shock when Sue Zee turns out to be your laptop. Let's hope he isn't expecting Suzi Quattro!" and with that, Fleece roars with laughter so much that I hear a clatter at the other end of the line. It takes a moment before he's back again, still laughing.

"Sorry, Captain, I just thought it was an amusing idea. Priceless, actually."

I don't know what to say.

"You still there, Captain? Speak to me?" He's still laughing, but I still don't know what to say. "Go on, Captain, just reassure me that you haven't told Tam that we've got Suzi Quattro as our bass player."

"No, Fleece, I haven't told Tam that Sue Zee is Suzi Quattro."

"Thank Christ for that."

"But, the thing is, then again… I haven't told him that she isn't."

That silences Fleece. "You'd better hope he thinks it's funny that our sexy bass player is actually an inanimate computer."

"Do you think we could pass Bev off as our bass player?"

"Bev? Don't be silly. She has many talents, as you've obviously noticed, Captain, but music is not one of them. She couldn't even switch your laptop on in time to the music."

"In which case we'd better hope Tam thinks it's funny," I agree. Tam, and his heavies as well.

34

The World's my Oyster

This next morning, Monday, brings an Edinburgh weather speciality: haar. 'Haar' is an old Norse word which describes a cold, miserable, damp mist which rolls in from the North Sea, and a January haar is the grimmest haar of all. Fortunately it's a non-working day, so I read in bed until almost nine o'clock, having risen to make a cup of tea and taken it back to my bedroom. I'm actually trying to force myself to think of things other than music at the moment, because I've begun to worry that it's taking over my life, so I'm immersed in an Ian Rankin Rebus detective story. This is quite successful until the action takes Inspector Rebus – who in the TV series is another blighted Hibs fan – into Leith. I'm suddenly reminded that our rendezvous with Tam Cantlay will be in a sound studio somewhere in the area, so that I find myself getting up and looking up 'recording studios + Leith' on Google. There are two, but since one appears huge and the detailed list of all the engineers who work there doesn't include someone called 'Duffy Coates' or anything like it, I guess it's the other one, called Sounds Great, with just a basic entry, and which has an address in Mitchell Street. I've never heard of Mitchell Street but the wonders of Google Maps show it as running east off Constitution Street, itself an extension of the main Leith Walk artery that runs from the east end of Princes Street right down to the port area.

There are a number of really nice restaurants close to Mitchell Street, and I phone Becky to see if she's free for lunch, thinking that I could check out the studio at the same time, but Becky's busy. So too is Harry, as it turns out, but he surprises me by making another suggestion.

"I know Danni's down at a course in Victoria Quay this morning, though." He's right; Victoria Quay, the headquarters of the Scottish Government Civil Service, isn't so far away. "Why don't you give her a try? She might take pity on a lonely old man." Why did he have to add that last sentence?

"Thanks, I might just do that," and ring off after a few pleasantries. I don't even have time to tell him about the recording.

To my delight, Danni says she'd love to join me for lunch. Her course is just about to start, but she'll have an hour to herself from one till two, and we settle on the King's Wark, agreeing to meet at the junction of Bernard Street and the Shore as soon as she can make it. I decide to take the number twenty-two bus again rather than my Honda, because I'd like to offer Danni wine with her lunch.

By the time she appears, I've already checked out Mitchell Street, a narrow one-way street full of buildings which might have been whisky bonds in a past life but now seem to have been converted into anything from offices to small car workshops. The offices are of the fourteen-in-a-building type, each of the street entrances festooned with large name plates announcing tiny firms with next-to-no employees. I've managed to find 'Sounds Great', which looks suitably unprepossessing, but the nameplate does reveal one thing: 'Managing Director: D. Coates' is written in small print below.

The weather is still horrible when Danni appears at just after five past one. Class is written all over Danni's clothing, bearing and demeanour. Dressed in a perfectly fitted grey skirt, deep red jacket and white shirt – it's a shirt, not a blouse – she greets me with a kiss, and it occurs to me that she's never kissed me when Harry hasn't been there before, and what's more it's in full public view, so that a casual observer might be mistaken for thinking of us as easy lovers. But part of the secret, I suspect, is that Danni is confident that she knows me well enough and that, while I like her company, I like my women to be older as much as she likes her men to be younger, so that neither of us presents any threat to the other. Why has the sexuality chess-game become so difficult? The easier its morality has become, the more difficult its language, it seems.

"This is a nice surprise," she says. "To what do I owe the honour?"

"Believe it or not, I was in the area. Harry suggested you might be available for lunch, so here we are."

We find a seat in the King's Wark, which is filling up. "Anyway," I continue, "I know you share my love of oysters." The restaurant, unsurprisingly for a dockside eatery, leans towards fish in its menu.

"Oh, we'll see. I'm not sure I fancy oysters today."

"Whatever takes your fancy," I reassure her. "Would you like wine?"

"I think I should give wine a miss, Brian."

"Not like you," I say to her. Danni loves her wine, especially good earthy reds from Spain and Italy, some of which cost a fortune.

"Perhaps I shouldn't when I'm on duty," she says. "Even a training course counts, I think. I'd better stick to water."

Water it is, then, the ubiquitous San Pellegrino, and Danni chooses a fish soup, while I refuse to be deflected from the oysters, and we both choose the fishcakes to follow. While we wait for the first courses to arrive, Danni and I catch up on some news. We ask each other about work, then I ask her about holiday plans for the summer, but she says they haven't got round to anything yet, perhaps they might consider a last-minute deal to some nice place in the Highlands. Harry and she have booked a couple of concerts, though, which prompts Danni to ask about something else.

"How's your band going, Brian? Harry showed me the new clips – there seems to be a lot of interest."

I fill her in on the latest developments, and she's suitably impressed.

"I have to confess that I was down here this morning looking for the studio. But this is a real bonus."

"I'm amused that this guy thinks some leather-clad pop female icon of the seventies is your bass player when it's actually a computer."

"I'm not sure how he'll take that, frankly."

"You need a bass player, don't you. A real one," Danni says.

"We do. Can you play bass?"

"Not quite. I know a guy who does, though."

"That's a major problem. In a weak moment I gave our non-existent computerised bass player a female personality on the website. It's going to be hard to find a female bass player."

"You could always ask Jane," Danni says, laughing.

"You're right, she does play bass, but I think she's ruled out on health and safety grounds." Danni's expression tells me I have to expand. "She threw lots of stuff at me, Danni."

"Did you deserve to have stuff thrown at you?" This is interesting. Danni's questions go places neither Becky nor Harry will go; Becky doesn't want to hurt me, and Harry thinks we're both simply behaving stupidly. Danni, in her direct but gentle way, has just asked a question I've never been asked before.

"The answer's yes and no, Danni, my love. No, in that no-one should be subjected to having missiles thrown at them by their partner. Do you and Harry throw things at each other?"

"No. And you can't even see it as something for 'consenting adults' can you?" I love the way that Danni treats me as a complete equal in our relationship, as much a brother as a father-in-law, although technically I'm not even that. She presses on, quietly. "But you said 'yes' as well. In what sense?"

"Because if anyone deserved to have stuff thrown at him, it was probably me."

"Why? I don't see you as violent or anything."

I smile, she's got the wrong impression, I realise. "No, Danni, I was never violent. In some ways that was the problem, I wasn't anything at all. I was just nothing in our marriage, I contributed nothing except money, and Jane got fed up with me. Often. Just out of frustration. And that's when the crockery started flying."

I discover I'm a little emotional and take a deep breath to recover myself. She places her hand on mine, which actually makes things worse, but I'm saved by the arrival of half a dozen oysters and Danni's soup, which proves to a bowl of fabulously creamy seafood chowder. My eyes light up, partly at the food, but mostly at the chance for distraction.

As we study our respective choices, she says, without looking up, "Sorry if I blundered clumsily all over your private life, Brian. I think I went too far."

"Danni," I say, looking her directly in the eye, "you're always welcome to ask me anything. You certainly didn't go too far. If anything the problem is that no-one else has the courage to ask, and they all seem to want to avoid the subject. Sometimes they seem to want avoid me altogether."

"I'm sure that's not the case, Brian."

"What about Jane?"

Danni laughs. "I don't think she counts, Brian."

"No, I don't suppose so. And this is lovely, Danni, lunch with you."

Lunch in fact, leads us completely to different, easier topics. But two plates of fishcakes later, we're sitting with a couple of lattes before us in lieu of dessert, and Danni raises the subject of Brunhilde again.

"Brian, what are you going to do about Jane?"

Her directness is actually quite refreshing. "I'm not quite sure, Danni, but I need to contest the agreement. Whatever I signed, whatever I agreed to, it wasn't fair, I don't think, and I'm open to all suggestions on how to reopen negotiations. I really can't afford to hand over half of my pension. And I don't think Jane needs the money."

"She's not that well off, Brian."

"She doesn't need to live in that house. It's too big for her now."

"She doesn't want to move. I can understand that, too. She's upset, too, and needs stability."

"I know, I know." I look at her. "You sound like you're on her side."

"Absolutely not," she says firmly. "I'm simply being the devil's advocate. But you need to think everything through."

"I suppose so. I need to sort this out. I can't keep avoiding things."

"I don't think you can. But whatever happens, we'll always be around."

"That's the best news I've heard for weeks, Danni." It really is, too.

35

Citizens' Advice Bureau

Tuesday, the very next day after I've had lunch with Danni, is of course one of my Costa days. It's routine enough, with the usual bursts of action around mid-morning, mid-afternoon, and particularly lunchtime. Sometimes it seems that the world and its next-door neighbour eats in my Costa at lunchtimes, but I suppose it's not surprising given the number of offices there are in the West End. In fairness to Costa, they wouldn't put a café here if they didn't think people would use it, although it never ceases to amaze me how many junior office staff can afford to waste vast sums on my lattes and cappuccinos (should that be cappuccini?), either to go or to sit in. As usual, we cope, especially as the part-timers have shifts that overlap at lunchtime, so that the morning shift runs from eight till two while the afternoon one runs from midday till seven. I'm on all the time, as is a young Polish woman called Kleopatra – honestly – who spends much of her time washing dishes in the kitchen, but who comes out for half an hour each morning and afternoon to give me a break and to help brush up on her English. She's actually a foreign language teacher from Krakow, completely fluent in French but also qualified to teach English, and now she's in Edinburgh for a year trying to become fluent in English as well. She's not quite there yet, but she's making progress. She herself has two school-age children back in Poland, who are being cared for by their father, and whom she misses terribly although she did manage to get home to see them for a fortnight at Christmas. Incredibly, she informs me that she makes more money working in Costa in Edinburgh than she did as a teacher in Poland. I suggest that a teacher might be treated with more respect in a Polish school than a Scottish one, to which she replies "Pshah – your cheeldrren behalve rreally budly heerr. You urr corrreckt." I couldn't have put it better myself. They're almost as bad as some of the headteachers, in fact.

Anyway, during my Tuesday afternoon break, Kleo – that's how she's known, of course – comes through to the kitchen to tell me that "thurrs a men her to zee you, Brrian", and she promises "to look uvtar the cufé" if I need a little time with him. I'm not sure what that means – is it the police? – and it is with some trepidation that emerge into the main shop, only to be greeted by the bald, camel-hair-coated, fine figure of respectability that I know as Walnut but the wider world calls Duncan McIntyre of Marsden McKinlay McIntyre Bell, Writers to the Signet.

"Goodness me, Wal- Duncan," I say, thinking immediately that I've spent too much time in Geoff's company lately. "What a pleasant surprise."

"I was passing, on my way walking back to the office from a meeting in Tollcross, and I thought I'd pop in." Walnut craves gravitas, and has tried to achieve this by lowering his previously squeaky voice by two octaves. "It saves you the effort of trailing all the way along to Multrees Walk."

"And the cost, I hope," I say, smiling amiably.

Walnut hesitates. "And the cost," he agrees, smiling a little less amiably.

"What can I do for you, Duncan? Can I get you a coffee or something?"

"That would be nice. Could I have a large latte with a couple of extra shots, please?"

Walnut's legal training shines through. He's chosen one of the most expensive coffees in the shop.

"The thing is," he begins, "the thing is, Brian, that I'd like to help you, but I'm finding it difficult."

"Why's that, Duncan?"

"Because I'm not sure your heart's in this. If you want to play this 'signed under duress' card, you really have to look a bit more 'under duress' than you do at present."

"Don't I look under duress?"

"Brian, you've been the most over duress person I've ever met."

"Over duress? That's new. Is it a compliment?"

"It's a pain in the arse when you're meant to be under duress."

"So what's the story? What's my position? Has it changed at all?"

"From what we might refer to as the 'Harry position'? 'Utterly fucked'?"

"Yes."

"No."

"So why are you here, Duncan, if there's no hope?"

"Why not try to negotiate? You might be able to compromise," Walnut suggests. He's the true solicitor, actually; he'll do anything to avoid a fight.

"You remind me of Neville Chamberlain, Duncan. And I can just picture Brunhilde marching all over me in jackboots once I've compromised."

"This could be nasty, Brian. Don't say I didn't warn you."

"Nothing could be much worse than having crockery fly past your ears."

"At least she missed."

"Only when she was trying to hit me. When she tried to miss, she was deadly."

Walnut is still smiling wryly at my description of life in the Reid household, when there's a yell from the doorway.

"Fuck me! Two for the price of one!" Who else? – Fleece, who has popped his head in.

The café is busy at the moment – this is potentially embarrassing. I have to put on my best stage whisper and most polite accent to ask Fleece to tone his language down. I sense approval from the customers.

"Listen everybody, I'm sorry," yells Fleece to all and sundry as he waddles in. "I just got excited when I saw a couple of friends here."

I point to a framed piece of paper behind the counter. "Do you see that certificate on the wall, Fleece? That's a commendation from the last time you came in here. Remember? Everyone here thought you were a beggar."

"They pay beggars' wages in the Civil Service," he says. He turns to Walnut. "Walnut, my boy, how are you?"

Walnut, of course, does not like being called Walnut, and he likes references to his baldness even less.

"That's a real spam-heid these days, Walnut," Fleece says, making squeaky noises as he rubs Walnut's naked skull, after which he sits down beside us. "Matches the voice. How are you?" He turns to me. "Listen, Captain, go and make us one of those giant pails of coffee like the one you made for Walnut here. Would you like another one, Walnut?"

"A small one, perhaps," says Walnut, in as deep a voice as he can manage.

"You heard the man, barista," Fleece says, snapping his fingers.

It takes a few minutes to make their coffee, and then to serve two other customers who have had to come in at the same time as these two intergalactic figures. By the time I return, Fleece and Walnut are actually deep in conversation.

"You didn't tell me about your music video, Brian," Walnut says. "Fleece here has just been filling me in."

I'm pleased to see that Fleece is really interested. "Actually, Duncan, we might have a further use for your services." Turning to Fleece, I say, "That'll be eight pounds, Fleece," which he treats as if I were speaking Swahili.

"Oh? What services of mine might you need, the pair of you?" Walnut says suspiciously, which I can understand, because so far he's not received a penny in payment for acting as a mercenary soldier in the war against Brunhilde.

"I think it would be helpful if you'd look over our contract." Silently, I hope he won't charge.

"You've got a recording contract?" Walnut asks, incredulous.

"No, you daft twit," Fleece clarifies. "With this agent Captain was talking about."

"Back in the early eighties, there was a Long Tom Cantlay who sang a song called *Any Way You Want Me I'm Ready*," Walnut says. "This is not the same guy by any chance?"

"I think it might be," I confess, recalling that one of Walnut's talents was an encyclopaedic knowledge of pop and rock music.

"Tiny wee guy – four foot three or something – and paraded as some sort of freak in the days before that sort of thing became politically incorrect. George Watson played keyboards, Dave Norman played guitar, Mickey Malone played bass and a pair of twins played percussion. What were their names? – Yes, Robert and Norbert Simpson, that was it."

Fleece can't get over the last pair. "Norbert Simpson? The poor guy's parents called him that? What a shame – was it a family name or something?"

This question would be beyond most human beings' abilities to answer, but when it comes to rock trivia, Walnut is not of this earth. "Apparently his parents weren't expecting twins, so they'd organised only one boy's name, Robert. When the father went to register the births, they still hadn't thought of a second name, so he registered Robert first, then when the registrar asked him the name of the second twin, he said, 'Well, it's no' Robert anyway.' The registrar misheard him and wrote it down as Norbert."

Normally, such a tale would be apocryphal, but when Walnut is talking rock, it can be accepted as gospel truth.

"Was the song any good?" Fleece asks.

"Best avoided," Walnut nods sagely. "Peaked in the charts at number twenty-three. Stayed in the twenties for a couple of weeks in the run-up to Christmas, then sank without trace."

"Impressive display of knowledge there, Duncan," I say. "Remind me to be in your team for the next pub quiz."

Fortunately, it seems pub quizzes are not beneath Walnut, and he takes it as a compliment, which is how I intended it, to be fair. Then he suddenly looks at me in alarm.

"This contract you're going to show me – you haven't signed it already, have you?"

"I gave some sort of vague assurance of good faith over the phone, but nothing else."

"That's a sort of contract, too, Brian. When will you ever learn? But in practice, a verbal contract isn't worth the paper it's written on."

"That sounds like a quote."

"Sam Goldwyn. Responsible for lots of quotes, actually."

"My favourite's 'Nobody ever went bust underestimating the intelligence of the public'," Fleece adds.

"That was H. L. Mencken. Famous American journalist and satirist," Walnut corrects him sharply. Fleece acknowledges his reprimand with a Frankie-Howard-style "Ooooh."

"Fleece says this Tam Cantlay sent it to you as an email attachment," Walnut carries on, and I nod confirmation. "Can you forward it to me, then?"

"No problem. You're welcome to come along on the day, if you want. Are you doing anything a week on Sunday?"

"Nine hours is a long time, Brian. I suppose I could look in for a bit, though," he offers to my surprise. "I'd like to hear you, actually. It could be entertaining."

"You mean, it could be hilarious," Fleece suggests.

"Now that you mention it, it could be. Are you selling tickets?" Walnut asks, laughing.

"It might be the only way we'll ever make any money, Duncan," I suggest.

36

The Labours of Geoff

The ten days or so leading up to the studio session are, to say the least, hectic. Tam telephones to let me know what I've already discovered, that the studio is in Mitchell Street, under the name of Sounds Great, and that we need to be there at nine sharp because we're paying for every minute. Of course we have to practise the numbers we are definitely going to record and film, but there are other issues, too, especially the decision to prepare a couple of new songs in case we get the chance to record them, too. Everyone is up for an intensive series of rehearsals at Little Joe's, and now we practise recording all the time, absolutely everything we do, so that Little Joe suggests that we need to look after the hard drives they're being recorded to in case they're stolen and later used for bootleg sales. Only Little Joe could possibly get that carried away, though, and needless to say his older brother rips him to shreds for it. Another matter is that all the songs need to be written out in proper music form for Geoff's benefit, something I can do on my laptop but which is hugely time-consuming. We've decided on two more songs of mine, *Get A Grip Of My Life*, and another one called *Leave Me Alone*, which is about promotion-seekers at work who espouse the latest fads, force others to follow these fads, then get promoted and bugger off to leave the rest of us to clear up the mess.

All this work is essential, though, because if we don't, there's a serious danger that one of Little Joe's rasta-jock songs will have to be recorded. That in itself brings yet another problem, because I daren't let on that we're trying to save the world by preventing Joe's music from going live, so we have to practise that, too, which in turn means I have to write out the music for Geoff, and so on, and so on. And to be honest with you, I really don't understand how to write reggae music down on paper, so that when I play it back on the computer, it sounds like a folk-song turned into a complete joke. Mind you, that's what it sounds like in real life, too, but it's a different complete joke from what I'm committing to paper. But at least I'm trying, as much for Bev's benefit as for Little Joe's or the band's.

And of course there's the bass part. Sue Zee at least does exactly what I ask, and in fact I'm starting to get the hang of the bass part, which is the one thing we can't change – we all have to practise playing along with a computer. It's just that it all takes time, and in the second week I even have to postpose a treasured Wednesday lunch with Becky in a lovely little restaurant in Thistle Street, much to her amazement.

And I get a letter from Walnut, telling me that Brunhilde's lawyer has racked up the pressure on me, so that if I don't part with half of my pension, she'll sue, and if I lose the costs may well gobble up the other half. Selling the *Big Issue* looms before me. I used to tell my pupils that it was very easy to become homeless, it wasn't just drug addicts and the very poor; now I threaten to become living proof.

And, to cap it all, last weekend Hibs lost at home again, this time to a goal scored in the very first minute, which hardly anyone saw because the fans were all outside demanding a change of manager. Which would be a good idea except they don't have one at present. They're not quite bottom of the league, but that's only because two teams are even worse.

On the plus side, Walnut has emailed me to say that he's shown Tam's proposed contract to a colleague in the office, who assures us that it's a pretty standard format, it's safe to sign, and we should expect all to have to sign it. Tam is committed to 'promoting' us, which means that he has to make some sort of visible effort. The contract will expire in twelve months' time, when all parties can review it and start all over again. I email him back immediately to say thanks and hope to see him at the recording.

Geoff, however, is giving me a little cause for concern. We've arranged a dress rehearsal for Saturday, the day before our planned recording, and when he collects me in his convertible (incredibly, in mid-January, he's driving around with the top down), I make the usual mistake of asking him how he is.

"Goodness me, Brian, I'm not so good at the moment. I'm struggling a bit just now to tell you the truth, goodness me, I'm certainly struggling a bit, yes."

It is a noble thing I do now. "Tell me about it, Geoff."

"Kind of you ask, Brian. Well, there's a number of things." I was afraid of that. On he goes. "I've still got quite a few aches and pains around my neck and shoulder area, and I've been having a bit of trouble with constipation lately. Nothing that a couple of suppositories won't sort, though." Did I have to know that, Geoff? "But the doc seems a bit concerned about the water works. He wants to get these tests done."

"You seem to have been waiting a while, Geoff," I suggest.

"It seems there's a lot of people in my position. Long waiting list, I suppose."

"That's a bit unfortunate," I say. To be honest, I don't know what to say.

"Well it's certainly very worrying, Brian, goodness me, I will say that. Actually, this band stuff of yours has been a very welcome diversion, to tell you the truth."

"Well that's one good thing that's come out of it."

"It's a lot of fun," he says, "although my guitar teacher is suspicious. He thinks the songs don't 'challenge' me enough." Geoff finds it funny, although I don't – is that teacher of Geoff's trying to insult me, saying my songs are simple? (Actually, they *are* simple, but I'm not admitting it. I'm also thinking how long it takes me to write them out especially for Geoff's benefit – where's Clapton when you need him?)

Even as we speak, though, I can tell Geoff is in discomfort. He frown-frown-frown-smiles, and I know he's not right, although he's just about back to himself in a couple of minutes, distracted by trying to dodge his way around crowds in Dalry Road as they gather for a Hearts home game. But once we've made it through the maroon-clad hordes, we're at Bev and Little Joe's house just a minute or two later. Geoff somehow manages to help me escape from his straitjacket-on-wheels and we emerge out into a gloriously sunny, if freezing cold, sunny afternoon in Merchiston Place and stagger up the path to their front door. They've painted it a different colour, a deep red colour, and for another change, it's Little Joe who answers our ring of the doorbell.

"Hi guys," he greets us, looking lovingly at the front door, as he waves us inside..

I get the hint. "I see you've repainted your front door, Joe. Nice colour. Do it yourself?"

"Thanks. Glad you like it, and yes I did, thanks. If you want a job done well, I suppose, you should do it yourself. It's four-D-forty-five of course, one of the most popular colours, with a zero-E-fifty-five to surround. Both BS four-eight-hundred."

"I'm sorry, Joe, I really have a clue what you're talking about. Is this Joe the ironmonger speaking by any chance?"

Little Joe chuckles. "Sorry – I tend to think of colours by their trade paint names."

"I can just picture you on a romantic evening with Bev. 'Look Bev, what a glorious four-D-forty-five sunset it is tonight.'"

"The sunset is more likely to be four-E-fifty-three sunset against a twenty-D-forty-five sky. Flame orange against chelsea blue. You might get one later, actually."

I wish I'd never asked. "I'll take your word for it, Joe."

Ever the polite host, Joe asks Geoff how he is and to my horror I'm treated to a re-run of Geoff's constipation, shoulder-pains, and trouble with the water works. Joe is a decent sort, and listens patiently, offering his sympathies where appropriate.

Bev appears. "I'm sorry, boys, I was in the loo when you arrived." This comes as a shock: surely Bev and the Queen are exempt from bodily functions? As ever, she treats me to one of her aspirated kisses, and even Geoff receives a chaste peck on the cheek now, which he clearly appreciates from an attractive woman over ten years his junior.

Then Bev asks, "How are you, Geoff?" – condemning me to a third straight hearing of bowel and bladder stories. Of course, Bev manages to say all the right things as she leads us through to Little Joe's studio, and Geoff is still giving ever more intimate details as we arrive. Fleece is battering his drum-kit to within an inch of its life, but he stops when he sees us, cheerily asking… "Captain, Geoff, how are you?" My reply takes five seconds, Geoff's five minutes, at the end of which Fleece's eyes are visibly rolling.

Bev watches while we begin to get set up. "I'll leave you to it today, since this the last rehearsal before tomorrow. Cheese scones when?…"

Little Joe is in really serious mood. "Perhaps we should skip the cheese scones today, Bev."

Fleece is having none of it. "Certainly not, Bev. Your cheese scones are what makes putting up with all this rubbish worthwhile."

"How about an hour and a half from now?" Bev suggests, and we settle for that as she leaves.

"Before we start," Geoff asks, "can I use the little boys' room?"

Fleece mutters under his breath, Little Joe looks impatient, and I'm increasingly worried about Geoff, but he's back in a few moments. There are no explanations this time, which is ominous.

The plan is to rattle through all the songs, once each in turn, as if we were doing a live gig, and then practise what seems worst. Little Joe suggests we should leave time to include a couple of rasta-jock numbers, and no-one has the heart to suggest otherwise. The two songs now available on the website and on YouTube, *Right Here Lovin' Me* and *Bird*, sound the tightest, unsurprisingly considering how often we've been playing them, but even the new ones are just about presentable. This could be less bad than we all feared. Geoff keeps having to go to the toilet every now and again, and even Fleece and Little Joe have expressed some concern about him, but when the scones arrive we're all able to report a degree of readiness to Bev.

"And here comes the Last Supper," Fleece announces loudly.

"I'm sure tomorrow will go better than that," Bev soothes. "You're being noticed, I gather. Joe showed me." The musical press has discovered us, and we're developing a small cult following which is partly boosted by the air of mystery that surrounds us.

"Seems like it, Bev," I reply. "Tam has managed that cleverly, actually."

"So – tomorrow – what are you hoping to record?" she asks.

I explain that we've got a list of songs, most of which she's heard already.

"Are they all yours?" she asks me, looking across at Little Joe.

I've ready and waiting for this one. "Mostly, Bev. We're also thinking about a couple of Joe's." I don't enlighten her on what those thoughts might be, and for once she's unable to read my mind, and gives me one of her spine-melting smiles instead. Maybe it's something she adds to the cheese scones...

37

The Studio, Part One

The agreement is that we'll have nine hours of recording time from nine o'clock through till six, with the sound engineer being allowed from one until two for lunch. Tam has said that "Duffy's a good guy, he often works his lunch break", although he adds rather ominously that he's more likely to help out bands whose music he enjoys. That rather suggests that he must not hear anything by Little Joe or he might down tools altogether.

Because it's a Sunday and parking will be easier, I insist on taking my own car down to Mitchell Street, which at least means I haven't got cramp even before we start. Although I get there ten minutes ahead of time, Geoff is there already as he and Sheila are early risers even in the winter, and he's probably been up since before six. Now that I think of it, Geoff's guitar teacher likes him to do his scales and arpeggios first thing in the morning, so that's what Geoff will have done. Seeing my Honda drive up, he gets out of his tiny little car using only the driver's door, the soft top of his Nissan Micra Sports remaining firmly on. He catches me staring at him and gets the wrong idea straight away.

"Hello, Brian, anything wrong?"

"I'm gazing in wonder at your ability to get out of the side of that thing rather than straight up out of the top," I explain.

Geoff frown-smiles. "But there's a knack, Brian, yes. Yes, goodness me, it's all down to having the knack."

"It might have something to do with the fact that you're supple and without a spare inch of flesh, whereas I've got a belly to manoeuvre round."

"I don't think that's true," Geoff frown-smiles.

"What isn't?"

"I'm not that supple, really, there's a knack."

"I rather hoped you were going to say that my middle wasn't that big, Geoff," I say, wryly.

Geoff frown-laughs at this, but he still doesn't say it.

"You seem a bit better this morning, Geoff." Oh, no! – Why did I say that?

"Well yes, Brian, feeling quite well today. Maybe the effect of double-helping prunes with my breakfast – "

I decide to cut in. "You seemed in discomfort yesterday, Geoff. You're sure you're up for this?"

"Goodness me, yes. Goodness me, wouldn't miss this for the world. Been up since five practising."

"Five?! Five o'clock?" That just seems out of all perspective, especially in mid-January.

"It's just like getting up to go on a foreign holiday. Off to do something different in a different place in the middle of winter, except without the passports."

"It's a novel way of looking at things. Did you bring some cash?"

"Goodness me, of course, Brian. I wouldn't let you down in that department. I wonder when the others will get here."

"Good question, Geoff. Fleece isn't always the most reliable."

In fact Fleece arrives only just after nine, mainly because he's been dragged down by Little Joe in Joe's ironmonger's van, turned for the day into a roadies' van for Fleece's drum-kit. He looks awful, actually, as if he's only just been dragged out of bed by his younger brother.

"Hi, everyone," Little Joe says brightly; it's good to see one of them looks fine. "Sorry we're late but I had to get Fleece up when I called for him." As predicted – and is Fleece still wearing his pyjamas under his trousers?

Fleece manages to come up with a primeval grunt in response. "There's good news and there's bad news, Captain. The good news is that I'm here." Christ almighty!

Is that the good news? – I shut my eyes, waiting for the blow to fall. "The bad news is that I've not been able to get to a cash machine so I can't pay my share."

The bad news could have been worse, and I've brought some extra in case, but I'm not letting Fleece off that easily.

"That's all right, Fleece, Coates collects the money at the end of the session, not the beginning," I tell him.

"Oh that's fine then! Great."

"We'll all pay our share and Duffy and Tam can set their heavies on to you."

Fleece looks alarmed. "What heavies? I thought you said this guy Tam was tiny."

"Perhaps you could nip out to a machine at lunchtime, I suggest." This produces another primeval grunt from Fleece. I resume my 'up-and-at-'em' mode. "Right everyone, let's do it."

I ring the bell, and an enormous bearded lump appears at the street door.

"Jesus, are you one of Tam's heavies?" Fleece asks immediately.

The giant frame produces a high-pitched voice with a slight lisp. "Sorry? I'm Duffy Coates, the proprietor of Sounds Great. Are you The Flying Saucers?"

It's absolutely the first time I've heard anyone ask that question, and it sounds great.

"We are," I say, thrusting out my hand to shake Duffy's as ostentatiously as possible in order to divert attention from Fleece's sniggering; in fact he might not be the only one. All I can hear are schoolboy whispers of "duffle-coats" behind me, and I abruptly make them all focus by introducing them each in turn.

"Welcome to my lair," lisps Duffy, lumbering across the room. It's surprisingly empty, although it's not helped by the bareness of the walls. At one end stand some screens and quite a fair number of boom-microphones, while beyond that lies a control room not so dissimilar to the control room in

Little Joe's studio. There's a lot more kit in Duffy's control room, though, and in any case Little Joe really hasn't a clue what to with the stuff he does have. The main room isn't even rectangular in shape, it's more of an L-shape, and there appear to be a couple of cupboards off it to my left.

"I can see you're looking at the room. Is this your first time?"

"We've never recorded anywhere," I reply, "except in Joe's house here."

"Although it does have proper recording facilities," Little Joe insists.

"Which you don't have the slightest idea how to use, Little Joe," Fleece says, "Otherwise we wouldn't be here."

"Well it helps to have a room that offers different echoes, depending on where I place you all. It offers all sorts of options. Over there I also have a small single recording studio for solo work," he adds, pointing to one of the door off.

Fleece looks round the studio. "Where's this guy Tam Cantlay? Is he hiding somewhere?"

Just at that moment, there's a sound of a flushing toilet, then a moment or so later the other door in the side opens and a pocket-sized figure emerges. He might be five foot two, but he might be a lot shorter, but he's in perfect proportion. He looks like the Incredible Shrinking Man, a part of the way down the trail.

"I'm Tam Cantlay," he announces. "Sorry I was otherwise occupied when you arrived."

"And I should say that if you need to go to the toilet, that's where it is," Duffy points out. I can see Geoff adding it to his mental list of 'favourites'.

Tam looks bemused. "But where's the band?"

"You're looking at the band, Tam. I'm Brian Reid, otherwise known as 'Captain'. This is our rhythm guitar and backing vocalist, Little Joe Mackay, on drums we have Fleece, whose real name is Josh Mackay, and finally on lead guitar there's Geoff Arrowsmith. Together we make up The Flying Saucers."

"Jesus Christ." Tam's looking up at the four of us, a stunned expression on his face.

"Is there something wrong?" I ask, knowing full that there is. I just want to hear Tam say it.

"Jesus Christ," Tam repeats, which doesn't much help.

It's Duffy who comes to his rescue. "Tam gave me the impression that The Flying Saucers were a new young band, that he wanted me to record today."

"Well he's half right," Fleece says. "We're new."

"A third," Tam corrects him. "It's not even a band yet. Where's your bass player? Suzi? She is coming today, isn't she?" He pauses. "Actually, on second thoughts I think I'm not going to like this."

"Sue Zee," I announce, enunciating the two syllables quite separately as they appear on the website, "is this, Tam," producing my MacBook and starting to power it up.

"Holy Mary."

"Tam actually doesn't swear very often, I can assure you," Duffy says. "He'll be all right once he gets over the shock of seeing you."

"Goodness me, are we that ugly?" Geoff asks, frown-smiling, and trying to lighten the mood a little.

"Little Joe is," Fleece says.

Little Joe himself is looking at me accusingly. "Have you misled this guy, Captain? Have we done all these rehearsals for nothing?"

"I didn't mislead anyone," I reply, bristling a little. I'm the one who's had to do all the negotiations here and I'm not happy at Little Joe's tone. "I haven't said anything about our ages, and nothing about our bass player either."

"You misled me all right," Tam says sharply. "You could have said. You could have told me I had the wrong idea about your band."

"But I didn't know what your picture of our band was until your son produced that cartoon showing a band full of youngsters, did I?" I know, that's bending the truth a little. "By then it was a bit late."

Tam sinks down on the nearest seat, shaking his head. "What a shambles…"

"And lots of people seem to be looking at the video clips," Geoff says, still frown-smiling. He's doing his best.

Tam looks up at him. "That's the problem. The whole world will know I've been made a fool of. Can you imagine what my credibility will be like when this gets out? Someone in my job depends on credibility for everything. The big boys know that when I find talent and say it's good, then my word is worth listening to. What's going to happen now? I'll be a laughing stock."

"Surely it's not that bad?" Geoff is still frown-smiling, but there's more doubt in his eyes now.

Tam is back in head-down-and-shaking mode. "I'm ruined… I'm ruined…" There might be tears in his eyes.

There's not much I can think of to say at the moment. Fleece can't make up his mind whether he's angry or whether the whole thing is hilarious. It's Little Joe is the one who acts like a businessman.

"Look," he says to Tam. "As far as I can see, you heard us sing a couple of songs, and on the basis of that you phoned Captain to take things a bit further.

Tam replies with a nod, then goes back to despairing head-shakes.

Little Joe is firm with him. "On the basis of your calls, we've given up a lot of time, come along here ready to do a recording – at our expense, mind you – and we've even taken legal advice on any possible contracts that we might sign. I hope you're not going to go back on your promise now, Mr Cantlay." As his six foot three towers menacingly over Tam, I am forced to ponder the incongruity of 'Little Joe' next to 'Long Tom Cantlay'.

Fleece looks a little worried, perhaps remembering the Tam's 'heavies' that I told him about earlier. "Careful, Little Joe."

Tam mistakes Fleece's words as a warning to Little Joe not to rough him over too much. "You're quite right, gentlemen, the fault is partly mine," he says. Little Joe and Fleece give him the stare. "Perhaps mostly mine." More staring from all of us, except Duffy, who has drifted into his control room to get out of the way.

"All right," Tam says. "It was my fault." I can't believe how easy that was.

"So where does that leave us?" I ask, to no-one in particular.

"Well, I'm here to do a recording, and I'd like to get on with it," Little Joe says.

"So am I. Goodness me, so am I," from Geoff. Meanwhile Fleece just laughs and shakes his head.

"And you're employed to manage and promote our band, Tam. However you can," I point out. "You get twenty per cent of our take. It's time to start earning your money. We're making a demo or two, and you're producing a film of us." Along with the others, I start to get organised.

Tam looks up at me in despair. "I can't do it boys, I can't do it. I've presented you as a young five piece band with a female bass player. I can't change the image now."

"That's your problem, isn't it?" I suggest, trying not to sound too aggressive.

"That depends."

"Explain."

"If I launch you as a bunch of old geezers with a laptop for a bass, I reckon that's the last we'll hear of you, however good the music is. Captain, right at the start I told you that your music needed a good video to be successful. Nothing's changed there. The video still needs to be right."

There's a moment of silence as we all take in what Tam has just said.

"So, as I asked before, where does that leave us?" I ask him.

Tam looks up at me. For the first time he looks a little more confident. "I think I might have an idea." Slowly, he explains his plan to us.

"You've got to be kidding," I say to him, but he's not.

38

The Studio, Part Two

"Goodness me, boys, it seems we really *are* ugly," Geoff says, frown-smiling furiously. He at least thinks the plan's hilarious. Little Joe is not so sure.

"Let's get this straight, Tam. You want us to make the recordings, then you're going to get actors to mime our parts in the videos instead?"

"That's the plan," Tam says triumphantly. "Any better ideas?"

"But we'll never ever be able to play live on stage," Little Joe bleats.

"In your case that'll be a good thing," Fleece puts in. "Alternatively, we could issue everyone with a paper bag to put over their heads so they can't see you."

"If it works, you make the money only from recordings. No live shows at all. Plenty of bands have done it before," Tam points out.

"It sounds like fraud to me," I suggest.

"Only morally, I think," Tam says. "Plenty of immoral things go on in the music industry."

"Most of them involve sex and are more fun," Fleece roars.

Tam winces – he hasn't become acclimatised to Fleece yet. "It would still help if we could get hold of a female bass player just to be on the safe side."

"Bass players are hard to come by. Female ones are like hen's teeth," Little Joe says. "No-one who thinks they have any talent ever wants to play bass. It's just so boring, don't you agree, Geoff?"

"Goodness me, I don't know anyone who even possesses a bass guitar, I don't think."

I do know someone, and am keeping very quiet. The Apple Macintosh is the better option. "In any case," I suggest, patting it, "the bass parts are all written for this thing already. We might as well record it and see what Duffy has to say."

Tam goes into the control room and brings Duffy out.

"Has peace broken out?" he asks.

"Sort of," and I explain what we'd like to do. Duffy ponders the problem for a moment.

"Actually, that might work. It might even speed things up a little." He explains that his normal technique, especially for first-timers, is to record all of us together as a master track, then to record each of the parts in turn playing along with the master track. He then uses the mixer to get a good result. Sometimes he includes the master track, sometimes he leaves it out, but it's the methodical recording of each part that takes so long. On the other hand, he can record our master track and the bass part separately and at the same time, so that helps straight away.

The first song we decide to do is *Right Here Lovin' Me* because it's structurally very simple, and although we spend twenty minutes or so getting the sound levels set correctly the first time, Duffy's experience proves invaluable as he manages to get us through a first master take. Because we're using the laptop as a bass, we're even able to record a second master track that he can use for comparison later; he says it'll still work, and he can even use them both if he wants to experiment. Once we've done the masters, he has each of us doing our part in different parts of the studio – me in the little cupboard, for instance, Fleece round the L-shaped corner, as we sing or play along while listening to our previous recordings through headphones. Although much of this is new to us, Duffy's expertise helps us pick it up quite quickly. I have to say I like this dishevelled monster, and he seems to have limitless patience. Tam's sole contribution is to record the master tracks on DVD from different angles for some reason. Other than that he spends the whole morning reading the Sunday papers.

It takes us until lunchtime to make something Duffy feels he can work with on *Right Here Lovin' Me* but after lunch we make quicker progress with *Bird*. I manage to get a good vocal sound on it immediately, and to my amazement, Little Joe's extra bit sounds better with some interesting effects. Duffy gets us to do second recordings of the vocal parts, promising to explain later. Again, Tam takes a break from the papers to make DVDs of our master tracks when we're all playing together.

Towards the end of *Bird*, a light goes on above the entrance. It transpires that this lets them know that someone is outside ringing the bell in the street, because of course there's no bell in the studio itself. Tam goes off to see who it is and returns a moment later with a spectator.

"Walnut!" Fleece roars. "Welcome to the dark and seedy world of underground music."

Walnut nods to all of us, and I introduce him to Tam and to Duffy. He looks totally out of place, still sporting his camel-hair coat, and apart from not wearing a tie he could be headed for the office. I explain that Walnut is our lawyer, and he said he'd pop along if we were thinking about signing anything.

Tam seems suspicious of anything that might remotely be termed 'legal'. Walnut picks this up on his antennae.

"It's all right," he says. "Everything looks fine, Mr Cantlay. It's all fairly standard, although I gather twenty per cent is quite a big take."

"Yes," Tam replies, "but of course it's also my job to move them into a bigger league, where they'll be able to negotiate a better deal."

Walnut's not sure about the logic of this, but says to us, "If you guys are happy, it seems fine."

"It's not as if people are beating a path to our door, Duncan," I point out. "If things do change, the contract only lasts for twelve months."

"It puts the onus on me to impress them over that period, Mr McIntyre," Tam says.

"I suppose so," Walnut says, looking less than sure. "How's it going?"

"Not too bad. We've laid down two tracks so far."

Fleece bursts out laughing. "'Laid down?' 'Laid down?' What sort of language is that?"

"You've got to talk the talk in this business, Fleece," Tam says. "You'll learn that quick enough."

"Must I?"

"It all helps the image, which all helps make more money."

"In that case, Walnut, we've 'laid down' two tracks, so far," Fleece says, laughing. Then he stops to think again. "Wait a minute. We don't have an image. You're going to use someone else's image to go with our music."

"Good point, Josh," Little Joe says.

"Eh?" says Walnut.

Tam gently explains that the music will be mimed to by younger actors.

"But that's surely fraud?" Walnut says. This word concerns me a little, especially when a lawyer uses it.

"We're not actually saying that these particular actors are the actual singers and performers of the music."

"It's implied," Walnut points out. "There's also the small matter of the non-existent bass player."

"It's been done before," Tam says. "It's like The Archies."

"Oh, sweet Jesus," Fleece mutters, while Geoff frown-smiles in recognition of a shared pain.

"Who?" asks Little Joe.

I try to fill Little Joe in on a little musical history. "A couple of session musicians had a smash hit with something awful in the seventies called *Sugar Sugar*. They produced an animated cartoon to go with it. Seemed to stay at number one for months."

Walnut corrects me. "Nineteen sixty-nine, to be exact." My scars are deeper than I'd realised.

"It was like a bad smell that wouldn't go away," Fleece says. "You, younger brother, were too little to have to deal with it. Be grateful to your elders and betters."

Little Joe will have none of it. "My era had to put up with Wham! and that awful McCartney frog song. Every generation has its cross to bear, Josh."

"And don't sneer at The Archies, gentlemen. They made a fortune," Tam points out.

"I've suddenly decided not to sneer," Fleece announces. Holding the lapels of his fleece like a defence lawyer in court, he declares "I will prostitute my art for a fortune. Only a fortune, mind you."

"And as I say, the Archies didn't have a bass player either," Tam says.

"Nor did The Doors, as far as I know," I add. Walnut, the walking musical encyclopedia, nods his agreement.

"Goodness me! Really? Goodness me!" says – well, you know who says it by now.

Fleece clears his throat loudly. "Em, Captain, I hate to break this to you, but you ain't no Jim Morrison."

"I sing better than he does nowadays," I reply.

"You might be right there. But it's a close-run thing. Morrison's still better than Little Joe."

I can see Little Joe is wilting under the attack.

"Leave him alone, Fleece," I say. I'm trying to change the subject anyway. "Listen, Walnut, I don't mean to sound rude but we're paying a lot of money for our studio time here. Can we get on with some more recording and we'll look at the contracts later?"

"Of course," Walnut replies. He hasn't noticed or picked me up for accidentally calling him Walnut. He turns to Tam and Duffy. "Can I stay and watch for a while?"

"Sure," Duffy replies. "You have to be quiet, though." Pointing to Tam, he explains, "Please stay in the control room. If you listen to this morning's stuff you occasionally hear that balloon Tam rustling his Sunday papers in the background. He should know better."

"Has he ruined the recording?" I ask, glaring at Tam.

"No, don't worry. That sort of stuff happens all the time in recordings. People fall off their drum-stools, folk laugh too early or start clapping. It adds to the texture of the music."

In the next two hours we manage to record another couple of songs of mine. Walnut is absolutely transfixed, insisting that he's not been so entertained in years. He says he can sing a little, so I invite him to join us for the backing vocals on the second song, which completely thrills him to bits. It's almost half past five when the light goes again to indicate that someone else has arrived at the front door. I'm annoyed that we've been interrupted while things are going so well, and in my irritation I volunteer to go to the door to send the person away.

But when I open the door it should be dark – it's well past sunset in mid-January, after all – but a light shines before me in the form of Bev.

"Brian," she breathes. "I do hope you don't mind. I just felt that I've heard so many of your rehearsals that I couldn't miss out on the real thing. Is this all right? Will I be in the way?"

How could Bev ever be in the way? "Of course not, Bev. Walnut dropped in, as it happens, and he's stayed on to watch. Do come in."

As she comes in, she quickly kisses me, and then brushes a little closer than is entirely necessary. "Lead on, Brian," she commands, softly. As I lead her, the dark corridor seems to be lit by her luminous presence.

We emerge into the main studio. "Look who's here?" I announce.

"Bev!" Fleece roars. "Where have you been? I need my cheese scones!"

"Double helpings next time, Fleece," she replies, but kisses him in compensation; Geoff is treated to a kiss, too, as is Walnut, whom she knows quite well. I feel a faint pang of jealousy, even of Little Joe, whose wife she is after all. Then she's introduced to Tam and Duffy.

"How's the recording going?" Bev asks.

"Brilliantly," I reply. "Making great progress."

"Have you recorded any of Joe's music? Or is it just yours?" Bev asks, quietly, but looking at me. All of a sudden I want to be somewhere else. Anywhere.

Little Joe tries to help out. "I'm not sure my music is what was on the agenda, today, Bev."

Bev smiles wonderfully and with understanding, but I can feel the cold steel of her smile sliding right into my heart. I can't stand it.

"Listen," I say. "We've come to a natural break in things here. Why don't we try something of Joe's now?" I look towards Duffy. "Can we do it, Duffy? Have we got enough time?"

Duffy shrugs his shoulders. "We've still got a good three-quarters of an hour. Maybe a little more. You've spent a lot of time arguing. But I like you, so I'm happy to help out."

"You like our music?" I ask in wonder.

"A bit. I've heard worse. But I like the fact that not one of you has called me 'Duffle' all day. Nobody else has ever managed that before."

I look around, expecting this compliment to go down well, but the reaction to what has happened is mixed. Geoff is frown-smiling rather doubtfully, but Little Joe is utterly overjoyed that *The Jute Mill Song* – his least-bad offering, after all – is getting a formal recording. By contrast, Walnut, Tam and Fleece, who all know what to expect from rasta-jock, are horrified at the prospect. Duffy is oblivious to the impending danger – he doesn't realise he'd be safer standing on a railway line in front of an express train.

I don't need to look at Bev; she has infused me with her warm glow once again. Using her telepathic powers, she makes me positively feel the spine-tingling words: *Thank you, Brian.*

39

Hard Negotiations

It takes me fully an hour to make my peace, first with Duffy, then with Tam, and finally with Walnut, who has chosen to stay behind to supervise the signing of contracts with Tam, and the payment of Duffy's studio fees. Duffy, furious that I subjected him to the horrors of rasta-jock, spends much of the time trying to negotiate extra out of us, first as overtime, then as danger money (rasta-jock is a health and safety issue, he insists), but Walnut silences him by enquiring gently why he needs all his money paid in cash. Duffy softens his tone after that, which allows me to explain gently that Little Joe's music is his entire life, and he, Duffy, has made Little Joe happier than he's ever been before. I also point out that Bev showed some typical appreciation of Duffy's work, too, which he acknowledges with some embarrassment.

It's almost seven by the time we leave, but it's been a good day. Tam promises to get back to me with details of his next move. He's become quite adjusted now to the idea of his new clients – signed up on the dotted line with a great many pieces of paper flying around – being just a little older than he'd imagined at first. We're old enough to compare notes on some shared experiences sixties and seventies music, and I allow him to feel he's impressing me with some top-of-the-range name-dropping. This takes forms such as "Rod Stewart and me were sitting in a bar and Rod says to me…", or "Jagger and I were on stage together in Portsmouth when…", or utterly improbably, "Mercury was my pianist for a while, of course." I find myself at one point wishing he'd been "on same plane as Buddy Holly the night the music died". All this from a man who seems to be shrinking by the minute – even his five feet nothing turns out to be boosted by a pair of cuban heels.

He tells me that the next move in question is to round up a group of young actors he's worked with before, and in fact are part of his 'stable' of clients. This term has me leaping off at a mental tangent trying to work out which of any of the four of us, Fleece, Geoff, Little Joe or me, could remotely be described as 'thoroughbred'. My train of thought rejoins his ramblings as he describes these young actors, who he claims have some musical experience and "should fit the bill nicely".

"Who's paying for them to 'fit the bill', Tam?" I ask him.

"Em… Why shouldn't it be you? This is all for your benefit."

"No, it's not, Tam, it's for yours. We don't see the need to have them. This is your idea. To save your skin, to save your reputation. What's more, you've dragged the four of us along with you in a conspiracy to mislead the public. And we're not to be allowed out to play. Ever."

"Eh?"

"On stage, in public."

"I suppose not."

"So you can bring in your 'actor' friends if you want, but my wallet remains firmly closed," I say firmly. "As is the subject."

"I don't think we've done anything illegal, mind."

"Hmm. Keep it that way."

"In the meantime, Captain, the sooner we can do this footage of the actors, the better. It's good if they can copy your style of playing – it helps the actors to have a vision of what they're trying to copy. When can you manage?"

"We always practise on Sundays. Where did you have in mind?'

"We need a recording studio as a backdrop. I'm not sure if Duffy can do it next Sunday, though."

A thought comes into my head. "The room we practise in is actually Little Joe's own personal studio. We could use that, I think." I give him Little Joe and Bev's address in Merchiston Place.

"The guy's got his own personal studio? To play that crap of his?"

"The studio keeps the sound in, safe from the world. But don't ignore it, Tam. Make sure you give a little time to Joe's songs as well. Please."

"His wife's a nice piece." I think: to describe Bev as 'a nice piece' – how coarse.

"She's a very nice woman, yes. And an extremely successful businesswoman. Don't mess with her, Tam. Seriously."

Tam's taken aback by this warning, but takes it as 'man to man'. "So provisionally, next week at Merchiston? In the meantime, Duffy will mix the songs, and I'll round up the band of actors."

"You'll need something else, Tam. We haven't got a bass guitar."

"Don't worry, I've told you, I've got a girl in mind."

"No, I mean we need an actual guitar. A bass. None of us possesses one."

"Ah." It dawns on him at last. Then he adds, "But I know where to go."

"Sounds fine to me," I say, and as we let ourselves out of Duffy's studio together, I reach down to shake his hand.

40

Harry Phones

"So how did it go, old boy?" It's Monday, and this is Harry on the phone.

"Interesting. We've signed a contract with an agent."

"Really?" He's impressed. "So you're making some money, then?"

"So far, not a penny."

"How does this agent get paid?"

"A percentage. Quite a big percentage, in fact, twenty."

"Wow. That's twenty per cent of nothing, which is er... nothing?"

"Correct."

Harry is at a loss. "So let me in on the secret. Why is this guy – Tam, you called him? – acting as your agent for twenty per cent of nothing at all?"

"Because he seems to think that fairly soon it'll be twenty per cent of a fair bit. Maybe not that big a bit, though, which will be why he wants twenty per cent."

"How on earth do you hope to make any money?"

"I think he's got designs on selling downloads. You know, mp3s, iTunes and so on."

"I know what a music download is, Dad. Out of interest, do you?"

"Not much, I suppose. Only what's on my iPod."

"Well, I've got news for you. Mp3 files get ripped off all the time. Lots of top-class bands give them away for free these days."

"So how do they make any money?"

"Doing live concerts. Huge money to be made there."

"Ah. Well, that's not an option for us." I explain Tam's idea. Long before I finish, Harry's in hysterics.

"He thinks you're too old and ugly? That's a bit harsh."

"That's unusually generous of you."

"You might be ugly, but you're not too old. Half the stadium rock circuit would qualify for a bus pass."

"The Stones, The Who, Tom Petty, Dylan, the guys from The Band, Clapton, I know."

"They're the young ones. McCartney qualifies for extra on his state pension next year, I think." Harry continues to think like an accountant, even when discussing music. "And then there's the super-old, the ones you thought were dead already, like B. B. King and Chuck Berry. So there's plenty of time for you yet. But there's a real problem about your ugliness."

Harry has an astonishing ability to get me to laugh about myself. "Let's see how it goes over the next week or two. I'll keep you informed. How's Danni?"

"Oh, she's keeping well," he replies, using an odd turn of phrase. "We were out at Mum's last night."

"How is she?"

"Spitting blood. She's angry with you, Dad, that's for sure."

"It's self-defence, son."

"I know, but I want to keep out of it. Maybe one day you two will be able to speak to each other again."

"You're quite right to keep out of it. And actually, I don't like not being able to speak to Mum. I seem to miss out on a lot."

Harry's quiet for a moment, then he says, "I think you probably do."

Now it's my turn to pause before I continue. "I miss her, too. It might surprise you, but it's true. But we just can't live together, it seems. It should work but it doesn't. And then the crockery flying around my ears just made it downright unsafe. And daft to stick around."

I can hear Harry's hesitation. "Did you never throw anything at her at all?"

"Not once. It was a one-way street," I assure him. "You should ask your mum for confirmation of that, though. But I'm sure I deserved it. I drove her up the wall."

"How was that?"

"Again – you'll have to ask her, although I can guess. There was nothing else, though. No-one else, no drink, no gambling, nothing. Maybe that was the trouble. But really, Harry, you'd have to ask Mum."

"I find it difficult to understand, Dad. Becky, too."

"I know, I know. That's why I'm so grateful you've got Danni and Tommy, the pair of you. I know you're OK when you're with them. One less thing for me to worry about. By the way, I had a lovely lunch with Danni last week."

"She told me. She enjoyed it, too, although precisely why you insist on paying for lunch when she earns twice you earn is quite mystifying."

"That's a bit rich from you," I protest. "You're the one who insisted that every time I took you out for lunch at my expense, I was evading inheritance tax."

"So I did. Now I'm being inconsistent. I'm from the inconsistent generation," he announces, laughing.

"I told Danni that I thought she didn't need to grab half of my pension, and that she's got plenty money, but Danni told me Mum wasn't that well off. Is that right?"

Harry hesitates again. "No, Dad. Mum's loaded. Her job pays well, she's got a nice house, and she has very few expenses."

"So she's just trying to screw me into the ground."

There's a silence at the other end of the phone, which this time Harry doesn't break.

"I'll take that as a 'yes'."

"I want to keep out of it, Dad. I told you."

"And that's right, son, that's right. In the meantime, I don't know where this whole business with your mum is going, but when I do, you'll be the first to know."

"Can we talk about something else?"

"Sure. How's work?" Safer ground there, surely.

"Things are a bit rocky at the moment, Dad. The recession is biting hard. Even giant firms like ours get affected."

"Is your job all right?"

"Well, nobody's safe, Dad." This is all I need, although Harry is legendary for trying to cross bridges that simply never come anywhere near.

"Oh dear." I can't think of anything better to say, so I don't say it.

"We'll have to wait and see. There's a big staffing review going on at the moment, and they've warned us that some people are bound to be emptied out."

"With a package?"

"Possibly. But what do you do to get another job? It's a competitive world out there just now. We might have to move away."

"What about Danni?"

"She'd get a job all right, especially in London."

This really would be heartbreaking for me – I depend on my children for family company, and I've no-one else in Edinburgh at all. I try to remember that this is Harry, who likes to pretend he's devil-may-care but in fact is quite neurotic underneath, a worrier like his father. Like me, he's constantly seeing disaster round the next bend, although in his line of business it makes him extremely good at his job. Becky should be in the more vulnerable job, but her up-and-at-'em attitude tends to keep her ahead of the game all the time.

We talk about football, the weather, a couple of alterations Danni and he are making to their Bruntsfield flat, the possibility of them moving up a level once they know where the job situation lies, and about my dead upstairs neighbour. We blether on for a few minutes about nothing in particular, and he rings off, promising to look in to see me very soon, either to my flat or to Costa.

After he rings off, I'm struck by the fact that I was full of enthusiasm for life before he called, but that now I've sunk into a bit of a depression. And that's what bothers me – a phone call from my son should be uplifting. Something is wrong, but I can't pin it down.

41

The Fruits of our Labour

By Wednesday evening, I'm really excited again, which is entirely down to an email I receive directly from Duffy, although Tam copies it to me again later on. It contains a link to a Dropbox-type website – it seems all these guys use this sort of stuff – where our demo tracks are parked. There are five in total, and I download each to my desktop before listening to them.

Duffy has done a truly sensational job. All four of my songs actually sound like they've been recorded in a proper studio, and I suppose they were, of course, but I mean they sound like the sort of things I might actually buy myself on a CD or on iTunes. I can't believe we sound that good, to be honest, and the bass actually sounds like a top-class bass guitarist. Then I brace myself for Little Joe's effort.

There's no escaping it – it sounds awful. But then I didn't like punk either, and that was supposed to be a purist's attempt to get back to clean musical roots. At least that's what my punk-rock friends said. Whatever people make of this rasta-jock tripe, Little Joe will certainly get the credit for being the first. Hopefully the last, too, although he might achieve a footnote of notoriety such as a page in Wikipedia all to himself. Having said that the music sounds awful, Duffy really has given it his best shot, bringing up some interesting guitar echoes to offset the funky rhythms of new-wave rasta-jock. I'm trying my best here. I forward the email on to the others, adding a health warning to Geoff and Fleece which I don't include in Little Joe's.

Little Joe is on the phone immediately, so quickly that he can only possibly have listened to one track.

"Captain! Captain! Isn't it great? Isn't it great?"

"I assume you mean *The Jute Mill Song*. Yes, I've listened to it. Duffy's done a good job on all of the songs, hasn't he?"

"Eh, yes, Captain. He has. They all sound good." He's lying, unless he had them all playing at once. Come to think of it, *The Jute Mill Song* actually sounds like a number of quite different songs all being played at once.

"OK, Joe, the plan is that we're all coming to your house on Sunday, and we're going to run through the songs with these mime artists there." I have a sudden vision of people with white-painted faces all moving around in strange jerky movements. "They're going to watch us, then copy our movements for the film shoot."

"All the songs?"

"Each of them in turn?" Joe asks.

"All four. Tam plans on launching our first EP, on CD eventually, but to start with on mp3. It'll be seventy-nine pence a track or two pounds ninety-nine for all four."

I can hear Little Joe's brain winding up to this. "Where do I fit in? I mean *The Jute Mill Song*?"

"I'm not sure, to be honest, Joe. Perhaps we don't need any subterfuge for you. We could just make a film of you as you are, singing on your own." Unspoken, I think: it will also allow the rest of the band to dissociate itself from rasta-jock.

Little Joe's spirits pick up instantly. "Do you think so, Captain?"

"Let's see what your agent says. You're paying him for advice, so ask for it."

"I suppose so."

"Do you have anything else in the pipeline?" I'm being polite. I keep hoping that this particular well will finally run dry.

"One or two things, Captain." I was afraid of that; I was just hoping beyond hope. "But I'd like to keep them under wraps for the moment," he adds. Is that a threat or a promise?

"In the meantime, expect lots of people to appear on Sunday afternoon – all the usuals, plus five people who are pretending to be us, Tam, and Walnut said he'd maybe come along again. Could you let Bev know that? There might be a big call for cheese scones."

"Aye, aye, Captain. Walnut had a good time, then?"

"Definitely. He said he hadn't laughed as much for years."

"Did he think we were that bad?"

"No, of course not. I was kidding." I can't quite bring myself to tell Little Joe that Walnut wanted rasta-jock to be referred to The Hague as a war-crime. "He was just very interested, that's all. I think he sees us as potential clients, too."

"I suppose we might be."

"We mustn't get ahead of ourselves here, Joe," I warn him. "Remember that this exercise on Sunday is designed to keep the real Flying Saucers hidden from view. Tam clearly doesn't think we have much of a future as four old geezers."

"It's better than nothing, Captain," Little Joe says. For some reason he's being unusually rational. We discuss exact arrangements for Sunday, and he naturally turns down my offer to contribute something in the way of refreshments.

"Don't be daft, Captain," he says. "You know it's a labour of love for Bev – she loves doing it, having us around, you know."

"I know. She's a saint."

"You can say that again, Captain."

So I do. "She's a saint."

Little Joe rings off laughing. It's great to hear him so genuinely happy, but I wonder how long it can last.

I have no sooner returned the handset to the cradle than it rings again.

"Get off the ruddy phone, ye bugger!" roars the voice at the other end.

"Good evening, Fleece. How are you?" I answer.

"Fifty pence less well off than I would have been if you didn't spend so much time gabbing on the phone. Your number was constantly engaged so I pressed that button five as that stupid bloody woman tells you to, only to discover 'you will normally be charged for this service'." He mimics the artificially posh accent of the female BT announcer.

"So you got the email then?"

"I did, Captain, I did. The man's done a remarkably good job of turning sows' ears into silk purses. Or in the case of Little Joe's tripe, turning horse-shit into fertiliser. Thanks for the warning on that one, by the way."

"Happy with the percussion then?"

"Well, I have to admit it, Captain, your man Duffle Coates smoothed over some of my... idiosyncrasies. Has Geoff been in touch?"

"No. Geoff doesn't really do modern technology – he doesn't check his emails and keeps his mobile switched off. Anyway, he's probably in bed by now."

"It's only ten o'clock, Captain!" Fleece is incensed at the thought.

"But he's up before five. His guitar teacher tells him to get up early and practise before dawn, so that's what he does," I explain.

Fleece laughs at this insanity. "Does his guitar teacher tell him to say 'Goodness me' all the time as well?"

"Goodness me, I never thought of that," I reply. Fleece however has the attention-span of a gnat, so he's not managed to listen to both ends of that sentence.

"Listen, Captain," he says a little breathlessly. There's a pause, followed by a gulping sound that suggests 'beer-can' at his end of the line. "Is this guy Tam really planning to bring in kids to mime to our music? I can hardly believe it."

"That's the general idea, Fleece."

"Who do you think he'll get to play me, then?" Aha – now we get to the nub of Fleece's call.

"What sort of person do you think would be appropriate, Fleece? Brad Pitt? Matt Damon? Julia Roberts?"

"Julia Roberts?" he laughs. "Fuck off. How about Johnny Depp? He ought to be free."

"Hmm. I'm not sure he's quite right. How about the guy from the Harry Potter films. He should be free."

"You mean Daniel whatisname? Young and dashing? He could dump the glasses, I suppose."

"I was thinking more of Robbie Coltrane."

"See my earlier answer, Captain. As in 'fuck off.'"

Ignoring him, I say, "It's certainly going to be interesting to see what Tam comes up with. He insists he knows 'just the people'. He keeps saying they're perfect."

"And you say Tam's paying for this charade, Captain? He's surely not going to spend lots of his own money then, is he?"

"No, I wouldn't have thought so. But this whole plan was settled on before he knew he was paying. Maybe they owe him a favour," I suggest.

"God help us if we ever end up owing that wee guy a favour. After all, he's got heavies."

Does Fleece really believe that? Or does he know something I don't?

42

Acting Out the Music

Geoff and I travel early on Sunday, once again in his wheeled deckchair. I want to go with him because I've had little chance to discuss the music that I sent him and, sure enough, he hasn't checked his emails and he's heard none of it. He's only heard of today's arrangements because I was able to speak to Sheila on their land-line and leave him a message.

"I did try to phone you, Geoff," I say in exasperation.

"Oh, goodness me, Brian, but I was out at my guitar teacher's."

"On your mobile, too. I left a message."

We're driving along the road but he insists on digging into his left trouser pocket to rescue a battered but barely used Nokia silver mobile phone.

"Oh, I'll switch it on and see what the message was."

"Geoff, there's a police car behind us," I shout, grabbing the phone from him. "You'll get done for that."

"Oh goodness me," he says. "Goodness me, I suppose I might now. I never thought."

"Anyway, it's all right. If you haven't listened to the message, it doesn't matter now. I can just tell you right this minute."

"Goodness me, of course you can, of course you can, Brian." Geoff frown-smiles happily, giving me a quick glance and so missing the wagging finger from the police car as it overtakes us. I wave the phone in acknowledgement.

I've brought my iPhone, and I manage to play two tracks through Geoff's car radio, and unsurprisingly he's suitably impressed in a suitably Geoff manner.

"Goodness me! Goodness me!" Then after a pause – during which we nearly miss a phase of traffic lights – "Goodness me!" He's frown-smile-smiling a lot here.

"They're not bad for beginners, are they?"

"They're not. Goodness me, Brian, they've turned out far better than I thought they would. What about Little Joe's song?"

"*The Jute Mill Song*? Well, let's say it's not made it on to my list of iPod favourites, but there has been progress. Little Joe's excited by it at least."

"That's good, that's good," Geoff nods. "I'm pleased for him." Geoff is a seriously nice guy.

By the time we arrive at Merchiston Place, I've managed to fill Geoff in on the day's programme, which entails an hour or two of rehearsal of all five songs (we can't ignore the execrable *The Jute Mill Song*) so that we'll be ready to go when Tam arrives complete with the miming actors. Tam seems to think this will take very little time, although I fail to see how these poor souls can rapidly learn the music and mimic our style in four separate songs. Hours upon hours of painful toil surely lie ahead for all involved here.

As ever, Bev greets us at the door. It's the end of January by now and the daylight is getting better, but there's a glow around Bev which boosts it and lights our way as she guides us through to Little Joe's studio. She ushers Geoff in, but stops me at the door.

"Things seem to be going well, Brian," she breathes softly into my ear. "I've not seen Joe this excited for years." As she says it, she softly rests her hand on my left pelvic bone, with predictable impact.

"Bev, I know how much this means to him. It means a lot to all of us, but I'm not sure what's going to come of this. I can't honestly see how Tam's going to get this to work." I look into Bev's eyes, probably for longer than is appropriate. "I hope you don't have lots of pieces of Joe to pick up some time."

She looks down and nods her head. "I know, Brian, I know," then she looks up at me again. "But you'll never know until you try." The hand that had been cupping my hip now pats encouragingly a couple of times to reinforce the point.

As usual, Fleece and Little Joe have set themselves up, and Joe has placed some boom microphones around in convincing-looking places around the studio, even including one for my acoustic Angelica guitar although it has a pickup attached to it. Bev departs, and for the next ninety minutes we slog our way through the various numbers. Geoff suggests doing Little Joe's first for a change. I understand his thinking, that we can get it over with and it will make Joe feel more important, but, excruciatingly, *The Jute Mill Song* is so bad that it takes seven attempts to get it right. Not that anyone has the slightest idea what Little Joe's concept of 'right' actually is. The other songs are fine when we manage to get round to them, although another side-effect of playing *The Jute Mill Song* first might be that we have simply lowered our standards thereafter.

Around two-thirty, Bev knocks on the door and comes in.

"Your visitors have arrived, boys."

I've been nervously awaiting this moment all day, and my nerves are not eased as Tam comes in, followed by four young men and a young woman. The young men are all roughly the same age and height at just under six feet, three of them blond-haired and casually dressed and broadly similar in appearance, while the fourth is clearly of Indian origin. The girl might be slightly older, and she's also a little shorter, perhaps five foot four. She's also dressed from head to toe in black leather.

Tam looks pleased as punch with the people he's rounded up for the day.

"Gentlemen, let me introduce you to Magda, and these are Jimmy, Evelyn, Quentin and Omar, otherwise known as the C-U Jimiz from Falkirk." He pronounces 'Evelyn' like a girl's name.

"The fucking whats?" Fleece yells, although to be honest he's simply expressing a collective surprise. Both Geoff and Little Joe are open-mouthed at what stands before them.

Tam enlightens us. "The C-U Jimiz are one of Scotland's foremost boy-bands"

"Em, why haven't I fucking heard of them, then?" Fleece asks, forensically.

It's the Indian-origin lad who answers. Interestingly, he has a broad Falkirk accent. "We've still some work to do on our act, Tam reckons," he answers. Join the club – does Tam collect these sorts of acts?

Fleece becomes a civil servant for a moment. "What aspect of your work do you feel most needs work, er…?"

"Jimmy. I'm Jimmy," says the Indian-origin lad, to Fleece's bemusement. "Tam reckons we can't sing."

"That's a bit of a problem for a boy-band," Fleece suggests.

"Is it?" Tam interjects. "Have you heard any of them? They're just miming along to the voices of studio singers, most of them." Ah – Tam's plan has just become crystal-clear. "But I think I should introduce each of you in turn," a process which of course threatens to take ages thanks to the numbers of us present.

Indian-origin Jimmy turns out to be some sort of self-appointed boy-band leader. "I'm Jimmy Macgregor," he announces, to gales of laughter from the entire cast of The Flying Saucers. Jimmy, to his credit, takes this in good part. "No, not that Jimmie Macgregor, I'm the other one. He spells his name with an 'ie' at the end." I didn't know that.

"Does that mean you *can* shove yer granny aff a bus, then?" Fleece asks. He thinks this is hysterical, and actually I'm quite impressed with young Jimmy's patience with him.

"And I don't sing songs about yo-yos either," he says. "I'd better explain. My family own a chain of Indian restaurants, but my great-grandfather was actually white, a Glaswegian soldier who married an Indian girl in the days of the Raj and brought her back home.   Unusually, all of their children married into Scots-Indian families."

"So your family produce the legendary Macgregor's Pakoras, do they?" I ask him.

"That's us.   And Macgregor Vindaloo and Chicken Tikka Macgregor."

"What the fuck is Chicken Tikka Macgregor?" Fleece demands to know.

"Family secret," Jimmy says. "But I can reveal that the base for the marinade includes a lot of haggis." The very idea of this stops Fleece sufficiently in his tracks to allow Jimmy to finish his introductions. He waves his hand at each in turn.

"This is Quentin Hickmott, who's a student at Glasgow Caledonian University."

Quentin, who has a Home-Counties English accent, raises his hand and says, "Hi."

"Then there's Evelyn Kerr.   He's Eeevelyn, not Ehvelyn, by the way," Jimmy says, pointedly looking at Tam. Evelyn keeps his hands firmly in his jeans pockets, but his grunted "Aye" suggests central Scotland. Jimmy supplies no background information for Evelyn.

"And this is Omar Thompson here. Omar's works in a call centre at night."

Fleece is off again. "Omar?"

"Hi everyone," Omar replies in a well-spoken Scots voice. "I'm afraid my mum liked the name. She claimed I was conceived on the living-room rug directly after she and Dad had watched *Dr Zhivago* for the ninth time."

Fleece chuckles. "Thank your lucky stars she hadn't just watched *Shrek*."

"Customers to the call centre are convinced they've called India when they speak to me. They all start shouting as if I'm far away."

"But Omar's not even an Indian name."

"People who call centres are very stupid." I'll bear that in mind next time I'm calling a call centre, I think.

Jimmy has one more introduction. "Finally, there's Magda Czeslawska here. You'll probably guess she's not one of the C-U Jimiz," he says smiling.

Magda steps forward with authority, hands on hips. She wears glasses. "I am Magda, I am Polish, and I am here to learn English for a year. I am twenty-five and have a boyfriend in Krakow. In the meantime I am working as a waitress in All Bar One in George Street." She has a deep husky voice and a thick Polish accent: she is "verking uss a vetress" in All Bar Vun, to be exzakt. She also has attitude. A wholesale introduction session and shaking of hands follows as we introduce ourselves, Bev included.

Tam takes charge insofar as is possible for anyone who is five foot nothing including cuban heels. "OK," he says to us, the band, "the idea is that you guys play each of your songs in turn, and then we run through them again with the band miming to the song in the style in which you sing or play. Did you provide me with copies of the lyrics as I asked, Captain."

I hand over five copies of the words of each song. "As requested. What do we have to do here, Tam? I don't get it."

"Your guys don't have to do anything, Captain. Just play your song as usual, that's all. It's their job to fit in with you. It'll be easy because you're actually both working to the same computerised bass."

"Really?" I say doubtfully.

"These are professionals, Captain. Watch and learn, watch and learn," he says, smugly. There's something about the combination of his five foot nothing and cuban heels which makes me want to punch his smug, arrogant little nose. Perhaps he can read my mind, because he takes a step back from me. What with him and Bev both in the room, how's a man supposed to have any secrets any more? Perhaps they know when I last went to the toilet?

Just before midday, Brian. You'll be needing to go again some time soon. Now that is scary. I turn round to see Bev shimmering at the side of the room. She turns towards me and smiles. *This will be fine*, she adds.

Tam claps his hands and demands that we set off playing something, and as *Right Here Lovin' Me* remains the easiest song in terms of structure, I suggest we do that one first. We know this song well now, and play it slickly and cleanly right through to the end, while Magda and the C-Us study us very closely. They're kind enough to give us a polite round of applause afterwards.

"I've heard vurse," Magda announces, "although mostly in Poland." It transpires that three of them, Magda, Quentin and Omar have even taken some notes while we've been playing.

Then Tam announces that it's time for the mime performance.

"What does the band do now?" Little Joe asks.

"I told you, nothing," Tam replies. "They mine to your recording, not to you. Take a seat and watch this. They'll need your instruments, though."

Geoff asks a question I haven't thought of, for some reason. "Out of interest, who's playing who in the band?"

It turns out that the band haven't thought of that either, and they all gather in a huddle with Tam to decide. Magda, of course, is expected to play bass, but the others all claim they can mime anything, and a good deal of squabbling now ensues. Quentin, it seems, hasn't been allowed to pretend to be a drummer before and reckons it's his turn, but Evelyn's view is that Quentin hasn't been allowed to play the drums because he's hopeless at it. Evelyn makes this point with some force, seasoning all of his sentences with the words 'stupid', 'posh', and 'tosser'. Omar, meanwhile, is complaining that he's being landed with having to be Little

Joe, and Little Joe can hear all of this with dismay. Jimmy rides to the rescue, arbitrarily declaring Omar to be the drummer and taking on the role of Little Joe himself. Quentin is to be me and so Evelyn is left with being Geoff, which he regards as acceptable.

Tam then gets his iPod out, together with a fancy little lead with white wires and colourful plugs at each end, and he connects all of this into two of our speakers. He hands Magda a bass guitar, which he says he picked up for twenty pounds at Duncanson's, a pawn-shop on the corner of Queen Street and Frederick Street. He counts them in, and the iPod starts playing.

Then, before our very eyes, a remarkable thing happens. We can hear our own voices and instruments from the speakers, but it doesn't appear to be we who are singing or playing them. Instead, in perfect time to our music, these five youngsters manage to make it look as if it is they who are performing. Everything is in absolute perfect synchronisation. They've got our mannerisms, too, Omar's elbows capture Fleece's all-over-the-place drumming style, Jimmy does a fine job of copying the seemingly unique agonised singing of Little Joe, and Evelyn has in minutes managed to get Geoff's frown-smiling lead guitar. As for me, it's a very odd experience to watch Quentin, and although I have no real idea whether he's got me or not, I feel he might be uncomfortably close to it as he stands, sings, strums the guitar, and frankly does not a lot else. The four of us watch them, utterly stupefied, but we manage to pull ourselves together to applaud our imitators, and not out of mere politeness either. But we can say nothing. Eventually, a voice breaks the silence.

"What was that?" Incredibly, it's Bev.

"Told you they were good," Tam says, smugly.

"There is one thing, though," I point out.

Because for once he's standing and I'm sitting down, Tam is able to look down his nose at me as if I were a piece of dirt. "Well?" he says, sharply.

"Why is Magda playing her bass upside down?" The string tuning pegs point down the way, when they should point up.

"Ah," says Tam, visibly deflated. "I didn't notice it was a left-handed bass guitar. That explains why it was so cheap at the pawn-shop."

43

Making Movies

Once we've regained our equilibrium, Tam immediately orders a complete rerun of *Right Here Lovin' Me*, only this time he's going to set up a number of digital cameras to film the event. No sound is required, of course, and the performance goes perfectly. The process is repeated for *Bird*, *Get A Grip On My Life* and *Leave Me Alone*, and Tam is delighted to hear that I have more songs in the pipeline. In each case, our job as a band is to play the song in our own way, while Magda and the C-U Jimiz study us in order to mimic our actions while the sound track is playing. They are a truly remarkable band, especially the boys, who clearly have rhythm and dance in their souls. Magda has less to do, because she's not required to sing, and she seems equally happy 'playing' her bass guitar left-handed as much as right. Her only concern relates to her clothing, her all-in-one leather suit.

"Tam," she says, demanding his attention firmly. The way she says it, it sounds more like "Tum".

"Yes, dear?" Tam answers, although I sense that this is not the way Magda likes to be spoken to.

"My leather suit," she says, pointing to her front.

"What about it, dear?"

"How far down do you want me to leave it open?"

"A fair bit, I suppose." I'll bet – his camera will be able to spend more time on her. But in the meantime, Tam is too busy setting up cameras and positioning the C-U Jimiz to give his full attention to this pressing matter.

"But exactly how far?" she insists. She slowly starts to unzip the front. "This far?"

"A fair amount, I said," Tam replies, but he's got his back to her and he can't see.

Magda pulls the zip down a little further. "Tell me when to stop, Tam."

By now, four middle-aged men are viewing this discussion from the best possible angle, and Magda, being a true professional, is not going to let an audience get in the way of her work.

"This far?" But Tam still isn't looking.

"Whatever, Magda. As far as you can, I suppose."

"This far?"

What we now have before us is a miracle of science. Magda's zipped – or should I say now-unzipped – leather suit is now open beyond her navel, and there is absolutely no underwear in sight so far. Nevertheless, she is just, maybe only just, decent, although none of the four viewers can quite work out why. None of us can say a word – and Fleece makes it clear he doesn't want us to – but eventually Geoff can't help it.

"Goodness me!" he says. Fleece gives a furious look that says – Traitor!

Tam spins round, and immediately homes in on the cause of the distraction. "That's kind of you, dear, but perhaps you could pull the zip up a little from there." Magda shrugs and does as she's bid. Tam asks her what we all want to know

"Em, Magda, em... are you wearing anything under that leather suit of yours?"

"No, of course not. You told me not to."

"Did I?" Tam looks embarrassed.

"I asked you, 'What do I need to vear on Sunday?' and you said that 'All I vould need was my black leather suit.' I do vot I am told. I am good girl."

"Ah," Tam says. "I need to be more careful with the subtleties of the English language in the future. Sorry."

"Did I do wrong?"

A chorus of male voices: "Certainly not." But Fleece needs to ask a question that's bothering him.

"Magda, can you explain something for me?"

"Yes?"

Fleece points to his own chest. "How does the suit not... you know... open?"

"Ah, Fleece," she replies, smiling. Her glasses add to her knowing look. "Double sided sticky tape."

At that very moment, Bev, who has disappeared for much of the filming, reappears with a huge tray of cheese scones and, moments later four large flasks of coffee and one of tea.

"How's it going, boys? Magda, too, I suppose."

Fleece replies, "Magda here has just been giving us some tips about the sartorial benefits of double-sided tape."

Bev raises her eyebrows, then gives Magda's leather suit a knowing look. "You couldn't be without it today, Magda, could you?" she says.

Magda laughs a deep, deep laugh.

"So how did you know, Bev?" Fleece asks, amazed. Bev just smiles one of her iridescent smiles, but doesn't reply. Instead I feel the answer, so perhaps the others do, too. *I know everything*, she says.

Bev, however, wants to know exactly what we've been up to, so Tam gives her all the details of the four songs we've recorded.

"None of Joe's songs?" There is a hint of reprimand to Tam, but it's more directed at me. *How could you allow this to happen, Brian? How could you? I trusted you.*

I can see Little Joe shuffling in his seat. "Bev..." he begins, like a small boy who wants his mummy to stay out of his playground battles.

I have a responsibility, but I can't resist it anyway.

"Tam, could we film something of Little Joe's?" Even as I say it I can see the look of shock in the C-U Jimiz faces. They've obviously been exposed to rasta-jock without the proper vaccinations.

Tam hesitates. "Captain, I don't really think it's fair..."

I can actually feel Little Joe crumpling, to say nothing of Bev's super-sharp steel Sabatier knife entering my heart. But in the nick of time I'm about to be rescued by a stroke of genius. "Look, Tam," I say, "why don't you simply film Joe actually singing on his own. No-one else has to be in it at all."

Tam looks at me. "Eh?" sums up his grasp of the situation.

"You could make it look like a solo video featuring Little Joe himself. It could be semi-animated, with all the background animation and Little Joe playing his guitar over it for real."

"You mean like Mary Poppins?" I can see a light going on inside his brain.

"Just like Mary Poppins. Can you do that, Tam?"

Tam is very interested in wriggling off the hook, and he realises that this way, we can all dissociate ourselves from rasta-jock. It'll be clearly Little Joe's project and Little Joe's alone. "I suppose that might be possible," he says.

"You could out-source it to Sam, couldn't you?" Tam smiles and nods, and I turn to Little Joe. "Are you interested in that, Joe?"

"That sounds great, Captain, that sounds great!" With one bound I am free, and Little Joe is happy again. All the rest of us will be happy once the excruciating *The Jute Mill Song* has been safely put to bed – 'in the can' seems particularly appropriate on this occasion.

It's not long in coming. I feel a *thank you, Brian* coursing through the marrow of my bones like a narcotic.

44

The Finishing Touch

"How long do we have to wait to see the results, then?"

Becky, bless her, is genuinely excited for me.

"Soon, I'm told. Young Sam just loves his work, and Tam says it'll be hard to keep him away from it. A bit like your Tommy, I suppose. How is he, by the way?"

Tommy, it seems, has a huge – and very lucrative – commission for his furniture in a grand West Lothian home which has recently been bought by an ageing former golf star with more money than sense. The golf star's previous home had been on the edge of Wentworth Golf Club in London, and when he stumbled upon Tommy's work in an exhibition, he demanded that Tommy's furniture fill his new abode. Tommy, I should explain, claims 'to bring metaphysics to cabinet-making', so that all parts of one of his 'Bowie' furniture can be analysed in relation to their value, either intrinsic or aesthetic. A chair, for instance, should be both functional and aesthetically pleasing. That's what his blurb, says, anyway. He therefore rejects Charles Rennie Macintosh chairs, which would instantly fall apart if Fleece was ever allowed to sit near a pair of them (if you can picture a Macintosh chair, you'll know why Fleece would need two side by side); he would class such chairs as 'sculpture', to be viewed and touched perhaps, but not to be used. His masterpiece so far is the 'Bowie Table', a solid-pine occasional table which is exactly the right height on which to place a television, and underneath which the solitary shelf is perfectly sized to accommodate a standard group of DVD players, Sky boxes and so on, and yet would pass for a coffee table or a magazine table without the hardware. You could even sit quite comfortably on one for a whole evening. It seems massively overpriced at three hundred and fifty pounds, but it looks beautiful. I have one myself, and a well-furnished room could take up to three. He sells well over forty a week, constructing them using a system of templates, and enlisting Becky to do some of the sanding and finishing work.

The fact that the ageing golf star wants an entire household filled with themed Bowie furnishings, including dining table, kitchen dresser, wardrobes and an enormous double bed, and wants them yesterday so that he can move in the day before, means that Tommy has been spending every available moment in his workshop. Hence Becky's rather at a loose end, and tonight has suggested sharing an Indian takeaway in Eton Terrace before I walk her up to the station.

"Oh, Tommy's fine. He's going to make a fortune out if it, I think, to say nothing of the publicity if Dean likes it and tells all his friends." Dean is the ageing golf star.

"You don't resent it?"

"Resent it? Of course not, Dad. This is great for Tommy – his work combines the two most important things in his life."

"It's some combination," I say, smiling.

"But stop changing the subject, Dad," she chides me, laughing. "This is astonishing news about your songs and the videos."

"Don't get too excited, Becky. I don't even appear in the video, remember."

"Yeah, that's a bit crap. Fancy describing you as too ugly and old," she says.

"Have you been talking to Harry by any chance?"

"Yes, why?"

"Those were Harry's words, not Tam's," I tell her. "Although Tam probably would agree."

"I should know better than not to believe everything my big brother tells me," Becky acknowledges. "So when do we see them?"

"Tam's going on about momentum, still, so the answer is – soon, I think. He's organising it as paid-for downloads on our website and on iTunes, that sort of thing. We'll not make much money, though. Everybody just copies everyone else's mp3 files, don't they?"

"I'm not so sure, Dad," Becky says. "Lots of people share mp3s, right enough, but plenty of paid-for tracks are downloaded, too. Maybe they share them with their friends, but that doesn't mean those friends would ever have bought them otherwise. And in the meantime, your music is getting a wider hearing."

I smile. "I love your optimism, Becky."

"Think how much stuff you've got on your iPhone, Dad. Stuff you never listen to, or they're CDs you've already bought and paid for. When was the last time someone shared a download with you and it then became something you listened to a lot?"

She might have a point there. My iPhone is full of all sorts of rubbish I could do without.

My iPhone's ears must be burning, because it decides to ring. The screen on the front says 'Tam Cantlay', and I'm tempted to decline the call, although I suspect all that would do is offend him. Personally, I hate people phoning me on my mobile when I've got a perfectly good land-line, which has better reception to boot.

"Yes, Tam?" I know I sound irritated.

"Is this not a good time to call?" Tam asks.

"I've got my daughter here with me, Tam, which is why I put the land-line over to taking messages so I wouldn't be disturbed."

"Ah well I'm glad I phoned your mobile then, Captain," he says, with a logic that defeats me. "I just wanted to let you know the latest news."

"Go on, then." I try to give Becky one of those sorry-I'll-try-not-to-be-too-long looks, and she in turn gives me back an it's-OK-I-know-this-is-important one.

Tam's already in full flow. "I told you Sam would come up with the goods," he's saying. "Everything's done. Took him less than an afternoon, he said, although Sam's concept of daytime is a bit strange. He gets up at midday and goes to bed at four in the morning, so I suppose 'afternoon' runs up till around ten at night."

"But you're pleased with the result?"

"The boy's a genius. Everything is perfectly synchronised. Quentin and Jimmy look great as singers."

I'm not sure how to take that. "That's good," is all I can manage.

"When will see it, then?"

"Now, if you go to the link I've just sent all of you by email."

I explain to Tam that Little Joe is probably watching it already, Fleece will if he's not in the pub, and Geoff never will because he thinks you switch technology off at the mains, pull out the plug, and put it back in the box it came in whenever it's not in use.

"I could send Geoff a postcard, I suppose."

"Go on then, have a look," Tam says, sounding very full of himself.

"How about if I do just that with my daughter Becky here – remember I mentioned her, Tam? – and get back to you later?"

Tam sounds doubtful and excited all at the same time. "Fine, I'd appreciate a call tonight regarding one small detail, but go and look at the five downloads now."

"Five? You did Little Joe's as well? This I must see." Actually, I'm not sure I must, but I undertake to phone him later tonight.

Tam turns out not to be kidding about the video downloads; they're seriously well produced, and his son Sam clearly looks like having an incredible future in computers and media. It's definitely the sound of The Flying Saucers' singing and playing, but it looks like it's being performed by the C-U Jimiz and Magda. Fleece, Little Joe, Geoff and I have simply transformed – there's no other word for it – into Omar, Jimmy, Evelyn and me respectively, while my MacBook Pro has become Magda. Becky is transfixed. Three times she makes to speak, only for her mouth to jam in an open, wordless pose.

I decide to play her Little Joe's *The Jute Mill Song* in lieu of smelling salts, and she's brave enough to take it on without earplugs. *The Jute Mill Song* is the same desecration with which I've become chillingly familiar, but Tam has obviously relayed my suggestions to Sam, who has Little Joe performing his deep knee-bends and backward, upward guitar jerks against a loosely-painted background of some Caribbean scenes. It does looks like a cross between scenes from the films *Mary Poppins* and *Scream*, but that serves to provide welcome distraction from the music in a mind-over-matter sort of way. Becky's reaction is hysterical giggles. I'm told some people have the same reaction to the shower scene in *Psycho*, too, and indeed both the camera shots and Little Joe's music bear striking similarities to that part of the movie. But the best part of all is that the rest of us are nowhere to be seen.

Little Joe's happy enough with it, though, and he's on the phone to me in no time.

"Great, Captain! Great, Captain! What do you think of it?" Not them, notice – there's only one track he's interested in – so I know what he wants me to say.

"His son Sam has done a good job on you, Little Joe. You're pleased then?"

"Thrilled, Captain. I'm really excited, actually!" You don't say, Little Joe.

"What do you think of the rest of it?" I ask him, steering the ship away from the rocky ground of rasta-jock.

"Great video, but a bit strange listening to us but seeing the C-U Jimiz and Magda."

"It is a bit, but that's what Tam said would work best. At least for *The Jute Mill Song*, you're allowed to be yourself, Joe."

"Yes," he says, "it's great isn't it, Captain?"

I think I've got the message, and I make my apologies and ring off. A call to Fleece's house suggests he's either out, out for the count, or both, and I'm unable to raise him on his mobile either, which usually means he's let the battery run flat.

With Becky still in my flat, I don't even bother with Geoff, but asking her forgiveness I call Tam back to see what was the other thing he wanted to discuss. It turns out to be something that I've forgotten about.

"This release of ours," Tam says – yes, I spotted the 'ours' in there, too – "is effectively a downloadable EP of four DVD tracks."

"So?"

"It needs a cover."

"A download-only EP needs a cover, Tam?"

"Definitely. Can I put Sam onto that, too? Do you have any requests? Special suggestions?"

"You've caught me on the hop, there, Tam…" Then I stop – how could I forget? "Hang on, Tam, I have one special absolute request. In fact it's essential."

"Really?" I explain to Tam. "Well in that case…" he says, and I ring off for a second time.

With another shrug and a smile to Becky, I dial one more number. It rings for ages before anyone answers.

"Geoff?"

"Brian? Goodness me, you got me out of bed!"

"Geoff, it's only nine-thirty."

"Yes, but I've got an early start tomorrow."

"Of course, guitar practice," I tell him about the video, not that he'll do anything until tomorrow after his scales and arpeggios, then I quickly get to the point. "Listen, this is vital. We need a cover for our EP. Will you design one?

We need your artistic skills." I've remembered that it was always his ambition. There's a moment's hesitation at the other end of the phone.

"Geoff? Are you there?"

"Goodness me."

"Geoff?"

"Goodness me. Goodness me, Brian, I'd be honoured to do a cover." I know he would. "When would you need it?"

"Tomorrow."

"Goodness me!"

We discuss details briefly, then he rings off amid a flurry of 'Goodness mes' and 'Wait till I tell Sheilas'. Then at last I can return to Becky, and I give her a quick resumé of what I've been talking about."

"Goodness me," she says, giggling.

45

Passing the Torch

Geoff may have waited all his life to produce an album cover, but he's well prepared for his moment when it comes, as it turns out he's spent much of the last fifteen years of his spare time cooking up imaginary ideas in *Photoshop*. Geoff asks me round to his house the following evening after my Costa shift to select from a number that he's prepared already. The 'number' in question proves to be over seven hundred, most of which already have some sort of title such as *Geoff Arrowsmith: Live At The Usher Hall* or *Arrowsmith in Action* or simply *Arrowsmith Plays The Blues*. I understand his point, though; all that needs to change is the title and the artist, and in keeping with the song *Bird*, he's suggested a possible album title of *Flying High*. It's as good a title as any, I reckon.

A lot of Geoff's covers include images of Geoff himself, some photographs, some stylised images, and it's clear that for years he's lived his dreams through his guitar and *Photoshop*. He's understandably a little embarrassed of them as well as proud, but I feel quite touched to be allowed into this private side of his life, and I tell him so. However, as he's the first to point out, such covers are entirely unsuited to adapting for The Flying Saucers, and instead what we're looking for is something abstract, perhaps with a plain front. Eventually, and after much discussion, he persuades me to settle on an extremely simple pattern of red and white stripes in front of a picture of a bird of prey – it's supposed to look captive – and with black lettering for the title. It looks a little like a punk rock cover from the seventies, although Geoff later confesses that it was simply the colours of his beloved Lincoln City football club, and that he's rather proud to have slipped it past me.

As soon as I get home, I send it off to Tam in an email, as he'd asked earlier. Within minutes, he's on the telephone, this time my land-line, and his opening is curt.

"Is that the best you could come up with?"

"That's what we decided on. We had a few ideas, in fact. Seven hundred, to be exact."

"No photographs of the band. Do you think that's a good idea, Captain?"

"We're happy with it, Tam."

"I think there should be pictures of the band, Captain."

"Which 'band' are you referring to, Tam?"

There's a silence at the end of the phone, then Tam says, "You know what I mean, Captain."

"My son called it right, Tam, didn't he? We're too old and ugly for your needs."

"That's not fair… but we've got to be realistic here, Captain. If you're ever going to make any money, you have to use Magda and the C-U Jimiz."

"No."

"What do you mean, 'no'?"

"I mean, we're the band. You can do what you like, but we're the musicians, so we're the band. We're maybe not great, but we're all we have. Don't take us away from us." This last sentence makes sense to me, but I can understand why this might cause confusion in other minds, and it doesn't take much to confuse Tam.

"Anyway," I add, "so far we've received nothing whatsoever, and thanks to you we're out of pocket for the recording studio. You get nothing until that's paid off, by the way, and then we start counting. You get twenty per cent of our net take, not of our income." I have no idea if that's true or not, but I'm feeling a little insulted by Tam and I don't like the direction this conversation is heading.

Tam decides not to argue.

"OK, Captain, we'll go with Geoff's cover. We can always re-issue it later if we want to." I think: he's not learning is he?

"Good. Now what, Tam?"

"You leave the rest to me. You've done your bit. Go back and make up some new material for a possible second album."

"And keep working on the first one, too, of course," I point out.

"If you want." Tam's tone is ominously dead.

"When will we get some money?"

That produces a laugh. "When we make some. As I say, that's my job, Captain."

"OK, I'll leave it with you then." And that's exactly what happens – I leave it with Tam.

46

The True Value of Fame

Whatever I say about Tam, and whatever reservations we've had about him, there is little doubt that he has contacts. In no time, *Flying High* is available as a download album, and effectively there are eight tracks, four of The Flying Saucers' original sound-only recording, and the same four tracks complete with video for computer screens. All for just three pounds, too. As well as being available on our website, he has it on iTunes and a couple of other download distributers.

Moreover, Duffle Coates has contacts of his own, arranging for radio play, first on local radio stations and then on all the major music stations. Tam insists we should launch *Right Here Lovin' Me* as a proper single, and with some judicious plugging, the track is such a success that the decision is taken to release *Flying High* as a genuine CD. The price – still only two pounds ninety-nine – is a huge selling point. Tam arranges for further video footage of Magda and the C-U Jimiz to accompany our EP, and the play-time these get on music channels make The Flying Saucers' music famous in every gym throughout the land. *Right Here Lovin' Me* runs at a perfect speed for a powerful burst on the cross-trainer, while as a dance-to track, it's to be heard any Friday or Saturday night in clubs across the land. There are even requests – all of which Tam accepts, of course – to include the song in computerised keep-fit dancing machines.

Tam has also correctly gauged public opinion about the band's public image. All the teenage girls currently argue about which of the C-U Jimiz – Quentin, Evelyn, Jimmy or Omar – they would most like to jump in bed with, funny Omar, Indian-Scottish Jimmy with the bright eyes, cuddly posh Quentin, or the dark, brooding Evelyn with the murky past. Meanwhile the teenage boys simply salivate over

Magda and her black leather one-piece suit. Magda has mastered the use of her zip to gain maximum attention, and causes a storm when the band are interviewed one morning on *This Morning* by appearing to pull the zip well below her navel for Philip Schofield's eyes only – she turns away from the camera to do so. And of course, she has no bass guitar to hide behind either, since Tam has categorically refused all requests for live performance. The tabloids have a field day, especially since Philip denies anything actually happens and Magda is clever enough to provide a series of no-comments, but general interest is heightened after Tam releases issues a press release where the zip most certainly has been pulled well down, as far down as is possible, in fact, without Magda being arrested. The *Sun*, true to form, takes this as a cue to start a reader debate, to be continued with online voting: does Magda shave? Magda, no fool, continues to play her audience along, in the meantime signing up a contract with Vision Express to promote glasses, using a slogan which carries the words 'The New Object Of Desire', a picture of Magda, and below her, 'Glasses from Vision Express'. Intriguingly, the poster itself doesn't show much below Magda's waist, so the open zip disappears off-page.

For our band, this new-found fame for The Flying Saucers comes with just one small problem: the band itself doesn't seem to be part of it.

By our second practice in March, the troops are beginning to get restless. As Fleece, Little Joe, Geoff and I set up our instruments in Little Joe's house, Fleece is the one who voices the band's concerns most succinctly.

"Captain, are we being fucked about here? Is this 'Tam' friend of yours screwing us over?"

I take a deep breath, knowing that Fleece is only expressing the frustrations everyone feels. "Fleece, in the first place, Tam is no friend of mine, he's simply our manager, and he's signed a separate contract with each of us. In the second place, I don't know any more than you do."

"That contract says Tam's supposed to be getting twenty per cent of what we make, so at the moment he must be getting paid twenty per cent of nothing," Little Joe says. "He can't be getting anything either."

"Aye, right," Fleece says. "Do you really believe there's no money yet?"

Geoff frown-smiles at the expression, one of his favourites. "Only you Scots can turn a double positive into a negative. It's in your nature, the same as 'ye'll have had yer tea'," he says, then he deploys the double negative himself, "but I don't believe there's no money."

Bev is still with us, waiting for instructions on when to bring the cheese scones. So far she's said nothing, but she softly says to me, "Brian, why don't you try to get in touch with Tam right now? You have his phone number, don't you?" The moment she asks me, the phone call is as good as made.

"I suppose so," I say.

"You'll not rehearse well today until you know how the land lies, boys," she adds, as I take my iPhone out and start to dial a number I don't remember having in my list of contacts. Do Bev's psychic powers extend to tampering with my mobile as well?

Astonishingly, there's a reply.

"Tam Cantlay speaking. Who's there?"

"Hi, Tam, it's me, Brian Reid." At my end of the conversation, I look around me and see four pairs of ears, between each of which is an anticipatory smile. I've no idea what they're looking forward to.

"Who?"

"Brian Reid," I say, more slowly. The smiles have subsided already. "Captain to you, Tam."

"Captain! How nice to hear from you!" His voice can be heard by everyone at my end, although they can probably here the lie in the second sentence, too. The smiles reappear.

"We're all here practising, Tam, and the thing is... the thing is we wonder when we're going to see some money, Tam."

Tam hesitates. "I thought I'd explained that, Tam."

"You thought you'd explained what, Tom?" The smiles subside again.

"Well, you must understand that the fees for the appearances should really go to the people appearing. That's Magda and the C-U Jimiz."

"So all the money's gone their way so far." The smiles are now frowns.

"Yes."

"Less your twenty per cent." Deeper frowns.

Tam hesitates. "Of course. As per contract."

"There's just one thing, Tam," I say, confidently. The smiles at my end are starting to reappear.

"What's that?"

"It's our music. In fact they're my songs. We own the copyright." Bigger smiles now.

"The fees for your personal copyright don't come through till much later, Captain. They get paid every three or six months." I don't tell the band about the fact that the copyright fees are to be mine alone. I'd guessed that already.

"What about the fees for playing our music? *This Morning* and so on? Perhaps Magda and the C-U Jimiz appeared, but ITV must have paid fees for playing the music, too."

"Why?"

"Because they played the music in the introduction to the show, complete with one of the videos. That's got nothing to do with Magda and the C-U Jimiz," I say. Big smiles at my end. Geoff, who is frown-smiling a lot, punches the palm of his left hand with his right as if to say, Gotcha!.

There's silence at the other end of the phone. "Listen, Captain, I said you were to leave it to me, and you should do that. You employed me as your manager, and I said I'll look after you. You'll get what's due to you eventually."

"Meantime Magda and the C-U Jimiz get paid now. How much, by the way?"

"What for?"

"Let's say, the *This Morning* appearance."

"I'm not at liberty to say."

"YOU'RE NOT AT LIBERTY TO SAY?" I scream at him, causing the four smiles to turn into look of shock – at my response, I should add, because they still can't hear Tam. Regaining my composure, I say, "Tam, this is our band, this is our music. That's what's being played at discos and parties, and on radios and iPods across the land. I think we're entitled to know what we're earning for that privilege." The heads beside me are nodding now, with a 'thumbs-up' from Little Joe thrown in for good measure.

"Captain," Tam says, "I really think you should consider this again – "

I cut him off. "Tam, do I have to get our lawyer onto this?"

"Think about it, Captain, if you create too much fuss, the public might find out that Magda and the C-U Jimiz can't play a note. Then you'd just be a bunch of sad old geezers acting out their fantasies on guitars and drums."

"A bunch of sad old geezers who'd be acting out their fantasies but are due a lot of money for doing it," I point out. There is anger at my end that Tam has clearly referred to us as 'sad old geezers'.

"Who says you're due a lot of money?" Tam asks.

"You did, last time we spoke," I reply. "You said we'd sold a mountain of CDs and downloads. And by the way, last time I looked, we were at number one on the indie charts."

"That doesn't mean much these days," Tam says.

"Bullshit, Tam. I feel a lawyer coming on," I warn him. More frowns at my end.

"That might be a bad idea."

"Why? It sounds like Magda and the C-Us are doing all right. Now it's our turn – remember, Tam, the musicians? The ones who make the noise?" Much nodding of heads beside me.

"I wouldn't clash with the C-Us, Captain."

"Why not?"

"It's not good to get on their bad side. Quentin's seriously well off. He's got friends in high places. And then there's Evelyn."

"What about Evelyn? He seems an ordinary boy from Falkirk, although I wouldn't blame him if had a chip on his shoulder about his name."

"Evelyn's never lived anywhere else except Falkirk, actually. Polmont, to be precise."

"So?"

"Polmont Young Offenders' Institution."

"Jesus. Why?"

"He killed someone five years ago while he was still at school. Managed to skip the murder charge somehow but still got put away for a lesser offence. Some guy had borrowed five pounds and didn't pay it back on time. Evelyn's only just been released. I'm giving him his first job, a chance to start again."

"Is that by way of a threat, Tam?" All four of my fellow listeners instinctively recoil. Bev holds Joe's hand.

"I don't make threats, Captain. I tell it like it is."

"All right, Tam. Let me think about it." I ring off.

"Well?" There's a chorus of voices around me.

"I think we need Walnut's help," I suggest. The faces fall again, and the frowns return, and this time they stay there for the rest of the evening. Things are so worrying that Bev actually forgets to make any cheese scones.

47

Courting Disaster

"Your troubles seem to be piling up, old boy, just when you would think you should be in the clear." I'm sitting in Walnut's ridiculously and overly expensively furnished office in Multrees Walk, having just laid out the state of play concerning the The Flying Saucers. Throughout, he's chosen to sit back in his high-backed, swivelling leather chair, hands together in that pointed triangle against the mouth that people do when they're trying to pretend they're listening and thinking at the same time.

"You supervised the contract, Duncan," I remind him. "Is everything in order?"

"The contracts are fine, Captain. I checked them this morning after you made the appointment."

I'm interested that he calls me 'Captain', but he doesn't like anyone calling him 'Walnut'. "In that case, Duncan, how do we enforce it?"

"Hmm. First of all, we have to establish that any money has been made. We could do with getting in touch with these... C-U Jimiz, couldn't we?"

"Even the hired killer?"

"This 'Evelyn' character? A hired killer?"

"Well, he's a killer, Tam's hired him."

"Don't believe everything you hear from Tam. It may all be a story to frighten you."

"In which case it succeeded."

Walnut ponders. "Don't we have any contact details for these C-U Jimiz or Magda at all?

"I don't even know their second names. The only time I heard them was when we met for the first time."

"And we can hardly ask Mr Cantlay," Walnut points out.

"Hardly."

"So, do you want me write to him instead to ask him formally for what you're due?"

"I can't see much else we can do," I acknowledge in resignation.

"In the meantime, Captain, there's the little matter of your wife." Just when I thought it couldn't get any worse, I know it's about to. "Jane's solicitor has written to me saying that she really has no option but to go to court on this."

"Who – Jane or the solicitor?"

"Both, actually. And this could be very expensive, I should warn you." Walnut pauses for a moment, to see how well I'm absorbing this, then continues. "Listen, Captain, do you really want to go ahead with this? If you want to call it off, I'll not charge you my share of the fees. At this stage, Sue Gunn's fees are still Jane's problem, but if we go to court, that all changes. What's more, the fees for a court hearing will be astronomical."

"You think I'll lose, don't you?"

Walnut sighs. "If I were Sue Gunn, I'd be feeling very, very confident indeed. And rubbing my hands at the prospect of charging you for every single thing imaginable."

"But what about my claim that I signed under duress?"

"Well, the trouble is, you also signed a statement at the time saying that you weren't under duress."

"That's because I was under duress," I protest.

"I doubt if the courts will see it that way. They'll say that you signed it because you were stupid. And hasty, too."

"I needed to end it, Duncan. For my own safety."

"Can you prove that, Captain? Can you prove she actually endangered your safety to the extent that you were forced to sign contracts under such duress and were even forced to sign that you did it willingly?"

He knows I can't. "Years' worth of broken crockery have all been swept up, I suppose."

"This was all after Harry and Becky left, too. You can't say you did it for your children. Did either of them ever see it happen?"

"No. But I promise you it did, Duncan. You're not doubting me now, are you?"

"No, no, I'm sure it happened. For one thing, I've seen Jane in action when she's lost her temper with you at a couple of parties. It wasn't nice. However, you'll soon be getting money from your music, all being well. Can't you let her be?"

He doesn't understand. "First of all, Duncan, that money isn't here yet. But the other thing is that I don't trust Jane not to try to get a bit of that, too. I need to stop her in her tracks. She needs to agree, once and for all, to leave me alone, and that's what's been such a shock here."

"She really hates you, doesn't she?"

"Seems like it. With a vengeance that I can't quite get my head round," I say.

"Perhaps it's unfulfilled love," Walnut suggests. "They do say the two emotions are just two sides of the same coin." He looks at me, then together we both burst out laughing.

"I'll write to Sue Gunn straight away and ask if her client will reconsider," Walnut says. "That's just about all I can do."

It doesn't work; I didn't expect it to. Two days later, I receive a copy of correspondence between Walnut and Brunhilde's lawyer to the effect that war has been declared.

48

Thank God It's Thursday

Throughout all my troubles, the days at Costa have remained a rock in my life. I've heard people say how much they needed work to make them feel valued, but I never once felt that as a teacher, certainly as a Depyoot Head. I worked to live, not the other way round. But Costa provides a single, lonely man like me a chance to do the simple things in life, to make people happy, and to serve them the albeit simple pleasures of a large americano with an extra shot and room for cold milk in the top, or perhaps a flat white. Tuesdays and Thursdays have me going into work with a skip in my stride, although don't get me wrong, two days per week is enough.

At the moment, Costa is not only giving me a little boost to my income, it's also helping me forget my other troubles. Walnut may have had a rapid reply to his letter to Sue Gunn about Brunhilde, but the more pressing letter to Tam has gone unanswered; things are just not going my way for the moment. However, another benefit of Costa is that people know where to find me, although sometimes they find me even if they don't know.

Kleo is still trying to learn English, and in a sign of her improved confidence she has stepped up her time on her own with the customers to one hour in the morning and another in the afternoon, banishing me to the washing up, wiping down of tables, and general tidying during these periods. I don't mind – it's good to see her improving. If she needs help during these hours, she can always ask me to come through, but it doesn't happen often. So on the day after I receive the Brunhilde legal correspondence from Walnut, I find myself contemplating the meaning of life and the size of pensions in the kitchen while she's out in the front serving cappuccinos and those foul coffees with syrup which seem to be so popular. Kleo has had no need of my assistance at all, so when I eventually emerge to wipe down a few tables, I'm paying no attention to the customer she happens to be serving. It proves to be no ordinary customer.

"Kuptin? Kuptin?" I'm busy, and my back is to the customer making this noise, whatever it is, until quite suddenly I feel my shoulder being firmly tapped.

"Kuptin? Ur you deff?" the voice repeats.

Naturally, I look round, smiling inanely in case I upset the customer, to find myself facing a young woman wearing jeans, a thick woolly jumper with a turtle neck, and a duffle coat. I'm confused, but it's the glasses I recognise.

"Magda? Magda? Is that you?" I say, staring at her.

"Of course it's me, Kuptin," she says. "Or have you gone blind as well as deff?"

"You look so... different," I say.

"Of course. I do not wear my leather suit all the time. I only do that to make people think I am sexy."

I can't help it. "It works quite well, Magda." I brace myself for being so blunt. Will she hit me?

"Thank you, Kuptin. I like to think I can be sexy when I need to be." Phew – that could have been catastrophic.

Kleo, meantime, is watching with amazement. "You two know each other?" While Kleo is looking the other way, I shake my head vigorously at Magda. I think she's understood; the world still thinks that she and the C-U Jimiz are The Flying Saucers.

"We have met professionally," Magda says.

Kleo looks at me dumbfounded, then her expression changes to an astonished wide-eyed one. "You dirty old man," she says to me. "I'd never have guessed."

I look back towards Magda, completely at sea. "I don't understand this, Magda," I say, although in truth I'm beginning to.

"I think my friend Kleo misunderstands. I don't mean professionally that way," Magda says, turning to Kleo to reinforce the point.

I'm still digesting this, but I need it confirmed. "So you...?"

"Sometimes," Magda replies. "How else is a Polish girl supposed to earn money here if she sometimes has no job? People pay good money here for sex. I can pay my guss bill in an hour. I only do it with people I like."

"Fair enough." What else can I say? Addressing them both, I ask, "So how do you know each other?"

"We live close to each other in Leith, Brian," Kleo explains. With the intense practice, her accent is now actually significantly better than Magda's. "Near the top of Easter Road. Lots of us live there. We have become friends, and Magda keeps me company when I'm homesick for my family. Today she's called in to see me here. But why does she call you 'Captain'?"

"It's a joke," I say, before Magda can reply.

There's a small queue building up, so Kleo apologises for being rude and goes to serve them. I suggest to Magda that she brings her latte across to a corner table and joins me for a moment.

"I've been desperate to find you, Magda."

"That surprises me, Kuptin. I'm surprised you're not hiding from us." She rolls her 'r's venomously.

"Why would we be hiding from you?"

"The boys and I seem to be doing a lot of work for your band."

"I assume you're glad of the work, aren't you?" It registers that she doesn't regard herself as truly part of The Flying Saucers, though.

"Only iv ve are pedd for it." Magda's accent is so thick that it takes a moment or two for her meaning to get into my equally thick head.

"Are you saying that Tam hasn't pedd – I mean – paid you?"

"No. Not a penny, Kuptin. And ve are nutt happy." Her accent becomes thicker as she becomes emotional.

"Magda, we haven't been paid anything, either. He says he's given you all the money so far, but we don't believe him. Our lawyer's sent him a letter, but Tam hasn't replied." I fill her in on some of the details of my phone call with Tam.

"So it looks like Tam is playing – how do you say? – both ends against the middle?"

I smile. "Both ends against the middle will do very nicely, Magda." It sums it up perfectly, actually.

"This lawyer of yours – is this your friend Walnutt? The one who vas so interested in my black leather suit that day when ve did our first video?" Magda asks.

"Yes. Was he particularly interested?" I ask. I seem to having been slightly distracted at the time.

"He vus the vurst. By miles."

"Oh." I'm relieved to hear it.

"It's fine," she says, shrugging her shoulders. I can see her eyes clearly behind her glasses, and her smile looks extremely genuine, "I vus pedd to verr it, so it did its job. Except that I haven't been pedd."

"Which is where we came in."

"I think *I* came in, Kuptin. You verr here alrreddy." Magda has a lot of English colloquialisms still to learn. "In the meantime, can ve also use this lawyer of yours, Kuptin?"

"Of course. Why not? I'm sure he'd be glad to help."

"I might not be able to afford his fees."

"Just wear that black leather suit each time you call on him," I suggest, which to my surprise brings out the deepest laugh I've heard from Magda so far.

"You err a badd man, Kuptin," she says.

49

Walnut Mobilised

Walnut is hard to get hold of until late on Friday afternoon, and by the sound of things he's already enjoyed a first-class corporate lunch by the time I speak to him on the phone. Eventually he confesses to having eaten at an insurance firm's expense in a new restaurant in North Castle Street.

"Where Cosmo's used to be?" I ask him.

"That's the place. It's been through a few hands and now it's gone seriously upmarket. Glad I wasn't paying."

"Which insurance firm was it, out of interest?"

"Durham and Northumberland."

"My house contents policy is with them. My premiums paid for your meal, Duncan. Expect an invoice from me in the post."

Duncan laughs. "So which of your disasters is this about, Captain? Jane, or your band? Or have you got a new one for me? They say these things come along in threes."

I bring him up to date on my visit from Magda.

"Well this certainly changes the complexion of things a bit, doesn't it? First of all, Brian, you can tell Magda that I'd be glad to have her as a client. Nice-looking girl, that. I suppose if the others want help, they might as well come along, too.

"Second, if what Magda says is true, it rather looks as if our friend Mr Cantlay has been a bad boy. At best it would be incompetence, but if it can be shown that he's deliberately misleading his clients and pocketing the money himself, then that would be fraud, pure and simple."

"Are you suggesting that we go to the police?" I ask.

"It's always a good idea to hear what Tam has to say for himself first. Give him the chance to provide a perfectly innocent explanation."

"And some money, too."

"And some money. It's important to act quickly, though, so what I suggest we do is first of all, I'll send him a letter by courier, and I'll also try to phone him."

"Not me?"

"No. If he telephones, ask where your money is by all means but don't get involved in any negotiations. If you do, there's not much I can do for you after that. Are you practising on Sunday?"

"Yes, we'll need to. We didn't get much done last week."

"OK, well, I'll come along and see you at Little Joe and Bev's house. Can you see if Magda or any of the others can come along, too?"

I ring off, promising to round up anyone I can. A telephone call to Magda immediately produces an enthusiastic response, along with a promise to bring along as many of the others as possible, and I also telephone Little Joe at his ironmongers to warn Bev that she might need extra cheese on Sunday.

"I never liked that wee guy," Little Joe says, wonderfully wise after the event. "You should have shopped around a bit."

"I should have shopped around? I wasn't aware that it was my job to provide any manager at all. And in any case, as I recall, Tam Cantlay came to us and he was the only one who did. He's got our music this far, Little Joe. Don't let's get ahead of ourselves."

"I suppose so."

Ringing Fleece and Geoff later in the evening, I get similar "you should have done better" reactions, which I inwardly resent given how happy they were when things were going well. I know it's best to hold my tongue, but on the next day, Saturday, I'm meeting with all of my 'family' in town – Becky, Tommy, Harry and Danni – for yet another catastrophically expensive lunch courtesy of my credit card, and I can let rip a bit. We're sitting in Café Rouge, which may be part of a UK chain but somehow manages to feel both intimate and unique, and in front of me I have my favourite lunchtime platter of mixed cold meats and cheeses. Becky is dressed wrapped up in about seven woollen layers and scarves, while Harry, once he's discarded his leather coat, is only wearing jeans and a tee-shirt. One of them looks hopelessly wrongly dressed. Tommy looks more sensible attired, in head-to-toe blue denim, while under her coat Danni is wearing a loose-fitting crochet-style dress over a pair of red trousers.

"So you think you're a victim of a villainous bunch of fraudsters, Dad?" Harry asks. "I can see the headline in the *Evening News* even now: 'ELDERLY PENSIONER BAMBOOZLED BY HEARTLESS MUSIC BUSINESS CHEAT'." He never misses an opportunity.

"Try 'middle-aged half-pensioner' and you might be nearer to the truth," I reply.

Becky chips in, "I really can't see why Mum's being so difficult. It seems so unfair." Harry looks at the floor; he knows better than to get involved. Tommy and Danni happen to be sitting together at one end of the table, and begin a whispering conversation of their own about something else, anything at all to avoid being part of this.

I end up having to defend Brunhilde myself. "She's doing it because I signed an agreement that said I would give her half my pension. She's doing it because she can. She's doing it because..." Brunhilde is doing it because she hates me, that's the honest truth, but saying that is just a step too far.

"Why does she hate you that much? Why? I don't understand," Becky says. So they can read my mind, too, as well as Bev? Well, that's not so bad, they are my children, after all.

"You mustn't take sides, either of you. Both your mum and I need to be able to see you when we can. I don't want to drive you into making a choice between us."

"Scared you'd lose?" Harry asks.

"I suppose so. You would be, too, in my shoes. How is your mum, by the way?"

Becky replies. "Oh, she's fine. Enjoying her job, definitely."

"That's good. I'd like you to be able to tell her that I was asking after her, but I think she'd regard that as provocative. She and I did exchange Christmas cards. Despite everything."

"Christmas cards? All is not lost, then, for my mum and dad," says Harry with a triple dose of sarcasm. He reinforces the point by shaking his head in despair.

I'm feeling more than a little depressed by the turn of this conversation, and it will only get worse when the bill is presented to me by a tremendously good waiter who seems to be there whenever needed but disappears into a wall somewhere behind me otherwise. Sure enough, even although it's only lunch-time, I've been relieved of in excess of almost a hundred and fifty pounds. Maybe I'm subconsciously trying to spend it all my cash before Brunhilde can get her hands on it.

Then Harry asks a question which lifts my spirits immensely.

"These rehearsals of yours," he says.

"Yes?"

"Are they a private joke or can anyone come along to watch?"

"They're not private, of course not."

"Can I come tomorrow for a bit? Danni's meeting some friends in town and I'm at a bit of a loose end. Little Joe's house is just round the corner, after all."

"Of course you can come." I point out that there may be some others present, but that just makes him all the more interested.

"No, no, I'll definitely be there, if that's OK," he says.

"Of course. Are you around, Becky? You and Tommy are welcome, too."

"I'd love to, but Tommy's still very busy in Bathgate and I need to help him get on top of things. Can I take a raincheck? I'd really like to hear the live act as well as Harry."

"Well it looks like the only way you'll ever hear us live is if you come to one of our rehearsals," I say sadly. "That's if Tam has his way, anyway."

50

A Grand Gathering at Bev's

The following day, the last Sunday in March, is the first where there's a noticeable improvement in the temperature, and because it's also a beautiful sunny day Geoff's tiny little toy car doesn't seem so cold. I've acclimatised throughout the winter, of course, which may also have made a difference, but I'm in quite a cheery mood for the journey across.

"You got my message, then, Geoff. About Magda, and how Tam seems to be double-crossing us all."

"Goodness me, yes," he says, frown-smiling at me and then immediately having to swerve to avoid a line of parked cars in Melville Street. He looks at me again. "Goodness me, that was close, Captain." Goodness me, I think, even Geoff's calling me Captain, now. In the meantime, I've worked out that every time he looks away from the road in front of him, he steers in that direction, so that we veer left when he looks to talk with me, and right when he's spotted something in fields on the far side of the road. But we make it to Little Joe's house, and as ever it's Bev who greets us each with a kiss and a smile. As has become customary, as she reaches for me, she places her hand on my hip, sending shivers throughout my body. Her magnetism seems even stronger than usual today.

As she leads us through to the back, the spring light glows behind her through a stained glass window, enhancing Bev's natural glow, and eventually we find ourselves in the studio in the back garden. As is always the case, Little Joe and Fleece are each doing their own thing.

"Fleece," I say, nodding in his direction, which he acknowledges with a nod and a murderous thirty-five second drum break using everything he's brought with him today. This may be unbearably noisy but it at least has the side-benefit that Little Joe can't be heard, not even by himself. But all bad things must come to an end sometime, and eventually Fleece runs out of steam.

"Hi, Captain, hi Geoff," he says, almost completely out of breath.

"Hi," I reply. "Little Joe, how are you?"

"Not too bad," he says. "I've been working on some new stuff." This I can do without. Let's hope he forgets what it is.

As Geoff and I start to set our gear up, Bev asks me if I know who else is likely to turn up.

"Magda said she'd be here soon, and she said that at least two of the C-U Jimiz were coming, too. Walnut's due within the next half hour as well. I'm afraid your guess is as good as mine when Harry will appear. If there's football on telly I suppose he might not come at all."

"It's nice that he's interested, all the same. I hope he makes it," Bev says, and suggesting that it might make sense to discuss the time the cheese scones once Walnut is here, she leaves us. As ever, the room feels emptier as a result.

But we've only made it into verse two of *Bird*, when she's back, and behind her, all five members of the official version of The Flying Saucers have made the effort to come. It's great to see them, and they seem glad to see us. Even Fleece gets off his stool to go and greet them.

As a goodwill gift, Jimmy has brought a huge carrier bag of Macgregor pakoras, which are devoured within five minutes. He explains, "Magda filled us all in, and everyone agreed we needed to sort things out. We agreed to meet beforehand in a bar just down from Holy Corner so that we'd all come together. Safety in numbers and all that."

"We're certainly needing to get together given that we seem to be getting messed about by our manager," I say to him. "It was only luck that Magda and I ran into each other during the week, otherwise we'd all still be cursing each other."

Fleece then launches off into a rant about Tam of which cursing is very much a core ingredient. Geoff's repetition of "goodness me!" is partly in shock at the new levels of vitriol in Fleece's language, and partly in agreement with his sentiments. When Fleece finally runs out of steam – it's been like an honorary drum break, actually – the entire room gives him a round of applause, which the man himself acknowledges by standing up and taking a bow. Meanwhile, Bev has slipped away during Fleece's orgy of profanity, and I wonder if he's overstepped the mark but moments later she returns not only with Walnut, but also Harry, whom I am delighted to see.

"Saw your son out there on his way up Merchiston Place, Captain, so we came in together. Safety in numbers," Walnut says.

"That's the second time today someone's been scared to enter my house alone," Little Joe says, although he probably isn't being serious. I hope not, although there might be a danger of falling under Bev's spell, like Odysseus and the Sirens.

"Welcome to Mordor, and the Land of Little Joe Mackay, the Dark Lord," Fleece announces. Geoff, a long-time *Lord of the Rings* fan, finds this so funny that he doubles over in a coughing fit of 'goodness mes'. Then he grimaces and, realising that he needs to go to the toilet, he leaves us for a moment, muttering all the time about his 'water works trouble'.

His absence allows the rest of us to catch on each other's versions of Tam's duplicities, and Omar calmly describes how Tam has been telling them that all fees have been paid to us, and that it's our responsibility to pay Magda and the C-Us. The man, it seems, even had the nerve to suggest that he too was still unpaid, and that we, The Flying Saucers, had betrayed him to the point that legal action would almost certainly be necessary. Omar and his friends already know that we've received nothing either, a fact which Walnut readily confirms. Walnut tells everyone that he's written to Tam and also left a message on his answering machine, but has received no reply.

Magda sums Tam up perfectly. "He issa sneck," Then, addressing Walnut, she says, "Walnutt, vill you be our lawyer too?"

Walnut, who is now having to come to terms with the fact that, however we address him to his face, we all call him 'Walnut' behind his back, sees a chance to earn more money and agrees.

"Not bad for a day's work, Walnut," Fleece remarks. "Five new clients in one visit."

"Better still," Walnut replies with a grin, "I have nine of my clients here all consulting me, but I can send out nine separate bills."

"You can send them, but we won't be paying them."

Geoff has returned, looking if anything worse than before he left. Meanwhile Harry has been standing at the side of the room, amused.

"Excuse me asking, but is this all you ever do at your rehearsals? Stand around and complain about not being paid?" he asks. "If so the world of big-time rock music is a sore disappointment to me."

"Once you've heard us, you might wish we'd stuck to complaining all the time," Fleece replies.

"The lad's right, Fleece. He and I have come a long way to hear you," Walnut says. "The least you can do now is deliver."

Fleece is outraged. "A long way? Harry's just walked round the corner. You've only had to drive your four-by-four whatever across the mountainous terrain from Corstorphine." He pronounces it 'Cor-stor-FINE', with a heavy emphasis on the last, mispronounced, syllable.

"But goodness me we should play for them, boys, we should play," Geoff says.

"And vot are ve all supposed to do?" Magda asks, referring to the C-U Jimiz as well as herself.

"Mime? Dance?" I suggest. "It's what you seem to do best."

"There are spare electric guitars of mine across in the shed. You could all have one each," Little Joe says. It's a little sad that he has so many of these things yet he's never really learned to play any of them. "You could play a guitar as well, Omar, seeing as there no spare drums."

Five minutes later, we have finally resumed *Bird*, and we then follow it with the other three songs from the EP, because I feel it's important that these at least are perfectly prepared. Harry and Walnut are captivated by the performances of Magda and the C-Us, who seem to be able to follow our every movement, anticipate our every turn, especially the boys, whose art I have now come to regard in such high esteem. It takes just over forty minutes to play each of the songs and then review our performances, during which Harry, and particularly Walnut, have some interesting observations to make. I keep forgetting that Walnut may not play any instrument – apart from a harmonica when he's drunk – but his encyclopaedic knowledge of all forms of popular music since 1950 has made him quite expert in techniques nonetheless. He even manages to suggest a slight alteration to Little Joe's rhythm guitar which improves his work on *Bird*.

By a quarter to four, we've covered our EP material, so I start to tell the band about a new song that I've been working on which has a slightly different feel, a more political song called *River of Tears*. But I don't get far, because there's a knock on the door and Bev comes in. She's not carrying any cheese scones – it's too early for them anyway – and instead she's followed in by a diminutive figure in cuban heels.

"Ah, Mr Cantlay," Walnut says, "so glad you could make it this afternoon."

Tam looks around the room and sees twelve faces, eleven of whom he recognises.

"Allow me to introduce my son, Tam," I say to him. "Tam Cantlay, Harry Reid. Harry, Tam." Tam moves across doubtfully to shake hands. "I think you know everyone else." He nods.

"You've tricked me, Mr Walnut," he says. Fleece greets this with a roar of laughter, Geoff frown-smiles furiously, Little Joe wonders what's happening in his own home, with twelve people in his studio, at least ten of whom are prepared to beat one of the others to death. Speaking of which, my eye is on Evelyn, whose dark brooding countenance has become significantly darker and broodier since Tam appeared.

Tam has now discovered that shaking hands with Harry was a mistake, because Jimmy from the C-Us and Walnut have moved to cover all the exits. Tam is here until we say he can leave. Everyone in the room has suddenly become extremely impressed with Walnut's ability to set this meeting up.

"You told me that The Flying Saucers had urgent work for me, Mr Whatever-you-are," Tam says to him.

"The name's MacIntyre. Duncan MacIntyre." Walnut would like to add "licensed to kill" but he can't while he's wearing a camel-hair coat. "I said I had work for you with The Saucers, but I didn't say you'd be paid. In fact, Mr Cantlay, you're going to work for me and then you're going to do something you haven't done for a while."

"Which is?" Tam asks nervously.

"Pay these people the money they're due."

Tam's shaking. "I can't," he says.

"Can't – or won't?" Walnut says, towering over him.

Bev approaches and says softly to Tam, "Why don't you take a seat, Mr Cantlay. You don't look too well." She pulls up a chair and guides him into it. Now Walnut looks even taller, of course, and Tam is beginning to get a crick in his neck looking up.

"I... I... I can't. I don't have the money."

"Why not, Mr Cantlay? Where is it?"

"Ne... ne... necessary expenses."

Walnut bends down to look him directly in the face. "In other words, Mr Cantlay – " he says the name very, very slowly and clearly – "you've spent it, haven't you?"

Tam looks down. There are tears running down both cheeks. "Yes."

"Oh dear, Mr Cantlay. You have been a bad boy, haven't you?"

Tam nods sadly. "Yes. I'm sorry."

"Sorry's not good enough, Mr Cantlay. I think they want their money. And soon."

"Yes."

I'm almost feeling sorry for Tam, but before we forget everything, I want to take the chance to change how things are to be done in the future.

"Tam," I say, gently, "I know you'll get the money for all of us. I'm sure you can go to the bank and take out a nice big loan. Or borrow it from one of your Falkirk friends."

"No! Not the Falkirk Friends, please! Don't make me do that! Anything but that!"

"That's up to you, Tam." I've no idea at all what he's talking about. "What I want is a live gig for The Flying Saucers."

"But you can't," Tam says. "Then everyone will know that I've been passing Magda and the C-Us off as you."

"That's your problem, Tam," I remind him.

"I think most people would say that what you've been up to is fraud, Mr Cantlay," Walnut continues. "You've defrauded the The Saucers, you've defrauded Magda and the C-U Jimiz, you've cheated the media, you've cheated the general public. Shall I call the police, perhaps?"

"Not only my problem," Tam says defiantly. "When they find out you're just a bunch of old geezers trying to be rock stars, no-one will want to know you."

Tam recoils from a hard kick in his right shin, although I can't tell who delivered it. Oh, it might have been me.

Little Joe pipes up. "There have been whispers about us, lately, Tam. Whispers that we can't play live at all. We can't do it outside the studio. NME called us 'the new Archies' this week."

We're all shocked. "They didn't, did they?" Geoff asks. "Goodness me, goodness me – The Archies!"

"And it'll be all your fault, Mr Cantlay," Walnut adds. "All your fault," he repeats.

"I'll get you a gig. A live gig. I'll think of something."

"And something forr uss too. And our missing money," Magda adds.

Tam nods, but adds plaintively, "But you can't sing or play anything."

"Your problem," Walnut repeats.

"I'll come up with something. I promise."

A menacing new voice speaks: Evelyn. "Yes you will, Tam. I'm from Falkirk, too, remember. Polmont, to be exact."

Tam nods.

"I know where you live," Evelyn says, menacingly. Tam has gone as white as a sheet.

"I'll do something." He looks around the room, desperately.

"Let the rat out of the room," Walnut says to Harry, whose job it has been to cover the door. "We know where to find him."

Tam gets up and races out of the room into the garden, and guided by Bev, jumps a garden gate towards the street. Everyone has seen the sweat stains have soaked right through the under-arms of his suit jacket.

Harry quietly closes the door after the fugitive.

"Now that's what I call entertainment!" he declares.

51

The Missing Link

"That was impressive," Fleece says to Walnut.

"That's my job," Walnut says. "I gently promote my clients' interests."

"Are all lawyers like you then, deep down?"

"The good ones."

Evelyn chimes in, wearing a wry smile, "I could have told you that. When I most needed a good lawyer I was given a fucking tosser." Even his grunts have everyone's attention: ignore a convicted killer at your peril.

"Captain told me you might have some sort of... a past," Walnut says.

"I think you all know I've done time in Polmont," Evelyn growls.

"Is it true that you killed a man?" Magda says. Perhaps her relative clumsiness with English makes it easier to ask blunt questions; perhaps Magda is simply a blunt speaker.

"Yes." There's a shocked silence, then Evelyn adds, "I killed my own father."

"Jesus," Fleece says. Thankfully, Geoff's too shocked to make his usual comment, while mentally, Little Joe is far away in Jamaica.

Walnut, however, is watching Evelyn intently. "Go on, son. I'm sure there's more," he says, quietly.

Evelyn stares down at the floor. "He was beating my mum up again. I was trying to stop him, but the courts said I overdid it."

"So what did you do, for fuck's sake?" Fleece asks.

"I beat him over the head with a frying pan."

"And that killed him?"

"It was one of those Le Creuset things. My dad had nicked it from John Lewis as a Christmas present for his woman on the side. My mum discovered it and they had this fight. I arrived in the middle and picked up the first thing that came to hand."

Needless to say, Fleece and Walnut and – I'm ashamed to say – my own son manage to see black comedy in the idea of 'death by Le Creuset', but Walnut pulls himself together just enough to manage an apology.

"A decent lawyer would have kept you out of Polmont, Evelyn. You're probably right there."

"It would have helped to have had a posher accent than mine, too," Evelyn adds.

"That, too, I'm afraid. I'm sorry. The law's crap sometimes. And I bet life's tough in Polmont for a boy named Evelyn."

"Funny thing, that wasn't a problem. Everyone was really nice to me. Either they felt sorry for me, or they'd all heard *A Boy Named Sue* – you know, the Johnny Cash song?"

Fleece laughs. "Where he beats the living daylights out of everyone to make up for being a girl's name? Interesting. I think I'd prefer to play safe and stay out of jail in the first place."

"It's the better option, believe me. That's where the Falkirk Friends get recruited."

"So tell me," Fleece asks. "Who are these Falkirk Friends I keep hearing about?"

As if they've rehearsed their lines, all four C-Us chorus reply at once, "You don't want to know."

Fleece looks around at everyone else. "Well that's that, then. It seems I don't want to know."

"Even I've heard of the Falkirk Friends, Fleece," Walnut says. "Believe me, you not only do you not want to know, you don't want to know why you don't want to know."

Evelyn tries to restore sanity. "But now I need a job, so I'd actually be quite grateful to Tam if he could get the C-U Jimiz up and running. Although I need the money, too."

"So maybe we should just get back to rehearsing for the moment," I suggest. "At least that way we'll be ready to play a gig if we're asked to."

Harry, who long ago has grabbed a chair and sat down, wants to hear some music. "What was the new gem we were all going to hear, Dad?" he asks.

"Goodness me, don't mock your dad, Harry," Geoff frown-smiles at him. "Goodness me, no. It's his songs that have got us where we are."

Harry does a mock-thoughtful look, stroking his chin. "Let me see, now. That's the same songs that no-one will let you be seen dead singing, you never get paid for, and you're one step away from a mysterious terror organisation called the Falkirk Friends, whom you don't want to know about?"

"Exactly," I reply. "But I may as well run through this new 'gem' as my son so kindly described it."

I run through *River of Tears*, a song about which has a folky feel to it. I've produced a bass line on the MacBook Pro and written out a lead guitar part for Geoff, but I can be sure that both Little Joe and Fleece can play their instruments well enough to produce the rest by ear. Perhaps it isn't a dance-to number, but the lyrics are decent and it might provide a welcome break in the rhythm of a live set. It's become a tradition for Bev to join us when I give my new songs their first airing, and thanks to her, I find my song's world premier being applauded by eight onlookers.

"It's very good," she breathes at me. "Very powerful, Brian. It's different from the others."

"Thank you," I say, rather embarrassed at the attention.

"It'll be easy enough for us to pretend to play as well," Jimmy of the C-Us says. "You don't exactly do very much."

"No, they don't, do they?" Harry remarks. "But then they are old geezers. Maybe Tam's got a point." He really likes winding me up, but this time I'm ready for him.

"Harry," I point out slowly. "Age isn't everything. The youngest member of our band just sits and does nothing at all. The MacBook Pro is less than a year old."

Harry delivers a sardonic smile in my direction. "Very good," he says in a measured tone. "For a pensioner."

"Is this what it's like having children, Brian?" Bev asks good-naturedly.

Geoff replies for me. "Oh goodness me, yes, Bev, goodness me yes. Mine are just the same." I can only laugh, but there are knowing nods of agreement from Fleece and Walnut and Geoff as well.

Around about now, Little Joe returns from his mental Caribbean holiday, during most of which he's sat with his head nodding, guitar jerking, and knees deep-bending. As usual, everyone else has ignored him; it's safer that way.

"Listen, everyone," he suddenly announces, excitedly, "I've got something I want you to hear as well."

"The question is, little bro," Fleece asks, "do we want to hear it? Will we still be alive at the end? Will you?"

Bev gives Fleece a cold look. She's worried that Little Joe might be put off, but she needn't be; this time he's completely unstoppable.

"Listen, everyone." Little Joe's repeating himself and I suspect his blood pressure might be rising as well. "I've been bouncing an idea around in my head for days and I've just cracked it."

"You have cracked your head, Little Joe?" Magda asks. "Is your head empty?" Another phrase lost in translation, but of course at least eight of us think her question is magnificently apt. Little Joe ignores her, or perhaps simply hasn't heard her because he's so carried away with himself. He doesn't even need Bev to make me give him a helping hand.

"Listen, everyone." He keeps saying "Listen, everyone", but Little Joe manages to tell us this time. "I think I've discovered the missing link."

"The missing link?" Fleece asks, incredulous. "My little brother has made the greatest anthropological discovery of all time?" he asks. Then he says slowly, threateningly, to Little Joe: "Or does this involve rasta-jock, by any chance?"

"Of course it involves rasta-jock, Josh! It's been my life's work, it's been my life's work. And now I've cracked it!"

Harry, who is blissfully unaware of what fate has in store for his ears, actually encourages him, although there are heads furiously shaking all around him. "Sounds interesting, Joe. What have you discovered?" As he asks the question, I feel a familiar female voice pulse through my spine: *What a nice young man you have for a son, Brian.*

Little Joe stands up and starts to play the all-too-familiar reggae beat on his guitar, and Harry briefly has to look away to compose himself as Joe gets into gear with his knees and guitar-jerks. Serves Harry right, but I suppose he has to learn the hard way like everyone else. Now Joe starts to sing:

Scots wha hae wi' Wallace bled,
Scots wham Bruce hae aftimes led, –

Around the room, fingers are surreptitiously making their way towards ears.

Welcome tae your gory bed,
Or tae victory
Now's the day and now's the hour,
See the front o battle lour,
See approach proud Edward's power,
Chains and slavery.

We assume he's going to stop there, but it turns out that Little Joe actually knows the words – he later confesses he was forced to learn them at school – so we get verse two.

Wha will be a traitor knave,
Wha can fill a coward's grave -

By now a rather amusing thing is happening, which is that the C-U Jimiz and Magda have decided to dance to Little Joe's demolition of this iconic anthem, and although it's pricelessly funny, Little Joe is taking it seriously and giving it all he's got. Fired up by this seeming appreciation of his talents, he uses verse one as a chorus, and demands we all join in.

Scots wha hae wi' Wallace bled,
Scots wham Bruce hae aftimes led, -

Of the band, only Geoff tries to join in, and he doesn't know the words, although Harry lends his voice, albeit he's racked with laughter as he does it. He has to assist, I suppose – it's partly his fault that Joe's out of control. And Joe really is. Oh no, he knows verse three as well...

By oppressions woes and pains,
By your sons in servile chains -

And then, of course, we're doomed to receive verse one as yet another chorus...

Scots wha hae wi' Wallace bled,
Scots wham Bruce hae aftimes led,
Welcome tae your gory bed,
Or tae victory
Now's the day and now's the hour,
See the front o battle lour,
See approach proud Edwards power,
Chains and slavery.

Then – mercifully – it's over.

"What the fuck was that?" Harry asks in a shocked stage-whisper.

"Don't say you weren't warned," Fleece replies. "Little boys shouldn't play with matches."

"What do you think?" Little Joe asks, wide-eyed and utterly delighted with his new song. "It takes rasta-jock to a new height, I think."

"Try going in the other direction," Fleece suggests.

Bev looks towards me. "Brian, what do you think of *Scots Wha Hae*? Do you like it?" She's testing me: can I give the right answer without her help, she's wondering?

"It's interesting, Joe. It might indeed be your best yet," I suggest.

"Do you really think so, Captain?" Little Joe asks. "Best yet?"

"Best yet." That doesn't, of course, mean much. Nevertheless, I feel a *Thank you, Brian, I knew I could rely on you* shivering through my central nervous system. I have done well.

Then there's a major shock.

"I like it. It's queerkee," says Magda.

Fleece agrees. "It's certainly in a queer key, Magda. Fortunately, I'm only the drummer, it's not my problem."

"No, I mean it. It's quirky," she insists. "We can all danz to it. It is musick to danz to."

Little Joe is overjoyed at the praise he's receiving, and I do believe he's grown a little taller suddenly. Perhaps some of his hair will start growing back next. In the meantime, though, I foresee a problem.

"I'm a little concerned about how the public will view one of our greatest national songs being played as rasta-jock. You might alienate them badly. It's potentially very controversial."

"Goodness me, but it's been done before, Brian," Geoff says. "Remember the Sex Pistols did *God Save The Queen*? That was all good fun. It's a classic now."

I explain to him that the title may have been "God Save The Queen", but it they didn't actually use the national anthem's words.

"Goodness me!" he says. "Goodness me, well there's a thing. I never knew that. Tell you the truth, I could never make out a word they said anyway."

In any case, Little Joe is not discouraged by my concerns – far from it.

"No, Captain, you don't understand. It's precisely because *Scots Wha Hae* can be played as rasta-jock that it's so anthropologically important!" He looks and sounds like a mad professor, and indeed he has us all spellbound. "Don't you see? Don't you see?"

As we all look at him, I wonder if we're about to discover that it's the rest of us who have been mad all along.

"Playing *Scots Wha Hae* in reggae proves that West Indian music influenced Scottish music much earlier than previously thought." Little Joe is almost screaming with excitement. "It means that the tune for *Scots Wha Hae* was probably written by Jamaicans. This is how it was meant to sound originally."

"It's a Burns poem, for crying out loud, Joe. Give us a break!" Fleece says, desperately. He's experimenting with the sound of beating his forehead against the snare-drum.

Little Joe is unstoppable. "No, you don't understand, Josh, you really don't! It's *much* more important than that. *Scots Wha Hae* is Robert the Bruce's address to his army before the Battle of Bannockburn. It means that African reggae and Scottish culture have been linked since 1314! It means Jamaicans almost certainly fought for Bruce at Bannockburn! It means Scotland was the world's first multicultural society! How about that? How about that? Now do you see why it's so important?"

No-one, not even Bev, says a word. I'm only relieved to realise that I'm really not as mad as Joe. Bev gets up and walks across to Little Joe, glows around him, then gives him a consoling kiss on the cheek.

"I think I should get the cheese scones, now, Joe" she says, and leaves the room.   The light seems a little dimmer.

The silence continues for a moment, then Magda says, "Well I still think it's quirky."

52

For Whom the Bell Tolls

On Wednesday, I ask Harry and Becky round to my flat, as I have an important matter to discuss with them, and them alone. Neither of them asks what it's about, but I'm well aware they can both guess – it's about Brunhilde and me, of course. They've both agreed to arrive around six, to allow Becky to drop in after work and so that she won't have to make a special journey in from Bathgate, and Harry has amazed me by announcing in advance that he will run Becky all the way home. And of course I know the reason why he's so keen to do that, too – to give time to debrief with her afterwards.

I know he's concerned by the fact that, for once, there's no attempt to wind everyone up by arriving late; he might even have been waiting around the corner to arrive at six on the dot, because George Alagiah is just beginning the BBC *Six O'Clock News* when I have to switch him off because they're at my door. As they enter, Becky gives me a kiss, and he, quite formally, shakes my hand.

There's a little small talk, a declined offer of a drink, even coffee or something soft, then I say, "I think you've probably guessed what I wanted to talk about."

Harry nods. Becky replies, "We've each seen Mum already this week. We know about the hearing."

A date in August has been set to hear the sordid details of my marriage to Brunhilde, and I explain that I'm anxious that Harry and Becky don't get caught in the crossfire.

"To be fair to Mum, she is too," Becky says.

"I just think you're both behaving like total fuckwits," Harry says. "How long were you married? Over thirty years? And this is how you've ended up? Talking through lawyers and the courts?"

I open my mouth to defend myself, then I realise that I'm forgetting the very purpose of asking them round.

"I was about to say something stupid there," I say, "but I managed to catch myself just in time. Of course your mum and I are behaving like total fuckwits, Harry, but that's our business, not yours. Don't let us infect you. I'm aware this could get very nasty over the next few months between your mother and me."

"You two have said a lot of stupid things in the last few years," Harry says.

"I know. I'm not proud of my part in it all. But the damage is done now and the way things are looking, I stand to lose everything. In the meantime, what are the pair of you going to do?"

"Keep our heads down," Harry says. "Emigrate?"

"Dad, what happens if you lose here? What will you do?" Becky asks.

"I'm not sure, Becky. I'd probably have to give this place up for a start and rent somewhere, unless I won the lottery. Or I could try and get a full-time job, but in this recession who's going to give a job to someone of my age? I suppose there might be benefits I could claim. I don't know, to be honest."

"So why did you ask us round?" Harry asks.

I take a deep breath. "I've been thinking a lot about this. The one thing I don't want to do is to make you take sides."

"You've said that before," Harry says, quite sharply. "You're worried that if we take sides, we might choose Mum's." It's difficult to judge if this is a threat.

Becky gives him a reproving look. "Leave Dad alone, Harry. This is hard for him."

"And for Mum," he says.

"I haven't made myself clear, Harry," I say. "You siding with Mum isn't the worst-case scenario. The worst thing would be for one of you to support Mum and the other one to side with me. Then we'd split you. That would be awful for me. Probably for Mum, too. That's what I'm most afraid of."

I'm not quite sure how this is going down, and although I don't mean it, I have a suspicion that Harry thinks I'm closing in on emotional blackmail.

"For fuck's sake..." he says.

"What I'm trying to say is that I'd rather you two remained friendly with each other, and if the price of that is I don't see much of you, then it's a price worth paying." It's a hard thing for me to say. "As a parent, you just want your children to be happy."

Harry responds with his usual level of sympathy. "Get a grip, Dad, and don't be so pathetic."

Even Becky doesn't come to my aid this time, although I thought I was trying to make things easier for them.

"We've heard this speech before, Dad," she says, sighing. "From Mum, last night."

"Except hers was accompanied by floods of tears," Harry says, "which by the looks of you might happen here any moment." Of course he's right, and it does. Becky gets up and crosses to the sofa beside me to give me a hug.

"This is where we came in," he says. "A pair of total fuckwits."

53

The Prodigal Son

By early April, we've still not heard from Tam, although our recordings continue to get coverage in the music press. Alerted by Little Joe, I've started to notice more and more little references to The Flying Saucers as a 'studio band', and surfing some blogs on the internet reveals that the general public has serious doubts that we even exist. One thread refers to us as 'The Drowning Saucers', and the word 'fraud' is mentioned many times, suggesting that the paying public has been cheated. 'Zorro' – why do these bloggers have such daft names? – reckons we should all give our money back to the customers. That would be an interesting idea if we'd ever been given any to return.

We carry on rehearsing, but for Fleece and me at least, it's hard to stay motivated. Geoff's guitar teacher has finally decided that playing in a band is good for him, and of course Geoff will do whatever his guitar teacher decides is good for him. Meanwhile Little Joe remains on the rasta-jock planet, far, far away from Earth. But Fleece and I are wavering.

One Sunday, he decides it's time to have a beast-to-man talk with me on the subject, and he decides to open with a deeply philosophical question.

"Christ, Captain, what in the name of God are we doing here, you and I?"

Little Joe, who is attempting to teach Geoff the rudiments of rasta-jock guitar, is perfecting *Scots Wha Hae*. Geoff is frown-smiling a lot.

"We were born into this world to suffer and die, Fleece," I suggest. Little Joe sounds as if he's doing both, slowly and painfully.

"I didn't mean like that, you daft twit," Fleece replies, laughing. "I mean, is there really any point in rehearsing?

Do you really believe Tam's going to come up with anything?"

"Walnut's done a good job on him, keeping the pressure up. He's been on the phone several times in the last week asking about our money, and also about a live gig." It's true, my respect for the legal profession has soared. "You've got to hand it to him, Fleece. Walnut keeps dropping dark hints about these 'Falkirk Friends' of his."

Fleece smiles. "These are the Falkirk Friends we don't know about, don't want to know about, and don't want to know why we don't want to know about them. Is that right, Captain? Does that make sense?"

"I don't know, Fleece. I don't know if it makes sense, and I don't want to know if it does."

Fleece chuckles. "Whoever they are, they had Tam worried for sure."

"I know what you mean about rehearsing, though. When there's nothing to rehearse for, and nothing to show for our efforts, it's hard to keep motivated. But both Tam and Walnut insisted that we keep rehearsing so that we were ready for a gig."

Our rehearsals have certainly lacked zip lately, while my songs have dried up and the EP is sliding down the charts. I've noticed that Geoff says "goodness me" less often when he's bored, which I suppose is only to be expected. Even Bev's aura seems affected. The light around her seems dimmer than in previous months, and her cheese scones seem heavier as well.

"I'm inclined to ignore anything that pint-sized rodent tells us to do," Fleece says. "He's just at it. But Walnut's proved to be worth listening to."

"Walnut texted me earlier to say he would drop in to our rehearsal this afternoon," I tell everyone. Little Joe's rendition of *Ho-Ro My Nut-Brown Maiden* grinds to a halt.

"Has he got any good news for us, do you think, Captain?" he asks hopefully.

"Haven't a clue." I sound grumpy; I don't mean to, I just can't help it.

"Sorry, Captain." Now I've upset Little Joe. At this point Bev arrives to announce that there's been a phone call from Walnut saying that he'll definitely be here at half-past four, but then she spots her husband in the corner and, after studying him for a moment, she glances at me coldly and with a touch of anger. *Brian – how you've disappointed me.* It's a crushing experience.

I apologise. "I didn't mean to snap at you, Joe. We could do with hearing something, couldn't we?" It's obvious, I suppose, but true. Even my apology doesn't stir any sort of response from Bev, I note, and it's now clear that she is indeed afflicted with the general malaise.

Little Joe wants to play some more rasta-jock, and because no-one really has the energy to resist, we find ourselves playing along. I've worked out that the bass lines for his music fall into three categories, fast for songs such as *Willie's Gone Tae Melville Castle*, medium for *Ho-Ro, My Nut Brown Maiden*, and slow for songs such as his latest desecration, *Loch Lomond*. All I have to do is to pick the right bass track, and Little Joe will do the rest on his guitar. On the 'if you can't beat 'em join 'em' basis, Fleece has agreed to play along on drums, although he continues to signal his contempt for rasta-jock in general by reading the sports pages of his *Sunday Mail*, spread out across the snare and side drums. He tells Little Joe that he's giving each song his fullest attention, but it doesn't take long to spot that the drum he chooses to play depends on whether the Hibs report is on the left or the right page each week.

Meanwhile Geoff, being a thoroughly decent fellow, tries to make some sense of this garbage on his guitar, shaming me into doing the same. Not that there's much one can contribute to a reggae number on an Angelica acoustic guitar, but Bev still clearly feels I've betrayed both her and Little Joe, so I have to make an effort. Geoff has been working on the knee-bends and the guitar-jerks – which he somehow combines with continuous frown-smiling – and now he insists that I keep him company.

"Goodness me, Brian, if an old dog like me can make the effort to learn new tricks, a young man like you can, too," he says. I don't mind the reprimand, but I'm stung by the 'make the effort' bit. So, for the sake of harmony, I throw myself into *Loch Lomond*, complete with staccato chords and the slow reggae bass track from my MacBook Pro. As we hit the chorus – hit it like a train crash, actually – Bev nods at me and I feel a slightly warmer glow from her. It's been a while since my spine tingled, though, and I miss it. I want to tell her that I'm doing my best, but I'm afraid she'll simply say my best isn't good enough. Perhaps it isn't, but we're all very tired. Instead she slips away out of the studio door, having achieved her aim of getting a little attention for her husband.

We are halfway through the third chorus of *Loch Lomond* when Bev returns. We don't stop when she comes in and out these days, we're quite used to her, but the discordant wall of sound – it could never be called music – crunches to a stop instantly when we see who's behind her. Bev is followed by Walnut, who has turned up at four-thirty just as promised, but with him is a small figure who looks as though he's been washed at too high a temperature.

Fleece has fallen off his stool.

"You, ya wee bastard, where have you been?" he says, picking himself up. Remember this is Fleece: it takes him time.

Walnut looks rather pleased with himself. "Gentlemen, look who's joined us today."

"What was that?" Tam replies. "Is that what The Flying Saucers are playing these days?"

Little Joe, looking devastated by Tam's comment, limply replies that it's *Loch Lomond*.

I intervene on Little Joe's behalf. It's not Joe's fault we're reduced to playing rasta-jock, we're at a loose end because our manager has failed us completely.

"We play what we want to play, Mr Cantlay," I say, brusquely, "That's what musicians do. Your job is to find us opportunities for us to play, and to make sure we get our money when we do. You're paid to do that, and you're paid handsomely. Kindly restrict yourself to your business."

That produces a response. *Thank you, Brian, and well done. The man's a charlatan.* With a mixture of relief and pleasure, I feel that spinal shiver for the first time in a while.

It produces a response from Walnut, too, and a surprising one. "I think we need to give Mr Cantlay a little credit, gentlemen. He's made some progress for us."

"Has the bugger made some money for us?" Fleece roars.

"That will come, Fleece, that will come," Tam replies.

Now he has our attention, although Little Joe hasn't quite managed to get a good view of the tiny being who is standing close to Walnut. Tam seems to regard Walnut as the nearest thing to safety in Little Joe's studio.

"Is that man here?" Tam asks. He's looking around for someone he's clearly anxious to avoid.

"Is it Evelyn?" asks Walnut, remembering the 'Falkirk Friends'.

"No, Evelyn's fine, he's just a laddie. I meant your heavy from the last time. The one who stopped me getting out."

I realise he's mistaken Harry for a thug, which is ironic because he's a bit of a verbal thug but otherwise a complete pussycat. However, Tam needn't know that, nor need he be reminded that the 'thug' in question is my son. And nor will I tell Harry, whose ego is large enough already.

"He's available if needed," I say, threateningly. It has the desired effect on Tam, but of course the others have no idea what I'm talking about. "Meanwhile, why don't you get to the point, Mister Cantlay?" I've learning fast from Walnut; the more you appear to be respectful towards someone, the more likely they are to fear you.

"I've got a gig for you, Captain. A real gig.'

"A live gig?" Fleece asks, disbelievingly. "As in, where we play and sing and people listen to us?"

"Yes."

"Far out!" Little Joe cries, excitedly.

"Goodness me! Good...ness me!" From Geoff, of course.

"Christ almighty!" Fleece roars, and looks round at us all. "What's the catch?"

"No catch," Tam says. "And a very big fee, too, probably."

I'm still a little cynical. "From which you'll get twenty per cent," I point out. "Less what you already owe us. But there's something I don't like already, Tam." I've slipped back into calling him Tam, which is careless.

"What's that, Captain?"

"It's that word 'probably'. I want to see a contract, with guaranteed sums, with a promise that some friends will be round to see you if you don't deliver."

The very mention of the word 'Friends' has a powerful effect.

"This is the deal, boys. My friend Duffle Coates – remember him? – has pulled a couple of strings for us. There's been a late cancellation at a new rock festival and you've been offered the chance to fill the slot instead. You'll get a share of the take – five pounds for every ticket sold. If lots of people come, you get lots of money."

"OK," Fleece says, "where's the festival?"

"Peebles."

"Peebles??"

"The Peebles Rock Festival in June."

"You're telling us that there's to be a Peebles Rock Festival?" Fleece roars at him. "You're expecting us to believe that?"

"Just outside Peebles, actually. Some rich dude wants to relive his youth by starting a rock festival on his land."

"Peebles is full of retired folk, Tam. Assuming they're still alive come June, they'll all want to listen to Vera Lynn and George Formby."

"We'll see, we'll see," Tam says confidently. I'm amazed to discover he actually is wearing his cuban heels after all. "Do you want the gig or not?"

Geoff is enthusiastic. "Well I'm up for it, boys. Goodness me, why not? What have we got to lose?"

"Geoff's right," Little Joe adds. "There's no point in doing all this rehearsing if we're never going to play anywhere. We've got to start somewhere."

Fleece is thinking. "The Peebles Rock Festival... What do you say, Walnut? Is this a good gig?"

"I'm the one who brought him here, Fleece," Walnut replies. "I wouldn't have wasted a good Sunday afternoon otherwise."

"There was me thinking you liked our music, too."

"Can you remember what you were playing when we arrived?" Walnut says.

Fleece is forced to recall *Loch Lomond*. "Point taken, Walnut, point taken."

It falls to me to remain the cynic.

"Listen, Tam, where does this place you? I thought if we played live, it would blow your cover. That's the end of Magda and the C-U Jimiz."

"Is it?" Tam asks. He's got some plan, I can tell, and it's a plan I'm not going to like.

"Should I be phoning my friends up before I hear what you're going to say next, Tam?" I ask him.

"No need to be so offensive, my boy. The C-Us and Magda get to do their thing as well."

"I'm definitely not looking forward to hearing this, Tam."

"This is the plan. You play behind a stage curtain, they dance and mime in front of it." Tam says it quickly to get the words out and the shock over.

Tam has left me speechless, but others can respond for me.

"Goodness me!"

Even Little Joe is able to speak before I can get the words out. He takes a few steps towards Tam, who requires twice the number of steps to keep the same distance between them because of his short legs.

"Tam," he asks, "are you telling me that we're not to be allowed to be seen on stage, although we'll be heard?"

Tam is unrepentant. "And then we can do it again and again. And it'll help your album sales, so you'll make shed-loads of money."

"We haven't seen a penny so far, Tam," I point out, still the cynic. "I thought we were making shed-loads already."

"You'll make ten times as much as you've made so far, Captain, promise," Tam says.

Walnut puts his head in his hands, but it appears that only he and I appreciate that ten times nothing doesn't amount to very much. He steps in to help Tam.

"I can understand Captain's concern here, Tam, and to be honest I share it. But I think we both understand that if they don't see all their money this time, I'll be sending some friends round."

Tam visibly pales. "I understand."

Fleece is trying to get his head round the details.

"Look, Tam, the idea is that Magda and the C-Us mime while we play, is that right?"

"Yes, that's the idea," says Tam.

"And there's a stage curtain between us. We're hidden behind them, yes?"

"Correct."

"But how do they know what we're playing? How do they know how to keep in time and so on? It's not as if you can do it by trial and error like a recording."

Tam replies as if he's been waiting for this all afternoon.

"Not a problem, Fleece. First of all, they'll all have little earpieces to hear what you're doing. All bands do that in concerts nowadays anyway to make sure they can hear instructions over the crowd. Second, you and the ones in front of the curtain have something in common – Captain's MacBook Pro is the bass. Your bass never varies, so you have to count in anyway. If both sides of the curtain are keeping in time to the computer bass, you're bound to be together all the time."

Fleece, Little Joe, Geoff and I are too astounded by the brass neck of this plan to answer.

"In addition," Walnut says, "I'll be conducting from the wings as a safeguard."

There's a massive crash of cymbals. Fleece has fallen off his stool again and is convulsed with laughter. He can't get up easily – he's too fat to get past the drum kit – so he sums up the plan while seated on the floor with his back to everyone. His arms are waving a bit.

"OK, so we've got us playing a set in this Peebles Rock Festival behind the curtain, Magda and the C-U Jimiz in front pretending to be us – Magda pretending to be a laptop, mind you – and finally Sir Simon Rattle here conducting the whole thing from the wings."

"Correct, Fleece," Walnut replies. "It can't fail."

"It can't fail," Little Joe repeats. "Really?"

"Guaranteed success, Joe," Tam insists. "It's not as if you're the headline act for a big festival. This is a one-day affair. The organisers hope it'll grow in years to come. This is just a starting point – for them as well as you."

I don't know why I ask this question.

"You said we're filling in a slot because of a cancellation, Tam."

"Yes, that's right. You're second-last on, actually. Six-number slot just before the main act. There's a lot of interest in your band after all the recent publicity. Might be some TV coverage, too. You get five pounds for every body through the gate."

"OK, I get the five pounds bit, Tam. So who's the headline act?"

"Yes," Walnut says, "You were a bit coy when I asked you before."

"Didn't I tell you?" the smug little rat says. "Coldplay."

There a silence of what seems like a whole minute, then one voice from one corner of the studio manages, "Goodness me. Goodness me."

54

At Cantina Mexicana

"So you'll have to start with this from the beginning, Dad. Remember Tommy and I have never met half of these people," Becky says.

"Neither have I, Brian," says Danni. "Harry's tried to give me a picture of these people, but you know what he's like – if it's not very interesting he'll just make it up," she adds, giving her beloved Harry a pat on the arm. He, for his part, spreads his arms to protest his innocence. Danni and he, Tommy and Becky are all sitting with me in Cantina Mexicana, a Tex-Mex joint in Rose Street. My wallet seems to be floating away already and we haven't even yet ordered. I give a silent prayer for the invention of the credit card and the embarrassment it saves.

"We need you to corroborate one of Harry's claims straight away," Tommy says. "Is this guy Tam really well under five feet tall?"

I put on a serious expression. "I hereby solemnly confirm that Thomas Cantlay, esquire, must be no more than five feet tall, and that includes a stupidly high set of cuban heels which would fail any health and safety test in the world."

"Even Cuban health and safety rules?" Tommy asks.

"I can't speak for Cuba, Tommy, sorry. But the man walks on stilts."

"Right," says Harry impatiently. "So exactly how has this poisonous little Falkirk midget managed to ingratiate himself back into your good books?"

"He's got us a slot in the Peebles Rock Festival."

This is greeted with ribald laughter by all four of them, but not for the reason I expect; for a start, they're all actually aware that the Peebles Rock Festival is indeed due to take place in June, although it's understood that the organiser, the Fourth Earl of Delatho, is struggling to fix a line-up. With only two weeks to go, the headline act is yet to be announced, and a couple of the publicised acts have already cancelled.

"Everyone agrees it's a bit of a joke, Dad," Harry says, this time being more sympathetic, as if for a foolish old man taken in yet again by con-artists. "The Peebles Rock Festival might happen, but no-one will go, no self-respecting band will want to be part of it, and generally speaking it'll be a complete disaster. Sorry to let you down."

I certainly feel down, crushed, even.

"The Maplins – they're a dance-electronica mob from Easterhouse, Brian – pulled out just last week," Tommy says, who is proving to be the font of all knowledge on local music gossip. "Two of the band were given three years in Barlinnie for handling stolen goods. Thieves were selling them speakers and PA equipment, which they would then use on stage, then sell on branded 'as used by The Maplins'. Quite a clever scam, when you think about it."

"Clever right enough," Harry says. "It might be The Maplins' slot you've been asked to fill."

"Might be," I agree. "The timing's right."

"This Earl of Delwhatever boy must be desperate," Harry adds, kindly.

"I'm sure he is. But so are we, or at least I am."

"And you say a contract's been signed?" Harry asks, still slightly bemused.

"Five pounds for every punter that turns up," I repeat.

"So it would be good if you get a big name for a headline act, and you could make lots of money."

"Correct."

Danni has said nothing until now. "You say there's still no sign of a headline act, Brian?"

"Nothing's been announced," I say.

There's a chorus of "aha!" from around the table, which brings the waiter across to take our order, and we are distracted onto discussing the relative merits of nachos, enchilladas, quesadillas, and virtually every stereotypical Tex-Mex dish known to the western world. It's fully ten minutes before Danni remembers to probe me about the headline act again. Or perhaps she's just being polite.

"Nothing's been announced, as I said before," I tell her.

"Aha – as we said before!" the four of them chime as one; that has to have been planned when I wasn't looking – yes, probably when I nipped away to the toilet for a second.

"Well?" Harry asks.

"Well, what?" I reply.

Tommy has a satisfied smile on his face, but it's in appreciation of someone else's detective work. "Danni here, who's sharp as a tack, reckons you must know who's on the bill. Especially who the headline act is."

Sure enough, Danni looks pretty sure of her ground, and although she's saying nothing, that's because she doesn't need to.

"It *is* Peebles, so they'll like dead people," Harry says. "Jim Reeves? Buddy Holly?"

I'm not giving in that easily.

"Roy Orbison?"

My lips stay closed.

"Kenneth MacKellar?"

This is unbearable; my son should have been in the Gestapo. I have to confess.

"Coldplay."

Tommy: "Coldplay?"

Becky and Danni: "Really?"

Harry: "Bullshit."

"That's who it's supposed to be, honest," I assure them all. "Chris Martin and this Earl of Delgado were at boarding school together, and then the same university, it seems. The Earl studied music, but never made anything of it."

"Martin did have the right musical training – Latin and Greek," Tommy adds. "Studying any art form's usually disastrous if you want to play anything. All they teach you is what not to do."

"Is that why metaphysics is good for cabinet-making, Tommy?" Danni asks with a smile.

"A perfect example, if I may say so. Most people see no connection, which is why they don't interfere with the creative spirit," he explains. Tommy likes talking about his work, and he's in demand as a speaker in the local colleges, too. He's offered an apprenticeship to a college student who comes up with the best design for a bed which takes into account its three most common uses, sleeping, reading and sex, a competition which has stimulated lots of entries, as well as an interest in testing prototypes.

"I still don't believe it," Harry says, "but if it's true then five pounds from each ticket might turn out to be quite a large sum of money."

"It could solve a lot of my problems," I point out. "Playing behind a curtain may not be ideal, but I can hardly afford to turn it down in the circumstances."

"How much will your Magda and the C-U Jimiz cost?" Harry asks.

"Tam wants them to get twenty per cent. They won't have a lot to do. The hardest job is Omar's – he has to make it look like he's hitting the drums without actually making contact at all. Fleece says Omar's actually got a bit of talent. I suppose it's the rhythm thing."

"Magda has to do her undressing thing, though."

"Hidden by a bass guitar. She doesn't have to reveal too much."

"Glad to hear it," Danni says. "I wasn't comfortable with the use of Magda's body as a sex object."

"I think Magda got over that personal hurdle a long time ago." When I see raised eyebrows all round, I just shrug my shoulders.

"Well I'm excited, Dad. I'll close my eyes and pretend I can see you all on stage," Becky says.

"I'll close my ears and pretend I'm listening to Kings of Leon," Harry adds, receiving both a chuckle and a punch in the side from Danni at the same time. "Actually, I'd love to be in the wings watching both parts of this nonsense at the same time. Will you be selling tickets for that?"

"Staff only, I'm afraid," I reply.

Tommy is contemplating, and of course being a professional contemplator I'm aware that this is likely to be high-calibre contemplation.

"But you'll need roadies," he says, in a measured tone.

"You're a genius, Tommy!" Harry yells, although the place is so noisy that no-one notices. "You're a first-class fucking genius!" He's ecstatic, and in a weak moment offers to pay for the wine.

You're a genius, Tommy, I think. *You've just saved me thirty quid.*

55

Sacred Music

The band turns out to be better prepared than we'd feared, as we now find ourselves rehearsing the six numbers for the set – no covers, all songs written by yours truly, and absolutely nothing whatsoever of Little Joe's rasta-jock. Joe has accepted that, since Magda and the C-Us have never been seen singing his songs (let's call them 'songs' for the sake of argument), it would be better if he himself took full credit for any live performances. Geoff and Little Joe have begun to get along really well, and it is usually now Geoff who reminds us at the end of each rehearsal that we have a duty to continue to assist Little Joe with his project, and of course Fleece and I have to agree through gritted teeth: we are using Little Joe's studio, after all.

Geoff has actually begun to try playing some funky little guitar with Little Joe's rasta-jock, and it is the appearance of this new aspect in his playing that has made his guitar teacher finally give up on him. Geoff and Sheila have been getting up later in the morning, a quarter to six now, and at long last he's learning to play some music by ear.

We've stepped up our rehearsal programme, however, so that we practise the music mid-week on Wednesdays (to suit me), and rehearse the whole show complete with Magda and the C-U Jimiz, Walnut, and anyone else who happens to be available, on Sundays. Tam has been showing up on Sundays, too, although in recognition of his size, Fleece suggests it would be better described as 'showing down'. In any case he arrives late and leaves early, taking in little more than two or three numbers and Bev's cheese scones, constantly referring to Bev in her absence as 'that tasty piece'. I can't stand the man, but since if anything Little Joe seems to be flattered by having a tasty piece for a wife, Fleece suggests that we should leave things as they are.

The C-U Jimiz and Magda are in top form; I can't believe how professional they are. Magda, Walnut and Tam discuss her key contribution to the concert, the degree to which her leather one-piece suit is unzipped at the front, and Magda is firm that she need go no further than just below the top of her bass guitar, despite Tam's suggestion that for 'artistic integrity' she should pull the zip down a further ten inches. The C-Us are agreed on all-black outfits to match up with Magda, although none of them really fancies leather apart from Quentin, which seems to be something to do with Quentin's personal tastes in other directions. Omar has perfected 'silent drumming' and even Evelyn concedes that he's proving to be an inspired choice on percussion, while Evelyn himself is thoroughly enjoying the role of dark, brooding lead guitar player, retaining Geoff's frowns and ignoring his smiles. My favourite C-U remains Jimmy, ever-cheerful and happy to see the good in anyone, added to which he invariably arrives on Sundays laden with pakoras, samosas and a different jar of pickle or chutney from the restaurant each week. These last are home-made, made by Jimmy's mother Ina who, Jimmy informs us, looks and dresses as Indian as they come but in fact is as Scottish as a deep-fried Mars Bar – his words – and is a season ticket-holder at Partick Thistle Football Club.

Meanwhile, Walnut has developed his very own version of rehearsal. Having picked up a job lot of different-coloured curtains in the IKEA sale, he's erected them most of the way across Little Joe's studio, and now insists on having what he calls 'curtain rehearsals' where he conducts our playing on one side, and Magda and the C-Us' miming on the other. It's as well that's he's doing this, as he looks spectacularly stupid, and we all need to get used to Walnut's antics before the big day. Thankfully, the real conductor and keeper of the beat is of course the more reliable MacBook Pro which provides our bass.

But if I'm honest, the show is fine, and we just about all know our parts in our sleep. Tam has confirmed that on Saturday 18th June, we'll be second last on, just before Coldplay, the headline act, although our own presence in our maiden live show has created considerable interest in the music press, including an apology from the smart-arse in *New Musical Express* who had questioned our very existence. In fact Tam's demand for an apology is driven by a wish to get the subject into the news again, and to stir up a little more publicity he manages to get some coverage of the squabble in the national media. Meanwhile, his friend Duffle Coates has put together a disc of all six songs which will be for sale immediately after the Peebles Rock Festival, and has arranged for twenty thousand copies to be produced in a 'limited edition', which concert-goers will be able to buy if they can produce a ticket for the Peebles event.

Two weeks before the concert, we've played the songs at least four times already, and Little Joe is getting is getting frustrated; it's clear he has something new to tell us, and what's more Geoff is in on the idea as well. Duffle Coates has just appeared to let us each see the now-ready CDs, when Joe asks him if he could manage to make a recording of some rasta-jock.

Fleece is horrified. "Sweet Jesus. Please, no."

Duffle is bewildered. "I've never been called sweet before," he says.

Now it's Fleece's turn to be bewildered, but being Fleece he blunders on anyway. "Duffle's a guest in your house, Little Joe. Does he deserve to be subjected to this rasta-jock stuff?" It's just as well Bev isn't present.

But Little Joe now receives support from Geoff. "I think there's something in Little Joe's concept," he says. "Goodness me, yes, he and I have been working on the rhythms for some of his music, and he may have a point. Listen to this."

Geoff begins to play *The Flowers Of The Forest*, the traditional air about the defeat of James IV at Flodden in and the death of ten thousand men or more. It should be a dirge, but Geoff and Little Joe have racked it up into rasta-jock, slow mode, and it sounds like music to have at a hideous barbecue.

"I just can't do it, I'm sorry. I just can't stand it," Duffle says. "And I'm not sure my insurance policy would cover the recording equipment being used for it." Little Joe is devastated.

"Goodness me – surely you'll record it, whatever you think of it." Geoff asks. "I had you down as a professional, Duffy. Goodness me, I certainly did." Geoff is frowning a lot here, and I can tell he really is on Joe's side.

The C-U Jimiz have been hiding behind the curtain devouring Bev's cheese scones, but Magda is fed up with their company and appears just at that moment. She wants to know what she's missing, and is appalled to discover that Duffle is reluctant to "do his duty" as she puts it.

"That last tune – what vas it?"

"*The Flowers Of the Forest*," Little Joe says.

"I like it. It's quirky."

"You said that about the last one, too," Fleece says. "*Scots Wha Hae*"

"That was quirky too, yes. And the one you played last week, Little Joe."

"*Loch Lomond*? Thanks," says Joe, genuinely delighted.

"That's the whole point," Geoff says. "Goodness me, don't you see that's the point? Magda's right. It's quirky."

"Jesus help me" says Fleece in desperation. "Please!"

Duffle surrenders. "Look, I'll do it. But get this straight. It's not my fault my first name happens to be Jesus. Blame my parents, but Jesus Duffy Coates is what I'm stuck with. I'll put up with 'Duffle" but I like 'Duffy' better."

With that he stomps off in a sulk and sits down on one of the chairs at the side of the room, but to complete his moment of humiliation he sits on an uneaten cheese scone that's fallen on the floor and been set aside.

Magda goes across and whispers some words in his ear. As if by magic, Duffle looks happy again, and although he can't quite ignore the stain on the seat of his jeans, he's ready to help out. As Magda passes me on the way back to work with the C-U Jimiz, she whispers in my ear that she's arranged that Duffle can come back to her flat afterwards, where she'll wash his jeans for him.

"OK, what do you want to record?" Duffle asks. "*Loch Lomond? Flowers Of The Forest? Scots Wha Hae?*"

"Well actually," Little Joe says, "Geoff and I have been working on yet another number."

"Goodness me, we have, yes. Something else. It's good."

Fleece has his head in his hands, but then the pair of them begin the racket bringing the C-Us out from the other side of the curtain. No-one can say a word while they play right to the end, and our appalled silence continues eerily for several seconds afterwards. The C-Us are frantically posting Facebook messages.

"That's sacrilege, Joe," Fleece says quietly. "You'll be burned at the stake for that."

"Is that wise, Joe?" I ask. "Is it really wise? Is that not a step too far?"

Even the normally composed Walnut is concerned. "Joe, I know this sort of thing is illegal in lots of other countries, but I'm not sure about the situation in the UK. It's risky."

Magda, however, has a different view. "I like it. I think it's great. It's quirky – very, very quirky."

56

Meet the Earl

William Marston Thackeray Scobie-Jones, Fourth Earl of Dalatho, 'Wullie' to all who know him, came into his title precisely at the turn of the millennium when his father stood too close to a fireworks display and had his life extinguished by a powerful roman candle. The first earl had purchased his title from Lloyd George in the nineteen twenties, in the days before it became necessary to pretend to be a party donor or generous benefactor to a worthwhile charity such as whichever major English football club the current prime minister supported. All the earls seemed to have a desire to put on large public displays, and the RAC Rally, balloon races and a variety sporting events had been put on over the years at the estate's expense. The second earl had tried unsuccessfully to attract events from the 1948 Olympics, while the third earl had experienced a similar lack of success with the 1966 World Cup. However, the present earl had a better sense of the possible, and three years ago managed to capture a stage of the Tour de France for an enormous fee, and now Wullie was determined to start an annual Peebles Rock Festival just south of the sleepy town itself. There had been some local objections, but Wullie believed strongly in a carrot-and-stick approach, combining significant bribes to 'helpful' local figures, at the same time as more recalcitrant opponents were finding their four-by-fours the victims of a series of mysterious catastrophic fires. By the summer, Peebles was, on the surface at least, looking forward to the Inaugural Peebles Rock Festival, headline act: Coldplay, not-so-headline act: The Flying Saucers.

Six of us are on our way to the Dalatho Estate exactly two weeks before the one-day rock festival is due to happen. Walnut is driving, as he's suggested we take his 'car', an upmarket Land Rover - of exactly the same colour as his Barbour jacket - which he feels might be useful if we have any rough terrain to navigate. Because of his size, Fleece is in the front passenger seat, while Little Joe, Geoff and I are shoe-horned into the seat behind. The rear of the Land Rover is fenced off for Walnut's large but friendly black labrador, but that area also contains a small seating area which faces out to the back, and Tam has been dumped in there beside the slobbering hound. Ostensibly because he's the smallest by miles, in honesty it's because that seat is all he deserves. Saturday or no Saturday, Tam is wearing his suit, and Herman – that's the labrador's name – is rapidly ruining it, which bothers the rest of us not a jot.

We're heading to Peebles to check out the lie of the land for the big day two weeks hence. Tam has been informed that Wullie has had the stage, the lighting galleries, and many of the facilities installed already, and it seems a good idea to find out exactly what will happen on the day, especially since none of us has done anything like this before. Dalatho turns about to be a large park area, surrounded by a few fields which have already been identified as car parks, and when we arrive we are greeted by some security staff wearing luminous orange tabards emblazoned with words '2F SECURITY' in large letters, underneath which is apparently printed – in Latin – the firm's motto *Nulla Excreta*. One of the guards welcomes us at the gate.

"Right, pal?" he says to Walnut, who has the Land Rover's window down already because of the heat, "Can I help you?" The security guard, who has a broad Scottish accent, sounds as if he has no intention of helping us if he can help it.

"We're from The Flying Saucers," Walnut says, thankfully just managing to avoid adding "my man". "We're here to check out the stage and so on for the eighteenth. Lord Dalatho is expecting us – we have an appointment at three."

The security guard checks his watch. "You're a bit early," he says – it's only five-to, right enough – but shrugs his shoulders then says, "Carry on down that road for about a quarter of a mile and you'll come to the stage. Wullie's the one with the big cigar." For some reason he chooses to bang the side of Walnut's Land Rover as if he were sending a horse on its way. Watching him disappear into the distance through the rear window, I suddenly become aware that Tam has disappeared and may have fallen out, but we discover him flat on the floor, seemingly in a warm embrace with Herman. Herman's got the wrong idea, however.

"Security guards make me nervous," Tam explains. "They're too big, it's not fair." His suit has changed colour from light grey to a deep, damp charcoal, and he probably smells of dog now as well.

A minute or so later, we've made our way down a bumpy track to the stage area, where lots of people seem to be working, busily nailing, fitting electrical cables, installing safety lighting and erecting security fences designed to keep the crowd and the performers apart. Walnut puts Herman on a lead, and we all get out, including Herman, and look around for the man with the cigar. There's no obvious 'boss figure' but then Geoff spots a barrel-chested man in blue denim dungarees and a tee-shirt, sporting a grey beard and a thick head of grey hair tied back in a ponytail. Most importantly of all, he's smoking a cigar, and not just any cigar, either; Fleece immediately identifies it as a Cuban Jaime Partagas thing which costs nearer twenty pounds than ten.

Just to be on the safe side, Walnut approaches him without making any assumptions.

"Excuse me, we're trying to find Lord Delgado."

"You've found him," the cigar-smoker replies. "Everyone calls me 'Wullie', though. You are?"

"We're The Flying Saucers," I say, offering my hand for him to shake. "Tam here phoned on Thursday to make an appointment with you." I point towards Tam, who seems to have shrunk still further, although this time I realise that Tam's cuban heels have sunk somewhat into the damp turf. Tam steps forward and proffers his hand with a murmur of "Your Grace."

"You're not who I expected to see today, gentlemen," he says, shaking my hand but turning his back on the admittedly disgusting figure of Tam. "I was expecting four rather younger lads and a young woman with glasses." He is well-spoken, but his gravelly voice is clearly the worse for wear after literally thousands of expensive Cuban cigars.

"Ah," Walnut says, "all is not as it seems with The Flying Saucers," Walnut explains.

It's easiest to be honest with Wullie, I decide. "Tam here, who's our manager, thinks we're too old and ugly to be seen in public, so the five youngsters you see mime to our music."

Wullie has a problem; he finds it difficult to smoke a cigar with his mouth wide open in astonishment. I take the opportunity to introduce the rest quickly.

"This is Little Joe Mackay, our rhythm guitar, Geoff Arrowsmith is lead guitar, and Fleece here, who's Little Joe's brother, plays percussion. I play acoustic guitar and sing lead vocals." Each of them in turn shakes Wullie's hand, while the earl himself, though still unable to speak, has recovered enough of his composure to be able to return the handshakes while smoking his cigar.

"And you are?" he asks, nodding towards Walnut. "You can let your dog off the lead if you like. He looks like he'll be fine."

Walnut slips Herman's lead off and they shake hands. "I'm Duncan McIntyre, of Marsden McKinlay McIntyre Bell, solicitors for Messrs. Reid and Mackay here, and I'm their stage manager, too." This last is news to us.

Lord Wullie takes a long puff on his cigar. He doesn't blink much, but he narrows his eyes when he's sizing people and situations up. Looking towards Tam, he says, "I think

I'm due an explanation from someone, probably you, Mr Cantlay."

Tam has a new friend in Herman, who has clearly decided that Tam is another labrador, a bitch in heat at that, so that he's spinning round and round in circles trying to avoid the dog's further embarrassing advances.

"Your Grace," he says, "The Flying Saucers are a musical act combined with a visual stage act. What we have here is the musical section, the orchestral portion, if you like, and there's a visual presentation, which the public is familiar with, in the band's videos."

Lord Wullie studies him, puffs on his cigar, and narrows his eyes again.

"Bullshit. The young ones mime, don't they?"

"It's a visual and a musical extravaganza," Tam insists.

"I signed a band called The Flying Saucers. I signed a live act. I didn't sign people who mime to other performers' recordings."

"But the band is playing. The Flying Saucers are playing," Tam says desperately.

"It sounds like fraud to me, Mr Cantlay. And I don't like being defrauded." This is going badly. "This doesn't really sound good to me, gentlemen. My rock festival fans expect a proper live concert and they won't be cheated. The fans have been done once – they bought tickets expecting The Maplins to play, and now half the band is in the Bar-L. That's why I've made the contracts so strict in your case."

Four of us don't like the sound of what Wullie has just said.

"Can you explain what you just said to us there, please, Wullie?" I ask him.

"Don't you read the contracts you sign?"

"Our lawyer – and it appears our stage manager – both negotiated the contract for us and advised us to sign. The contract had a lot of pages, in small writing. It all seemed to be one big sentence," I say, making it clear that Walnut has some questions to answer here.

"That's how lawyers work, Mr Reid," Wullie says to me. They keep their clients guessing by making their contracts incomprehensible, and then they make lots of money helping them sort out the mess. "And you, gentlemen, are in a mess. There's a penalty clause in that contract – didn't you notice?"

"Walnut – I mean Mr McIntyre here – said it would give us a guaranteed five pounds per head," Fleece explains.

"Indeed. Better than that, gentlemen, even if the concert is cancelled you get a fee based on a notional crowd of twenty thousand tickets sold."

"Goodness me," says Geoff, "that's a guaranteed hundred thousand!"

"It is, Mr Arrowsmith. But it's a two-way thing. If you fail to deliver, you have to pay me a hundred thousand pounds. You'll be liable jointly and severally. So if I think you're trying to defraud me, as I think you are, that's what will happen."

"Goodness me! Goodness me!" Then, after a pause, "Goodness me!!"

"I won't be able to pay my share of a hundred thousand," I say bleakly. "I'm still trying to sort out a divorce settlement."

"Me neither," Fleece adds glumly.

"Jointly and severally, Walnut," Little Joe repeats anxiously. "What does that mean?"

Lord Wullie doesn't give Walnut a chance to get a word in. Exhaling cigar smoke throughout, he menacingly leans towards Little Joe and growls: "It means that I'll get it out of you somehow. And if you don't, I'll have all your joints severed."

"Goodness me."

"Jesus," Fleece adds, looking heavenwards in prayer.

"I wasn't involved in the contract, Your Grace," squeaks a voice in between licks in the face from a black labrador. If

Herman stands on its hind legs, they're the same height, so he has no way of avoiding its attentions.

"I don't care, Mr Cantlay. I hold you responsible as well. You brought them to my notice, and that's good enough for me." Worryingly, he doesn't seem angry, he just keeps narrowing his eyes and puffing his cigar out from above his barrel chest. It's Lord Wullie's very calmness that's so scary.

"And if you don't have money, I'll come after you, don't you worry. I'll come after you with some friends."

Not for the first time, Walnut shows why it's important to have a good lawyer in a crisis. He's being studying the contracts, which he'd produced earlier from a small leather briefcase in his Land Rover.

"Lord Wullie," he says confidently, "I don't believe we're in breach of contract at all. All the contract requires The Flying Saucers to do is to play a six-number set in a live performance on the eighteenth of June."

"Yes."

"The contract doesn't say that the audience has to be able to see them. So if we forget the people we have in the front, we'll have met our requirements." As Walnut explains what we plan to do, Wullie's eyebrows rise higher and higher.

"You're saying the band will be playing at the same time as your young people mime?"

"Yes," Walnut says. Lord Wullie's eyebrows rise a good two inches further, and there's a delay of three cigar puffs before he speaks again.

"I suppose I might have to accept this. Let's hope no-one finds out, and that you can make it work. You do realise, gentlemen, that if it goes wrong, I have many friends who will help me recover my money?"

"Friends?" Tam asks nervously.

"I'll introduce some of them in a minute," Lord Wullie says ominously, with more puffs of a cigar and an evil smile.

"In the meantime, I'm concerned about one aspect of your contract."

"Which is?" Walnut asks.

"I signed a live concert for The Flying Saucers, understood to be a five-piece band." I can see what's coming here. "There are only four of you gentlemen. Where's your bass player? The Flying Saucers have a bass player, don't they?" He puffs on his cigar, then when he sees our expressions, smiles.

"Please tell me it isn't a computer you play along with, is it?" Wullie asks.

No-one dares to answer.

"Is it? Is it, now?" His face is just about lost behind cigar smoke but we can all see enough of his smile to know that we have a big, big problem.

Wullie has more to add. "I said I'd introduce you to one or two of my friends." He calls over some of the tabard-wearing security staff. "Gentlemen, I'd like you to meet my friends from 2F Security. They used to be known as 'FF Security', and then before that as 'Falkirk Security'. I find they're very... reliable."

They may be very reliable; we are very, very scared. Tam gasps, "Fal.. Falkirk... Friends."

"Jointly and severally, gentlemen," Lord Wullie repeats. "Jointly and severally."

57

Desperate Measures

"Dad, you can't just let this happen to you," Becky says, despairingly.

We're sitting in a French deli-cum-restaurant near Haymarket station, where she's agreed – demanded is a better description in fact – to meet me to discuss my plight, and by extension, the band's.

"Got any ideas?" I ask her pathetically. "Tam Cantlay plans to emigrate, although I'm not sure his idea of emigrating to Berwick is quite as safe as he thinks it is. Walnut has ordered extra security for his house. Even the security staff are afraid of the Falkirk Friends, though, so they're looking at hiring attack dogs which never get fed."

"Is it that bad? They're not just trying to scare you?"

"They've managed that already. No, Lord Wullie wants his live five-piece band with a female bass player and what Lord Wullie wants is what Lord Wullie tends to get."

"You need a female bass player, don't you?"

"I think that's the obvious statement of the year, Becky." She looks hurt by my sarcasm, and I apologise. "I'm sorry, sweetheart, I'm being selfish at the moment."

At that moment Harry appears through the door.

"Did I hear you describing yourself as being selfish?" he says. "You've finally worked that out. Only taken you six decades."

"Nice to see you, too," I reply, using my most sarcastic tone. "I didn't know you were invited, too."

"I wanted him here as well, Dad," Becky said. "I can't discuss this alone."

"We're both here because we're worried for you, you cretinous fuckwit," Harry clarifies. "We may have a complete fuckwit for a father, but you're the only dad we've got and we'd like to look after you as best we can."

"Promise to visit me in hospital," I say sadly, looking down at the table. I haven't touched the mille-feuille in front of me. "In the meantime, Harry, it's nice to see you, really it is. I'm sorry to be giving you all this grief.

"I know, I know. I shouldn't be making things worse, I suppose. You know what I'm like."

It's a rare admission of weakness from my son. Both Becky and I acknowledge it with a smile. Harry orders a small shot of coffee which comes in seconds. Sipping it, he says, "And of course we all know who could be your female bass guitar a week on Saturday if you'd allow it to happen, the pair of you. The female bass guitar player from The Blonde Bombshelles is available. Aka, Mum."

Nobody's actually dared to bring the subject up before.

Becky spells it out. "Dad, why don't you ask Mum? She could do it."

"I can just see your mum taking time out from her court case against me to fill in for a gig with my band," I say. "Somehow I don't see it. She might even ask for a ticket to watch the 'jointly and severally' event."

"Have you anything to lose, Dad?" Becky asks.

"A limb or two."

"That'll happen if you do nothing," Harry points out.

I'm being attacked in a pincer movement. I study them closely.

"Someone been speaking to you two, haven't they?"

"Well, yes, they have," Harry confesses. "I've had a visit from both Little Joe and Bev as it happens, and a phone call from Fleece. I gather you even cancelled yesterday's rehearsal."

"Duncan McIntyre phoned me today at work," Becky says.

"Even Walnut?" I'm surprised, because he must have made some effort to track Becky down, and I'd have thought he'd be the last person to consider anything that might compromise a client's position in a legal dispute.

"The guy is scared, Dad," Becky says. "He was quite hysterical over the phone. He says your guitar player Geoff is talking about booking a holiday in China for him and his wife, leaving the day before the concert, and with a one-way ticket only. You need to try something."

I'm hesitant, but only because I can't see how this will make any difference. Brunhilde is only likely to enjoy my discomfort even more.

"OK, I'll phone Walnut first thing tomorrow. You never know, Mum might have met the man of her dreams, be head over heels and in love, and say she'll forgive me and do it."

Both of them give a sigh of relief. Then Harry produces a small compact camera.

"Can I take a photo of your face while it's still in one piece?" he asks, laughing. Becky is not impressed, and nor am I.

"Bastard," I mutter quietly at him. "Bastard bastard bastard bastard."

58

Legal Correspondence

Marsden McKinlay McIntyre Bell
Multrees Walk,
34, St. Andrew's Square,
Edinburgh EH2 2AD
7th June 2012

Susan Gunn,
Robb Merriman,
18, Rutland Square,
Edinburgh EH1 2BB

Dear Sue,

Jane Reid (née Forrest) v Brian Anthony Reid

I refer to the above pending legal dispute between the two parties above.

My client wishes to approach your client with an unusual request. You may be aware that both parties have some history in the music industry, and my client has a forthcoming appearance planned at the Peebles Rock festival on the 18th of this month.

My client's band is in need of a bass guitar player at short notice, and I have been instructed to approach Mrs Reid, through you, to ask if she might be available to play on the day. A significant fee will be paid.

Time is of the essence in this matter. Could you contact her please as soon as possible and get back to me by return?

Yours sincerely,

Duncan
(Partner, Marsden McKinlay McIntyre Bell)

ROBB MERRIMAN, W.S.
18, Rutland Square
Edinburgh, EH1 2BB
7th June 2011

Duncan McIntyre
Multrees Walk,
34, St. Andrew's Square,
Edinburgh EH2 2AD

Dear Duncan,

Jane Reid (née Forrest) v Brian Anthony Reid

Thank you for your letter regarding the current dispute action my client is bringing against your client, which I received earlier today. As requested, I immediately contacted my client Mrs Reid for instruction. She has given me clear instruction on the exact responses I must give to Mr Reid's request.

My client wishes to make it clear that she is delighted that he is in need of a bass player and even more delighted to be able to refuse him. She is interested to hear that he needs a bass player and hopes he completely fails to find one.

My client is delighted that your client is likely to be disappointed by this response. She wishes to assure him that he will be in her thoughts on Saturday 18th June.

Yours sincerely,

Susan Gunn

(Partner, Robb Merriman)

Marsden McKinlay McIntyre Bell
Multrees Walk,
34, St. Andrew's Square,
Edinburgh EH2 2AD
7th June 2011

Susan Gunn,
Robb Merriman,
18, Rutland Square,
Edinburgh EH1 2BB

Dear Sue,

Jane Reid (née Forrest) v Brian Anthony Reid

Thank you for your prompt reply to my letter of earlier today.

My client is extremely disappointed that your client is unable to assist, and begs her to reconsider her position. He is aware that their relationship is not a good one, but wishes to come to an accommodation. He is prepared to make over his own entire fee for the concert, in addition to that originally offered in my letter of earlier today, if she is prepared in turn to abandon her forthcoming action against him. Mrs Reid should be aware that this is likely to be a substantial sum of money, although neither he nor I can say at this stage what that fee is likely to amount to. It would, however, require Mrs Reid to perform on stage with his band on the 18th June.

My client would like your client to be aware that the consequences for his own personal safety may be extremely grave if a bass player cannot be found. Indeed my own safety may be compromised. He begs your client to reconsider her decision, and look forward to hearing from you as soon as possible.

Yours sincerely,
Duncan
(Partner, Marsden McKinlay McIntyre Bell)

ROBB MERRIMAN, W.S.
18, Rutland Square
Edinburgh, EH1 2BB
7th June 2011

Duncan McIntyre
Multrees Walk,
34, St. Andrew's Square,
Edinburgh EH2 2AD

Dear Duncan,

Jane Reid (née Forrest) v Brian Anthony Reid

Thank you for your second letter of today, which I received half an hour ago.

Understanding the urgency of your request, I once again contacted my client Mrs Reid for instruction, and again she has given me clear instruction on the exact responses I must give to you and to Mr Reid.

My client has instructed me to state she absolutely will not assist Mr Reid or his band, and that it has 'made [her] day' that Mr Reid's personal safety is a matter of concern. Of course she condemns violence of any sort, but she can understand and sympathise with those who might lose patience with your client.

My client now regards this correspondence as closed.

Wishing you personally all good health,

Yours sincerely,

Susan Gunn

(Partner, Robb Merriman)

59

The Truth about Brian

"Well that didn't exactly work, then," Fleece says, summing up the flurry of correspondence that has taken place between Walnut and Brunhilde's lawyer earlier in the day. It's Wednesday, and we're in Little Joe's studio at our midweek rehearsal, having decided to keep working and hope something will turn up, like Mr Micawber.

"In the novel, Micawber ended up in Australia," Walnut points out, "and that may be a good option for you guys as well." He's untied the red ribbon from a manilla file – why do they use these red ribbons? – and has started to spread all the relevant documents and contracts in front of us on a card table in the middle of the room.

"You as well, Walnut," I remind him. "Lord Wullie seemed to think you were as much part of this as we are."

"I suspect you're right, Captain. I should have known you were trouble from the start." He looks around the room, where we have been joined by Bev, Harry, Danni, Tommy and Becky, but there's one person missing. "Where's the disappearing Mr Cantlay?" Walnut says.

I look at my phone, which receives texts on silent, to discover that Tam has been in touch. "Aha – it seems Tam's just texted me," I tell them. "It seems he can't make it tonight, and he may be away for some time. At least I think that's what the message says – it doesn't have any vowels in it."

"He's on the run, if he's got any sense," Fleece suggests.

That sounds like good news to me. "We don't actually need him any more, actually. If he really does disappear, all it means is he doesn't get his twenty per cent share."

"The price of life is set at twenty per cent, then." Fleece can still raise a laugh, gallows humour.

"Personally, I'm not sorry to see the back of Tam Cantlay," Little Joe says. "He's a nasty little man." These are strong words from Joe, and when Bev nods her head in agreement I'm even more surprised; she sees the good in everybody.

"Goodness me – nasty – that's a really good description for Tam, isn't it?" Geoff frown-smiles furiously. "Nasty, yes, goodness me. That's so apt."

"But easy to laugh at," Harry says. Of my children and their partners, he's the only one to have met Tam. "The Norman Wisdom of music management," he suggests, to more laughter.

"How about Stan Laurel?" I suggest.

"As in 'this is another fine mess…'?" Walnut asks. This time the laughter is muted as we all remember our plight. "This is getting us nowhere. Where are we going to find a female bass player?"

"Is there really no hope of persuading Jane, Captain?" Little Joe asks.

"No chance, Joe. It's there in black and white," I say, pointing to Walnut's file. "The more I ask, the less likely she is to agree."

"That's probably right," Walnut agrees.

"Tell me, Brian, why does Jane hate you so much? What on earth did you do to annoy her so much?" Walnut asks the question, but it's clear Little Joe has no idea either and wants an explanation of why my marriage has fallen apart. Everyone goes very quiet waiting for my reply, but I'm not really ready to lay bare my soul to a whole group of people, including my children and their lovers. It might feel like it at the moment, but this is not Alcoholics Anonymous.

Geoff is still frown-smiling. At least he seems to be able to smile a little, perhaps just putting a brave frown-smiling face. He decides to shed some light.

"I've known Brian for a long time – goodness me, a very long time – and I regard him as one of my dearest friends."

Then he turns towards me and says, "Even you, Brian, would admit that you got a bit negative and cynical in your old age." I'd admit it, Geoff, but only privately. Not here. Geoff continues in my silence. "Goodness me, Brian, you could be quite hard to work with sometimes. People would come up with what they thought were good ideas and all you'd ever see were the problems. I thought it was funny. So did lots of your friends. But anyone who didn't think you were funny — goodness me, they wanted to strangle you. Is that a fair statement?"

Harry and Becky probably would be the first to acknowledge this, too, but say nothing. I wasn't negative towards them, actually, but they know what I thought of my job, and many of those I worked with. Becky knows I'm upset, and she discreetly squeezes my arm.

"It's fair, Geoff." There, I've said it.

Fleece is interested. "So Brian is being a bit negative when he says his head was a cold, stupid, talentless bitch, then?"

"Goodness me, Fleece, Brian is spot on there," Geoff says with some passion. "I wouldn't use the word bitch, maybe, but that's just me. But goodness me — cold, stupid, talentless, definitely."

"And what with Brunhilde and her temper — and boy does she have a temper — you and she were a marriage doomed to fail," Fleece adds. "Christ, I've felt her temper, Captain, haven't I? Do you remember the night we came back to your house from the Hibs game when they drew four-all with Hearts?"

"Hibs lost two goals in injury time. Felt like a defeat. Referee played far too much extra time."

"Brunhilde started ranting about how it must have been great to see such a good game and we never got beat. Remember? Then off she went about a whole host of wars in Africa where nobody gave a fuck about Hearts 4 Hibs 4. Her words. Do you remember, Captain?"

"I do, Fleece. I remember it well." I can laugh about it now. It's getting on for ten years ago, too.

"Then she starts producing atlases, every atlas she could find in the house. Every one. Becky and Harry's school atlases, the lot. The *Readers' Digest* was the heaviest. Turned to the page with Africa, held them up at us, then hurled them across the room."

"She was passionate about what she believed in, Fleece."

"A bit unhinged, too."

I'm not so sure, actually. Jane was probably right, really, but it maybe wasn't what I wanted to hear at the time. In the meantime I shrug my shoulders, say nothing, and smile sheepishly to hide my thoughts.

"This is getting us nowhere," Little Joe says. "The fact is that we need a bass player and it seems like Jane Reid is still our best bet."

Bev has been silent until now, but picking up on her husband's cue, she looks towards Harry then Becky. "Are you sure you've got no influence, either of you? Couldn't one of you ask her, for your sake rather than your dad's?"

"I can see why you're asking us, Bev," Harry says, "but you really have to understand that these two fuckwits – sorry to have to be so blunt – are lost causes. They know we want them to get on better, which just gives them each an opportunity to blame the other for something else."

Becky agrees. "Harry's right. We're not happy that they don't get on, and they blame each other for that, too."

It's a very uncomfortable feeling being talked about in the third person, by the way – it's as if I'm not here at all. In the meantime, we seem to be at a dead end.

Then Becky adds something more. "But I'd like to give it one more try." My emotions are confused; one half of me is glad she's making one more effort, but the other is afraid she might fall out with her mum, and I don't want that.

Harry obviously feels the same way. "I'm not sure that's wise, Becky. Mum would never agree just because one of us had asked her nicely, and in the meantime she'll think you're taking sides."

"Of course she'll probably think I've taken Dad's side, and it might be true that I don't want to see him get hurt," she says. "But she might do it for someone else."

60

Condemned Men Eat Cheese Scones

By the weekend, each of the band, as well as Walnut, has received a postcard from Tam, posted in Dubai, although none of us is to know where he's flying on to from there. He explains that he's been called away suddenly and that he will no longer be able to act as our manager, although he will be sending us an invoice for services rendered thus far. Given that he's done nothing for us, this enrages the band members, to say nothing of the fees he's pilfered, but Walnut suggests that we should simply write off Tam as a bad debt. On the whole it's good to get rid of him. Privately, Walnut's also told me that he has located most of my royalty fees for radio plays of songs I've written, and then being the typical lawyer that he is, he explains that almost of all of the money will be required to pay his legal fees.

Walnut has persuaded us all to keep rehearsing, and that if we can produce some sort of sound on the day – including a laptop-generated bass – Lord Wullie might settle for leaving us alone and paying us no fee. Well, I suppose it's possible, but Walnut always was an optimist.

So on the Sunday before our first live concert, everyone has assembled, including Magda and the C-U Jimiz and Walnut, who now sees himself as conductor of the Royal Merchiston Philharmonic Orchestra and is ordering everyone around. This is to be a dress rehearsal, he says, and we've even to wear what we'll wear the following week. Summer or no summer, he still arrives wearing his camel-hair coat, but underneath he's wearing a dinner jacket and bow-tie.

We need to fill the C-Us and Magda in on our various problems and how they've yet to be resolved, but the curtain has been erected across the middle of the studio again. Magda is delighted to see the back of "that sneck Tam".

Harry and Tommy have agreed to act as stage hands, so they're present as well, as are Becky and Danni simply because they've nothing better to do. The band is about to play its first number, *Get A Grip Of My Life*, when Bev appears at the door – she's been organising cheese scones, of course – to say that we have a visitor, who follows, carrying a guitar-case, behind her. The visitor is a woman in her late fifties, around five foot eight tall, whose bleached-blonde shoulder-length hair has a few dark and grey streaks in it. She's wearing a pair of quite tight jeans and a dark green tee-shirt that somehow matches her eyes, and she looks not bad, not bad at all. A lot better than when I last saw her.

No-one else can really find anything to say, not even Bev, and it falls to me as it was always bound to. I daren't go anywhere near her, though.

"Hi, Jane. Nice to see you. Thanks for coming."

"Don't push it. Let's get on with this." Brunhilde hasn't changed that much, then.

None of the band have the slightest idea how she's been persuaded to come, but with salvation at hand, we've no intention of asking right now.

Brunhilde surveys the studio. "What on earth is that?" she asks, pointing to the curtain.

Walnut gives her a brief explanation of how we've ended up with Magda and the C-U Jimiz as our front act, but that we play the real music behind the curtain. Jane is to take over from the laptop, which I feel is being cruelly discarded after such loyal service, but I daren't say a word. In any case, I'm still stunned by the miracle that she's here.

"I like the curtain," she says to no-one in particular. "I can sit on the other side from you-know-who." This is going to be a long day, indeed a long week. Even Brunhilde knows that isn't really possible, but then Jane *does* come up with an idea – she suggests that to keep the rhythm of the bass constant, she can have an earpiece playing the bass line from the laptop into her ear and then all the rest of us will follow along. She gets ready in silence, plugs her bass guitar into one of Little Joe's many spare amplifiers, and in five minutes she's ready and tuned up. The air is thick with tension.

"Six songs, Jane," Walnut says. "The four on the CD, and two others called *Saturday Blues* and *River Of Tears*."

"For goodness' sake! *The Saturday Blues?*" Jane says, dismissively. "That old thing." I'd forgotten that it dates back to the days before we were married; she's actually quite familiar with it. "Becky left me a copy of the CD so I know them, too. I don't know this other one you're talking about." She's cold, it's as though I'm not here.

Communication is mainly through Fleece or Walnut. I know Brunhilde met Little Joe once, but it was over thirty years ago and both have changed a lot since then and they don't remember each other. Jane has met Geoff more recently, but as one of my colleagues from the latter years of my school career she regards him as an enemy combatant. Geoff, who can sense this, is reduced to frown-smiling at her; Brunhilde thinks he's laughing at her.

"What's so funny, Geoff? Am I the circus freak or something?"

Jesus, this woman is angry.

"Jane," I say, "I promise no-one is laughing at you, least of all Geoff, who in my experience is the most pathologically friendly man I've ever met. It's me you're angry with, feel free to be as unpleasant as you need to be with me."

Brunhilde studies me, unblinking. "That can come later." She takes a deep breath. "OK, Fleece, start by telling me about these songs. I know about *The Saturday Blues*, because that's his crap," she says, indicating me with a sideways nod of her head. "Who's responsible for the rest?"

No-one replies, certainly not me. The silence tells Jane all she needs to know.

"Don't tell me he wrote them all?" She laughs mirthlessly. "I might have guessed. Well, Brian, I suppose your songwriting has improved a little bit in forty years. Marginally."

"I don't know how to take that, so I'll assume it's praise, Jane," I say. "In which case, thanks."

"If you thought I was trying to be nice to you, please be reassured it was completely unintended."

I think – I think – that statement might be a genuine back-handed compliment.

Meanwhile, Magda has been studying Brunhilde. "I am to coppy this woomann?" she asks, bewildered.

Jane has temporarily forgotten about Magda and the C-Us, and the side-show where they're pretending to be us. Now that Magda can see a real-life female bass-player – if as Brunhilde could ever be described as 'real-life' – she's having second thoughts about her role. However, Walnut sees an opportunity to regain control of the proceedings, using his best Edinburgh-establishment solicitor skills to pervert the English language to his needs.

"I think we need to move forward on this one, Magda," he says. He's really speaking to Brunhilde, but he's too scared. "Now that Jane's kindly agreed to step in on bass, let's do the song we were going to do, then run through the rest. Leave *River Of Tears* to the end. Do the easier ones first."

"Sounds a good idea, Walnut," Fleece agrees. Geoff frown-smiles. Little Joe might be on the planet Neptune with his rasta-jock, or perhaps he's thinking about where he's going to display his new range of Bosch tools. Much nodding and high-fives from the C-Us. Jane just shrugs her shoulders. Magda does, too – she's got the idea already, I think. Meanwhile Tommy and Harry try to look busy behind the scenes, and Danni, Becky and Bev simply keep their fingers crossed.

Walnut lays a copy of the music and words to *Get A Grip Of My Life* in front of Jane and announces that this is where we'll start, directing Magda and the C-U Jimiz to their positions behind the curtain in the middle of the studio.

"Remember we can't expect Jane to just slot in as if she's been part of the band all along," he says, and we set off, Jane taking her lead from the MacBook Pro.

Did Walnut say we couldn't expect Jane just to slot in?

On the contrary, everyone, even me, has failed to take into account one simple fact: Brunhilde is a class bass-player. Seamlessly, she plays bass along with the rest of the band, making it sound much, much better than it ever did simply using a computer. Walnut sees a small problem to start with; Jane is capable of playing, and naturally tries to play, more subtle and complex bass than I've set down on the MacBook Pro, and therefore Magda is familiar with, but Jane understands, and after a few words with Magda, adapts. That's it. She makes us look what we really are – total rank amateurs. She listens once – only once, mind you – to the single song new to her, *River Of Tears*, and plays it second time around as if she's played it all her life.

When we've played our six songs through, Geoff simply says admiringly, "Goodness me, Jane, that was a pleasure to watch and hear you play. I've been trying to learn to play guitar for years but I'll never have your natural skill. It's quite depressing, really." That's quite a speech from Geoff, and only one 'goodness me'.

Brunhilde is assessing Geoff. She might say something nasty but she thankfully settles for, "Thanks, Geoff." She might be mellowing.

"Are we allowed to applaud at all, Mum?" Becky asks.

"Is it worth applauding? Or just a load of shit? I'm not sure all the chords are right." Brunhilde was always more into augmented fifths than me.

"Sounds good to me," Harry says. "You maybe set high standards, Mum."

"It's the best way."

"Maybe we need to remember what's possible between now and next Saturday," Walnut says. "We've got something to work with here."

"I can see the light at the end of the tunnel at last," Little Joe says.

"I can see life after next Saturday," Fleece adds, laughing. It's been a long time, too long, since I heard that head-back roar. Despite the murderous female looks across the studio from me, things are looking up, and everyone is in a better mood.

Behind the curtain, the C-U Jimiz and Magda have been gyrating away out of site, so that the band has never seen them – only Walnut, our self-appointed lawyer-cum-manager-cum-stage-manager-cum-conductor, as well as any onlookers. For the moment the onlookers are down to Tommy, Harry, Becky and Danni, because Bev has left us to prepare refreshments. Now one by one they appear from their purdah looking a little bored.

"Listen, guys," Jimmy says, "all we seem to be doing is dancing about endlessly here, but we're not so sure we're really needed any more today."

Walnut looks nonplussed. I'm left to answer for him.

"Don't you need to make sure you've got all the songs right?"

"I think Walnut would say that our bit of the show seems fairly secure," Quentin points out. "He's never once said there's anything even remotely suspect." It's strange how you can know someone for so long without noticing their lisp.

Evelyn is more succinct. "Wasting our fuckin' time here going over the same stuff over and over again."

Walnut gets the point. "I get the point, Evelyn," he says. "So long as Jane can repeat the bass part, you guys are just doing what you've always been doing. Lord Wullie said that the stage will be completely ready by Thursday, so I can check it out, then I can brief you if there's anything you need to know."

"Should we all be there?" Little Joe asks. "I can't really close the shop until six."

"I think it would look better if only a couple of us were there, actually," Walnut says. "The band looks a bit amateurish if it can't trust its manager to do its work for it." Now Walnut is definitely our new manager.

"You *are* a bunch of amateurs," Jane says, sarcastically. She doesn't miss a chance.

Walnut ignores her, and tells the C-Us and Magda they can go home, promising to keep them in the loop before Saturday. Omar complains that he hasn't even had his cheese scones, yet, so Joe suggests they call in at the kitchen as they leave to collect cheese scone takeaways.

Once they've departed, Jane is invited to say which songs she feels we most need to practise.

"All of them, really," she says, but this time she says it without rancour. "The more you can rehearse for a big live gig, the better. You really have to be able to play the music without thinking, because you don't know what's going to happen on the night. And I've never done anything remotely like an open-air pop festival. There's a lot more to think about in a festival – the crowd are a lot less predictable, might not be so well-behaved and so on.

"But on the plus side, they're all fairly simple songs, basic chords, basic structure, and you all seem to know the lyrics well enough. You don't even have to work out how you're going to appear on stage, because as far as the crowd's concerned, those young people who have just left do that for you. They seem nice, by the way, and they're good – where did you find them?"

I decide to take a chance on speaking to explain. "Our disappearing manager, Tam Cantlay, found them. They're a boy-band, although I don't really know what Magda does." Actually, I do know: she wasn't one of Tam's clients, he was one of hers, in the days when she couldn't be so choosy about how she made money.

Jane doesn't acknowledge that I've spoken, but neither does she bite my head off, so I wonder if we might be making progress towards an armed neutrality. In Norse legend, Valkyries rode across the battlefield deciding who lived and who died, the demons of the dead; pinching myself, I think the demon has passed me by for the moment.

"So," Fleece says, "you think we should go through the lot again? In order?"

"Yes," Brunhilde replies, "I'm afraid I do." As Geoff frowns-smiles, Little Joe is writing something down on a scrap of paper – I shudder to think what it might be this time, and hope it's to do with the price of nails in Mackay's Ironmongery. Fleece just looks exhausted and ragged, but then he's looked that way all the time I've ever known him.

Walnut claps his hands in a 'luvvy' manner to indicate he's once again the director of the show.

"OK, izzie-wizzie, let's get busy!" he announces.

"What?" the Valkyrie asks. Let's hope she's not about to take another sweep across the studio battlefield.

"I mean – let's go, everyone," Walnut says, sheepishly.

Strictly speaking, we don't need him now, but on Saturday we'll need to take our cue from him, so we may as well do it now, too. He counts us into *Get A Grip of My Life*, and it sounds fine, especially after a couple of sound balance alterations at Tommy's suggestion. We've just reached the end – this time the non-combatants do provide applause – when Bev appears at the door with tea, coffee, and, of course...

"Cheese scones!" Fleece announces. "It's all I come for, you know."

It's interesting that although Bev glows, she does so much less now, for some reason. Perhaps I'm getting used to her, perhaps it's the competition from the Valkyrie. Surely it isn't that I still find Jane attractive? Of course she's attractive, otherwise I'd never have married her in the first place, but she terrifies me.

Minutes later, we're sitting tucking into Bev's huge plate of cheese scones – they help the glow a bit, actually – when Jane puts her plate and mug of coffee down.

"These are pretty special, Bev," she says, with a friendly smile – Jane has no quarrel with Bev. "This is why they come, isn't it? I thought a couple of them had put some weight on," she adds. It might be a joke at my expense, and at poor Fleece's, but then again Fleece has put weight on so she might just be stating a fact.

"Thank you, Jane. It's nice to have you here." That, Bev, is the understatement of the century.

"I've just been thinking." Jane is studying me, and I sense Brunhilde the Valkyrie is about to make another sweep of the battlefield. "That name for your band – The Flying Saucers."

I know to say nothing; let's be clear about this, the demon of the dead has me directly in her sights.

"I've always thought it was because one of you guys was into UFOs," she says, slowly. I'm not convinced that that smile on Jane's face isn't a front for an altogether different emotion. "You know," she says, "like some daft boys are. Are you interested in UFOs, Little Joe?"

"Not much?"

"You, Geoff?"

"Goodness me, no."

"Fleece?"

Fleece is prepared to try to cover up for his old pal. "Well, yes, Jane, as it happens…"

He's not allowed to get any further. The Valkyrie rises to her full height, ready to bring down her fury on her prey. "Don't waste your breath, Fleece, he's not worth it. I know why you're The Flying Saucers," she says, then her voice rising to a high pitch scream, "I KNOW WHY YOU'RE CALLED THE FLYING SAUCERS!"

Bitter experience has hardened me to what's coming next. In the absence of saucers, Jane picks up the nearest missiles and propels them with all her venom and ire in what she hopes is my direction. But instinctively I also know to stand still and Brunhilde's aim is so squint that I'll be safe and they'll all fly safely past me. On no account, duck or take cover – that way lies her accidental success. Less than twenty seconds later, everyone else in the room, the band, Walnut, the four youngsters, even Bev, has been hit by one or more cheese scones, but I'm still untouched. Frustrated, Jane moves forward to finish me off, pummelling my chest with her fists until I prevent myself – and her – from real injury by putting my arms around her tightly, the first physical contact we've had in well over a year. Eventually, as she's bound to, she runs out of steam.

Kissing her on the forehead, I say, "Sorry." Jane doesn't look so much like a Valkyrie now: a Valkyrie would never allow herself to be seen with tears running pouring down her cheeks, tears of rage, tears of frustration, tears of embarrassment. And all this in front of her own children.

Eventually, Fleece looks around at the scone-mess on the floor, on clothes, on musical instruments.

"Bit of a waste. They were nice, those scones," he says with a wry laugh.

"I should go and make some more, shouldn't I?" Bev says, standing up to leave.

61

Hidden Memories

Jane wants to leave, but Becky and Danni move on to prevent her. Becky reminds her that she's here for a reason, but it's Danni's influence that is stronger this time, displaying a tenderness that is all the more effective because she's normally so level-headed and sophisticated. In any case, Jane's a bit of a basket case at the moment, and Becky insists that it would be dangerous to drive a car in her present state – better to leave it for a while.

While we clean up – I help a lot here – Geoff goes off to the toilet muttering about his water works, and his return prompts me to ask him about his visit to the hospital. I've always tried to avoid health topics, but anything's welcome at the moment to take attention from Jane's discomfort.

"Well, Brian," he begins, "Goodness me, I had such a lot of tests. Goodness me, ever so many, you know."

"And?"

"Well, it's not actually great news, actually. Goodness me, you could hardly say that, no."

Walnut, Fleece and Little Joe are starting to tune in, understandably concerned.

"Well are you going to tell us, for crying out loud?" Fleece complains.

"Well, it's not good."

"Geoff!"

"It's the big one, boys, the big one. Goodness me, I'm afraid it's the big C." He's frown-smiling bravely.

A chorus of "Oh, Geoff," and "Sorry to hear that."

"What will they be doing for you?" Little Joe asks. "Will they operate?"

"They say there's no point. It's inoperable." More frown-smiles.

"Jesus Christ, Geoff. That's awful."

"Have you made a will, Geoff? I can help you there," Walnut says.

Geoff ignores him. "They can help make things better, less pain, control the water works, that sort of thing, but I'm afraid that's all they reckon they can do."

"I'm sorry to hear that," Fleece says. He's keen to cut to the chase and find out if Geoff's going to die any time soon. "So... did they give a prognosis?" 'What's your prognosis' is such a delicate phrase for 'how long have you got?', isn't it?

"Goodness me, you mean how long have I got?" Geoff asks. "Why didn't you just ask?"

"I just did, Geoff." Fleece might strangle him anyway, rendering the entire question academic.

"Oh, well, goodness me, they said a good twenty-five years. Goodness me, that anyway."

We're all looking at him, stunned.

"Twenty-five years?"

"It's very slow-growing, they said. Best to do nothing. Goodness me, yes, best to do nothing except help pain and so on. Quite common, apparently."

Now Geoff is in mortal danger. Fleece's hands have risen above waist level, and the fingers on both hands are twitching.

"So there isn't a problem, Geoff, then?"

"Well I'm terminally ill, Fleece. Goodness me, I'm terminally ill. I'm going to die."

"By that measure, we're all terminally ill, ye daft Lincolnshire goat. We thought you were going to die soon."

"I think Fleece envisaged an earlier demise than twenty-five years," I add, quietly.

"Goodness me, boys, are you that desperate to see the back of me?" Geoff asks, frown-smiling.

"Stick around until Saturday at least, Geoff," Little Joe says. The crisis has passed, and Fleece's hands have returned to his knees; instead he's in head-shaking mode. Walnut, at least, manages to see the funny side of it.

"I don't know, I don't know," he's muttering.

Bev returns with quite the fastest-cooked replacement cheese scones I've ever seen, surely ten minutes at the most, this time glowing at full force. Her scones look, act – and smell – like a great, powerful unifying force across the whole room. There must be an argument for listing cheese as a Class A drug. In no time, Jane is back on her feet, determined to put aside her recent hiccup and reassert her strength in our band.

She marks her return to action with a new problem for me to think about.

"That song we just played could have been written by Rab Noakes, you know," she says, looking at me.

"I thought that, too. I don't think it's one of his," I reply. "I wondered if I should write to him but I never got round to it."

"Didn't you?" Walnut asks, anxiously. His lawyer mind is already into 'lawsuit' gear.

"Well, you can never be sure that anything you write is original, can you? I just half-hope, half-assume."

"It's called cryptomnesia," Walnut adds.

"Sorry?"

"Cryptomnesia. Hidden memories. You think you've made something up but really it's just a memory you've forgotten. There have been a few court cases about it in the music industry over the years." Walnut sees everything in terms of legality – or to be precise legal fees – so he's enjoying this. "And really it's not that new. Away back in the seventies George Harrison had to hand over royalties because he'd used someone else's tune for *My Sweet Lord*. Then there's *Creep*."

"Tell us about *Creep*, Walnut," says Fleece. "You're going to anyway, so why not just do it with our blessing?"

"Thom Yorke had to share the royalties of Radiohead's *Creep* with the guys who wrote *The Air That I Breathe*."

"The Hollies' song?"

"Well, it was actually written by Albert Hammond and Mike Hazlewood a couple of years earlier. Yorke has to give them half the royalties because the songs are so alike."

"Away ye go!" Fleece says, "They're as alike as Portobello Beach and the Scott Monument."

"Nevertheless," Walnut says, adding for good measure, "Hammond came from Gibraltar, by the way, Fleece."

Fleece can't take it. He shouts theatrically, "Gibraltar! Gibraltar! God spare me from Gibraltar!"

Walnut goes in for a quick kill. "Hammond and Hazlewood wrote *Little Arrows* for Leapy Lee as well."

This is doing my head in. The idea that *Little Arrows* and *Creep* were written by the same person is just too much to take.

"I really don't think I've pinched the song from anyone, Walnut," I insist.

"Ah, but did you check?"

"Check with whom?"

"I thought you were going to check with Rab Noakes," Jane says. I so wish I'd never mentioned it.

I've had enough of this. "Listen, that's only the first song. I'm not arguing over the copyright for every single bloody song in the set. They're mine, they're only mine, and they're all mine. So there."

Walnut, Little Joe and Fleece combine in a camp "Ooooo."

My turn to take control. "Next song." Jane is smiling quietly, presumably laughing at my strop.

We play through each of the remaining songs in less than thirty minutes. It's been decided – we all agree we can do no more. All of us except Little Joe.

"We haven't played any rasta-jock today," he complains.

"This is a dress rehearsal for next Sunday, Joe," I point out.

"We're not in full dress," he reminds me, helpfully.

"I'm really not sure..." I begin, but I can see he's disappointed, and moreover I can feel two forces counter me. The irresistible Bev has invaded my spinal column at full power – Brian, surely there's time for one song? – but Jane rides to his rescue, too.

"Do you write songs, too, Joe?" she asks.

"I'm working on a project exploring the links between Scottish folk songs and the music of the West Indies – you know, reggae and so on. It's the slave connection."

"It's all slavers, Jane," Fleece roars, laughing. "Don't encourage him."

"Play something for me, Joe. Go on," Jane says softly. This is bizarre; the spirits of Ingrid Bergman and Bev have combined in Jane to give Little Joe inner strength.

Little Joe stands up and asks the other three of us to join him, which we do, like condemned men going to the gallows.

"Let's play that one from the last time, the one Magda liked," he suggests.

"I'll just take this opportunity to go to the toilet," Walnut says.

"Must we?" Fleece asks.

"Why not?" Geoff says. "Goodness me, that's a good choice! Just the one."

We start to play. It's a new experience for Jane, who listens, and after a moment or two sits forward, smiling, her head propped in her hands, her elbows in turn supported by her knees. It's a pose taken by all in the room, Harry and Danni, Tommy and Becky, even Bev, whose radiant smile glows more than ever. The sound is excruciating, but eventually the last chorus grinds to its miserable conclusion, and a round of applause from the audience of six.

Only in the last couple of lines do I realise that the pose adopted by each onlooker has been chosen to allow them to sit with their fingers discreetly in their ears.

62

Curtains for Walnut

In the event, only Walnut and I head for Peebles on Friday, the day before the Festival. When we arrive, the venue is definitely ready, with car-parking, loads of clear signs, toilets, first-aid, assorted rest-rooms, and – to my surprise – television gantries as well. I don't know of any plans to show the concert live. Walnut is wondering aloud if this entitles us to more money. He's brought the contract with him, and quickly checks to make sure television rights are not included.

"Is that our business, Walnut?" I ask him. We're still sitting in his four-by-four.

"Definitely," he replies. "We're getting five pounds for everyone who comes, so it's arguable that we should get a share of the television viewing public fees, too."

"I don't get it."

"You will. Just leave the talking to me," Walnut says confidently.

We get out and set off towards the stage, passing some friendly 2F Security staff on the way, and find Lord Wullie, Fourth Earl of Dalatho, marching about in a haze of cigar-smoke on the stage giving directions. He hails us with a mixture of disbelief and amusement.

"I wondered where you were, gentlemen," he says. "A little bird told me that your little reduced-calorie manager friend had disappeared off the face of the earth."

"Gone east," Walnut replies. "Probably masquerading as a terrapin somewhere in Borneo."

Lord Wullie puffs on his cigar and himself briefly vanishes.

"No, gentlemen, you don't understand me. He's disappeared off the face of the earth," he repeats, and then again becomes a puff of smoke. I'm not sure what Lord Wullie is saying but I don't think it's good news for Tam. Perhaps the terrapin has gone to sleep with the fishes.

Lord Wullie continues. "I do so like my business associates to honour their commitments," he says, menacingly, "which is why I'm so glad to see you. You will be a five-piece band tomorrow?" His contemptuous smile returns.

"Yes," Walnut replies, "plus our front of stage act."

The Earl's eyebrows rise noticeably, then disappear in four more puffs of smoke. Conversations with Lord Wullie take a while.

"Good," he says. There's a faint hint of respect in there, perhaps. "As I said, I like my business associates to honour their commitments."

Walnut points to the television tower. "I see there's a gantry up there. Is there live TV as well?"

"BBC Four plan to show highlights on the red button some time after midnight and the repeat of *Match of the Day*."

"Nothing live?"

"No live UK broadcast, promise. I'd have told you."

Walnut picks up on the comment. "No live UK broadcast? Ireland?"

Lord Wullie puffs a lot of smoke. "No."

"Germany?"

"No." More smoke, and I sense the good Lord is getting irritated.

Walnut will always go the extra mile. He's an Edinburgh establishment lawyer. "Tell me there are no live broadcasts to anywhere here on Earth, or on the planet Mars, and I'll stop pestering you."

"Mars?"

"Little Joe, our rhythm guitar, has a cult following on the planet. He tours regularly," Walnut tells him.

Lord Wullie is amused, thankfully, and I breathe a sigh of relief. "China," he reveals in a moment of weakness.

"China?" I say. "But…?"

"The act that's on before you, Otis Farrell and the Upbeats, are red hot in China," Lord Wullie explains. "The Chinese will pay telephone numbers to see shows where they play."

"But the Chinese surely don't understand…"

"Doesn't matter," Lord Wullie explains, "no-one else does either, so they feel they can appreciate it just the same as we can in the West. They'll be up at breakfast time to watch Otis and his chums."

Walnut maintains concentration. "So are we not entitled to some of the share of that? They're sort of paying customers, aren't they?"

Lord Wullie stops, puffs on his cigar at least eight times. Now I'm worried.

"You're a lawyer, aren't you, my friend?"

"Yes," Walnut replies. "Duncan McIntyre of Marsden McKinlay McIntyre Bell, Multrees Walk, Edinburgh." He goes to produce a card from his brief case.

"Don't waste your time," he says. "You're not getting a penny of the television rights. Tell you what, though. Christ only knows how you fell in with that Cantlay guy. Behind your backs, he'd negotiated an extra two pounds per customer commission for bringing you to me. You can have his share as well."

This final act of betrayal by Tam has taken us aback completely.

"How about that? Deal?" the Earl repeats.

He offers his hand to Walnut to seal the deal.

"I'd like to see that in writing – " Walnut begins, but I stop him, and, looking the Earl in the eye directly, I shake on the deal.

"I think Lord Wullie is a man we can trust, Walnut," I say. "When he says that's seven pounds per head, that's what he'll deliver." The Earl's handshake is firm, and I think

I see a warm smile before it disappears into many puffs of smoke.

"Is there anything you need to know, gentlemen?" Lord Wullie asks.

Walnut and I get up onto the stage and look out over the field. I get a cold, weak feeling in my bladder at the thought that there might be thousands of people there the next day. But in the manner of all humane executions, I'll at least be blindfolded – I'll be shielded by a curtain.

"The curtain is powered," Lord Wullie says.

"Do they not use ropes any more?" I ask, surprised.

"Nope. Health and Safety say it must be possible to lift it easily, so it's driven by a motor. There are a couple of buttons for 'up' and 'down'. Make sure you don't touch the buttons by mistake. You'll want to lower the curtain between Otis Farrell and the Upbeats' set and your own, then your stage hands can set you up behind it and your phoney act in front. And you say you have a bass player now?"

"Yes," I say. "A female bass player." I've got my fingers crossed behind my back as I say it.

"Well, I wish you luck. If you've survived Cantlay, you've done well. Don't make a mess of it, though. I don't like to be let down."

"No," I say. "We know that. There's a lot at stake for us, too. We want to make the Festival work as well. If this is the first of many, it would be nice to tell our grandchildren that we helped make it a success."

Lord Wullie disappears in even more puffs of smoke than before.

Then he quietly says, "Good answer."

63

Doomsday

Lord Wullie has given a lot of thought to his organisation of the Festival. He's decided that for security reasons, each act will remain based at the brand-new nearby Travelodge, which he's booked for them already and paid for as part of the fee. Coldplay will be the exception, staying with the Earl himself in his country retreat. Each act will be collected at the appropriate time, then returned to the hotel afterwards, so in fact we are unlikely ever to meet anyone other than the acts immediately before or after us. That's fine with Walnut, a massive Coldplay fan, who's looking forward to a brief close-up of the band after we've played.

The wisdom of letting the Chinese televise the Festival also becomes clear when it turns out that the Travelodge can receive satellite channel Beijing 4, which allows us to watch the events on stage from our rooms and in the hotel lounge if we can manage to ignore the incomprehensible Chinese commentary. Even as we arrive, we can therefore see the first act is already on stage, a husband-and-wife singing duo whose sole claim to fame came two years ago when they came fifth in *The X-Factor*. I remember this pair – the man wears dark glasses and pretends to be either blind or Roy Orbison, although he's neither. The woman smiles like a synchronised swimmer, and sings like one too.

They're followed by a school band called Target who have won the right to sing three numbers at the festival by winning a 'Battle of the Bands' contest. For them – probably for most of the acts, really – the Festival is the by far the biggest thing they've ever done, and they're nervous, taking too long between numbers and mumbling to the audience. It seems a big crowd, but television shots can be deceptive and Chinese television shots more so. They in turn are followed by The Hot Spurs, a girl-band whose special feature is to prance about on stage wearing barely – and barely is a very appropriate word here – long enough Tottenham Hotspur football shirts over thongs. It's not clear if they've factored in that they're playing on a significantly raised stage, but the Chinese camera production unit seems to include an inordinate amount of audience-level footage from the front of the stage. The girls succeed in attracting a lot of attention. No-one cares that they sing like muppets.

The Paramedics follow. I've actually heard of The Paramedics, who are on Harry's rather esoteric iPod collection. They play a funky mix of folk and jazz-rock, and their line-up includes a fiddle, an accordion, and a decent-sized brass section as well as the usual rhythm and bass sections. I'm not certain their music quite works, but of course Harry's glued to the telly. Afterwards, there's a ridiculous interview, in Chinese of course, in which the accordion player talks about his playing and the accordion itself, which turns out to be 'Made in China'.

By now it's well after six, and our date with destiny looms. A band arrives on stage called The Homewreckers, who are really a bunch of washed-up musicians from long-disbanded groups in Scotland and the north of England. They play a lot of covers, at last getting the audience vaguely interested in some music, and they're tight enough if not even remotely original. We're not going to be able to see much of their act, though, as we get a call to say that we'll be leaving for the venue in a few minutes, and it's only when Fleece squints at the television briefly that he suddenly exclaims, "That's Hannah!" and then, to reinforce the point further, "That's fucking Hannah!"

The woman he's peering at is one of trio of backing singers. Fleece, of course, knows this woman quite well: he's married to her. So, too, does Jane, her one-time colleague in The Blonde Bombshelles, a band which brought its four members a considerable secondary income until Hannah suddenly left both Fleece and band for the airline pilot from Gibraltar. From behind, I see Jane do something quite tender; she puts her arm around his waist – it's a bit of stretch around Fleece's waist, mind you – and leans against his shoulder. Am I experiencing a pang of jealousy?

"I can't be sure," he says. "I think the drummer's the airline pilot from Gibraltar, too."

"You're better off without her," Jane says. "She's just a dirty low-down cheat, Fleece. She's cheated you and me both."

Fleece nods his head. "There was always so much less to Hannah than everyone assumed."

"I'm glad you said that, Fleece. I always felt that she contributed very little, there was no substance to her."

"She looked good, but she left you feeling empty. A bit like lettuce," he says, causing Jane to laugh, something I haven't heard for almost two years. She has her back to me, but now she turns round and I'm sure she catches sight of a sadness in my eye before I get the chance to look away.

"Come on," she says sharply, "we need to be going. With any luck you won't see Hannah tonight, Fleece. She'll be coming back here just after we leave, and my guess is she'll be avoiding you anyway. After all, she must have known you would be here – The Flying Saucers' appearance has been big news."

The vans are piled up ready with what we need, less than usual for a concert because Lord Wullie has hired PA equipment from a big supplier in Edinburgh. All we need are our instruments, albeit that we need a set for our musicians and also a set for our alternative selves, Magda and the C-U Jimiz. All personnel, including stage hands, are to be shuttled in a luxury coach, and once loaded up, we set off for the stage a little over an hour before we're due to go on stage. Becky, Danni, Bev, Walnut's wife Zoe and Geoff's wife Sheila have been allowed to join us on the bus, although they will be allocated reserved spaces in a fenced-off safe area at the front of the audience to one side of the stage. They talk a little, but no-one else does, each of us now feeling nerves we've never previously experienced as the bus bumps its way down tracks and across fields towards the stage area. We pass a huge array of cars – far more than I expected – and there must be between fifty and a hundred double-decker buses, I can't count them, lined up for later use as well. Our coach has deep-tinted windows, so outsiders can't see in, but looking out lots of people are watching our bus and wondering in much the same way that the Prime Minister's car or a prison van containing a serial killer attracts attention. It occurs to me that once we've played our six numbers, we too might be classed as serial killers.

The drop-off area is tightly enclosed by 2F Security staff, who actually couldn't be more helpful to us. We alight and Harry and Tommy unload kit with the aid of some of Lord Wullie's own stage hands, while for us there is much kissing, hugging and wishing 'good luck' from the women who are destined only to stand and watch from the audience. Bev has reserved something special for me. I'm not telling anyone what it felt like, ever. Then she goes to Little Joe last of all.

Joe is of course excited by the act before us, Otis Farrell and The Upbeats, who happen to be one of the rising reggae bands in England. He has all three of their albums, and the Upbeats are mentioned as a major influence in his rasta-jock project, so they have a lot to answer for. To get the feel of the stage and the atmosphere, Lord Wullie advises us to watch the last part of the act before us from the wings, and in any case Tommy and Harry will need to be there with the Festival's stage hands to be ready to set up drum-kits, put guitars in place and so on. There's also the little matter of our MacBook Pro, which is still needed to keep the beat for Jane and Magda even although it won't be heard. Lord Wullie is suspicious that we're still not a live band, but I manage to persuade him that it's only necessary for Magda's benefit. I point out that we shook hands and that I'm a man of honour; that thankfully seems to swing things.

While we're standing on the stage, Walnut – who by now is sporting a white bow tie in keeping with his role as conductor – has one more surprise for us. With contacts everywhere, he's discovered that Otis Farrell and The Upbeats use a lighting engineer who was in his year at university, and he's persuaded Stella – that's her name and she's got a degree in astronomy, appropriately enough – to stay on for our set and do our lighting, too. Given that our band uses the MacBook Pro as its effective metronome, it's been easy enough for them to work out light changes for each number. He reports that Stella says it's the easiest job she's ever done. All Magda and the C-U Jimiz have to do is to keep to their stage positions, but they're all seasoned professionals so that will be easy. Just don't ask them actually to play an instrument, or to sing in tune.

Magda and the C-Us have made a huge effort. Magda has settled on around nine inches showing down from the neck in her black leather suit, while the boys have all spent some money at the hairdresser's over the morning. As I arrive in the wings, she's getting Omar to help her with some final adjustments to her suit, a job at which I've noticed each C-U gets a turn. Magda has her back to all of us except him, but it looks as if at the last minute she wants him to fit completely new double-sided tape, and judging by their respective reactions, the removal of the old tape is as illuminating for him as it is painful for her.

I'm standing beside Lord Wullie in the wings as all this is going on.

"How do you feel it's going so far?" I ask him. It's strange, I can see him because he has no cigar – even the noble earl has to obey Health and Safety rules.

"Not bad," he says. He's Scottish, so this means 'good'. "Good crowd, better than I'd hoped for."

"Go on then, tell me," I say to him. We both know the exact size of our fee depends on this figure.

"Thirty-eight thousand, seven hundred and something. We'll round it up to forty. I like men of honour."

"We've not played yet," I say to him. "We could be a disaster."

"You'd better not be," he says.

I'm aware that my life might depend on the events of the next forty minutes or so. I've only just become aware that our collective fee for the day is looking like topping a quarter of a million. I'm passing on neither that nor the size of the crowd to the other band members in case they take fright, and of course the band won't be able to see the crowd. They sound loud enough from here, though.

I'm awakened from my thought by the sudden realisation that Otis Farrell and The Upbeats have finished. We're next.

64

Otis Farrell and The Upbeats

Otis Farrell and The Upbeats actually take three attempts to leave, each time thwarting Little Joe who has brought a large black permanent felt-tip marker so that the Upbeat band members can autograph the back of his guitar. Lord Wullie has to tap his watch to indicate that the show is running late before they finally go. Now the curtain is lowered and two separate sets of musical instruments are set up, our real ones behind out of sight, and the C-U Jimiz' and Magda's pretend ones out in front and fully visible. Tommy tucks the MacBook Pro out of sight behind an amplifier, with an extended earpiece for Jane to keep to the rhythm. Magda and the C-Us will, as usual, use their essential cordless earpieces, but will also wear cordless microphones which are real but of course switched off. Walnut feels the need to conduct us from the wings, and in truth his being there will be reassuring.

Meanwhile, Otis Farrell and the Upbeats are in the wings, full of smiles and excitement after a good gig – it happens even to seasoned pros, apparently – when Little Joe approaches them with felt-tip marker, guitar and not a little trepidation. Geoff and I are watching, hoping this goes well.

"Excuse me?"

Otis Farrell greets Little Joe, "Hahlowmite!" Lots of Upbeat hands go up to give Joe high fives, let's hope he doesn't damage himself.

"Hawahyowmite!"

"Gowdtuhseeyuhmite!"

"Coowelgeegmiterite?"

Little Joe is utterly, totally confused.

"I really like your music," he says. "I'd… I'd be really honoured if you could all sign my guitar before we go on."

"Sawnitmite? Cawrsemite!" and they each start to sign it. Otis Farrell turns back to Joe.

"YowJowmite?

"Sorry?"

"YouLellJowMite?"

"I'm really sorry I don't understand your accent. I don't mean to be rude," Little Joe says. This is horrible for him, his worst nightmare. But Geoff comes to the rescue.

"Goodness me, Joe," he says, "Otis here wants to know if you're Little Joe."

"Oh," Little Joe says, bemused. "Please tell him I am, and I'm delighted to meet him."

"This is Little Joe and he's pleased to meet you," Geoff says

"Icemite", Otis says, delighted, and insists on shaking Joe's hand.

Little Joe remains utterly bemused. "Sorry?"

"Icemite. Yarr myeeowsicks icemite."

Geoff translates. "It seems Otis likes your music, Joe." Let's be clear about this, I am watching a conversation between a Scot and a citizen of West Ham – which is notionally all in the same tongue – taking place through an interpreter from midway between them, Lincolnshire.

"Ice? Oh, sorry, you mean 'ice' as in 'cool'. Thanks.

"Nowmite, Oimine ice. Nat-Bran Myden zice. Ice, as jeck, quayne, kain, ice, icemite. Oisideyarmyeeowsicsicemite."

Suddenly Little Joe understands, and armed with this Rosetta stone of the English language, the barriers between them fall away completely. They're like brothers in arms, equals in the pantheon of reggae heroes. Geoff frown-smiles away, his services no longer required.

"That's an amazing idea, Little Joe, mate," Otis says, "and we can liberate the West Indian slaves – and all their descendants – through the power of rasta-jock. It needs us both, mate, you and me together."

"You and me together, Otis," Little Joe repeats, nodding his head in glee. The pupils of his eyes are wide open, and it's just as well there no policemen are around or he'd be arrested on suspicion of taking cocaine.

Better still, once Otis learns that Little Joe has his own recording studio, he's ecstatic.

"Your own recording studio, mate? Your own recording studio? Stuff of dreams, mate, stuff of dreams."

"You should see it, Otis! Come up and see it some time! You could all stay with us."

Within half a minute they've exchanged mobile numbers, and Little Joe has promised to text Otis a few dates which might be suitable. Otis wants to make a fourth album, and he's keen to have Little Joe on as a guest performer, as it would offer new directions for The Upbeats, and to be able to record in Merchiston Place would suit perfectly.

In the end I'm the only one of the band who's been given the privilege of watching this life-changing moment in my friend's life. It's impossible not to feel overwhelming joy for him, and at least now I can say that, whatever else lies ahead of us in the immediate future, something good has come of this whole stupid adventure.

65

Live from Peebles

We're ready. The moment has come.

An announcer calls over the loudspeaker system, "Ladies and Gentlemen, the Peebles Rock Festival is proud to present, in their very first live performance, the one and only…"

There's actually quite a lot of noise building here. I wasn't ready for the wall of noise.

"The one and very only…"

Looking across to Geoff, I can see him mouth the words, "Goodness me." I can't even begin to hear him. We can't see a thing beyond the curtain, but I'm beginning to get some idea of what thirty thousand spectators sound like when they're drunk, out for a good day, and actually want us to play well.

"The one and only The Flying… Saucers!!"

Deafening.

Walnut has not forgotten his role. With a mighty sweep of his hand, he sets everyone off on *Get A Grip Of My Life*, Jane playing the bass in time with the MacBook Pro, me singing, and everyone else simply playing their instruments. Desperate to get it absolutely spot on, I throw myself into my singing and playing, performing at a blank curtain as if it simply weren't there. Walnut is conducting, but the fact is that, as Jane had said would happen, we don't really need him because we've all practised our parts so very many times. *Get A Grip Of My Life* has lots of verses, all much the same, and it's vaguely funny if anyone can hear the lyrics, but the most important thing is it's a simple confidence-building entrance number. Jane, Fleece, Little Joe, Geoff and I can only hope that our counterparts in front of the curtain are managing their parts as well, but Walnut seems happy enough and the fact that's he's giving everyone equal attention is very reassuring; it means no-one is hashing up.

The song ends perfectly, and there's a truly astonishing roar of acclaim from the other side of the curtain, which each of the band acknowledges with brief nods of the head to each of the others. Walnut is starting to think of the second song, *The Saturday Blues*, when I notice a shadow standing behind him in the wings. It's a tallish, lean-looking man in his late thirties, perhaps, too old to be Harry or Tommy, and both too thin and young to be Lord Wullie, who in any case likes to watch the start of each act from the 'safe area' beside the audience where Becky, Danni and the others will be. As I'm trying to work out who it might be, I suddenly remember that the next act on will be in the wings by now to get the feel of the audience, and realise that the figure with the folded arms is none other than Coldplay's Chris Martin. I therefore have to take some of the blame for what happens next.

Walnut catches my eye and realises that I'm looking behind him, and so Walnut glances behind to realise that he's in the presence of his all-time musical hero, a man he's defined as 'the genius', 'the great one', 'God's musician', and in one particularly slurred moment, 'God on Earth'. Walnut is transfixed. Unable to cope with the nearness of Martin's charisma, he takes a step backwards and to the left in the opposite direction.

Unfortunately, the path immediately backwards and to his left is not a clear one: a chair has been left there, in fact it's a chair Walnut left there himself when he was watching Otis Farrell and The Upbeats. So, not being an immortal god like Chris Martin, Walnut does what any normal person would do in the circumstances, he falls over it. This comedy turn results in my solicitor, manager, agent and conductor performing a backwards roll so that he quite literally ends up with his feet dangling over his own head, and his backside is now the highest part of his body. What's more, he can't get up. Chris Martin wants to help him, but Walnut is clearly not hurt so he remains, still in the shadows, still with folded arms, but now creasing himself with laughter. The five of us behind the curtain think it's pretty funny, too.

We're about to change our minds rather quickly. Walnut's fall over the chair, or more particularly his flailing leg, has accidentally caught the button operating the powered curtain between the five musicians at the back and the C-U Jimiz and Magda at the front. In a matter of less than six or seven seconds, it has risen out of sight so that we are now all ten of us completely exposed to nearly forty thousand spectators directly before us. Looking around, I can see panic, pure panic, in the eyes of each of my nine fellow performers onstage, and if there were a mirror to hand, I'd be able to see panic in mine as well. Both Harry and Tommy simply have their heads in their hands, unable to look. Down in the crowd, I've caught sight of Becky, Danni, and Bev who look shocked, as though they've just learned of a sudden close bereavement. Lord Wullie doesn't look too impressed either.

Chris Martin is untangling Walnut and helping him to his feet, though with some difficulty, when something remarkable happens: the crowd starts cheering. Suddenly, I realise – *they think it's part of the act!* Walnut is about to try to make the curtain go down again when I see the way out, and I frantically signal for him to leave things alone.

I pick up my mike stand and march forward to the front of the stage beside the bewildered-looking Magda and the C-Us.

"Good evening, Peebles!" I yell. This is greeted with a deafening, I mean deafening, cheer.

"Thank you, everyone. We are The Flying Saucers!"

Another roar of applause.

"That was *Get A Grip Of My Life* and I'd like you all to give it up for Magda here – "

A huge roar for Magda, and she gives them a double-handed wave by way of thanks.

"…And the C-U Jimiz here, Quentin – "

Another huge cheer.

"Omar – "

Yet another cheer.

"Evelyn – "

And another. Even the normally surly Evelyn has to grin.

"And Jimmy!"

And another roar.

"Give it up again for our dance-group, The C-U Jimiz and Magda!!"

Giant, giant roar.

"Thanks for your welcome. You're a fantastic crowd."

Fantastic, prolonged roar. Of course, praise the crowd, that's fail-safe.

"Are you having a good time?"

"YESSS!!!!"

I've cracked it. Crowds like this will cheer anything.

"The weather's been great this summer, hasn't it?"

"YESSS!!!"

It's actually poured most of the last three weeks. Let's test my theory.

"Hibs two, Celtic nil!!"

The sound of forty thousand derisive laughs is not the same as forty thousand roaring cheers. Clearly there's a limit.

"Well, we're having a great time up here, so thank you all for coming. It's great to be here."

Another roar.

"We'd like to play you a song about Saturdays called *The Saturday Blues*. It's forty years old, but some things never change."

I look around me to see where everyone is. Fleece remains at the back, of course, but drummers sit at the back. The others have all quietly moved themselves and their mikes forward to join me. Meanwhile, the C-Us and Magda have drifted further backwards, but they've clearly sorted something out. This is going to work, I know it, and I count everyone in.

"OK, everyone, take it away, one, two, three, four – " and we launch off into the old rocky number from my young days. The mystery of what Magda and the C-U Jimiz are up to is immediately revealed. Like the true professionals they've always been, they take my cue to become our dance-group, cavorting backwards and forward across the stage, winding up the crowd to dance, clap their hands in the air, all the things that people do when they want to join in. The number ends with a roar of approval from the crowd, but then I've already worked out they'll cheer anything. The main thing is that everyone seems to be enjoying themselves, most importantly the people on the stage. There's even a nod of approval from Jane.

"This is a song you haven't heard before called *River of Tears*," I say, and I tell them the story of its writing, about my days as a teacher and the awful things done to child soldiers in central Africa by other child soldiers, and of how I'd met African children who regard suicide as commonplace, so destroyed are their lives. It's greeted with great applause for a new song. I like it myself, but I'm glad it's over.

By now I'm enjoying myself so much that I decide it's about time to have some fun with the audience.

"What do you think we're going to play next? Something fast? – Nah. Slow? – Nah. Nah, nah."

There's a panicked look beside me from Jane – have I forgotten the script?"

The crowd take the hint, and repeat, "Na na na na nah, na".

"Nah, nah," I say, repeating the Scots negative. "Later, maybe."

This gets laughter from the crowd. That worked.

Without further comment, I count us straight into *Leave Me Alone*, which seems to be over in no time – another sign we're enjoying ourselves. The applause at the end lasts a long time, but I want to wait a moment for the intro to the next song, *Bird*.

"This song is one of the ones that first brought us to the notice of the public all those months ago. It's a song... well, it's a song addressed to the only woman there's ever been in my life, ever." I don't give its name, and don't look at Jane, deliberately.

As soon as I play the opening chords on my guitar, just me, there's the huge roar the showman in me was playing for.

Please understand I wouldn't hurt you,
Please understand I mean no ill,
Please try to listen when I tell you,
The love in my heart remains there still.

Then the chorus...

Set me free, Set me free,

...which the audience joins in with, but also to my amazement, they spread their arms out wide as they do so, like eagles soaring in the sky...

Let me spread my wings, And fly like a bird,
And soar beyond the sea,
A world is calling, A world is calling,
A world is calling, calling to me.

Aha! – looking around, Magda and the C-Us are at work behind me, prompting the crowd by doing the arms-for-wings thing, too. It's a bit dangerous, actually, as a few people get their eyes poked in the process. But they all seem to be having a good time getting their eyes poked, at least.

We make it into verse two.

Nobody came to try and tempt me,

Nobody tried to turn my head,
You're not to blame that this has happened,
Leave me to take the fall instead,
Leave me to take the fall instead.

Then off we go with another chorus, complete with arms outstretched. The second chorus is of course followed by a middle eight (actually with the repeated line at the end it's nearer a 'middle nine' or 'middle ten') in which Little Joe joins in with his slightly discordant bit that somehow works…

No matter how near, no matter how far,

But someone else is singing, too. Jane has come to join me right at the front microphone and is singing her own vocals, neither mine nor Little Joe's, somewhere in between, but she's obviously been thinking about this at home because it's perfect.

It doesn't matter, you know I won't care

I manage to catch Joe's eye, who nods his approval. Usually he's too intergalactic to notice anything short of a bomb blast.

I'll still be with you wherever you are,
There, I'll still be with you there,
I'll still be with you there.

Jane and I did many things during our marriage, but amazingly, we'd never actually sung together. It's taken just a few lines in the middle of one number to point the way to the future, and I realise that the divorce rate would plummet if married couples sang together more often. Verse three follows and then the chorus for the third time, with everyone joining in. And because it's repeated the last time, I have an opportunity to do what always works well at a big open-air concert full of young people – give them a chance to make a spectacle of themselves all alone.

"Over to you!" and taking their cue, the crowd sing the last chorus on their own, looking like a giant flock of drunken buzzards, until we join in at the end to slow it down towards the final top-note finish. If only earning over two hundred thousand pounds could be this easy all the time.

Once you've got an audience, don't ever let go of them. Even before the applause has died away, it's time to set the one remaining number in our set going.

"Na-na-na-na-nah-na." I put my hand to my ear to encourage them to sing it back, and louder.

"Na-na-na-na-nah-na."

"Not bad," I tell the crowd, "could do better." Jesus, even now, I'm still the Depyoot Head.

"NA-NA-NA-NA-NAH-NA!"

"Better! Keep that standard up!"

They do, a couple of times, then we add in our introductory riffs to match, before launching into *Right Here Lovin' Me*. When a large number of people take to you, the atmosphere is just electric, and I really can see why so many rock stars fall victim to drug addiction to fill in the gaps between big concerts. This could be dangerously attractive.

Magda and the C-U Jimiz are simply sensational here, whipping up the audience to jump up and down, another rock festival tradition, of course, but also to point to their friends in the audience. After four "na-na-na-na-nah-nas" and attached riffs, I get to launch into the first verse, followed by the simple chorus in which the whole universe seems to be taking part. The gap between each chorus and the subsequent verse is followed by a further four "na-na-na-na-nah-nas" plus riffs, and in no time we're in a loud repeat of the final chorus, and it's over. Fleece has great fun on his drums at the end.

Deafening roar.

More to the point, we've survived, and the Falkirk Friends can put their knives away. The ten people on the stage come to the front to acknowledge the crowd at various points on the spectrum, ranging from the C-U Jimiz' coordinated bows, to the faint nods and waves that Geoff and I manage. To be honest, I'd never considered the end of our concert at all; I didn't think we'd live that long. All I want now is to see my family, and looking down, it's less of a joy, more a relief, to be able still to see Becky and Danni jumping up and down in the safe area, and Harry and Tommy giving more measured applause in the wings. The others – Bev, Walnut and so on – seem incidental.

Eventually we depart the stage, to be greeted first of all by Walnut, who can't decide whether he should congratulate us, or to apologise for landing us in trouble in the first place. Right beside him in the wings, though, stands Lord Wullie, who seems absolutely delighted and wants to shake everyone's hand.

"That didn't exactly work out as planned," I shout in his ear over the racket.

"No it didn't," he replies. "Better. Much, much better. It's what the show needed."

Harry comes over. "Nice one, Dad. Not bad for a has-been." I give him a bow. This is an Olympic gold medal in the pantheon of Harry-praise. "But the crowd want an encore, I'm afraid."

So they do. And we can't give them one.

"It's bad form to give an encore at a rock festival," I tell him. "It messes up the timings for the next band." I've no idea if that's true or not but it sounds a good excuse.

Chris Martin is still standing there. "An encore's fine by me," he says, shrugging his shoulders. "Good set, by the way. Different," he adds, smiling.

"It's my festival," Lord Wullie booms, "and I say you should do one more." And when Lord Wullie booms, it's wise to listen out for the quieter sound of Friendly knife on Falkirk steel.

Nodding, I summon the band, Magda and the C-Us over to join me in a huddle.

"What the fuck do we do here?" Fleece asks.

Geoff says what we all know. "We haven't got another tune to play, Brian. Goodness me, what should we do?"

"How about just playing the last song again?" Little Joe asks.

"That'll look like we haven't got anything else to play,' Jane points out. "But then again…"

The C-U Jimiz look like rabbits in headlights, though to give them credit for their professionalism, they're panicking in time with each other. But Magda has an idea, which she shares with us.

"No."

"NO!"

"Goodness me, is that wise?

"For fuck's sake, Magda."

"Why not? It's quirky," she says, "verry quircky. They vil danz. I vil make them danz. Votch!"

66

Encore

"Ladies and Gentlemen, we'd like to thank you all very much for being so kind to us on this, our first live concert.

"I should introduce the people on the stage. We have an extraordinary team of dancers and musicians, The C-U Jimiz – Jimmy here – "

Big cheer, Jimmy waves

"Quentin – "

Same.

"Evelyn – "

Again.

"And finally Omar."

More applause.

"In addition there's the one and only Magda."

Magda gets a huge roar. She has her back to me, but her acknowledgement seems to involve the zip on the front of her leather suit, earning her a second roar, plus a good deal of laughter.

"Behind me is Little Joe Mackay on rhythm guitar – "

More cheers. Little Joe waves.

"Geoff Arrowsmith on lead guitar."

Cheers. Geoff frown-smile-nods acknowledgement.

"On percussion, Fleece Mackay."

Big cheer. Fleece simply stands up.

"Jane Reid is on bass." Boy, has she saved my life here.

More cheers. Jane gives a wave and a cheery smile.

"And I'm Captain Brian Reid." That's how it comes out, although it might include a comma in there somewhere.

There are even cheers for me.

"We'd like to try something out on you here. You all know the words, and this time Little Joe's going to step forward to take lead vocals."

Jane, Fleece, Geoff and Little Joe launch off into a horribly familiar reggae rhythm, Little Joe and Geoff working their knees and guitar-jerks in perfect time. While I'm working out how to join in, Magda and the C-Us have lined up along the front of the stage and are stepping left and right, clapping their hands in time to the island beat. Little Joe sets off.

Oh flower of Scotland, when will we see yer like again,
That fought an died for, yer wee bit hill and glen,

Then into the chorus, which all ten of us sing, even Fleece at the back. We'll go down on this together.

And stood against him, proud Edward's army,
And sent homewards, tae think again.

Hang on – the crowd have joined in as well! The C-Us and Magda have made it work. We know all three verses – including that middle one that gets left out at rugby and football internationals – and the crowd responds, well, as Scottish crowds do when *Flower of Scotland* is played. Saltires and Lion Rampants wave, as well as one or two other more surprising flags – because I'm a bit-part player this time, I have time to pick out a Welsh Dragon, an Australian flag, a Maple Leaf, a Greek flag, and something that I think might be an Iranian flag. There are also the usual banners, mostly things saying 'HI, MUM', or demanding world peace, although there's also one bearing the motto 'Chernobyl Ladies' Bridge Club'.

But soaring above all of this is Little Joe himself, whose life's work has finally come to bear fruit in less than three glorious minutes. As he sings his final chorus, he has truly sailed off towards the planet Mars, there to remain content for the rest of his days.

Rasta-jock has lift-off, and a star is born.

67

Travelodge

Coldplay are into their second number by the time we arrive back at the shuttle bus to take us back to the hotel. Not everyone is with us, however, as Fleece has delayed his return to talk to a woman who's been waiting for him at the performers' entrance behind the gents' toilets, and he sends a message via Tommy that we should go and he'll make his own way to the Travelodge. Meanwhile, Walnut has briefly taken the huff – Walnut, "a Writer to the Signet, too" – because Lord Wullie has refused to hand over the very, very large cheque to anyone other than me, as I was one "who shook hands on the deal". Following us out to the bus, Lord Wullie could not be more pleased, and he already wants to book us for next year. He's also pleased because, away from the stage, he can light up and disappear into a cloud of his favourite cigar smoke.

Playing a big gig can have one of two effects: either the participants are totally exhausted, or their libido is raised to spectacular levels, and both lead to the same destination. As soon as we enter the hotel foyer, Becky and Tommy, and Harry and Danni announce that they're simply going to say goodnight and head for bed immediately. Nor is it a surprise that Geoff and Sheila take their leave, as it's long past their bedtimes, goodness me. And Walnut and his wife Zoe disappear, too, Zoe promising as she passes that Walnut will be in a better mood in the morning, she can guarantee that. That doesn't sound like sleep.

The Travelodge lounge is an antiseptic affair, with faux-leather seating which it's easier to sit down into than to get out of, at least for anyone over the age of thirty. Magda and the C-U Jimiz realise that their days with The Flying Saucers are coming to an end now that we can admit to being the ages we really are, and she's decided that she wants to mark the occasion by spending some time getting to know each of the C-Us "a little more intimately" each in turn before they part. They're therefore perched on the edge of the sofas negotiating who's going to spend time with her first. Once that little matter's sorted out – I think the order is to be Omar, Quentin, Jimmy, Evelyn – they all leave us with a "goodnight", and for a "good night".

The only people left are Bev, Little Joe, Jane and me. As soon as the C-Us and Magda have gone, Bev surprises me by asking if she can have a word with me alone. I'm surprised – she's never actually sought my company away from Joe before, our private conversations have always been accidental, setting aside those where she invades my central nervous system. She seems to have some plan, and leading me down a couple of corridors, we turn into a dead-end. Immediately, by flinging her arms around my neck and somehow entwining her legs around me, Bev treats me to one of the most intensely intimate, sensuous embraces I've ever experienced. This is different in so many ways. She has always had strange powers, but never in all the time I've known her has she physically manhandled me, but now I can feel her, even smell her – and yes, I realise she's actually sweating, Bev glows for goodness sake, she doesn't sweat – as her body presses mine against the wall. This is all wrong.

"I'd love to have sex with you, Brian," she says, huskily. The voice hasn't changed, thankfully.

"Bev – "

"I'd love to, because I want to say thank you with every last part of my body. Every part. You deserve it for all you've done."

And all at once I realise that Bev has been set free, free from a lifetime of being at Little Joe's side, of being merely his loving wife, of being a drop-dead-gorgeous appendage on his arm that everyone covets but only Joe can actually have, a role that's exhausted her since she gave up her business enterprise to be his Olympic gold medal in the sex race. No longer will she have to spend hours each day putting on make-up, perfecting every last detail of her clothing, shopping for the perfect jewellery and perfume, judging how much to reveal and how much to hide. Or, for that matter, creating the perfect cheese scone. No longer will she be so tired that at the end of the day she has no energy left for Joe himself. What she has given for her husband has raised the meaning of the words true love to new heights. The joy of rasta-jock is that simultaneously it has released both the true musical spirit of Little Joe and the genuine human spirit of Bev.

She still has her arms around my neck, and as her head muzzles into my chest between the mostly-unbuttoned front of my shirt — both of us will need to readjust several items of clothing a little here — she kisses me, then looks up and smiles. Wordlessly, she buttons up my shirt and pats down my clothing, then attends to her own attire, her bra needing special attention. Then she takes my hand and slowly leads me back to the foyer where her husband and Jane are talking quietly. As we enter, Jane looks at me and gives me an approving smile and a nod; it must be some feminine intuition because she seems to know what's taken place.

There are only seven words exchanged between Bev and Joe, and Joe says none of them.

"Joe, I need you now, right now."

After they've gone, Jane and I find ourselves left alone. The plan is that Fleece and I are to share rooms, as a condition of Jane's participation was a room to herself, but there's no point in going to bed before Fleece arrives back because he'll just crash around making so much noise that I'll never get any sleep. Fleece needs to do his crashing around here in the foyer first, so I have little choice but to wait until he returns.

Jane, who's sitting on a sofa to my right, leans back.

"You did well tonight, Brian."

"Thanks, I think we all did. You made all the difference, though. I never realised you were so good."

"The Blonde Bombshelles were a decent act until Hannah went off with Gibraltar Jack. We were cut off in our prime. She thought she was the big star and we weren't worthy of her – and neither was Fleece – so it was very satisfying to see her on stage in that second-rate backing group."

"And she must have seen you and Fleece later."

"Quite," Jane says, satisfied. "But I'm serious, Brian, the man on stage tonight was the man I married all those years ago. You had passion, you enjoyed what you were doing, you believed in what you were doing. It came from the heart."

"Are we talking about teaching or music here?" I ask her.

"Both, I suppose. But once you began to get promoted, you lost it." I'm not enjoying this, but Jane wants to go on. "That last job, as Depute Head, that job, it, it poisoned you, Brian. It turned you into a cynical, negative, backward-looking miserable son-of-a-bitch."

"I allowed the job to poison me, I suppose."

"You were unliveable with. I thought you were a lost soul. Tonight I discovered you still had it."

I'm looking at her. "It won't work, Jane. We can't get back together. Too much foul water has flowed under the bridge."

"No, you're right, Brian, it won't work. We've had our chance and wasted it. Me too. I've got a shocking temper. I forfeited the right to live with any man when I started throwing Auntie Ethel's tea-service."

I smile at the memory. "Yes, that hurt. I couldn't work out the way her saucers swerved about."

She laughs, leans across, and slaps my knee.

Our conversation is interrupted as Fleece finally makes it to join us. He's red-faced, wild-looking, excited and out of breath, in other words just the same as normal. But he's concerned, and he comes up to Jane and me, he speaks in lowered tones so that no-one other than ourselves can hear him, even although we're alone in the room.

"Good night, you two, eh?"

"You can say that again," I reply.

"Good night, you two, eh?"

Jane closes her eyes in despair.

"Look Captain, Jane, I've got a little problem," he says. "I've brought back a groupie."

"A groupie?" Jane bursts out laughing.

"I know what you're thinking, but she's nearly our age. Christ she's a teacher, a head somewhere, I think she said."

"Heaven help her," Jane says. "Watch you don't catch something educational."

I'm looking at Fleece. "Fleece, forgive me for saying this, but what about your other matter, you know? Won't there be a problem – ?" I'm trying to put this delicately, although Jane has worked out straight away what I'm referring to.

"Oh, that's no problem at all," Fleece says, "the modern groupie comes armed with both condoms and Viagra, it seems. It's all these ageing rock stars, she says."

"VD, ED, come prepared," Jane says. "Is she a boy scout?"

"I fucking hope not," Fleece roars, laughing. "And vice versa, as Dorothy Parker nearly said. The thing is, you and I were going to share a room, Captain." He stands, waiting, shifting his weight from one foot to the other and back again.

Jane comes to his rescue. "Look Fleece, it's OK. Brian and I have shared enough rooms in our lifetime. One more won't kill us."

"Sure?" I ask her.

"Sure. I've not brought anything to throw at you. Are we going to meet her, then, Fleece?"

"She's a little shy. I think we'd just like to set off. Thanks for helping." There's clearly a female figure just out of sight behind the door.

"'Night then," Jane and I say to him.

Fleece waves as he takes his leave, me shaking my head at his departing back. He says something to the female figure, and as they head for their room, we catch a quick glimpse of her as she passes the open doorway. It's a quick glimpse, but it's good enough to make Jane and me gasp in disbelief.

"Not a completely talentless bitch, then," Jane says, gazing at the door.

"And Fleece seems to think she's pretty hot tonight," I reply.

Then it comes to us together. "But she sure is stupid!" It's great to laugh with her again.

Eventually I say to her, "So everyone has a happy ending except us?"

"Looks like it. Let's go and sleep it off."

Ten minutes later we're in our room, and Jane is in the bathroom brushing her teeth while I get the beds ready. It looks like a double bed, but in fact it's two singles joined together, and I'm trying to separate them when she emerges from the ensuite. She's completely naked.

"What are you doing, Brian?"

"Separating the beds. I thought you'd want – "

"Don't be so bloody silly. There's more room if you leave it as it is."

I start to take off my clothes, get to my underwear, then hesitate. Then I say, "I know – don't be so bloody silly," remove everything, then we fall into bed at last. It's been a long day.

"Tell me, Jane," I begin. "How did Becky manage to twist your arm?"

"She hasn't told you?"

"Told me what?"

"She and Tommy are expecting a baby."

"Hey! Whoa! We're going to be grandparents!" So perhaps there is to be a happy ending for us after all.

"It's early days yet, though. It's not for public knowledge."

"And you say Tommy's expecting a baby, too?" I say, trying to use humour to deal with my excitement. "That'll be a first for the human race." She laughs, and punches me in the upper arm – it's better than saucers. "So The Flying Saucers were saved by the power of an unborn child?"

"I suppose," she says. "And a few other people," she adds.

Taking a breath, I say, "I don't think I ever said. Thanks for everything, Jane."

She looks at me and smiles, propping her head up on her right elbow. "It was fun for me, too, you know." Then she lies back on the bed and closes her eyes. "I'll drop the court case, Brian."

I'm lying on my back, too, but I turn to look at her.

"Thank you. Sorry. By the way, you've got a share of a giant fee coming your way."

"That's not why I'm dropping the case, Brian. I know I was being malicious. I'm sorry, too."

If husbands and wives should sing together to preserve marital harmony, perhaps all warring couples should discuss their troubles with their clothes off.

"It won't work, Jane. This is nice but it won't work. People only remarry in the movies."

"We've done that conversation, Brian. Leave it."

"Harry says we've behaved like a couple of complete fuckwits."

She laughs. She still has her eyes closed. "I'm so proud of our son's analytical powers. He's right, though. We should be able to spend time with each other and enjoy it. For our children's sake, at least."

"And now our children's children," I add.

"Birthdays, Christmas, New Years, that sort of thing."

"Holidays with the grandchildren."

"I could even manage the odd weekend away with you without needing an excuse, you know. Holidays are more fun when you've got company."

"That sounds nice."

"Then Harry would have to stop saying we were behaving like complete fuckwits," she says.

"He'd find another reason."

Jane laughs. It's lovely. I never thought I'd hear it again.

"But it's time to move on, isn't it, though?" she says, after a minute or so.

"Where to?"

"I need to move somewhere smaller, that house is too big for me now." Then she adds, "And too many memories."

"There's a nice flat for sale directly above mine in Eton Terrace just now."

Now she opens her eyes wide and returns to her previous position, her right arm propping up her head to face me.

"Really? The old boy above you who didn't like your loud music? Banged his stick? Harry told me about him."

"Shuffled off this mortal coil a few months ago."

"Interesting."

"The old boy's death or the flat?"

"I'm not really interested in the old boy, Brian."

"It would make it easier for the family to visit."

"That's true." She's smiling, and thinking.

"You'll look at it?"

"I'm not making any promises, Brian. It's probably needing masses of work done."

"I'm told the downstairs neighbour's nice. Plays loud music, though."

"If you play any of Little Joe's rasta-jock I'll do more than bang a stick," she says, laughing.

I watch her as she studies my face. One of the consolations of ageing is that the women you age with appear, if anything, more attractive as you grow old together.

"Turn over," she says. I'm confused, so she repeats it: "Go on, turn over onto your front."

When Jane and I were younger, she used to massage my back, a tender, loving gesture which I treasured at the end of the day. I do as I'm told, close my eyes, and wait for her hands to caress me.

"OWWW!"

She gives my rear a massive whack with her hand. That was not in the plan.

"What was that for?" I complain.

"That's for calling your band The Flying Saucers."

"OWWW!" Again.

"That's for calling me Brunhilde the Valkyrie behind my back."

"But how – "

"It's funny, but don't do it again."

"OWWWW!" That one is really sore.

"And that's for behaving like a complete fuckwit."

"But we've both been complete fuckwits."

"True."

"So do I get to hit you back?"

"No. A man should never hit a woman," she laughs.

"Whatever happened to equal opportunities?"

Jane is examining her handiwork. "Heavens," she says, "I've left three red hand-prints on you. I'm sorry, I didn't mean to hit you so hard." Concerned, she says, "Brian, I'm really very sorry. Really I am."

"It's OK, honest."

"No, I overdid it. I'm sorry."

I'm still lying on my front. "It's OK, really it is, Jane." Then I whisper, slightly embarrassed, "I quite liked it, actually."

"You did?" She quickly pushes me onto my back. "Goodness me," she says, smiling, "so you did." She moves herself towards me, so that her head is now lying on me, and for the second time in an hour there's a woman kissing my chest. Then she adjusts her position a little, eventually sliding her left leg over me so that she's directly on top of me.

And then we do something that we haven't done for a very, very long time.

Acknowledgements

I'm indebted to a host of people for assisting the assembly of this book, including Professor Robert Hillenbrand and my cousin Ian McInnes for their early advice and encouragement, and Mike Rowley for allowing me to access his huge personal fund of music trivia. Stephanie Zia's book *How To Publish An Ebook - An Author's* Guide was an indispensible aid. Erick Davidson at Tayburn persuaded his colleagues Malcolm Stewart and Simon Daverin to give up their spare time to conjure up the cover. Meg Ross proof-read the novel – and gave so much more advice as well. Any number of friends were just very supportive of the whole idea. Most of all, thanks are due to my wife Katherine for her enormous patience, encouragement, and proof-reading skills, and for putting up with many days and nights of watching me sitting with a laptop quite literally on my lap.

All the characters are fictional except the obvious ones, and any similarities to real-life individuals are purely coincidental.

On the other hand, all of the songs mentioned in this book really exist, most of them complete. More details can be found at the website http://www.flyingsaucers.eu. The words of *Flower of Scotland*, by Roy Williamson © The Corries (Music) Ltd., are reprinted by kind permission, and finally I'd like to take this opportunity to thank Chris Martin and Coldplay for their contribution to this story.